this bright life

Also by Karen Campbell

Paper Cup
The Sound of the Hours
Rise
This Is Where I Am
The Twilight Time
After the Fire
Shadowplay
Proof of Life

this bright life

Karen Campbell

CANONGATE

First published in Great Britain in 2025
by Canongate Books Ltd, 14 High Street, Edinburgh EH1 1TE

canongate.co.uk

1

Copyright © Karen Campbell, 2025

The right of Karen Campbell to be identified as the
author of this work has been asserted by her in accordance
with the Copyright, Designs and Patents Act 1988

No part of this book may be used or reproduced in any manner
for the purpose of training artificial intelligence technologies or
systems. This work is reserved from text and data mining
(Article 4(3) Directive (EU) 2019/790).

British Library Cataloguing-in-Publication Data
A catalogue record for this book is available on
request from the British Library

ISBN 978 1 83726 061 4

Typeset in Sabon LT Std by Palimpsest Book Production Ltd,
Falkirk, Stirlingshire

Printed and bound by CPI Group (UK) Ltd, Croydon CR0 4YY

The manufacturer's authorised representative in the EU for product
safety is Authorised Rep Compliance Ltd, 71 Lower Baggot Street,
Dublin D02 P593 Ireland (arccompliance.com)

For Wren and Xander. Always follow the light.

'What do you want, you who are alive here today?
What do you want for the future?'

Alan Riach on Hugh MacDiarmid

APRIL

Chapter One

He hates his name. Flucken hates it. Hates the way it plops like an old turd. Gerard. *Jeh-rahrd*. He has hated it all through primary school, where it has been Gerbil and Germolene and Gerard the Retard, Gerard Butthole (from his namesake actor Gerard *But*-ler), Gerry Cinnamon Balls (because of the singer Gerry Cinnamon – he wouldn't have minded if it was just Gerry, but it was the Cinnamon Balls that stuck) and then for a brief, surprising while, it's been Gero – short for Geronimo. Gero's alright, he doesn't mind that. When his pals call it out, it sounds like he's an Italian gangster. Yes, he could live with being a Gero. He doesn't know who first said it – maybe Brian? But that's not the point – the point is, can he keep it? After the holidays, everything changes. They will move up to secondary school. Shit gets real then (which is a wank thing to say, he's not a New York rapper, but some boys can say these words and get away with it. Delivered in a low spit from a twisted mouth, it can sound hard as). Gerard may have an old priest's name, but he's not daft. Brian and Drew will go to Whitehill and he and Colm and Michael will go to St Roch's, and despite the fact they've all went to different primary schools and nothing has really changed, it will. It just will. The games will stop. No more football in the street, no more knocking fags and juice out the shops, no more stealing a workie's lawnmower thingy and driving it across Alexandra Park – and no more Broncos, because being in a gang named after a horse will get your head panned in at secondary. That's just life. Life happening like a big lazy river. Gerard's kind of given up paddling.

You're the fucking eldest! His ma shouts that at him, constantly, as if that is an excuse. Aye, no worries, Mum. *I'm the eldest.* What does that even mean? He checks his phone. Lunchtime. She should be up by now.

'You coming?' asks Michael. 'We're gonny head down now, see the flowers.'

The Broncos are off to see another statue. It's the anniversary of Billy McNeill dying, and he's an East End legend. Gerard doesn't really go to the football; he hates the way the crowds swell, how it becomes like one big panting animal, and the buzz you get off that. He hates the way that buzz makes him feel.

'Nah. I'm away home. Got stuff to do.'

'Babysitting again?' says Drew, sly-like. 'Your maw been on the nightshift?'

'Piss off, Dewdrop.' Gerard scuffs his bike backwards, so he can get a good purchase on the pedal, then pushes off. 'See yous later. Give Billy my love.'

'Gay-tard,' shouts one of them.

Gerard freewheels down the slope of Whitehill Street, feeling the air on his cheeks. What if that's the name that sticks? Stupid thought, hardly a thought at all, but he is aware of the panic starting, even as he pushes the feeling down: the breathlessness, the familiar pattering as his heart speeds up, and he pretends it is the fun of bombing it downhill. He closes his eyes, just for a wee minute, but it is enough to imagine what it might be like to keep going, never stopping, so it is just you and the rushing air and the bounce of the ground and onwards, across the junction of the main road with your eyes shut, your eyes tight shut so you can't see what's coming until it hits you. His feathery heartbeat is in his belly now, it's in every finger, all his skin, inside his head – and he bottles it. Opens his eyes as he squeezes the brakes, and makes a screeching loop onto the pavement. You're such a crapper, Jeh-*rahrd*. Come on, man. What's it going to be? Pedal under a bus or go home?

He chooses home.

Chapter Two

Margaret knows a lot, about a lot of things. She knows what it is to feel love, and loss. And pain, of course. You don't get to her age without that. She flexes her stiffened ankles. She knows about prisms and balloon-shaped hydrocarbons. About Hume and Adam Smith. She knows about the Druids and the Spiritualist Church in Berkeley Street and how Peploe mixed his colours and when the right time is to make marmalade. (January. You get the best Seville oranges then. Bitter, thick-dimpled on their skin.)

And Margaret knows how to live unseen. When nobody knows that you know these things. How we dwell alone. Because you can never truly know how this world feels for anyone else. You, looking out of your cage, all the bony vast hollows of your skull, your aching, lumpy legs, the curvature of your spine, the frame of brittle grey hair which rims your vision. Peering at folk, thinking: what makes you, you? Or me, me?

How do we ever know?

We don't. We only like to think we do. Take this building, in which Margaret lives. She's been here sixty-three years. Came as a young bride, into the home of her husband. Their together home. Although they're on the ground floor, they're also on the corner of the block. The lounge is light-filled; it has a deep bay window and a little extra one at the side, on which hangs a small picture of coloured glass. Margaret sits there as the sun comes up. There would have been stained glass once in all of the windows. Some tenements round here still have traces. But you've to go to the West End to see the good stuff: your languid, pastel roses, your bright ship's sails. Here, in the East End of Glasgow, the wealth never quite reached as far as was anticipated. When they built Dennistoun, the plan was for mostly villas, terraces, gardens. But the middle classes didn't pour in after all. What *is* it about East Ends? Is it the way the wind blows? If people move from the city centre to escape factory smells, does the badness follow them east? Margaret doesn't know that, actually. But they have a perfectly good library along the road, so it could be a thing she knows. If she wanted.

Anyway, the dreams of long vistas of townhouses for the upwardly mobile were subsumed by tenements (though there's still a beautiful clutch of villas scattered at the top of the Drives). Tenements are much more practical, each building housing layers of families instead of one. Tenements, some with little shops below, and the cafés, pubs, parks and prospects for what you would call the respectable working classes.

Margaret knows so many random things. It's hard to know what to do with knowledge when you're old. Eighty-two – that's quite old, isn't it? It is for here. Seventy-five is a whole life's expectancy if you're a woman in Dennistoun. (She hates knowing that fact, but it remains true, whether she acknowledges it or not.) If she lived in the leafy West End, she could be blessed with perhaps a decade longer on God's green earth. But, despite her mother's best efforts, Margaret's an East Ender. She sits here in her lounge, and she fills her head with facts, and she reads, and she misses her husband, and she watches shafts of coloured light play across her wrists as she holds her mug of tea. Folk wouldn't believe it if she said, so she doesn't, but the glass picture in her morning-light window was made by Margaret. Took herself off to a stained-glass workshop, so she did. Just along the road (run by a lovely, bearded fellow who was patient and kind when she cut herself or messed up blobs of solder). About a month after Bert had died; the house was yawning and sad and she'd such a need to be doing, doing some practical, useful action with her hands, now they were no longer required to lift and roll and wipe. She didn't find stained glass a pleasant craft – there were specks of glass under her skin for days – but she's awfy pleased with the result. It's a small, leaded rectangular panel, no bigger than a sheet of paper, hanging in the top casement of her window. The panel has one half of a beaming sun in one corner, beating on cloud-shaped trees and curvaceous hills. It's vaguely Art Deco, all cellophane blue and lilacs, with a beautiful pearly iridescent shard that is moonlight in the mist. She loves that wee bit best. How it winks at her. It's not as if she stole it. She only took a thing she really, really needed. They were given boxes of glass scraps to rummage through in the workshop. But she could see shelves of the real stuff, gorgeous barley-sugar slices of colour, and she'd noticed a few small glass squares arranged on a light-board below. Margaret couldn't resist that one pearly tile, the way the pinkish glass caught fire and shimmered into baby-blue then mauve. It reminded her of the wee matinee jackets she used to knit. So, she took it. Once she'd snipped and soldered it into place, what could the bearded lad do? He was very nice about it, even as he was moving the rest of the iridescent tiles away. But she only needed that one. She's not greedy. Except for her mind, perhaps. It still wants to devour stuff at a rate of knots.

She's reading a fascinating book at the moment. Margaret has a table where she keeps the book she's reading and the one just finished too. Just in case. You never know. You think a story's done and dusted, then some loose wisp of plot will hook you back, and you have to check it again. She wishes you could do that with life.

She fingers her book. A biography about a chap called John Maclean – a Red Clydesider, long gone now. Such pathos to his story. And who knows – they may be related, for Margaret was a Maclean once, before she became a Camberg.

After the Maclean book, she'll go for something light. A novel with a cursive, witty font. You should read as you eat – substantial courses, then a sorbet to cleanse the palate. The colour of the Maclean book matches her William Morris curtains. She's heard folk do that now. They call it 'curating'. She saw a picture in a magazine, where all the books on the shelves were in colour order. Imagine! Eschewing every thread of sense and language (*language* indeed, when it is books!) to sort your literature into some daft, random rainbow. How do you ascribe a hierarchy to colour?

You can't judge a book by its cover.

Her curtains have a wee cord which she can tug to glide them open. Margaret frequently says 'Ta-dah!' or 'Curtain up' when she pulls it. From her window, she looks out onto other tenements (ignoring her scrap of garden, which is a shame-filled state of rampant grass and weeds she pretends is no longer there), onto the new flats where the school used to be and the little grassy square with its statue. There's been a gang of boys there all morning, mucking about on bikes. But they've gone now. Buffalo Bill is all on his own. She wonders if he's ever appeared in a pub quiz? *Where in Scotland is there a monument to Buffalo Bill?* Outside Margaret's front room, that's where. A whole troupe of cowboys performed here once: Bill, his horses, Annie Oakley and several Sioux warriors too, all dancing outside her house. Her granny said they drove a herd of buffalo up Duke Street. Hard to imagine, even with the evidence of cast-iron Bill astride his bucking Bronco. It is so quiet in the Drives. You can't conceive of cowboys here. Well, not that type. The Drives are the douce part of Dennistoun: a handsome grid of sandstone streets sandwiched between the busy thoroughfares of Duke Street below and Alexandra Parade above. Close by, in Hillfoot Street, is a tailor's shop so quaint it's almost coming back into fashion. *Camberg's Suits and Alterations*, with its wide, sloping apostrophe S, and the little dark patch they painted over. Her husband's shop. His chalk still rests in a pewter dish on the counter, his tape measure curled limply like a dog awaiting his master's return. Margaret appreciates that Donald keeps it there, that he's barely changed the shop at all. Donald was her husband's apprentice, a 'boy' who's now in his sixties: slightly stooped, hair and skin as faded as the paper patterns pinned to the wall. Hardly anyone buys bespoke suits these days. They were going to let the lease go, but Donald's grandson – one of those irritating youths with groomed beards, the type who dress like lumberjacks and push liquorice allsorts into their earlobes – said the old styles were coming back. *So retro.* The way he said it, though, with a nasty smirk, when Donald tries so hard to keep up with the trends. Smirky Scott, she calls him. Always sneering at her and Donald.

Her. The shop has nothing to do with her, really. It is Albert's no longer. Bert didn't like the thought of Margaret working. He was quite strict that way – though she did do the books at home when she was younger. Before life got too busy. Bert had always hoped . . . Her heart begins to patter. She bangs a mild fist against her chest, as if that will restart things.

Donald, God love him, said he'd take the place over when Albert passed. Promised to pay the rent and everything. It's still Albert's name above the door, and she's grateful to Donald for that. He's taken on a pig in a poke, mind. She doubts he'll limp on through this year. Be as well pouring money down the drain. At least this flat is bought and paid for. All those tough times, all those years of scrimping. *I never want you to worry, yekirati.* Precious. That's what Bert called her. Margaret liked how it made her feel. To be precious is to be at the centre of somebody's world.

A drench of loneliness passes, like a cloud sliding over the sun, and she fumbles for the telly doofer. Some blaring game show, a programme about houses, the news, all the terrible news, and she snaps it off again, as if the telly's scalded her. She seizes her book, tries to read, but the words won't settle.

It's all that stuff in her brain – stuff she keeps shoving in, thirsty to fill the gaps and keep the noise down. She expects it's very messy in there by now. Music starts overhead. She sighs. All those lives above her, here in this tenement, where Margaret lives. It's a lovely close, mind, with its green-tiled walls and its worn, polished banister. Four floors, with two flats on each floor. She knows a wee bit about every one of those houses. Sharing the ground floor with her are a nice enough family – mum Jacqueline, daughter Sharon and grandson Ryan, who is two. Plus a parade of foster children, who come and go. One up, you have Gordon, a teacher who lives with his Peke. Across the landing from Gordon are a recently-arrived pair of girls – students who might be French, but since they only nod and murmur if you pass them in the close, it's hard to be certain. They are most definitely exotic. However, if they have one more party like the one last weekend, she'll be introducing herself formally very soon. Second floor – one flat is currently empty, and the other houses a doctor, his wife and their baby. Gorgeous wee thing.

On the top is a couple with outlandish spectacles. He's an architect and she's just opened a shop called 'Waste Not Want Not'. It resembles an old greengrocers, with fruit and veg piled high in crates – but Dennistoun already has the Asian man along Duke Street who sells fruit and veg (and fish and beautiful bright spices and mobile phone top-ups). And there's a Co-op. *But no*, says Zara with the black winged specs and asymmetric fringe, her store is unique – because you take in your own bags and they plop your purchases straight in. (Just like an old greengrocer.) They sell olive oils too, with bits of chilli in, and detergents in vast glass jars to be decanted into the customer's own bottles. It's a clever gimmick, and it's proving popular with a certain Dennistoun type, but Margaret wonders where the question of liability lies? What if you get your bottles confused once you get home and pour soap suds on your salad? She hopes it works out, mind – she's nice, Zara. Given Margaret some samples: a few filthy potatoes, two brown eggs and the greenest lettuce ever (complete with bonus slug tucked in the leaves). It was delicious.

And the other flat is . . .

Her mind's gone blank. If she took her time, she could probably remember the folk from twenty years ago. Forty even. Margaret's outlasted them all.

Changes. She's not sure what that's about. Every minute, every second, we change. A flake of skin falls, a tiny vein ruptures. Our brain holds one more fact than it did a page ago. Our heart has one less beat remaining. The sky shifts and the colour from the glass makes us think of the families from before.

She's going to go out soon. Get the messages for her lunch before they run out of rolls.

Chapter Three

Gerard's close is right on Duke Street, above the Dennistoun BBQ, which is a posh burger joint he's never been in. He rests his forehead briefly against their window. Breathes nice and slow. The burger place looks nothing like McDonald's; it is all dark wood benches and tables with squeezy plastic tomatoes instead of sauce bottles. Canny be that posh, because they've hardly got any lampshades on their lights, mostly just bare, coppery bulbs. People move inside. He sees a girl at the counter, reading a paper and scratching her nose. A man in a long apron lifts a pint glass high, polishes it with a white cloth. Each night, smells of cooking waft into their flat. Gerard and his wee brother describe what the folk downstairs might be eating, taking it in turns to shoogle the wean. He almost knows the menu off by heart. Pit beef brisket bun, hand-pulled pork – he'd even give the 'Meatless Jackburger' a go.

There's a man coming out their main door as Gerard approaches his close. Long and skinny, with a white trackie top zipped up to his throat. His eyes pierce into Gerard's. Glassy-grey. Skin below his eyes is pouched and shadowed, but the skin along the rim of his eyelids is crimson red.

'Alright, wee man?'

'Aye.'

Gerard tries to move past him, but the man stands his ground.

'You stay here?'

'Eh, naw.'

'You sure? Here – you're no Rissa's boy, are you? Marissa, I mean?'

The ground begins to bubble. Gerard shakes his head.

'You know her, but?'

Gerard's hands grip his bike. Hairs on his neck prickle. He tries to swallow, but even that is impossible, so he just waits, head bowed. The man rolls up the sleeves of his trackie. It is a deliberate action, so Gerard can see the tattoo on his forearm. A curious symbol. He keeps staring at it, waiting for the man to do whatever it is he's going to do. You think at first the tattoo is a gallows, like Hangman, but it is a line down and a line across the top and a smaller line along the bottom. It could be a fancy letter, but then there's a kind of half-circle round it, and a squiggle that might be a big R, but it might be a snake, because all the shapes start jumbling around; he squeezes his eyes, but he can still see them, squirming on the guy's arm.

The man slides his hand into his pocket. Guys like him are always carrying. Gerard can hear the noises of the street – people and cars and pigeons. But he could be a million miles away.

'If you do see her, will you tell her Davey called? Tell her I'm back, alright?'

Gerard manages to nod his head.

'Just say I'm needing a wee chat, OK?'

He keeps his eyes on the pavement.

The man puts his hand under Gerard's chin. It feels like ice. He presses his fingers, slightly, into Gerard's throat. 'Don't forget, wee man. Tell her it's Davey. And I'll be back soon.'

He waits until the man has gone, then wheels his bike into the close. Softly, he breathes out, then in. Out, then in. Leans against the door to shut it, but the stupid thing won't lock. The door entry's broken again, so he's to lug the bike up one flight of stairs. It may be old and beat up, but it's his. His mum said she 'won' it. He doesn't believe her, but he also doesn't care. The bike is the best thing she's ever given him. He could chain it on the landing, but he won't risk it, not with the door bust. Wee pair of bolt cutters and . . . wheech: *look what I found.*

It's what Gerard would do.

He tries to forget about the man. There are always people coming round here. Sometimes his mum borrows money off folk and forgets to pay it back. The close stinks of pish. He lifts his bike over the puddle in the corner, bumps it up the worn stone steps. When the outside door is locked, their close is actually pretty clean. For a wee while, their flat was too. The nearer he gets to their house, the slower he moves. He knows he should be hurrying, because he can hear the baby screaming from here.

'For God's sake!' He says it out loud, so the neighbours will know, know that he is outside, not inside, letting her bawl her head off. He bangs the door with his elbow, still holding onto the handlebars of his bike. 'Anthony!' he shouts. 'You in there? Gonny let us in?'

There's no point in shouting for his mum. If she's sleeping through this, she'll sleep through anything.

His wee brother comes to the door, tear-stained. 'Where were you? You said you'd get us breakfast.'

'Well, I got you bloody lunch, alright?'

Gerard pushes past him, props the bike in the hall and goes into the kitchen. He dumps a packet of Kraft Cheesey Pasta on the counter. 'Did you make her up a bottle like I told you?' He flicks the switch on the kettle.

'I couldn't. It's no working. Telly's not too.'

Electric must be off again. He goes into his mother's bedroom. The curtains are pulled tight, but one end is hanging off the rail, so there's enough light to see. The room is thick with stale air, but it is the smell of shite that hits him as soon as he moves towards the bed. He kicks an empty bottle out the way. It rolls over his mother's works, which she keeps neatly in a tin. It is the only neat thing in this house. A teaspoon and a roll of tinfoil lie next to dirty cotton wool. The baby is on her back, roaring and greeting, her face puce.

'Here, here. It's alright.' He lifts her, and the sodden, shitey nappy slides right off. It is that heavy. He leaves it where it has fallen, right beside his mother's nose. She twitches slightly but doesn't stir. Wherever she is is not here.

'Hey, hey,' he whispers into his wee sister's damp curls. She flails; warm shite is on his hands, all over his hands. On the bed, his mother mumbles. He can only make out the word *treasure*. It doesny mean anything. He used to think she was saying it to him, but it's just crap she mutters when she's out of it. He carries Miranda out of the stinking room. Prays there are some nappies left, and there is, thank you, Jesus, there's half a packet beside the toilet. He puts a manky bath towel on the floor, because it is cleaner than the floor itself, then lays his little sister on it. She's stopped screaming now; it's more of a pant, her eyes fixed on him. There's no wipes, so he does his best with bog roll and water from the tap. Her arse is red raw. There used to be some cream in a wee tub. He shouts through to Anthony. 'Gonny check the unit and see if there's any nappy cream?'

The first time he did this, Gerard was embarrassed, holding a wee lassie's legs up in the air and wiping her bum, but he knows it stops her crying. He cleans his hands on the edge of the towel.

'I can't see any.' Anthony is there in the hall, behind him. 'What are we having to eat, Gerard?'

He wants to scream at his wee brother, *You're flucken seven year old, you sort it*. Tries instead to feel the same gentleness he feels for Miranda (Miranda Macklin – wee soul. What a name. What is it with his mother and crappy names?). If he shouts at Anthony, he'll be just like his mum.

You're the eldest.

Does being the eldest mean his mother doesn't have to cook them dinner? Does it mean Gerard has to change the wean every time she's a rancid nappy?

'Where's my mum's bag?'

'In the room.'

'Go and get it.'

'But we're not allowed–'

'Just go and get it, Anthony.' He lets Miranda's wee legs kick about. Her skin looks so sore. Then she does this weird flip and wriggles over onto her belly. Gerard grabs her, before she rolls into more filth. Should babies do that? The health visitor doesn't come to the house any more, so he doesn't know if this is normal. What if she rolled over on the bed, shit he canny leave her lying on the bed any more. Where are they going to put her? They should've kept that stupid baby box, but his mum chucked it once they'd used all the stuff inside. Still on his knees, he holds his wriggling sister against his chest. His mother didn't actually chuck the box – he did, after she'd tried to burn it with her lighter. *Keep tripping over the fucking thing*, she was yelling, the flame burning her thumb.

He gets up, supporting his sister under her bare bum, the clean nappy in his teeth. He can't bear the thought of her red skin rubbing against dry paper. There must be something – would margarine work?

Anthony brings his mum's bag into the hall.

'Check her purse.'

His wee brother shakes his head.

Gerard snatches it from him, balancing the baby on his hip, but it's no use; she's slipping down. He goes into the living room, shoves aside a pile of clothes and toys so he can get a seat on the couch. Bounces Miranda on his knee. *Please don't pee on me*. Please let there be some money inside his mum's purse. Sometimes there is a wad of cash, and you can skim a tenner off, easy. But the purse is empty. Not even coins in it.

'See?' Anthony goes quiet. 'I looked already.'

Gerard stares at the wall in front of him, at the peeling purple and white striped wallpaper which they did not put up, at the black mouldy bits along the windowsill and the stains beneath, at the grey swirly carpet and the bunched-up Venetian blinds. Their house is as trendy as the barbecue café downstairs because they don't have a lightshade either.

'That letter's still there too.'

That letter. The letter that triggered this latest ... Gerard doesn't have the words for it. *Episode. Relapse.*

These are the kinds of words they use, those women who come with files in their arms and concern on their faces. And it wasny really the letter that set her off; his mum would've got here anyway. She was always heading.

'What does it say?' His brother thrusts the paper into Gerard's lap. Absently, he looks at the letters, which swim and wink on the page. 'I know!' Anthony's finger traces over a long eel-like shape. 'It's a huh and a oh and a uh and a ess – is it about our house, Gerard?'

It is the Loch Ness monster, the first shape, with a neck, a long thin neck, and his heart is going like the clappers again, so he grits his teeth. If he looks really hard and doesn't blink, sometimes you can catch them. But not this time, not with Anthony staring at him. Honisguhus. The markings dance and switch. Hsgnhoshoiusin. It's not just the letters, it's the whole big block of black, writhing and hammering at you like bricks smashing in your face. There was a teacher once, a student, who he thinks could suss what Gerard saw because she would sit with him, tell him to take it slow. But she was only there for part of primary four.

His throat tightens. Miranda farts. Begins to cry again.

'I'm hungry, Gerard.'

'Right.' He lays his sister on the couch, puts the dry nappy on her. 'Right, hold her. Sit down, Anthony, and take the wean. I won't be long, I promise.'

'You said that before.'

'Will you give me a flucken break?' he shouts, then immediately regrets it. He rubs his eyes, just enjoying the cool of his hands, just pushing up into his eyebrows. 'Here, wee man. Gonny take her. I canny make you pasta if the electric's off, so I'll away and get us some bread, OK? I've enough left for bread.' He doesn't. He doesn't have any money left at all.

'OK.'

He leaves his siblings in front of an empty TV screen. Swithers by the meter at the door, then shifts his bike so he can remove the top-up card from its slot. Outside, the air is brighter than he remembers; coming out of their house is always like coming out the pictures, only if it was a black-and-white film you'd just seen, and then the world outside was in colour. Gerard puts his hands in his pockets. Surveys the street. His mouth goes dry, like someone has sooked all the saliva out and they've taken the juice from his eyes too, because everything is a bit blurry, and then really, really sharp. He needs to do this. He knows there is a food bank at the church near where the Broncos hang. Everlasting Arms – it has a lovely name – you can totally see Jesus, pure standing there in his white dress and beard, arms forever stretching to *suffer the little children*. Good on you, big man. But it is only open Wednesday to Saturday and he doesn't think they top up your electric. Plus, what if it's him and not his mum that goes? They'd grass you up soon as look at you, church or no, because they all do, everybody does, whenever you try and ask, not even ask, just hint that you might need a wee bit help and it's all, *oh, wee soul, why did you not speak to your social worker or your teacher or* . . .

Or

Is there no one in your family? Who's your family? Oh, your mum? We thought she was coping fine.

Gerard has been in foster care before.

A big removal lorry is getting stuck between the corner of Duke Street and the side street that leads to the wee park. The wheels grind up onto the pavement and a woman walking there shouts *fucksake*, bangs on the side of the lorry. It stops, begins to go backwards, nearly hitting the car behind it. Another woman gets out the car, arms waving.

Gerard is being distracted. He is doing it on purpose, because he's a shitebag. He needs to sort this. His wee brother is hungry. Fucking fuck. He hates saying that word: *fuck*. Flucken fucksake, how is that fair, when all these folk out here are buying stuff and moving stuff and not giving a shit? Fucking Robin Hood. Fucking Bronco fucking Buffalo Bill. In his pocket, he makes a fist around the top-up card. His eyes are still greasy-feeling, as if the world is damp and folding round him. Panic is weird – it's slow *and* fast. You could suffocate in panic, and he thinks that might be quite a nice thing, for the sky to push down into your face and for the ground to sook you up, everything caving in slow motion while your breath is speeding and your heart is going mental; for your heart to just go for it, just fucking burst already, instead of kidding on it's going to, like it always does. Because that's exhausting.

The nice primary four teacher gave him a CD – he doesn't have it any more, but he minds it had white clouds on the cover, and some wee dude lying on top of the clouds, totally chill with his hands behind his head, and a big cheesy grin. They should have had him lying in the sea, though. That would have made more sense, because of what the man kept saying on the tape. *The feelings we get when we are scared are the same feelings we get when we're excited. So tell yourself you are excited. Ride the wave!* Gerard listened to it a couple of times – because he liked that teacher, he really did. Her name was Susan (imagine a teacher telling you her first name, like it was OK), and she was the kind of person you wanted to do stuff for. She always asked you nicely, and she was really happy when you did it. Whatever you did, even if it was a mistake. She had this big smile that came out of inside of her, it came out of her mouth and her eyes.

Ride the wave.

The street is moving the same way the words in his mum's letter did. When he thinks about his mum, lying there, his eyes ache. He squeezes them shut, just for a wee second, then opens them again.

Ride the wave.

The top-up card jags his fingers. That one thin slice of what he can see through his eyelids is all weird. It is like a magnifying glass. He sees: the shopfronts of the bookie's and the florist's and the fruit and veg man's with the sacks of muddy potatoes outside, the open crates of mushrooms and cut, pink-mouthed melons, and he is reckoning that that will be the best bet because of how the shop is laid out. It is long and dark inside, and there's usually just the one old guy and he's aye out on the street, fiddling with his display, serving folk like it's a market stall, so he'll just wait until the old boy comes out, then he'll run inside and dip the till, fuck knows how the till works, but he'll slam all the buttons, just slam it, it will be just like stealing sweeties and he's done that loads of times, what's the difference cause he's just taking money this time instead of Haribos, and his focus is narrowing, narrowing and sharpening harder as this old dear comes into view, all skinny and wee in her yellow cardie, how she is bent over the display of fruit, holding an orange like it really matters, and it's an orange for fucksake, who gives a fuck about an orange? How her purse is just sticking out of her bag, how her bag swings and hings behind her as she rummages and he is pumping himself up, the way he's seen his mum go, want a square go, *cunt fuck shit* she'll no even notice if he's fast, and he's fast, oh Christ, he is fast and hard-slamming into her because the stupid old cow turns, she bloody turns just at the point he is running at her, into her, grabbing the purse and sending her flying, he didny mean to touch, and she is falling backwards, sideys, over, he doesny flucken know just keep running, running from the awful, terrible noise she is making, and the shouting, the folk shouting so he just runs and runs and runs.

Chapter Four

Claire leans against the door of her Audi. She's still shaking. Mostly at the vitriol which spewed from that woman's mouth, when she realised the lorry was connected with Claire. Why did Claire say sorry, though? But she's also shaking at the fact she's just survived ten tonnes of metal rolling backwards, near into her face. The removal lorry must have made it round the corner; since she's been arguing with the woman, it's disappeared. She should follow them, but the guys have a set of keys, they've got the address and she just needs to compose herself. She knows her face will be scarlet, can feel the tightness in her cheeks. Her car's parked in at the kerb; it's fine, it's not blocking anything. And she wants to wait until the cow who shouted at her has gone. Claire feels the hardness of the metal at her back. Welcome to the neighbourhood.

The sky rumples greyly, but the air's quite warm. Seagulls bicker, and a beady pigeon eyeballs her from a crumbling windowsill overhead. It shakes its feathers, then flies off, deformed claws gliding above Duke Street. Her head feels tender. She's aware she's clutching onto the door handle behind her. It was a decent thing, to say sorry to that woman. What is wrong with kindness? As soon as you're kind, folk see the cracks in you. *Could of fucking killed me*, the woman screamed. *Glaikit fucking boot*. One wee thing. How can one wee thing burst your bubble? Claire is not glaikit. She has booked and organised the removers all by herself. She has found and (part) furnished a new home.

She can do this. She will do this, until one day it becomes second nature again to be untethered. She gazes down the street, which is the longest in Europe. Or Scotland. Or Glasgow – whatever, it's a long one. More importantly, it's on the up. That's what the estate agent kept telling her. *Way more for your money than out west. Get in while it's hot. Perfect timing.*

Debatable.

This morning has been horrible. Packing the guddle of their old life, not taking what she wants but what she is given, moving silently through the rooms of their home – their home, which he is keeping because he has no decency whatsoever. And the master bedroom had just been decorated – *that wallpaper cost a fortune* – and she didn't want it anyway, for how could she ever bear to be there: those walls imbued with all their hopeful memories? And now they – he and *she* – the other she, the new she – will lie there together in . . .

With the cot in the next room.

Breathing in hurts. Her stomach rumbles. There's a nice-looking coffee shop on the corner and an organic bakery she spotted nearer to the flat. Food has become her default lover. The comfort of soft, pillowy bites, of unctuous stodge. Seeking the heartiest solace she can shovel in. She knows this, and it has to stop. But the scabby rental she's been living in hasn't helped. This, here, her new life in her new home will be a watershed. New choices (because, let's face it, her old ones were shite). She will head up to the flat and settle the removers. She will resist the urge to cocoon herself from civilisation and lock the door forever. Instead, she will come back down to Duke Street and buy some food. Healthy food. Cram her cupboards with bounty. There's a bright display of fruit further down the road; Claire is considering the merits of half a melon versus a whole raggedy pineapple, which will be a well-intentioned but wasteful purchase, bound to sit splendidly in her new kitchen until it shrivels and starts to smell of pear drops – and then the half-melon is crashing to the ground; she watches it literally crash and erupt into jewel-pink vomit at the same time as a flurry of bodies collide and spill. It occurs so quickly, and is so very shocking, that it takes one deep pull of held-in breath to process what she sees.

And what she sees is this:

An old lady in a yellow cardigan falling to the pavement. Her leg buckles beneath her and her skirt flies up terribly. It waves its humiliation of undergarments and white skin, and there is a strangled cry, then silence

The traffic continuing to move, except for a bus which is screeching to a halt, right in the middle of the street, the driver jumping down from the cab and over the road, and this unthinking act of connection makes her heart leap

A young boy helping up the old lady, then he is not; he is wrestling and running away, he has on a grey hoodie and his hair is brown, that is all she knows, and he is running away

People gathering, Claire not being able to see what is going on, except she is running too, towards the fruit shop and the commotion of heads and smashed fruit and frenzied voices. She pushes through the people – why? What will she do, she doesn't know but you have to do

What?

There are maybe a dozen folk, all crowded round the figure on the pavement. The woman is a piece of broken china, pale and still, with her eyes not fully closed. The flesh on her visible, bent knee is torn and bleeding; the soul has come out without her tights on, no coat, just her cardie and her unprotected skin. An Asian man is making a pillow with his patterned jumper, but the bus driver is saying 'Don't move her head' as two women squat by the old lady's side, sharing her pavement and saying 'Oh, hen, oh, hen' over and over like cooing doves. Above them, in a chorus, other voices.

'Somebody call 999.'

'He is–'

'Am on it. The Royal's two minutes away.'

'What happened?'

'Did yous see what happened?'

'Aye.'

'No.'
'The old dear fell.'
'She was mugged.'
'No, she wasny.'
'I seen a wee boy.'
'So did I,' says Claire. 'A boy in a grey hoodie.'

The Asian man murmurs. One of the cooing women tugs on the ravaged skirt, pulling it down a little to restore some decency, but not so much that it brushes the injured leg. Suddenly, the old lady heaves and shudders, a terrible, gagging cluck rising from her mouth. She is choking.

'Put her in the recovery position!' shouts Claire, kneeling down.

'But her leg!' says the driver.

'Move her!' Claire tries to open the old lady's mouth, which is rigid with fear and choking. White froth pooling, Claire shoving her little finger in at the corner.

'Are you a nurse?'

Warm wet prising, her pinkie in, touching slevvery, flailing gums. 'I'm a lawyer.'

'Fucksake.'

The blaring of a siren, coming closer, closer. Hurry *up*. Hot blood, fragile skin. The old lady's lips are purple-blue. Claire shoves her fingers in deeper, forcing the wrinkled, gathered folds of the neck to crick, wider, and, yes, there it is – a smooth hard curve which she hooks deftly up and out. The old lady's dentures sit in her palm.

'Here.' Claire passes them to the driver, and is gently turning the old lady's head when she hears a voice you don't mess with telling her to 'move back', so she does, gladly, and lets the professionals step in. There are no choking sounds any more, no sounds at all.

She gets to her feet, an unknown hand helping her up. Police are arriving too, and the crowd negotiates their way onwards, dissolving whence they came, apart from the unlucky few who are stopped and corralled by the cops. Claire is shivery. She leans against the wall of the fruit shop. All she knows is that she can't remember her new address. The police will want her details and she will look so stupid.

'Here.' The bus driver returns the teeth to Claire. 'They're wanting a statement. I need to shift my bus.'

She should give the dentures to the ambulance crew, but they are busy, working inside the vehicle, in which the old lady is still silent. A pigeon pecks at Claire's feet. A policewoman comes and takes her details. Claire hears herself speak in a monotone: yes, she saw a young lad running away; grey hoodie, yes; quite wee – not a teen, well, maybe not, it's hard to say; no, she wouldn't recognise him again. She finds that she remembers her new address fine, and when she gives her occupation as 'lawyer', the constable nods, and she notes the imperceptible shift in her demeanour, which speaks of mutual respect. All the while, the teeth sit in Claire's hand. Smooth white gnashers, coated with a dying woman's saliva.

'Is she still alive?' Claire asks the constable. 'Is she going to be alright?'

The ambulance is moving off, blue-lit. The officer doesn't know. She will *be in touch* if there's anything else. Claire is free to go. She walks slowly back to her car, which she realises she's left unlocked. It is full of books and pictures, of lampshades and plants and bin bags of clothes (because her husband refused to split their set of luggage, and she no longer had the energy to fight). But nobody's stolen all her worldly crap.

She goes to open the car door, discovers her hand is still full of teeth. They leer at her. She should have given them to the cop. Claire turns, but the police are getting into their car now, further down the street. They look so vulnerable, the teeth. (Not the polis.) Homeless, and slightly sticky: in fact her whole hand is sticky. She had her fingers down an old woman's throat. Chattering teeth: it's not really them, it's Claire's hand, which is trembling. She gets into the car. A spike from her yucca pokes her in the eye. She turns the key in the ignition, and promptly bursts into tears. It is mostly neat, noiseless crying she's been doing of late, but this is something else. It is a shudder and a heave, it is the mirror image of an old lady choking, it is the up from the soles of your feet, soul-deep crying, it is your actual soul-being-split-in-two kind of crying, and on it comes, on and on, rolling over the top of her, unravelling in clear, hot ribbons. The teeth fall into her lap. Her mobile is ringing; she has no clue where her bag is. Claire cuddles the steering wheel. The only thing she can see is black vinyl and her two fingers, swimming in the tide. She keeps her face there and lets the steering column cradle the weight of her head, wonders, briefly, what would happen if she just nutted it and triggered the airbag. What if that was her last day on earth, that old woman? To finish it, prone on the pavement, after some wee shite has literally upended your life.

Eventually, she sits up. Rubs the heels of her hands in her eyes. Checks her hair in the mirror, and sees the flushed and furious face her mother sported, at the height of her menopause. At least Claire has that to look forward to. Her phone burbles; her bag is right there, has been there all along. It's a text from the removal men, saying they have given up waiting and are going for lunch and *does she know where she's going*?

Not really.

Claire places the old lady's dentures on top of the nearest box. Maybe she can post them? She checks her mirror a second time (for oncoming traffic, not masochism), indicates, eases out slowly, because the world is raw and vulnerable and vicious and cruel, and hard things hurt soft bodies, and it would be just her bloody luck to have a car crash to complete the morning. The side street is tight with parked cars. A white van flashes her, she drives slowly up the hill, hovers at the junction, then gingerly turns into her new street. Cars parked bumper to bumper, up on the kerb, rear-end into the adjacent road – how the removal lorry made it up here is a mystery. But there it is, parked in front of her new flat. No room for Claire, though, so she circles and prowls, inching further up the hill, into the next street, searching for a space. Realising this will be her future pattern.

Their old house had a driveway. Ach, stop this. Stop this endless, miserable comparison. *Onslow Drive. Armadale. Garthland.* She will need to learn these street names, reset herself in new surroundings. There are spaces here, but she's getting further from where she wants to be, is disorientated. The East End is a mystery to Claire. All she knows is that it starts with the Barras, bleeds into the Billy Boys of Bridgeton, then winds up at Celtic Park. And that Dennistoun is definitely 'on the up'. She drives past a fridge, proudly erect on the pavement, a cushionless couch alongside.

There is a flash of grey in the narrowness of alley that runs between two separate tenements; it could be the grey of a pigeon or bin bag, the reflected grey of a passing lamppost. Could be thin air. But it's an elbow. She watches it in her rear-view mirror. It is a figure, hands on knees. Smallish, male, the grey, upturned hood of his sweatshirt concealing his face. Claire brakes. Her stomach contracts. She thinks it is the boy. The mugger. She reaches for her phone as a car behind her toots.

She raises two fingers. 'Two minutes!' she mouths. The driver is pointing his finger at his head, then at her. Blares his horn again, longer; it is a horn that will brook no disputes, and her thumb is stuttering: what number is she going to call? Can she even call 999 – is this an actual emergency?

'Christ!' she shouts, at no one in particular; the car behind is edging ever closer to her bumper, virtually forcing her to move, and when she looks again, the boy – if it was him – has gone. The man behind goes to get out of his car – he looks like a bodybuilder. Claire drives off before he reaches her, turns blindly into the next street, realises, as the car stalking her blasts one final, furious trumpet, that she has just gone through a No Entry sign. She's in a one-way street. Wrong way down a one-way street. But there is a glorious, patient little space right at the corner. If she stops there, she can reverse out. Claire pulls into the space. Thinks about what she just saw. That lane isn't long. Just goes between two tenements. Perhaps it leads to back courts, which would be . . .

She gets out of the car. Locks it this time. East or west, most of Glasgow's streets, the tenemented ones at least, are built on a grid system. So, the boy could only go two ways. There's no harm in walking round the block. Apart from a young woman wheeling a pram, the street is quiet. Claire walks to the end, turns left. It would be this street the boy would come out on. She thumbs her phone – 101. That's it – she knew there was another number when it's not an emergency but you want to call the police. She should have taken that policewoman's name at the same time the policewoman was taking hers. But she wasn't thinking straight.

Claire is not a criminal lawyer. There is nothing darkly glamorous about her job; she doesn't hang around Barlinnie, or bang on courtroom desks, doesn't rock a flowing black gown. Mostly, she buys houses and divorces folk. And, yes, she does recognise the irony of this, has been much delighted by the sympathetic quips and comments that *at least you'll save some money*, so delighted that she mugs along with the jokes, each and every fucking time they come.

There is a ripple in the clouds, the tenements turning butterscotch and rose. Somewhere distant, a bell chimes. Maybe you can hear the cathedral from here. *Here is the bell that never rang.* She notes the name of this new street, works out that she is heading north. If she does see the boy, the police will need to know exactly where she is. She is being her best, most detailed self. A man, coming the other way, stops to let his dog pee. She moves to the side, skirting man and dog, passes a big skip full of rubble, and there he is, there, at the top of the hill, on the other side of the road. A boy in a grey hoodie. She still can't see his face, but he is a defiant wee shite, arms folded. Clearly does not give a toss about what he's just done; sauntering, Jesus, it is virtually a swagger, she can't be definite, but it is surely the same boy. It is not for her to judge. Claire presses three digits on her phone. Crosses the road: he won't know her, and she wants to get a closer look.

'Hello? Police?'

Her heart is thumping. Her plan is to carry on walking, then about-turn at the top and follow him. Keep him in her sights until the police get here. Arrogant wee prick. Not even got the decency to go properly to ground. His walk seems almost aimless, like time is unimportant and he owns the street. She's positive now that it is the same boy, has the vigilante certainty of the hunt.

She tells the operator it is urgent, explains the situation. Keeps her voice calm. Nearer and nearer, him walking, her walking. Her talking, him with his rolling gait. They have officers in the vicinity, the operator tells her. Claire makes a mumbling noise of assent because they are now virtually adjacent, her and the boy, and she doesn't want to spook him. But she wants to see, she wants to *see* the spite, the malice that must reside within his eyes because that will justify the rage she's feeling. She actually thinks she could reach out and punch him, no matter how skinny his wrists are, how shabby and threadbare and stained his hoodie is, and how he's wee, he's really wee up close. *Uh-huh* she says as the operator asks if she can still see the boy, and she is fizzing, Claire is physically electric with a desire to thrust this boy to the ground and twist and break his leg behind him and scream *You did that, you wee fuck, you did that to an old lady*. She steels herself to weigh the measure of him, this little smout, this height of nothing, who is continually, constantly, looking at his feet. But she, Claire, is looking full-square at him. At his small, tear-stained face.

And then she looks away, distraught.

'We'll have someone with you in two ticks,' says the nice operator down the phone.

Chapter Five

Gerard picks at the underside of the desk, keeps picking at it while they talk to him, and go away, and come back and talk again. He's been picking so long that a skelf has worked its way into his finger; he can feel it dig each time he flexes his knuckle, feels his blood beat along the wound. It's good. Reminds him who he is. You can get lost in here.

Gerard has been in here before. Not this windowless detention room, with its wire-glass and yellow strip lights, but somewhere else in this police station, in an upstairs office where a polis and a social worker interviewed him. Theft by OLP (breaking into a barn in the short-lived Wildlife World), theft of a donkey (which was bullshit by the way – the donkey followed them), vandalism (riding said donkey through a field of allotments). It was a laugh. Even the polis was trying not to smile, going on about the 'Wild West trail of destruction' and 'Which one of yous is Tonto?' They do that, the police, especially the younger ones, the gallus cool dudes with their cropped-in hair and big muscles and chewing gum. They talk like they're your pals, giving it all, *c'mon, wee man, just tell us who you were with, just tell us where you went.*

Just tell us, just tell us; it will be better for you if you do.
Will. It. Fluck.

Gerard is older now, and wiser. If you don't speak, then they can't interview you at all. They can ask questions, but your silence is yours. It's a thing to hold on to, to dig in as deep as this wee skelf. And so what if it's hurting you?

A tanned arm slides a plastic cup of water towards him. It's the younger of the two cops, the one with the Celtic knot tattoo.

'Your vodka, sir?' Guy's a prick.

Gerard's eyes remain fixed on the surface of the desk, on its pen marks and cup rings. His ears are constantly alert. He has learned to listen well. Your survival might depend on it. He bets if you asked an animal, like a wee deer or something, they'd say *oh aye, I need food and that but it's my ears that keep me alive.* Sometimes it's nothing more than a creak of furniture, an intake of breath, and then you know to tense or run. Other times it can be for power that you are listening, for some future fact or spilled-out secret which you can bargain with or protect yourself with later on. But you have to do that kind of listening really carefully. For little jugs get mighty flucken slaps.

The thing the polis can't get their heads around at the moment is what age Gerard is. Sometimes it pays to be a wee runt. You can only be arrested if you're twelve. He's sure they said that at school: a talk from some youth football fanny who runs the 'Streetwize Crew'. And Gerard is twelve. So this counts.

They've taken his phone. He's refused to tell them how to unlock it, but. Gerard has no idea of the time, of how long he has been away from home. Way more than an hour. A pain twists through his guts; it opens and closes like his mother's fist. He feels sick, has not stopped feeling sick since he hurt that . . .

'What's that noise?' says the cop.

It's Gerard's knee, banging into the table. He stops picking at the wood, presses his hand down on his jeans to make it stop. Anthony will be waiting for him. He's left his wee brother alone – good as – with the baby in that clatty house; they will be starving hungry and they will be waiting for Gerard to bring them some food – because he promised them he would. The baby is probably greeting again, and Anthony will be crying too, because he gets awful upset when Miranda cries, so upset sometimes that he pees hisself, and he'll be trying to shush her, feart their mum will wake and go berserk. Gerard cannot bear this. He tries not to see his wee brother's face, how it puckers before he cries, how his teeth sook his bottom lip scarlet, battling to keep the sobs inside. Worst of all, Anthony will be getting the dread, winding through him. The same dread that is in Gerard's belly right now.

He will be thinking Gerard has let him down.

Eskimos have hunners of words for snow, his da told him once. Because they have so much of it. Gerard knows hunners of words for fear. Dread is the very worst of them. It's not the kind of fear that keeps you on your toes, or gives you the energy to pure explode and do it, just do something, something to flucken help yourself even if it is to run into an old lady and smack her out on the floor. He shuts his eyes tight, against the image of her falling. No. Dread is when hope goes. And Anthony will be feeling it now. Because of Gerard. He will be just about to tumble over the edge, to stop trusting that Gerard will come back to them. Once that happens, you can't undo it, ever-ever. It's like death.

Another one.

'I reckon you're at least twelve, bud.'

Gerard opens his eyes. The cop is circling the room. He is bored; Gerard senses this and knows that boredom can be fatal. Boredom can lead to sport. He stares at the cup of water. He is really thirsty, but to take a drink will let them win. Gerard leaves the cop to his muttering, returns inside his head. Or maybe it's Anthony's head, because he's not seeing his brother's face any more, he's just feeling it. He can't remember the first time his mum left him. Or any one particular time: they flood together like a giant wave. It would have been before the wee ones were born, and it was only Gerard. And his dad. But his dad must have been away.

He does so remember his dad, no matter what his mum says. His dad came and went. Worked on the rigs, so he did. Except that was a lie. Gerard isn't sure who told him that or who else it was who laughed and told him *Your da lives in the Big Hoose, son*. Lots of people came to the house when his dad was away. His mum thinks he doesn't remember that either. Smoky parties and screaming, folk lying on the couch for days. They scared him, it all scared him, but at least the house was busy. It made all the other times worse. Only Gerard, in his bedroom, knowing the house was empty. It was an emptiness that terrified him, an enormous, yawning thing in which you could easily be swallowed up. He thinks that might be when he started hurting himself – not your mental slasher stuff, that's totally for losers. No, just wee jags like he's doing now. *I'll just be a wee minute, son.* You so wanted to believe her: his mum, being soft and nice with the thrill of going out when she was leaving you. Happy at the thought of being with other people, ones who made her glad, so happy that she could afford to give you a wee crumbly bit of gentleness. And she wasn't full of the drink, not yet, not angry, roaring drunk, just . . . like there was a tiny sliver of who she could be or used to be before you made her sad.

How many times had his mum said she would just be a wee minute? How many times did he believe her? Waiting for her to come back, waiting until darkness fell, until sleep would overtake him, fighting it, fighting it, because waking up was worse. Waking alone, and crying for her to come, for someone, anyone – but no one did – sobbing himself exhausted, then throwing himself on her later, when he would wake again and she'd be snoring in her bed.

After a while though, he stopped. Stopped crying, stopped waiting. He would just curl in on himself, watching the window until it was morning, long after he'd heard the door click and her come in. What was the point? It never made a difference. Gerard told himself that he didn't love her any more. That he
did
not
gie
a
fuck.
And now he is doing it to Anthony.
You are made of your mum. You see it in the mirror.
'You're a big boy now,' his mum would whisper, before she

went out. He must have been about four. Then, one day, his da came back and the parties stopped and they were a family again.

But only for a wee while.

'She's gonny die, you know,' hisses the cop suddenly, right behind Gerard's left ear. Gerard's face jerks down towards his shoulder, and he fights it. Will not give the cop the satisfaction of a reaction.

'How do you think her family's going to feel then? Fucking desolate, pal.'

Desolate. It is a sad word. Flat and final. But the man shouldn't have swore at him; cops are not allowed to swear at you if you're a juvey. He doesn't believe the policeman anyway. They are all bullshitters. He probably hardly even bumped the old lady at all. Gerard concentrates on staring at the cup. They are all lying bastards.

'Sheriff and jury for you. Culpable homicide when she snuffs it.'

Gerard hears the door open, and the light in the room changes briefly. The other one, the woman cop, is back. Goldie. She has a blingy gold tooth. She's the one that jailed him. She is quite fast for her age. At least Gerard knocked her stupid hat off as she grabbed him. Her hair is a horrible whitey-yellow colour, and her face has lines. Tons of wee lines round her eyes and her mouth. Her make-up was crusting at the edge of her mouth when she was reading him his rights, or whatever it was she was saying. He stopped listening after 'I am about to . . .'

'Listen, son.' She stands directly in front of him, on the other side of the table. Gold bangle jangling on her wrist. He ignores her.

'Ho! Wee man. Fucking look at me!'

The swear word jags him to attention. It's just a word, a word he hears all the time, a word he's started using himself, when he thinks he can get away with it. But it sounds louder in here. Louder, and wrong, and it makes him feel a wee bit like greeting. He screws up his mouth. Lifts his head.

The policewoman nods. 'That's better. See if you don't start helping us, how can we help you?' She pretends to smile. Takes a sip from the mug she holds. She puts another mug in front of the tattooed cop.

Help him? How can they? Gerard has definitely been away more than an hour. Definitely. His mum will still be comatose. *Para. Dead to the world*, all those funny things she says when she is making it a joke. Words like *Mummy's medicine*. How long until it is safe? If he tells them his name, they will know his address. They already have a file on him. Then the polis will go to his house and *see*.

They will see, and they will take them away.

But what about now? What's happening to Anthony and the baby now?

The table judders. Gerard tries to stop his knee from banging it. But it's not just his knee, his whole body is moving; it's almost like he is rocking himself.

Catch a grip, catch a flucken grip.

The policewoman is staring. 'You hungry?' she says. 'Want a wee sandwich? I can nip across to Greggs–'

The door opens again. Another, fatter polis. 'That's the duty Social Work, Elaine.'

The policewoman nods. 'Can you bring her along?' It's weird how the policewoman has got a name, like when he found out that nice teacher wasn't just called Miss MacKay, but was Susan too. Because then you think of them being a girl, like being your age and that, and being at school.

'Listen, my wee pal. We're going to bring the social worker in, and then we're going to have a proper chat, OK? And you better start talking, because there's an old lady lying in hospital, wired up to all sorts, and I've got folk nipping my ear, telling me it's all down to you. And I've got you, no even telling me your name, or where you stay, or nothing.'

The tattooed polis thumps his big mitts on the table. 'How do you think that looks for you, eh? See if she dies–'

'OK, thanks, Darren. Why don't you go give Callum Noakes a bell?' Goldie looks at Gerard again. 'You know Constable

Noakes? The community cop? I bet you do. And I bet he knows you. He knows everyone round here.'

'Is he no days off?'

'Yes, but he'll not mind coming in to help us out.'

'Aye, he will.'

'*Darren.*' She taps her fingernails, playing a wee tune on her china mug. Goldie gets a mug, tattoo-polis gets a mug, Gerard gets a skanky plastic cup. 'Yup. I think Constable Noakes will take one look at you and know who you are right away. Because something tells me you've been in here before?'

She's speaking in that smug baby voice folk do when they want you to think they give a shit. The man cop is getting up; he's grumbling, but she must be his boss because Gerard thinks he is actually going to go and phone Constable Noakes and of course Noaksie will ID him: Noakes the Joke, everyone knows him. He's aye hanging about the school like some sad paedo, trying to get them 'involved in sport' or talking shite about 'violence reduction'. Gerard needs to stall them for at least another hour. Even though Anthony will hate him forever and he doesny even know how long a baby *can* go without drinking; will Anthony think to give her some water maybe? Oh Jesus, his leg is away again, his whole body is shaking and tattoo-cop is grinning at him, shaking his head like Gerard's a loony. The policewoman is frowning: a nice frown, like. Her face is kind. Sad and kind. Maybe if he just tells her, she could go there on her own and not tell nobody else, just actually flucken help for once and get some nappies in and maybe a babysitter for when his mum has to go out. See if folk could just do that, then they'd be alright.

'Afternoon, all! How's it going?' A lady in a pink, jangly coat comes in. He can smell fresh air. 'Kate MacFarlane, duty social worker. Hello there, young man. How are you?'

She comes straight over. Puts out her hand like she wants him to shake it. There are wee bows on her cuffs. Witches and bitches. That's what his mum calls the Social. He stares at the woman's feet. Doc Martens. Flowery ones. There are two types of social work shoes. Weird auld granny ones or Docs. The granny ones usually come attached to someone who smells of cats and has mass-*oov* frizzy hair, while the Docs will be somebody younger. With wee round glasses and piercings.

'You'll get no joy out of him, I'm afraid,' the policewoman says. 'We're no for talking, are we, sunshine?'

'I see. And you arrested him when?'

'Just after one. And he's not been arrested – he's presently being detained.'

'But has he seen a lawyer?'

'Still waiting on the duty solicitor to attend.'

'Really? So this child has been here alone since–'

'He's not been alone. One of us has been with him throughout. Our inspector's already been in discussion with the Reporter–'

'And see this "child" you're on about?' Without even looking, Gerard can hear tattoo-cop do air quotes round the words. 'In the course of committing an assault and robbery, he's managed to put an old lady into a coma–'

They are lying.

'Look, our information's very sketchy at the moment.' Gerard watches the policewoman's feet move closer to the social worker's. Huh. She has Docs too. Immediately, the policewoman becomes more interesting. On her, Docs mean business. He can imagine the policewoman giving someone a kicking, which makes her . . . He doesn't know what that means actually. Imagine if she had the flowery Docs on.

'For now,' Goldie's saying, 'all we want to do is find out this young man's details–'

'Well,' says the social worker, 'if we can't get any information from him, we've got real child protection issues. As I'm sure I don't need to remind you. We're going to have to look at a Critical Referral asap.'

'I realise that.'

'Ach, I think we've enough to charge him now.' Tattoo-cop is right in Gerard's face. 'We've plenty witnesses – not to mention one poor auld dear at the GRI. Aye. Let's stick you in secure accommodation, then have you up in front of the Sheriff tomorrow morning. See if you burst then.'

There is a wee bit of dark stuff in between tattoo-cop's teeth. Gerard wishes you could screw your ears shut the way you can close your eyes. He is going to piss himself. He doesn't want to go to jail. He feels his chest inflate. The cop's breath is coffee and onions. It is rank. The cop's hair is all clipped and styled, but he canny even brush his teeth right. Gerard always tries to make sure Anthony brushes his teeth. He hates how his mum can smell, hates how folk he knows have brown stains or missing, gumsy gaps. It's like you are rotten on the inside, and if he can just keep Anthony and Miranda clean, just make them smell of soap instead of . . . cause what if they are the ones at school nobody wants to sit beside, the kid folk go 'aw, man, you honk – he's *stinking*, miss' and call you flucken horrible names and tell folk you've shat yourself when you've not, you've flucken *not*, and if they put Gerard in jail, what will happen to Anthony and Miranda? And his mum: if they take her away it will cut them all loose. Sometimes Gerard pretends they are all in the sea; they are inside a wee string bag which is bobbing on the sea, but it's them, all there and snuggled, keeping each one up, and the bag keeps them from drifting away from each other and there are times when his mum's face is so sweet and nice, you just want to stroke it. Put her fingers near your mouth so you can kiss them.

Muh.

'You say something, wee man?'

'Did you say *mum*?'

Gerard stiffens.

'Aw, *man*. You greeting for your mum?'

'Darren, please.'

'Your mammy can't help you now, bud. Here. What if that old lady was somebody's mum? Did you ever think of that?'

The old lady is going to die. She really is going to die and Gerard will have killed someone. He has hurt an old lady, he is shite, he is scum.

Muh. It is the noise again, coming from inside of him. He cannot stop his knee from jumping. The social worker is speaking, but there are no sounds; his knee, his knee is going mad, he has to get away; his knee is up and the table is flying, hands on his shoulder on his back *no don't hurt me please don't hurt me I'm sorry I'm sorry*, and he tries to duck down, only he can hear screaming and when there is screaming that is fucking mental you have to stop it make it stop, he punches and punches squashy skin and hard bone, break it, fucking break it all. Smash it up and make it go away.

'Away!' The weight inside his chest shifts. Bursts open so he can yell and scream, 'Away! Away!'

But then a Doc Marten decks him and his face is on the floor. He lies on the floor, beside all the feet. Folk talking and shouting above his head.

Chapter Six

It seems Margaret is back at the school. It's funny, though, because she's lying down. Flat on her back, eyes tight shut, yet she can hear someone calling her name. *Maar-ga-rett.* Sing-song voices, a playground chant. Is she inside or out? It feels warm, and Laurel Bank was never warm. But there it is. If she could sniff it – and she tries to, but there is something blocking her nose, so she tastes it instead. Yes, there it is – the smell of disinfectant which pervades the corridors. Perhaps they're indoors? Is she in Latin? Miss McGrory has a habit of making you lie on the floor, so she can stab you with an imaginary spear. *Pilum, girls. Pilum.*

Laurel Bank School for Girls. Margaret has to take a tram across town, but Mother says it's worth it. As are the fees. Mother is never done talking about the fees, which makes Margaret nervous and grateful all at once. *You must always work your hardest, Margaret. Look at us, working our fingers raw, so you can better yourself.*

Better than what? Than them? Mother says family is everything. Yet they never seem proud of how they graft for it. Mother works in a milliner's, takes in extra sewing, but it seems that kind of industriousness is shameful, for Margaret must NEVER tell anyone at school about her mother's work. Her daddy is respectable, though. She sparkles when she sees him. He is a manager in Glasgow Corporation –

A rough hand is pawing at her poor arm, squeezing and jagging some wicked pointed –

Pilum! Pilum!
Margaret tries to shout, but her mouth has disappeared.
Maar-ga-rett. She really should wake up. Lying on the floor is not bettering yourself.
And then you go and marry a German Jew!
If she could move, Margaret would jump from her skin at this revelation. But she is fixed and anchored. Turtle-turned. She hopes her underwear's not showing. The Laurel Park uniform is green and scratchy. The pinafore is loose, and prone to rising up if you run.
Running is ungainly.
Running is not bettering yourself.
Laurel Park teaches science and Latin. It teaches Scottish country dancing with other girls. It teaches Margaret that being better means being better than your old friends but not quite as good as your new ones.
Yet how is it that Margaret is married? How can she know that? Is that not daft? She hears a breath of laughter. It breaks over her like a sunshine-yellow egg, and her tummy twinkles. Her Stephen. He's come back.
Where were you? she tries to say. She sees his wee face, the light freckling where the sun has caught his nose. Hair like tender bubbles.
Margaret goes to chase him, but Stephen is off and running free – he doesn't care about being better. He just *is*. She knows it's him. He's wearing an unfamiliar cardigan. A zippy, grey thing. With a hood.
He'll not be back.
Back where? Margaret is confused. How can Mother be talking to her? She knows her mother is long gone. Did Stephen ever meet her?
There is something terrible behind her eyes. Where *is* she?
Margaret listens for clues, but there is only a lazy hum, as if bumble bees surround her. Rustling. Someone is touching her wrist now, but gently. She tries to move her hand. Such pain in her shoulder, her leg, her brain. It booms and blinds her.

Silly, silly Margaret.

Where is Albert?

More hands slip beneath her. Adjusting. Smoothing. Wet dabs at her face. Just as she did with Albert.

Margaret is frozen in time.

She is outside his hospital room, silhouettes moving beyond the fluted glass door. Something cruel is waiting for her here, and she wants to flee, but she's pinioned to the floor by the whispers and the sobbing, spinning above her head, and she is gripping tight to her handbag – how can she, though, when she can't even move her fingers?

Margaret does not want to be here, not back here; there is a wall of white, a smell of death. There is the shock of Albert's dear, empty face. DNR. DNR.

How could you leave me? Margaret says.

Her mother says.

Stephen says.

Stephen! She tries to call out to them, those many voices which vibrate the air. But nothing comes. And now that she is pushing uphill, the antiseptic smell makes sense. Terror as her body splits. She is too old. It's too sore. It is all they've ever wanted.

Oh, but how she wants to catch her boy by the hand. Tell him: *Don't go. I'm so sorry.*

How her heart hurts with the not-saying of it. The not saying. Ever.

Margaret's mouth is stuffed with wool. Something round her neck: she can feel a tightness, a deep pressure there. She is breathing other people's air, and she can't get out. She can't get out. Other eyes can see you. They watch you fight for breath. Do nothing.

Do nothing as your family fades.

Margaret tries to turn away from this knowledge, but still, she cannot move. She must fill her head with other . . . What are the . . . what is the square, papery . . . papery in her fingers. What was she doing last? Papery, holding, thinking. Margaret loves them. Sitting in her lovely lounge.

Margaret!
She finds it hard to fathom for she *does* know the word. Margaret is a clever girl. Oh, how her head aches with the thinking . . .
Ah!
Books!
You can't judge a book by its cover.
Margaret.
She is holding her book, and sitting in her lounge. From her window, she sees other tenements, and the new flats where the school used to be, and the little grassy square with its statue. There's a gang of boys there. Three of them, lolling on benches. One who is on a bike.

He is looking right at her. Moving closer, close as an arrow: the sharpness of his chin a blade. It stabs through, and the pressure bursts, erupts in colours of bright, stained glass, pinioning her; what a thin, fierce face; his eyes blaze with fury, except it is not fury if you know, if you've ever known, how an animal looks when it is shot but not yet dead.

This boy blazes with pain, their colours fuse, his and hers; hers bursting, his hurting, and the hurt is overwhelming. It knocks her from her feet.

And somewhere, Stephen is gone.

And somewhere further, Albert is waiting.

Margaret really should wake up now. She doesn't like this place.

Chapter Seven

'Right, young man. This way.' The woman is smiling at him, but Gerard doesn't respond. She's too shiny to be true. Shiny face, shiny earrings. He can see the line of her knickers winking through her dress, which is also shiny. Another woman brings up the rear. He thinks it might be the one who picked him up from the home and brought him here. This skanky old building. How come they never make these places nice? Tappity-tap go their shoes on the shiny floor. His high-heeled security guards. They couldn't chase him, no way; if he wanted to do a runner, he could just bolt now. Headbutt the one behind him in the stomach and just leg it.

'You OK, Gerard?' The one behind him puts her hand on him, but he shrugs it off. 'You know who's going to be in here, yes?'

His mouth is sticky. 'Aye.' He licks his lip.

They move down the long corridor towards dark, shiny doors. Yellow lights hum from the ceiling, those horrible long ones that trap flies inside. The hum reminds him of the police station. Reminds him of the home.

The home. Why would you call it that? Con you, so you don't go in screaming? Make you think you'll get slippers and hot chocolate? But they take you in anyway, march you in with a polis escort. Slamming doors, and zizzing lights, and adults in sweatshirts and trainers, all cool and gangly and *alright, mate* with flucken keys. *Kicked off*, he heard the polis say, when he was handing over Gerard's property to a blond guy with bumfluff on his face. They were talking about *him*, not football, sitting all cosy in the kitchen drinking tea. Gerard's property was a form inside a plastic envelope, and a chitty to say they'd took his hoodie. Took the electric power card too, to try and trace the meter number. Gerard didn't think they could do that.

He'd held out all that time, at the cop shop. Even the lawyer got nothing out of Gerard, and he kept saying, 'But I'm on your side.' Noakes the Joke failed to trap. Either they didn't phone him or old Noaksie couldn't be arsed. Why would you? He's called their community cop, but Gerard knows that's bollocks. Noaksie's weans do not go to Gerard's school. Can you imagine? Imagine if your dad was a polis?

Can you imagine your dad?

It was dark when they took him to the home. Or the 'Young Persons Unit' as the sweatshirt folk called it. Four hours, Gerard had reckoned. Way long enough for his mum to sort herself, and after that first long hour it wouldn't have mattered with Anthony and the baby. They would have cried and been hungry and scared already.

After four hours, they would be hating him hard. Hating him that sore, sore way Gerard hates his mum, hates her and loves her all rolled up together like the love is barbed wire in your skin.

He has only been in the home two nights, but he's already had a sore face off of this big fat lassie. (She was staring and staring at him, so what was he meant to do? And she *is* a massive fat cow, so he wasn't even lying.)

Tell the truth, Gerard.

Oh aye, and another boy has tried to feel him up.

'In you come, in you come.'

The two women take him through into a panelled room. It smells fousty, has high windows, but little daylight. More yellow lights. Below the windows, four people sit behind a table – two more women and two men. There are other folk too, sitting in a circle, in a horseshoe, in a big goldfish bowl, and they are all here to stare at him. He feels the horrible weight of them, watching. Their watching makes the air sing. Makes his head light. Gerard has not had any breakfast, so he wouldn't be sick, but thinks he might puke anyway, and it will be that rank, orange burny stuff coming up.

He hears a wee gasp. *Geh!* It is one half of his name: spoken, then silenced. He canny look. Somebody murmurs, then it comes louder: 'Gerard!'

He canny look. He canny not. His wee brother is over there, between two strangers. One of the strangers is trying to quieten Anthony with sweeties, but he's having none of it.

'Gerard!' he demands, standing up, in front of all these people. Anthony is braver than Gerard. Does he hate him? Is he going to come and batter him? Good if he does; he should kick the shit out of Gerard, for leaving them alone. For this.

'No, no, that's fine,' says the man at the big table. 'Would you like to sit beside your brother, Anthony?'

And the wee man is out of his seat and barrelling over to Gerard.

'Here! How can he no sit with me, then?'

Gerard knows that voice. It comes from the other side of the room, it rasps like fingernails pulling hair, like the carpet burning through your dragging knees. This time, he can so look. He feels Anthony, pressed against his side, hugging him so tight his eyes water; both their eyes are running, Anthony's nose too, and his mum will think they are crying, but fuck her.

Gerard stares at his mother. Sitting there. There is a man in a suit beside her, and she is wearing her best coat, the snuggly one like a teddy bear that keeps you warm. It is brown, and it always smells of perfume and cigarettes. She has a new dress, a nice one. It is green with wee yellow flowers and it covers right down to her knees. She looks so pretty, his mum. The man touches her arm, whispers to her, and she does a smile. The room has gone very quiet, or maybe Gerard has just stopped listening. The light from the window makes her shine. Her hair is washed; it's gone nearly curly. He hates when she flattens it with her straighteners – plus she always forgets to turn them off, and it's dangerous.

It's dangerous.

It's OK. He knows Anthony and Miranda have been with foster parents. One of the social workers told him. Jilly or Ginnie or Minnie bloody Mouse.

'Sorry,' says the man beside his mum. 'Please continue.'

She keeps smiling, but Gerard knows his mum is raging. She shakes her head a wee bit. Folk shuffle and move and make space for Gerard and Anthony to sit together. Everyone has a bit of one of the tables in front of them, except for Gerard and Anthony. He wants to keep holding his wee brother's hand, but he doesn't want folk to see. Instead, he pushes his chair as close as he can beside his brother, so their side-bums are almost touching.

Anthony is staring at his feet. Gerard kids on he's dropped something – he doesn't know what – maybe a pen cause they're all taking flucken notes so why shouldn't he? He gets his head in tight to Anthony's ear. 'It's OK, wee man. You've no been bad.'

'So,' says the man in the middle, the man below the windows. Gerard should give them all names. That one can be Mr Up-his-own-arse. And the one with the fat neck is probably the polis. Constable Rubberneck. 'So,' says the man in the middle, 'if that's us settled? Well, good morning, everyone. I'd like to welcome you all to this Children's Hearing, in respect of Gerard, Anthony and Miranda Bell.'

'No, it's not!' Gerard is on his feet before he knows it.

'Please, sit down,' says the man.

'But that's not our name! My name is Gerard Macklin.'

Anthony stands up too. 'And so's mine's. 'Cept it's Anthony, but.'

Every single pair of eyes in that room is wide, and popping out at them. Cartoon-popping. Folk look quite funny when you give them a fright. Is that bubble in Gerard's chest laughter? He doesn't think so. It still feels like puke. He didn't mean to do that, to shout out like that, but if they canny even get their names right. If they can't even –

If Gerard speaks again, his voice will be shaky. Sometimes he shouts because it's the only way his voice will come out of him. He knows this shout was different. It was what the doctor lady he saw would call part of his *anger cycle*. He can never remember the steps he's meant to follow, just those stupid words. Right away, you see a scowling clown riding a bike. He bites the inside of his lip. One of the women at the top table is leafing through a book. Maybe she doesn't know what to do either. Folk hide their heads in books, like pulling the blankets over. Books are meant to be magic. He wishes they were. But books just make you feel angry, and scared.

'You need to sit down,' says Jilly or Ginny or Minnie, tugging on his sleeve. What's Gerard meant to do? He can hear his own heartbeat. He sways slightly. 'Miranda's maybe a Bell, the wean. But we're Macklins. Ma da was Mac–'

'Um, you'll all be aware from the notes in front of you as to the particular circumstances of this family, in relation to the . . . um, father. So I think, with regard to the children being present . . .' The man in the middle smiles at Gerard. 'I apologise, Gerard. I will make sure your notes are corrected.'

It's his mother's turn to call out. 'Ho! They're my weans. I decide what they're called.'

'Look!' says the man. He's getting pissed off now – he wasn't pissed off at Gerard, but his mum has made the man angry, which means they'll all suffer.

'Mum–' Gerard wants to make her understand, how important it is. How his name is all that he's got left, but the man shooshes him.

'Gerard, please. I'm keen that we get started. So I think what we'll say is that this is the Child Protection Hearing in respect of Gerard, Anthony and Miranda – the children of Marissa Bell. Agreed?'

Now he has no name at all. Gerard sinks into his chair, pulling on Anthony's arm to do the same.

'Well, as most of you know, my name is Colin Parsons, and I'll be chairing this meeting. I'm pleased to see we have representatives today from Police Scotland, the family and their supporters, and of course, Social Work Services. To my right . . .'

Gerard tunes out. Folk will talk at each other for ages. They will talk about him and around him but rarely to him. He can zone out until one of them goes 'Gerard' in that sharp, pretend-friendly voice adults use. He hears the man say . . . 'have a Child Protection Assessment report in front of you.'

Hears his mother say, 'Aye, well, I want to object. See on page two—'

'Ms Bell, thank you. I'm aware you've already raised several points, and these are all noted, I assure you.'

'Aye, well, what the fuck does 'noted' mean? Does that mean binned?'

Gerard has been here before. He knows what everyone will say. And they will say it all in front of him. That's meant to be a good thing – it's a 'child-centred process' Ginny-Minnie told him. So why is Constable Rubberneck here, then? That cop's never seen him before in his life, so how does *he* know anything about Gerard? Banging on that Gerard is a 'disruptive influence'. Well, if anyone bothers to ask Gerard, he will say Constable Rubberneck is a fat old pig who smells like a butcher's shop. But it's not like a game where you take shots. After he's said his piece, they don't ask you *And what do you think of the policeman, Gerard? Is he telling the truth?* No, they say stuff like *Do you understand that, Gerard? Is this something you recognise, Gerard? How would you like to respond, Gerard?*

And they will keep repeating his stupid name, like it makes him theirs. He pushes the nail of his middle finger hard into his thumb, driving it between his thumbnail and the skin. He knows his mum is staring at him. How couldn't the man have let them all sit together? Gerard didn't say anything bad, he didn't say he didn't love her. He just said he loved his dad too.

They all know about his dad.

Hello. I'm Gerard, and my dad's dead.

Mainly, Gerard doesn't listen to these people because he's scared. Every single one of them has read his file. Right now – in front of him – they are all flicking through it. Look at them, gorging on his life. *Aye, I do know a word like gorge. I know it means to stuff your face.* Just because words on a page will not stay still for him doesn't mean he's stupid. You can listen to stuff on your phone (except he's no credit). Or on the computer at school.

If they felt like it, the people in this room could read every form and report and wee scribble that has ever been written about Gerard, or his mum, or Anthony, or the wean. These documents stick to him like lavvy paper on his shoe or like a big . . . a pure big chain that you drag around. Like a smell of shite that will never leave you. Every time you're at the Panel, or whatever this pish is called. Every time you see a new social worker or nurse or teacher. Your file gets lugged in too. And they always want to go right back to the start. Why can't they just start from now? Plus, they tell it different each time. The worst thing is when they stop reading, and just *look* at you, or turn a page and make a wee noise. These folk probably know things about Gerard that Gerard doesn't know himself.

What if you don't want to remember?

His dad. His dad is private. What the flucken-fuck has that got to do with any of them?

Gerard's thumb is hot and nippy. He pushes the nail down until he can't bear it any longer, then releases the pressure. For a rushing second there is nothing but the disappearance of pain.

He sneaks a glance at his brother. How much of this does Anthony understand? Sometimes they talk about his dad. Nothing bad, but. Only how they wish they still had him, how their mum would be so happy if their dad was here. Occasionally, Anthony will ask for Gerard to remember something about him, or tell him a thing he once said. Gerard's started making stuff up because it's getting harder and harder for him to remember. There was a counsellor once, in a wee room filled with dolls at the Family Centre. He made Gerard hold a manky old teddy. Told him to *return to the very first thing you remember. Trust me, Gerard. We'll walk through this together.* Aye, except counsellors get to ping a wee clock when the session's up and close their notebooks and move on to the next wean. Gerard never gets to do that.

'Yous canny prove fuck all!' His mother's voice breaks through Gerard's determination not to listen. There's no point even trying. He is like a dog, responding to her voice, whether he wants to or not.

'No, you're misunderstanding us, Ms Bell. Today is not about Gerard's guilt or innocence. All of this will be discussed at the Hearing.'

For a moment, Gerard feels quite chuffed. She must have been defending *him*. He sits a wee bit straighter in his seat.

'Thought you telt me this was the Hearing?'

'It is. This is the Child Protection Hearing. I'm talking about the Advisory Hearing, Marissa. With the Sheriff.' It's a smarmy voice. Posh, and deep like an actor. Gerard looks up, to see who's talking. It's the sharp-suit man next to his mum. 'We talked about this, remember? Today's about the welfare of the kids.'

She frowns. Her face is getting red. 'Right. I know that. And then he's got the Panel? So this isny the Panel?'

'No, it is. The Advisory Hearing's with the Sheriff?' Sharp-suit dude lowers his voice. 'Because it's serious, yeah? Assault and robbery, plus the police assault. They have to decide if Gerard remains within the Hearing system at all.'

'But I canny be at that one?'

'Apologies, Chair.' Sharp-suit smiles over at the top table, then speaks again to Gerard's mum. Gerard hates the way he is talking to her, like she's a daftie. 'You'll both be interviewed in advance of that.' Sharp-suit smiles again, this time right at Gerard. Gerard's shoulders shift backwards, away from the man's tractor beam. Big poisoned dart, that one.

His mum goes quiet. Gerard hears a woman say to his mum, 'We must do everything possible to avoid criminalising the child. Remember, this is about conversation, not confrontation.' That's his cue to zone out again. He hopes the wean's got her Ingiefant.

It's a blue elephant that used to be Anthony's, and they gave it to her in a panic one day when she was screaming the place down. She likes to sook on it, pure gives a wee gumsy smile when she's got it in her fists. Gerard hasn't got any toys left from when he was wee, he doesn't think. Maybe he had some when they took him into care before, but he doesn't know what happened to them. He doesn't really care about toys.

He wonders if they'll let him home the day. His mum looks totally fine. She looks like a normal mum. He's had a weekend lie-in, that's all. That's what big boys say when they've been locked up by the polis. At the weekend, they call it a lie-in. That is all this has been. After they've all said their piece, it will be Gerard and Anthony's turn to talk. If they both just say they want to go home to their mum, it will probably be fine. In fact, it definitely will be; nobody would of brought them in here unless that's what's going to happen. Obvs. There's no way any half-decent grown-up would put a whole family together again just so they could split them up. Gerard wants to tell them he's sorry about the old lady. Because he is. He really is. Fair enough, it might help if he says it too, but that's not why. He keeps thinking about her. Of how bony her body felt when he bashed into her. Keeps hearing the *crack* the ground made when she hit it. No one will tell him how she's doing, and he's feart to ask.

'Gerard? Do you understand?'

'Aye.' Gerard doesn't know who's just spoken, or what they said. There are too many people in the room. He thinks that sharp dude could be a lawyer. Does Gerard have a lawyer? His head is aching. All those papers and files, full of words he cannot read.

'So we have two functions before us today,' a man says. 'Firstly, we're here to review Gerard's . . .' Gerard looks up, because the man has said it funny. It's the one in the middle, the Colin one. '. . . personal situation. And his siblings too, of course. But we're also here to consider how best to take things forward.'

'I want ma weans home.' His mum has her quiet voice on, the one that scares the shite out of grown men. It makes him think of a blade, swishing through air.

'Ms Bell. As has been explained, it was necessary to obtain a CPO to remove Anthony and Miranda to a place of safety.'

'I wasny well.'

'Well, this is our opportunity to discuss all the circumstances that arose in the lead-up and what support and measures may be required going forward. If our concerns are such that compulsory supervision is necessary, then that will be conveyed to the Reporter. But, as Becca pointed out, we always aim for a voluntary, conciliatory approach.'

'I couldny help being ill,' says his mum. She's went all sulky.

Constable Rubberneck sticks his oar in. 'Can I remind you, there's a report before the Fiscal as we speak, with regard to Ms Bell being charged under Section 12.'

'Yes, quite.'

'Sorry, Chair, if I could interject . . .'

A woman starts talking about dugs; she breathes really loud out her nose. Gerard hears a chair scrape back – shit, his mum's totally kicking off now, she's on her feet, shouting, 'That is absolute bollocks!'

Ach, it's *drugs* they're saying, not dogs. Gerard feels his wee brother's hand creep into his. He holds it there, steady. Fuck them all if they want to laugh. But nobody does.

'Perhaps if the lads stepped outside?' Colin raises an eyebrow. 'We can discuss Mum's situation–'

'No, Gerard's entitled to hear all proceedings in respect of any decision made.'

Gerard is totally confused now. So, is the sharp-suit guy a lawyer right enough? Is he Gerard's lawyer too? Man, even if they all had name badges, it wouldn't help. Cause Gerard couldn't bloody read them. He can hear Anthony crying.

'Actually,' Gerard says as loud as he can, 'actually, can we go outside, please?' If he gets Anthony on his own, he can ask him about Miranda. He hopes they've been staying with nice folk. Plus, if they're not in the room, then his mum will stop acting up. She acts all big and tough in front of them, but it's to protect them. He knows that. But if it's just grown-ups, she'll calm it right down and do her "sorry" act. When she wants, she can be brilliant at saying sorry. Cries and everything.

'My wee brother's getting upset, and we want to go outside.'

'Well, Anthony, maybe if you want to leave the room–'

Anthony is gripping Gerard so hard it hurts.

'Naw.' Gerard tries to make his voice do that knife-swish, like his mum's. 'Me too. If Anthony goes, I go.'

'But, Gerard, this concerns you.'

'So?'

'So. Don't you care?'

A social worker is telling Anthony to come with her. She's tugging his arm, and he's trying to climb onto Gerard's chair. Fucksake, can they no see he's terrified?

'NO!' yells Gerard, pushing her away. 'Get to fuck! He's going nowhere without me!'

His chair falls onto the floor, and the woman trips over it, then she falls too. Gerard is trying to get to Anthony, and his mum is screeching, everyone's shouting, then two security guards come in and take him to another room.

'Gerard! Don't leave me. Please don't leave me.'

Gerard is kicking and struggling, but the fuckers won't stop pulling him away. Dragging him down the corridor, and all he can hear is Anthony, calling out his name.

JUNE

Chapter Eight

From Claire's top-floor corner window, she can see all the way down to Duke Street. Much of the window is filled with rooftops and evening sky, which is lovely – and squawking seagulls, which are not. They attack the overspill from rubbish bins and the black plastic bags outside the restaurants, but Claire is far enough above it that it doesn't matter. The plaster over the bay window is cracked, but there's original cornicing, and a ceiling rose, from which she's hung a copper-wire lampshade. When she switches it on, sunbursts fill the room.

Already, it feels like home. All this place needed was a wee bit TLC. She closes her laptop. Stretches her fingers, stiff from typing. A house sale has fallen through, and a day spent chasing tails and rainbows has left her with sixty-nine unattended emails in her inbox. Since she got home from the office, she's been sifting and sorting, trying to clear some of the backlog. Work is mental, all of them grafting at the same frenetic pace which never seems to stop. But work fills her day and fills her mind.

Keep it coming.

Claire leans back on her new couch. Mustard velvet – an excellent choice. Nico has done her a favour, really. Imagine if she had taken half their crap from the house. One fireside chair. Three wine glasses. His essence lingering where it wasn't wanted, like the smell of garlic after a good meal.

If only she could unpick him from inside her. She reties her ponytail, tighter. Instant facelift. Lowers her eyelids. Light to dark. To light.

Refocuses.

In between emails, she's been browsing too. Safe browsing, not going near Nico's Facebook. Splinters lodge between her ribs. The baby's due any day now. She's sure some kind soul will alert her.

Dennistoun has its own Facebook page, a villagey forum where folk complain about parking or ask after missing dogs. One woman today is particularly exercised about the price she was charged in a café for coffee and a buttered roll. *Bloody gentrification* seems to be the general response. But it's full of good stuff too – local events, gyms, evening classes, several of which Claire has resolved to take, then thought better of it because it would involve talking to new people. She's only hovered on the periphery, until this evening. She's not sure what to do.

She reads it again. Two more people have posted.

Lindy Harper: I'll make a banner!

Zara K: Do you think she'll want a fuss? Maybe keep it low-key?

The chat is about an elderly neighbour, in a tenement two streets from here.

She needs to know we care!

Claire takes a sip of wine. A few days after the . . . accident? Incident? A few days after she grassed up a small boy to the police, Claire went to the GRI. The front of the Infirmary is a big Gothic sprawl next to the city's cathedral, the rear all modern, shiny blocks. Confusing to find the entrance. She'd wanted to drop off the false teeth. It was bothering her, having something of that old lady's property – her person really – sitting in her flat. A bit like having ashes, albeit wrapped in a tissue, stuffed inside a small Tupperware. The dentures needed closure. Claire did too. A pensioner mugged before your eyes, a kid carted off to the cop shop – great introduction to the neighbourhood. Claire had done her civic duty. Fine.

But those teeth. That row of pearly gnashers, clipped inside her

Tupperware. She could hear them chattering at night. She needed rid of them. Claire thought it might be easier to explain in person, up at the hospital, instead of on the phone. Apparently not.

Do you not have a name? The receptionist was distracted.

No. It was a few days ago. In Duke Street? She was brought in by ambulance.

Are you a relative?

I've just said I don't know her name.

That was probably the point at which the receptionist stopped being helpful.

Crabbit Claire and her nippy tongue. *That tone*, Nico would say. *Like you despise people.* So Claire had mumbled a curt *never mind* and walked back home along Alexandra Parade, dentures in her bag. She considered just chucking them in the bin.

But she couldn't.

She'd thought of burying them. A neat, respectful, hamster-sized grave. She could inter them in Alexandra Park. A dangerous ritual, no doubt condemning the owner to certain death. Like voodoo.

She'd thought of contacting the police, but

But she didn't want to know.

Claire still cannot unsee that young lad's face, at the point she was making the call. She cannot stop thinking, about him and his tear-stained cheeks, about the throttling gurgle the old woman made as Claire dug around her mouth. About the awfulness of it all, the awful randomness that she was there. Claire does not want to be involved. Fragile, healing Claire, caught up in the thrill of wading in and taking charge. To surge instead of shrink. But actions have consequences. Claire is exhausted by consequences.

Claire does not want to be involved.

So she's folded that day away. Done. Nothing to do with her. Where the kid is now, if the old lady made it. Other people's problems. And the police never did get back to her, and the teeth are buried far behind the towels in the airing cupboard.

She needs to just close the page. Instead, she clicks her laptop again. There have been developments. Zara K seems to be organising a rota. The call's gone out, and Dennistoun is responding. Zara is definitely the cheerleader. She's asking for volunteers to cook, visit and *generally keep an eye out for our lovely girl. Let's show Margaret how much this community CARES!!* Oozing enthusiasm, Zara has helpfully provided a potted history of the patient. Claire checks the thread. Margaret Camberg. Widow, 82. A photograph accompanies Zara's post: an old lady with grey, flyaway hair. The style is like a thirties bob. The face is unsmiling – a passport photo, or a bus pass maybe?

As most of you will know, after her terrible attack (here, Zara's put a handy link to an April edition of the *Glasgow Times*), *Margaret suffered severe concussion, a broken collarbone and fractured hip. We're getting a care package in place, and her flat's been assessed by Occ Therapy. She's all alone since her hubbie Albert died last year. Obv she won't be able to get out and about for some time, so one of the main things we need right now is for folk to get her messages (she's refusing to have meals delivered).* Wry face emoji.

It could be the same woman. Her skin tingles. Claire might have saved a life.

There's definitely some privacy issues to be addressed in this thread, though. Posting the woman's photo for starters. Safeguarding too – you can't just let any randomer loose like that. *Here, away you and take the keys to this vulnerable old lady's house. Yes, that's right, the one who's traumatised after being assaulted by a stranger. Och aye, just let yourself in and give her a bed bath. She'll no mind.*

Mind, it could be anyone. Margaret Camberg could be anyone. Claire goes to switch off the laptop. Her cursor hovers over the link to the *Glasgow Times* report. She clicks. Scans the article. *Duke Street. Fruit shop. Coma. Youth helping with enquiries. Police are appealing for witnesses.*

Margaret is appealing for her teeth.

Claire returns to the photograph. A nondescript old lady, wearing a camel coat, who has put a smear of lippy on for the camera. Claire may have been intimate with that mouth. She does think it could be her. The eyes, while not stuttering and wildly flailing—

They are familiar.

Back to the thread. Someone called Shaz has pitched in. She and her mum will *cover breakfasts Mon to Fri*. Gordon can do *a Wed teatime and Sun aft* and 'Doc' says he and his wife can *help out between shifts*. What shifts? Who are these people? Is Zara K administering any sort of quality control? They need to be Disclosure checked at least.

Claire's fingers are already typing. *Hi there. As a lawyer, just want to flag up you are doing all nec checks? Sounds like this lady is pretty vulnerable.* She posts. It looks so stark. She adds: *Great you guys are helping out, though.*

Zara K: *Hi Lawyer Claire.* That is not what she called herself. Just Claire. *Great you're up for helping! Thanks for the tip, but we're all neighbours. Known unto each other, and unknown to the law!! You close by? We could do with some Saturday cover if you can spare an hour? x*

Fucksake. The woman is like some philanthropic vacuum, hoovering up anyone who comes into her orbit.

Claire closes her laptop. She's already in her jammies, so could pretty much roll from here into her bed.

Fingers drum like chattering teeth.

Fuck.

Sake.

Saturday. Claire has an empty day. Two empty days – to not do any of those classes. To not get on her bike or go to a museum or sob over gin to a friend.

She opens the laptop. Deliberates. Would it do any harm just to have the address? Go once, take some messages. Drop off teeth. Get the things out of her house. Like biting off a thread: she could just leave them quietly on the kitchen counter. Then it's finished. Then she could stop thinking about the boy too.

*

It's a ground-floor flat the old lady lives in. Claire pushes past a wayward hedge to make it into the wee garden. The tenement, and the street on which it sits, slant sideways downhill: steep steps lead up to the main door. Someone with a bad hip would struggle. They'll need to put some kind of rail in. An old-fashioned tricycle sits at the foot of the stairs. It has a big basket at the front and a mini trailer-on-wheels behind. A silver logo on the trailer says *Waste Not* – with a green and blue Planet Earth replacing the 'O'.

Well, you'll no be riding that for a while, Margaret.

The strip of tatty garden straggles from the steps around the side of the building. It is a tip – a literal midden. What state is the old lady's house? Kids' toys and a football clutter the path, and someone has dumped a broken wheelbarrow upside down in what may have once been a flowerbed. But the nettles and brambles are so deep and entangled, it's hard to tell. Broken plant pots litter the ground, and a single, sad gnome pokes his hat up from a pile of discarded newspapers – the free ones nobody reads. But the door into the close is a fresh, bright red, and there's a wicker trough of herbs on the top step. Sage blue, olive rosemary.

Claire's mouth is dry. The teeth are in her jacket pocket, wrapped in a fresh paper towel. She didn't sleep well, has the bruised beginnings of a headache. What is she doing? They'll think she's properly weird. Who would keep old dentures all this time? But she's here now. So what's she planning to say? *Hello, here's your teeth. I saved your life by the way. And then I saved your teeth. I've kept them all this time, and I'm not sure why. But here they are. Right. That's me away. Cheerio. Hope you get better soon.*

Weird *and* callous. That's what her new neighbours will think. But if she says: *I feel really bad about how that kid hurt you. How humiliated and frail you were, lying there. Nobody wants to be reminded of their frailty. So I didn't . . . Do you know how angry I feel too? About everything, really. And how shocked that a wee kid could do that. Disgusted. And scared. And I feel sorry for him as well.* They'll think she's pathetic.

Claire is an overthinker.

Why she's no good in the cut and thrust of criminal work. Court scares her. No matter how you prepare, court is in the moment, full of smashes and grabs, like a frenetic game of squash. Fine detail, that's what she's good at. Folk are fair impressed when you say you're a lawyer because it implies sharp wit and a shiny sword of justice. But Claire likes ledgers and permissions. The fair division of assets. She kicks miserably at a headless Barbie.

'Hello, hello. Come away in.' A striking woman, roughly ages with Claire, opens the door. She has sharp black glasses and a matching black fringe. 'You must be Claire, yes? I'm Zara. Saw you hovering there.'

Hovering? And thus Claire is branded indecisive too. She can't explain the bloody teeth at all. Just get rid of them, Claire. This garden, you could lose – or find – anything in here. But Zara is beaming widely, watching her, and Claire is climbing up the steps; she's at the door of the close already, and there's the tub of herbs, and there's her hand slipping open. Teeth tumbling into soft soil. Christ, no, she missed. The teeth are lying on the step. Claire kicks them behind the wicker trough as Zara ushers her into the close, passing a blur of glorious, shiny green tiles, in towards a half-glazed door on the right, which lies ajar. 'She's a wee bit nervous,' Zara says. 'About meeting anyone new. After what she's been through, you can understand. But I told her you check out!'

'I'm sorry?' Claire is still thinking about the teeth. That was even more stupid. You just planted old lady teeth in a flowerbox.

'I showed her your photo. On your firm's website?'

'Sorry?'

'Thought you'd be impressed,' says Zara. 'Especially after what you said about checking folk out. So I googled your name, found where you work – you don't mind, do you?'

'No. No, that's fine. Of course.'

Claire finds herself in a russet-coloured hallway. Soft faded rug on wooden floor. A long, elegant clock, marking time. The flat smells musty, but clean.

'She's a bit . . . she's not like her old self,' Zara whispers. 'Did I say that when we messaged? I mean, she's always quite reserved, you know, but pleasant with it? Now, she's . . . well, it's really shaken her up, this whole . . . Here we are, Margaret. Look! I brought you a visitor. That nice lawyer I was talking about? Mind I showed you on the computer?'

She takes Claire into a neat, light-filled living room. The old lady sits on a velvet wing chair facing a deep bay window. The room's a little shabby, but it has Arts and Crafts curtains. Oak tables, books, and a slim, extra window to the side. Shafts of colour from a stained glass inset spill on the old lady's hands. All Claire can see of Margaret is her clasped fingers and her hair. Random hanks of grey tremble as the old lady touches her face.

'I don't want to see anyone.'

'I know that, pet. But I need to open the shop, and there's no one else to sit with you.'

'I don't need babysat. I'm not a child.' A flash of chin. More hair, and quivering hands.

'Well, the carers aren't coming until Monday, and it was you that insisted you weren't staying in the hospital a moment longer. So here we are. Sue me.'

They move further into the room. Margaret fixes on her coloured window. Her face gaunt. Deep lines and pouchy shadows. An old-fashioned walking stick leans against the chair. Zara crouches beside her. 'Look, I'm sorry, Margaret. I'm doing my best – we all are. But what if you have a fall? You know what the doctor said. You were lucky not to get pneumonia as it is. And that hip's still not properly healed.'

With difficulty, Margaret turns her neck. The sag of her jaw, the struggle of unkempt hair. Claire can see the muscle below her eye, twitching.

'I like your sunset,' Claire says.

'What?' For the first time, Margaret looks her way.

'The stained glass.' Claire nods at the little side window and the leaded panel hanging there. 'It's beautiful.' It's a simple design, curved trees and half a sun.

'I made it.'

'Did you? Wow.'

'Don't patronise me.'

'I'm sorry. I didn't mean–'

Zara rolls her eyes. 'It's OK. She gets like that. Don't worry. Underneath it all, you're still the same lovely old Margaret you always were, aren't you?'

'How would you know?'

Distractedly, Zara pats her arm. 'Margaret, I'm sorry, but I really have to go. I've got the shop to open,' she says to Claire. 'Waste Not Want Not?'

That explains the bike outside. The greengrocers in Roslea Drive. Zara K. Of course. Of course Zara K would run an eco-store. Claire keeps meaning to go in there, yet she hasn't. The shop looks too . . . friendly.

'I've left some lunch in the kitchen. Just salady stuff and some nice bread. We get it from the prison.' Zara gives Margaret another pat as she gets up. Margaret is unyielding.

'Prison?'

'Yeah, Barlinnie. They have a bakery there. You know, to learn a trade. Do the most amazing sourdough.' She lowers her voice. 'It's wee bit tough for Margaret, though.'

There is nothing wrong with Margaret's hearing. 'I don't have my right teeth. I told you that. They've given me someone else's. In the hospital.'

'I know you did, pet.'

'Please stop calling me "pet". And I stole the glass.'

'Right, OK, Margaret.' Zara shakes her head. 'That's me away. See you later, yes?' She shoulders a big straw bag. It's full of multicoloured carrots – purple and gold as well as orange. 'Right. I'm off. You've got my number, just in case?'

Claire nods.

'Oh – and I've given her an old iPad to keep her occupied,' Zara says. 'Maybe you could give her a wee tutorial?'

'What in?'

'Och, I don't know. I just thought it might give her a window on the world, you know? It's on the sideboard. Anyway, I'll be back around two – my partner will've finished work then, so he can cover the shop. Bye, Margaret.' Zara calls. 'Mind and do your physio exercises!'

Margaret continues to look out the window. Zara gives Claire a wee pat too. She's very tactile, is Zara K. 'She'll warm up, don't worry. She's a sweetie really. Thanks so much for helping out.' She shouts out a final *byee*, then the door thunks behind her. The flat is very quiet.

Why? Claire wants to say. Why are you thanking me? Zara has no more obligation to this old soul than Claire does. She's not their responsibility. Margaret belongs to nobody.

Neither does Claire. She stands, swithering. How will she fill four hours? Should she offer to make some tea? Take a seat?

'Oh my God!' It's Zara again, bursting through the door. 'Margaret! Look!' Her outstretched hand is holding a set of dentures. 'You were right all along! I thought you were havering. But look what I just found! Your teeth!'

Margaret starts. 'What?'

'Look! Are these your teeth?'

Claire tries to speak, she is going to say something, she is. She has to. But then she sees the old woman's expression. Margaret is ashen.

'I just heard something clatter when I lifted those herbs,' says Zara. 'And there they were, lying on the step. Incredible!'

'How? How were they there?'

'I have absolutely no idea. But are they yours, right enough?'

'I don't–'

'You must have dropped them. That day you were . . . Do you remember? Were they annoying you? Do you remember taking them out? Putting them in your pocket, maybe?'

Stiffly, Margaret gets to her feet. Her face is changing colour – it is blush-red and grey all at once. 'No.'

'Well, you must have.'

'No.' She is emphatic. 'I would never take them out. Not in public. Let me see them.'

Already, the moment for Claire to explain is slipping. Has slipped. She focuses on the pretty shimmers of coloured glass, hanging in the window. Bright circles of trees and a childlike sun. An emerald path leading beyond turquoise hills. Waiting for the storm to pass.

'Well, you must have. They must have been in the garden all that time.'

'No!'

Claire looks again at the old woman. Her hands are full of teeth, her eyes wide, darting, and instantly, Claire is back there, on the street, kneeling over her as she chokes and writhes.

'*He* did it.'

'Who?'

'Him. He must have. The man. He knows where I live.'

'Margaret, you need to stop being silly, it wasn't a man – I told you that. It was just a wee, stupid boy – and they've taken him away.' Zara glances at her watch. 'Miles and miles from here, I'm sure. Of course he doesn't know you.'

'It was a man I tell you!' Margaret shouts, gripping the back of her chair. 'I remember every single thing! He was looming over me . . . on . . . the ground. He was trying to choke me – that's what I see, every night when I try to go to sleep. And now he's coming back to get me. He put them there to scare me! The man!' The walking stick falls to the rug.

Zara sighs. 'Margaret, I know it was terrible, I know that. But it wasn't a man. You just fell over when a kid tried to steal your bag–'

'You're lying! You're all lying!' The chair shakes. 'He tried to kill me. And now he's coming back, to do it properly!'

Claire cannot bear her terror. She goes over, places her hands on Margaret's shoulders. 'Zara's right. It was just a kid.'

'How would you know? How would you know?' Her eyes are wild. 'Who even are you?' she cries. 'Get out. All of you! Just get out of my house and leave me alone.'

'Margaret. Please listen to me.'

'Don't touch me.'

Claire removes her hands. 'I'm sorry. I'm so, so sorry. I should have said this right at the start. It was me. I found your teeth.'

'What?' Both women speak in unison.

'I must have dropped them when I came in.' Claire improvises rapidly. 'I could see how scared you were. I was waiting until you were comfortable with me, to tell you. The reason I got in touch was so I could bring your teeth back.'

'But how did you have them in the first place?' Zara inserts herself between Margaret and Claire, forcing her to step backwards. All jutting elbows and baleful, squint fringe. She makes Claire think of an eagle.

'Because I was there. The day Margaret was attacked. I saw it happen. I think it's me you remember, Margaret. You'd fallen on the pavement, and you were kind of, you were choking on your teeth. So I hoicked them out so you could breathe. And then . . . then the ambulance came to take you away and I got left with the teeth . . .'

'But why on earth didn't you say?' Zara regards her.

'I don't know.' Claire wants to close her eyes, make this all dissolve. She tries to find some kind of truth. 'I didn't want to bring back any bad memories for you, Margaret. Please believe me. I didn't want to remind you of that day, or make you any more scared than you already were. I just wanted to . . . I just wanted to give you back your teeth. And make sure you were OK.'

'Well, she's not OK, is she? What a thoughtless, horrible thing to do. Come on, love.' Zara picks up the stick, helps Margaret back into her chair. 'You could have told *me* at least. Let me decide if you should see her.'

'I know. I'm so sorry. I wasn't thinking.' Claire feels herself unravelling. She cannot have another meltdown. She just can't.

'I'm not a child.' Margaret speaks quietly. 'Do we agree on that?'

'Of course we do,' says Zara.

'So in that case, I'll decide who I can see. What's your name?'

'Claire. I'm sorry,' she says. 'Look, I'll go. I should never have come. I'm truly sorry.' She can never say sorry enough. Her neck is bent. She can see polished wood, and the tip of her shoes. The edge of the faded rug. She wants to melt through that lovely wooden floor and find herself in her new flat, new start with the door locked fast. Work and home. That's all Claire is good for.

'You saved my life,' she hears Margaret say. A statement of fact, not a question.

'No. I . . . the ambulance was there in minutes.'

'But I nearly died. They told me that in the hospital. I nearly died. I was choking, and then I wasn't. And that was because of you.'

'I suppose.' She looks up. Margaret seems calmer. Her hands are in her lap.

'Right. You've had a lot of excitement. I think Claire should leave now, and we can have a nice cup of tea.'

'But what about your delivery? At the shop? I thought the organic romanescos were coming? All the way from Perth, you said.'

'Oh shit!' Zara checks her watch again. 'Shit. I'm going to miss them.'

'I'll be fine here with Claire.'

'Eh, no, I don't think so.'

'But she's my guardian angel.' Margaret gives a beatific smile. 'When you think about it. There's a tradition, you know. When one person saves another person's life, they're bound together forever.' She frowns a little. '"Whoever saves a single life saves the whole world". Or something like that. So, I am indebted to you, Claire.' Margaret gropes for her stick. 'I think I shall make the tea. Off you go now, Zara.' She pushes herself up from the chair.

'Margaret, I can't leave you like this.'

'I'm fine now. I promise.' She softens, reaching out to take Zara's hand. 'You have no idea how grateful I am to you, dear. For everything. I was just being silly . . . I got a fright. I was getting . . . muddled.' She nods to herself. 'Yes, I was just getting stuff muddled. The man wasn't trying to hurt me.'

'There was no man,' says Claire. 'Remember?'

'No, of course. No man.' Margaret winces a little, rubs her hip. She takes her seat once more, tea forgotten.

'On you go, Zara,' says Claire. Her head, her jaw is aching. She wants nothing more than to crawl into bed with two paracetamol. 'I'll stay till you get back – and we can talk more then. And if neither of you want to see me after that, that's absolutely fine, alright? But let me sit with Margaret now. You get on.'

Zara shakes her head. 'I'm just going to open up for the delivery. Then I'll see if next door can come in instead.'

'Fine.'

'Fine.' Zara goes out. Once more, Claire and Margaret are left alone.

'I'm truly sorry–'

Margaret raises her palm. 'So you've said. Just sit with me, dear.'

Claire pulls up a little tapestry-covered chair. They sit in silence, watching the coloured light dance on the wooden floor.

'It really is lovely. Your stained glass. I love the mother-of-pearl bit.'

'So do I. That's the bit I took.' Margaret gives her a sidelong look. A fleeting image of a young girl glitters. She is young, then she is old. 'I only needed the one.'

Claire admires the stained glass again. Unsure of what she's supposed to say.

There is another lull, then Margaret says softly, 'Can you tell me about that day?'

'Tell you what?'

'Everything?' She dabs at her lip. 'I can't . . . I'm not sure what I do remember. What happened when. Or what I've . . . made up, I suppose. Memory is a funny thing, you know.'

So Claire recounts to her what she saw, which is blurry and is not much, but it seems to help.

'Tell me what he looked like,' Margaret says. 'The boy. Can you remember?'

Can she remember?

'He was wee and skinny,' Claire says. 'He was wearing a grey hoodie and he looked about ten or twelve maybe.'

Margaret makes a sound. 'So young? He seemed huge. When I was lying on the ground.'

'But that was me, remember? I don't think he bent over you. In fact I don't even know if he saw you fall. He was just . . . pulling on your bag, and you kind of turned, and he kept going.'

Margaret covers her face with her hands. 'I remember someone, tugging at my underwear.'

'No. No, oh God, don't be daft. That was just two wee wimmen. They were sorting your skirt, to preserve your dignity, that's all.'

There's a faint tremor in the old woman's shoulders. 'Look, we don't have to talk about this. Tell me more about your career as a pilferer of stained glass. Or can I get you that cup of tea?'

'In a minute. Nobody has . . . I've not been able to talk about this.'

'But did the police not speak to you?

'Yes, in the hospital. I think so. Someone came. But I don't really remember.'

'What about Victim Support? You should have got the chance to see them?'

'Och, I don't know. They gave me so many forms and leaflets at the hospital. Folk assessing me, folk seeing if I was daft. I just wanted to get home, you know?'

Claire takes her hand. 'I do.'

'What was his face like? Can you tell me that?'

She hesitates. 'I didn't see it. Not then. But . . . I saw him a wee while later, walking in a street nearby. It was me who called the police again, actually.'

'You?'

'Yup. I thought I recognised him, so I got out the car and followed him until the police came. Then, that was that. I pointed him out from a distance. They put him in a police car and I went home.'

'What was his face like?' Margaret repeats.

'Thin. And scared. I think he was crying.'

'Serves him right. Getting locked up.'

'No. Before the police came. When I first saw him. Just after he'd . . . he'd hurt you. His eyes were all puffed up and red.'

'Oh,' says Margaret. She picks at the pattern on her skirt. Blue flowers and purple leaves.

'Why don't we have that tea, eh?' Claire goes through to the kitchen. It is a typical tenement kitchen, wide enough for a table, with the old bed recess housing the cooker. As she's searching various cupboards for mugs, the doorbell rings.

'I'll get it.' Claire opens the door to a large woman, whose fist is raised and ready to knock. There's a wee boy, not much more than a toddler, peeking from behind her legs.

'You the lawyer?' the woman says.

'I'm Claire. Yes.'

'Right, I'm Jacqueline from across the close. You alright, Margaret, hen?' she shouts, barrelling past Claire. 'Zara telt me you needed to go. M'on, Ryan.' The child smears chocolate-covered fingers on Claire's jeans as he totters past.

'No.' Claire. 'I don't have to go. I said I could stay till later.'

Jacqueline rolls up her sleeves. 'Eh, no. Zara telt me you needed to go. And now I'm telling you, alright?'

Claire is too tired and scunnered to argue. There is no coming back from being identified as a hovery, deceitful, unhinged threat to humanity. The guardians of the tenement have got the measure of her – and honestly? She doesn't care.

She returns to the living room, where Jacqueline is bustling, plumping cushions. Ryan continues with his artistic chocolate trail, fingering the William Morris curtains. Margaret's mouth is slightly open. She shifts in her chair.

Claire addresses the old woman directly. 'Well, Margaret. Apparently my services are no longer required. I think Jacqueline is going to get your tea. It was very nice meeting you, though, and I'm glad you're doing well. Bye bye.'

She turns, lets herself out. Pretends she doesn't hear Margaret, who's trying to make herself heard over Jacqueline's stream of chatter. She's done what she came for. Case closed.

Chapter Nine

'I told you it was a stupid idea!'
'How? They say it works for loads of kids.'
'Well, clearly not for him. Is the other boy OK?'
Gerard can hear them arguing down below. The way the woman says it. *Him*. They are talking about Gerard, of course. At least his mum screams it in his face: what she really thinks. Not these two. These two are all kid-on smiling, all sing-song posh voices going *Och, it's fine. Don't worry. These things take time. You know we're here for you.*

The same shite social workers say. Then, behind your back, you hear them tell the truth. 'These things' are Gerard's life. Are they fuck here for him.

Fluck.

Naw, *fuck*.

He looks out at the garden. He's quite high up here. You can see spindly front gardens, with hedges and nice flowers and big, skinny trees. He's been staring at this view for nearly five weeks now. It makes him feel very wee. Everything does. Everyone in this house is tall and thin like the trees. Gerard is a jaggy bramble. He scrunches his legs into his chest. He's sitting on the window seat in the room. 'His' room. Aye, so and it is. There is a whole wall of fitted wardrobes, but Gerard only has about half of one for his clothes. The rest are crammed with sports gear. There are skis and ski boots, rugby balls, golf sticks. Loads of crap he wouldn't have a clue what to do with. No footballs, but. The man, Craig, says he's a fan (some diddy team like Kilmarnock), but there are no footballs in the house. Gerard would of loved a game of football, out there in the street. It's a square actually – Queen Square. Full of big fuck-off houses like this. He thought it was another tenement when they brought him here, but, naw, his new foster home is a 'townhouse'. So the man said.

Mr 'Call-me-Craig'. Except, that's no his right name. Nobody in this house uses their right name. He's called Craig, but then he says his name is James. James Craigie Tannahill Thomson. He said it in a funny voice, like he was putting on being snobby. When he already is snobby. And the lady with the funny accent? (She has hers all the time). Well, she telt Gerard to call her Kris, but then the man says she's really called Eva Kristina. She's definitely something foreign. Their boys too – they're called one name, but everyone calls them another. What's that all about?

Two big boys. Both way over six feet – even bigger than their dad. They're alright, he supposes. Nice enough, in that they smile and say 'How you doing?' if they pass him in the hall. But they're always out somewhere, doing stuff.

He didn't know rich folk did so much stuff. Imagine just being able to swan out the house each day, off on some new adventure, with your leather music case or your split-new tennis shoes. Imagine not having to think about what's in for tea, or how long you've got before it all kicks off. Gerard tries to think of all the things he would do with that time. Just acres of shiny time. He thinks he would probably go somewhere and be quiet. Get on his bike and pedal to the park – no, the countryside. Or near the sea, where it is all wide open and you can run for miles. He wouldn't go places where folk shout at you, that's for sure.

He needs to ask Craig where his bike is.

The boys both have band practice, and rugby. One of them's going to be in a play. And there's a thing called a Youth Parliament, which the other one is standing for. The bigger boy, Xander. He gave Gerard a leaflet about it.

Cheers, big yin, but I canny read, he didn't say. He thought that would be in his file. 'Gerard is a diddy.' Right next to 'Gerard is disruptive'. A load of labels everyone can peel off and cover him with. He assumed a family who were taking in dangerous street trash like Gerard would of read his file. That they'd have to? Because then they'd know Gerard's real name, his superhero name, is ACE. Of all the shoogly, jittery words he tries to wrestle with, he knows those letters fine. Can see them jumping out a mile. Gerard is one giant Adverse Childhood Experience. He is packed full of ACE-y goodness. Badness.

He rubs his knuckles across his lips. The skin is all shiny. Red and skint, it really, really hurts.

Wee fud had it coming.

He *told* Craig he didn't want to go back to the gym. He hates it there. It honks of sweat and pumped-up lads who look like they want to murder you. Which is pretty much the same as walking down Duke Street, but in the gym . . . it's like he is raw meat. Can't stand the feel of the boxing gloves on his hands either, someone wrapping your fingers in clingfilm. How can you defend yourself if you've two big bawbags for fists? But his foster family didn't listen, and the youth worker didn't listen, and the man at the gym – the coach with the stupit beanie hat – didn't listen. That ginger boy was nipping away at him. Three weeks in a row. Holding his nose whenever Gerard passed. Sniggering to his mates. Punching his fist into his hand and giving him daggers. All because Gerard had to take a shite. He'd got overwhelmed that first day: with all the noise and the bodies, with the whip of the skipping rope, the way the air crackled with aggression. He'd never been in a boxing gym before, never even said a thing about it, but Kris 'n' Craig knew it would be *right up his street*.

'The gym's a great place to get it all out, eh?' Craig had been squeezing his shoulder. Gerard wanted to puke. How was hurting people fun? He'd felt his tummy churn, knew he couldn't hold it. So he went to the frigging lavvy. So what?

So the freckled wee bastard named him 'Shitehawk'. And everybody laughed. That was Gerard's new name at the boxing gym. Gerard could take any name they flung at him. But then, today, he heard the ginger boy say to his mate, 'Aye, his mum shat him out of her arse.'

It was just before the 'huddle', when they're meant to stop punching and sit in a circle to talk about 'their feelings' instead. That bit's even worse than being in the ring.

Gerard turns away from the window. Lays his cheek on his knees. On good days, his mum used to laugh when he cooried up like this. She'd go 'There's my wee cherub'. Maybe stroke his hair. His tummy aches. He wonders where she is. His social worker doesn't say – which means she is in rehab. They're always so full of it, when she's in rehab. Aye saying, *Oh, Mum's doing really well*. But what *is* she doing? What is his mum doing today? He fingers his new phone. Craig gave it to him. He doesn't know where his old one is, with all his numbers on. Well, it's not that many, but he's got numbers for Brian and Drew and Colm. He had a wee photie beside each one, to tell who's who. But he canny mind their numbers, so even if he wanted to, he couldn't get in touch with them. Maybe they're sitting with their own phones right now, thinking about him? Wondering why he doesn't answer a number he no longer owns.

He knows his mum's number OK, but. Knows it off by heart. He chants it like a lullaby, just so he'll never forget. Soon as Craig gave him this phone, he called her. Three rings, then it went to answer. But at least he got to hear her voice. *It's me, Mum. It's Gerard. I got a new phone. Can you call me?* She hasn't called. Not yet, but she's probably trying to get herself together. Finding them somewhere decent to live, away from all the shite that seems to follow them. Folk like that creepy guy with the tatts – there's always somebody hassling his mum. He thinks that's why she gets scared. Maybe she gets the same heartbeat-in-your-head feeling Gerard does before he loses it. He phoned her every day at first, but then he got worried about credit (Craig's never said if there's a limit), so he just phones once a week now. Tells her it's him, and that he's fine. He doesny ask her to phone back any more. He hopes she's somewhere good, with folk who're being nice to her. He knows where

Anthony and Miranda are, though. They're with a smiley old couple who live in Shawlands. Proper old – like grandpa old. The lady aye has sweeties in her bag, and the man could be in a picture book: white hair, tweedy cap and a blazer with his bowling club badge on. They *are* doing really well, the weans. It's brilliant to see them, laughing when Gerard pushes them on the swings. There are no decent swings at their bit. Bigger kids burn fag holes in the rubber. They break glass and smear dogshit and fling the swings so high that they wrap round the top, then nobody can use them. But there's a really nice park near where Gerard stays now, with a massive duck pond. And hardly any broken bottles. Shawlands is just the next bit down from here. He's not sure if they did it on purpose, or it's just luck that his brother and sister are so close. Miranda's nearly walking now. It's crazy. She calls him *Gah*. It hurts so bad when he has to say goodbye. Miranda doesny have a clue, but him and Anthony . . .

He bites at his thumbnail.

Actually, it's worse that they're so close. He's only allowed to see them once a fortnight. It was meant to be once a month, but Anthony kicked off, *properly* kicked off, when they told them that. Gerard wished he hadn't, but he was kind of proud of him too. Danny Macklin's boys will take no shit off nobody.

He shuts his eyes. Whenever he thinks of his dad, he has to. Helps to see him more clearly. He's big – definitely as tall as Xander. Bigger, probably. Way stronger than Call-me-Craig, that's for sure. Gerard's dad had jet-black hair. Bright blue eyes. He thinks he'd a scar on his lip: a wedge-shaped nick, with a thin, silvery line going from his mouth up to his cheek. He thinks too, that he can remember rubbing his finger along it, and his dad saying it tickled. He could be making that up, but. Every year that passes, his dad fades a wee bit more. Gerard used to have pictures of him, in one of his bin bags, but they got lost.

Travelling light. That's Gerard.

What is it with kids in care, and bin bags? They manage to keep entire lists of who did what to who in your files, but they canny find a way to keep your toys and pictures safe.

Or your mum.

His breath is getting funny. It's going too fast and he tries to pant it out, to focus on the window, on the tree outside the window, and not the scar on his daddy's face, nor the old lady, lying on the ground, or the sticky red that is everywhere. He holds his knees into his chest, rocking and rocking, say a prayer, say a song say a song, and he grasps one: *Mary, Mary, quite contrary, How does your garden grow?* Just humming the tune, and rocking, and he doesn't hear the man come up, not until he is fucking touching him on the back.

'Gerard?'

'Leave me alone,' he whimpers.

'OK. But can I sit with you a while?'

Gerard doesn't reply. He hears Craig creak down on the bed. After a while, his brain stops seeing the pictures, and he can stop humming the stupid tune. Eventually, he is able to lift his head up, but he can't look at Craig. He concentrates on the birds in the big tree outside.

'Did you know,' said Craig, 'they think that song is about Mary, Queen of Scots? The song you were singing. Do you know her? Mary?'

'Aye.' Gerard is scornful. 'She got her head chopped off.'

'She did indeed, poor woman. But they think she may be the Mary of the song. And her contrariness is her marriage to Lord Darnley. You've heard of Darnley?'

Gerard thinks for a minute. 'Is that the scheme near the big B&Q?'

Craig finds this hilarious. 'It is indeed, my lad! Well done!'

Why does the old fanny keep saying *indeed*?

'You know it's named for Mary's husband? The estate? His castle was nearby. And there's a huge old plane tree there, which they reckon was alive in Mary's day. They think Mary and Darnley sat beneath that very tree when she nursed him back to health.'

'What was wrong with him?'

'That, I don't know.'

'Thought you knew everything.' It sounds dead cheeky. Gerard keeks at Craig, to see if he's going to be angry. But he's shaking his head. Grinning.

'You're something else, so you are. Listen, do you fancy coming downstairs?'

'How?'

'Well, you just put your hand on the banister, pop one foot on the step–'

'Ha, ha. You're no very funny, are you?'

'Apparently not.'

Gerard hesitates before he says it, then thinks *fuck it*. He sticks his tongue behind his teeth and goes, 'Indeed.'

And then Craig starts laughing, proper laughing, and so does Gerard, a wee bit, until Craig stands up and says, 'Right. C'mon, you.'

'C'mon where?'

'Come and help me sort the tea.'

Cooking? Gerard perks up at this. He's surprised they're going to let him loose with knives. On their big swanky worktops too. They are totally white and shiny, with glass chopping boards and a ginormous green glass bowl which holds nothing but apples, which no one seems to eat. But they don't go into the kitchen. Instead, Craig takes him through the hall. It's his favourite room in the whole house. Dark green walls, crammed with pictures. Your actual, proper painting-pictures. Faces. Animals. Hills. Some are just coloured shapes. When you stare, you can see different things, like looking in a fire: big splodges, watery shimmers. They give him a spooky feeling under his skin.

'You like?' Craig clocks him eyeing a painting of a black-haired woman. Her lips are a gash of red and she's surrounded by mad flowers – purple and red and orange. Even though you can hardly make out her face cause the paint is so thick and swirly, she seems dead happy.

He shrugs. 'It's alright.'

'That's my mum,' says Craig.

'Aye. Right.'

'It is! Self-portrait. She was an artist.'

'Serious? She done all these?'

'No. Some of them are my dad's. He was an artist too.'

Gerard tries to get his head round the fact that Craig knows actual painters. It's like saying you're mates with Dua Lipa or your uncle's in the Premier League. It's crazy. Craig was *born* from actual painters. Gerard goes towards another picture, set high on the wall. It's of a field, or maybe the sea, at sunset. Lots of ripply blues and greens, then a smash of orange in the centre.

'That's the sun, isn't it?'

'It is. My dad did that one.'

'Were they famous, like?'

'Only to me.' Craig smiles at him. 'No. They worked as teachers mostly.'

Gerard feels deflated. Craig's just bullshitting him.

'But that doesn't mean they weren't artists.' He puts a hand on Gerard's shoulder. It's annoying, how he does that. Gerard doesn't like folk at his back.

'Check this one.' Craig nudges him towards this painting of a weird, angry monkey with clown skulls on its head. It's eating a big circle. So many colours and patterns dancing. 'I give you the Wheel of Life!'

Gerard squints. It feels like the painting is shouting at him.

'See there? The three poisons of ignorance, attachment and aversion.'

All he can see is a snake biting the arse of a cow or a pig, which in turn is sooking a bird's wing.

'Oh. Aye.' Craig has went full loopy. Gerard may have to do a runner.

From the middle, the picture moves out in rings crowded with animals and people and waves and clouds. It makes him dizzy. He imagines it spinning, and all the wee people falling off. The giant monkey is well creepy.

'Anyway, onwards, my young forager.'

Fluck knows what Craig is on about. He dunts him in the back again – *piss off, Craig!* – and they go straight past the kitchen, out the back door. The back garden is long and thin too, with high stone walls all the way round. There's a wooden gate leading into the lane. Gerard's been out exploring a few times (not that there's much to see). Visited a few of the neighbours' gardens that way too. Now he sees there's a big padlock on the latch.

'*Sake*. It's like the jail, this.'

'Sorry?' Craig is frowning.

Gerard has gone too far with his gallusness. He'll blame it on the fresh air. 'Nothing.'

Craig stretches his arm out wide. 'You like this, don't you?'

'What?'

'My wee oasis. I've seen you out here.'

'I thought we were making the dinner?'

'Oh, but we are, young man, we are. First, though, we have to find it.'

This guy is loop-the-loo. Did the Social Work not check him out? Maybe no one else would take Gerard. He wouldn't of cared if they'd kept him in that stupid home. He'd've been alright. Just needed to suss out who to avoid and who to keep sweet. Who you'd to batter too. Get in quick before they get you. That's why he hit that ginger kid at the gym. He *had* to; he didn't want to.

Another entry to go in his file.

Craig takes Gerard into his greenhouse. He's not been in there before – it smells funny. Smells green, like when you snap a twig or they've cut the grass verges. He stands, uncomfortable, by the door. Why is Craig taking him in here? He's getting busy with a watering can. Muttering. Jeezo – is he talking to his plants? Guy's off his heid. Craig is fingering a big bunch of tomatoes, just hinging off a furry green stem. Gerard didn't know they grew like a bunch of grapes. The smell is juicy-sharp. Is amazing. There are mysterious small implements with dirt on – a poker thing, a fork and a totey spade. Wee red things he thinks are chillis (you get them in Nando's) and trays of tiny, spiky lettuces, which lie on slatted wooden shelves.

'Microsalads.' Craig lifts one of the trays. 'Want to try?'

'*No way.*' They look rank.

'Here we are.' Craig pulls back some long green leaves on a kind of vine near the floor of the greenhouse. Two big shiny purple cucumbers peek out.

'*Voilà.* Tonight, young man, we are having aubergine parmigiana. Want to have a rummage and see if you can find any more? We need about four or five. I was hoping to get them outside this month, but the weather's not been great. Much better when you can taste the sunshine.' He's talking to himself, or maybe the plants again. Whatever. Gerard's tuned out. He canny get over the size of these things. Aubergines. They look revolting. They look kind of rude. He parts the carpet of leaves, finds another, then another. He cups his hand around an aubergine. It is so smooth. So shiny purple-black that it canny be for real.

'There you go. Just twist the stalks gently. Don't bruise them.'

He does, once, twice, and next thing, he has a giant purple tadger in each hand.

'Excellent. Like collecting eggs from a nest. That must be why they call them eggplants, eh?' Craig gives him a nudge. Gerard flinches. 'Only joking. You get wee fat white ones too. Hence the monicker.'

Listening to Craig is the same as trying to read words. Weird and jumbly.

'You're going to have to apologise, you know.' Craig is piling the aubergines into a basket. 'To William.'

Gerard stops what he's doing. Just stands there, with an aubergine half-off the stalk. William is that ginger kid. He thought Craig was on his side. Wanker. He's no even flucken asked, about why Gerard did it, or what the kid said. He presses his fingernails into soft purple flesh. Little half-moons of white squish out. Unhappy smiles. Gerard is bad. Gerard is wrong.

'Next week, before class starts I want you to say you're sorry. OK?'

Gerard gouges out a bit more aubergine. The white gunge goes under his nails. 'I'm no going back there. No way.'

'Fine. But you'll still have to apologise.'

'Am I fuck.' He tugs off the aubergine. Throws it on the floor, where it bursts like a big fat slug.

Craig ignores the massacre. 'Now, Gerard, we've talked about this. I'd rather you didn't use language like that in the house.'

'We're no in the fucking house.'

'You're in our home, and we have rules here. Don't we?'

Is he waiting for Gerard to rhyme them off? Gerard notices wee white seeds inside the aubergine's guts. They give him the boak. He feels his tummy boiling.

'Respect. That's it really, isn't it? That's all we've asked for – and offered you.'

'No F-word,' Gerard shouts. 'No C-word. Say please and thank you. Eat your greens. Talk to us when you feel upset or worried. Don't go out without saying where you're going, and when you'll be back, and who with. Wipe your arse. Blow your nose–' He's plucking random leaves, tearing and pulling them and letting them float to the floor. He can sense Craig getting closer. Knows the man is itching to touch him, and if he does, if he fucking does, Gerard will pick up that fork . . .

'Gerard, this is the contract we agreed to.' Calmly, Craig moves a tomato plant out of Gerard's reach. 'I mean, do you even like it here?'

He's left with a bunch of furry leaves in his fist.

'Gerard?'

'It's alright.' He's frightened now. This is the start of another conversation. The one which ends with him getting shunted someplace else.

'Well, it doesn't look like it, from the damage you're doing to my poor plants.'

Gerard scuffs his foot along the floor of the greenhouse, raking all the pebbles into a rut. What he wants to say is *aye!* What he wants to say is: You've a huge big house. And it's a massive room I'm in, and you and Kris make nice dinners, and I never hear yous shouting much, and maybe if you thought about it, yous could take Anthony and the wean too, just for a wee while, so we could all be in the same house and not be scared? Just to see what that was like?

'It's better than the home, eh?'

'Aye.' Gerard glances up at him. Craig still doesn't look angry, even though Gerard has trashed his greenhouse. 'I thought they were gonny send me to a secure unit.'

The days after the first Hearing are blurry. He did get taken back to that shithole home, and he did get threatened with somewhere worse. He *knows* he did, even though they'll all deny it. But he remembers some torn-faced man with a jaggy chin, right in about him, telling him he was going to get done with all sorts – assaulting a social worker (yay!), assaulting a polis (again) – and probably murder too, if the old lady pegged it. He does so remember that: the man coming to his room, after they'd flung him on the bed, and he was curled up all wee and tight. This lanky prick, standing over him, reading the riot act. *Bad influence on your siblings. Uncontrolled outbursts. Don't know how lucky you are.*

The usual crap. Gerard had just kept hunched over in the bed. He minds biting his knees, to stop from listening to the man. He'd teeth marks on them for days. They're no meant to talk to you like that. He could of got them all the sack, if he'd said anything. Nebby bastards. They wouldn't tell him where Anthony and Miranda were either. For days and days, no bastard would tell him, not until he trashed their manky 'chill-out room'. Who knew there were that many wee polystyrene balls in one bean bag? And that, really cheap beanbags, you can rip open with your teeth. Oh, Gerard was definitely going to jail after that.

Except he didn't.

They had him up in front of the Panel again, about a week after the first Hearing. But this one was about the old lady. Tattoo-cop was there, leering at him as they droned through every wrong thing Gerard has done. A Hearing for Gerard's Greatest Hits. He was sure they'd lock him up somewhere really, really bad. But no. He got sent here instead.

His mum didn't even come to the Panel.

Craig is still talking at him. 'Well, they must have thought you were worth another try.'

'I just want us all to be together,' he blurts out.

'You and your brother and sister?'

'Aye.'

'I understand that, Gerard. It must be so, so hard for you, I get that. You've been looking after them for ages. But now it's time for us to look after you.'

'Why can't we, but?'

'Stay together?' Craig half-sits on the edge of a wooden shelf. 'Lots of reasons. Different foster carers have different . . . well, for example, Richard and Helen's, where the kids are staying, they specialise in helping babies and toddlers.'

'Our Anthony's no a toddler.'

'No, but remember at your Child Protection Hearing. There was a wee bit of ructions, wasn't there? So I'm told.'

Gerard shrugs.

'I mean, that social worker really hurt herself, when you–'

'When she fell.'

'Indeed. But I think they maybe thought that, because Anthony looks up to you–'

'That he'll turn out as shite as me? So they need to keep him away from me?'

'Ach, Gerard.' For a third time, Craig squeezes his shoulder, and Gerard just stands there, willing it to be over. But knowing that the squeeze won't lead to his ear getting grabbed, his head pulled down within kicking range. Knowing, yet not believing it. Sensing the pain of your skull cracking off concrete, even when it's not happening. The shock of that jolt. The sensation of first your feet, then your stomach, slipping away, and the black, falling, bursting pain of your soft-hard head on the hard-hard ground. Again, he sees her lying there. The old woman. Her happy wee cardigan all dirty on the pavement.

'Do you know what happened to the old lady?' Fuck, he's said it out loud, the thing they've never spoken about since he got here.

'Who?' Craig is glaikit, then his eyebrows go up, and he gets all flustered. 'Oh, you mean–'

'She fell and all.' Gerard wants to stuff the words back in his mouth; he doesn't know why he said it, like spewing. He is nipping the sides of his legs with his fingers, really hard. Nipping and twisting the flesh through his jeans. He wants to see blood come out.

'Did she? The old lady?'

Gerard nods. He can't speak now.

'They haven't told us. I think they try to keep what happened before and what's happening now a bit separate, you know? But they did say they were holding off deciding any charges till the outcome for the lady was known. And, as you haven't been charged–'

Gerard's eyes are screwed shut, but he knows Craig is looking at him funny. You can hear it in his voice.

'But it's not alright, son, is it? Jeez, look, I'll see what I can find out? I'll ask, I promise.'

Gerard opens his eyes. 'What about the weans? Will you ask if they can keep us together?'

Craig is scratching the base of his neck. It's what folk do when they're tired. He smiles at Gerard. 'There's some folk called Who Cares? Scotland I'd like you to meet. They're a charity. They help young people who're in care – they kind of advocate for them.'

'But I amny in care now. I'm here, with yous.'

'This is still care, Gerard. You know? You're under supervision. It's an interim Compulsory Supervision Order they've put you on. They explained that at your Panel, didn't they?'

Gerard shrugs.

'Nothing's been decided yet. They've given you three months to see how you're getting on. To not get into bother, be on your best behaviour. You know that, don't you?'

Gerard nods.

'Look, we really love having you here, but it's a temporary foster placement.'

His heart stills. He'd not heard them say temporary before. No one has said temporary. Of course he knows he canny stay here forever. He doesn't want to stay here forever. But he thought –

He thought . . .

He doesn't know what he thought. That it might be up to him? The glass on the greenhouse starts to shimmer. It turns into water, silvery water pouring and shaking, all the windows rushing like his blood, in gloops so hot and hard they hurt you. It must be him, making windows shiver, his fault that they are gonny crash in and kill them. His fingers open and close, they fumble onto a hard thing which tings as it strikes the watering can. It is the wee jaggy thing, the fork. He picks up the fork and he lobs it at the moving glass, because it needs to stop moving. There is a moment of silence then a glorious crack, and the tinkle of music, before he feels Craig's arms go round him from behind, and he is wriggling and struggling, trying to kick backwards onto Craig's shins, but the bastard won't let him go.

'Come on, son,' he's saying. 'Let's get you into the house.'

Gerard feels Craig's weight, pushing him on, and he lowers his head, ready to fling it back and smash his stupid face in, but instead, he slumps. He just gives up, because he canny stop crying.

Chapter Ten

The familiar wrought unreal. Margaret pauses by the window, afraid to look out. Unsure as to where she should direct herself. Returning to your own house should be a pleasure. But she is Alice in Wonderland; she has passed through glass into a world that is backwards and upside down and wholly malevolent. She holds fast to the top of her wing-back chair. Its shoulders bulk, blading the air. Her rug is nothing but a trip risk. The curtains hang like funeral drapes, cutting her off from help. All her lovely objects rendered menacing. See how that bureau looms, threatening to absorb the light. That mocking mirror. The dangerous coloured glass that twinkles and could cut your face to ribbons if you get too close.

Margaret runs her tongue along her upper gum. Even her own teeth feel wrong. They fit, yet they don't. She won't look in the mirror. She is scared of shadows: the shadow that trails behind her shuffling feet and the ones inside. What strange dreams she's been having.

She touches her books. *Strange*. Means alien. Unfamiliar.

She's appalled with herself. Margaret Camberg, whose life is shrunk to this one decrepit shell. A crone so frail that a child would see you and think to knock you down. There's no secret to Margaret any more. What you see is all there is. Her hand trembles, yet it's wasted energy. Her grip on the chair, feeble. She strokes her collarbone. The bony lump persists: a knot of new bone, knitted over old. Margaret moves awkwardly. The steady ache in her hip has joined all the other aches and pains, the can't-complains, the daily drains on your soul becoming indelible.

Of all the facts she has consumed, nothing remains. Her pile of books form a recriminatory tower. She will ask Zara to take them away. Her eyes are too muddy to discern words. Her mind too pummelled to translate them.

Her throat burns.

Margaret the husk. She wipes her eyes. If she's not careful, she will rust. What would Bert say? *Come, yekirati. All will be well.*

Zara found Albert's old stick inside the wardrobe. Margaret hates the zimmer frame they foisted on her at hospital, but this stick is a comfort. Her hand on top of his hand, almost. It's a simple cane, polished wood, with a brass tip.

'Oh, love,' she whispers, 'what a mess I'm in.'

She manoeuvres, so the stick is in the opposite hand from her sore hip. Takes herself into the kitchen, but she's not hungry. All the kind food her neighbours bring: mince and tatties from Jacqueline, lurid fruits from Zara and a nice shepherd's pie from the doctor's wife. Lovely girl. She forgets her name. Furtively, she investigates the master bedroom. She wants her bed moved, away from the window. How can she sleep below a sill that sits so close to the ground? Barely seven feet separate Margaret from the pavement. A tall man could easily vault it. Or punt a boy up on his shoulders. Perhaps she should try sleeping in the spare bedroom – but that would involve making up the bed, and she doesn't have the strength.

It's not the spare room anyway. It's Stephen's.

Margaret eases herself to sit at her dressing table. Runs her hands across its surface. The wood is satin-smooth. Such strange, strange dreams. When she was hovering there, in the hospital. Opening up her old selves. She thought school was buckled inside her ancient satchel. She remembers the day Mother bought it, in Campbell's Girls' Shop. It's tucked on a shelf ben the hall press, full of photographs. Photos which break her heart, but which she cannot throw away. She doesn't need reminding of all the things she's lost.

Her battered wee brain, however, thinks otherwise. What a clamjamfrey of memories have been shoogled up. Daylight-vivid they came, all the time she was trussed with tubes and bleeping monitors. Bright, buried fragments of her life. She was so positive she was there, walking the corridors of Laurel Bank. Her skin prickles, and she fans herself with the back of her hand. She could *hear* Stephen's laughter, see the sun catch his hair. Standing by Albert's hospital bed. Feeling him die all over again. Adrift in her own head, it had felt as if time flowed through her. Margaret's fingers stray to her jewellery box. She opens the catch. A tangle of tat coils and gleams within. Jewellery she'll never wear, for people and places long past. Mother's wedding ring. The pearls Albert gave her on her twenty-first. She holds the pearls to her lips. Returns them to the box. Untangles a locket. If she unclasps the front . . . No. She cannot release more memories. Beside the locket is a clean but yellowed lace hankie. Margaret unfolds it. The linen is embroidered with thistles. She cradles the fabric. Lifts it to her face. Glimpses herself in the mirror – a stupid old woman, sniffing a hankie. Hurriedly, she slams the lid of the jewellery box. The hairbrush on her dressing table rattles. The handkerchief drops to the carpet.

This will not do. This is not her.

Stick in hand, Margaret resumes her pacing. The grandmother clock in the hall chimes two. Well-meaning Zara will be here at four, bringing more knobbly green foodstuffs. The leftovers other folk refused to buy. Margaret is grateful for her kindness, but she doesn't want her to come any more, and doesn't know how to say. Doesn't want any of them, morning and night. Breenging in like they own the place. Margaret wants them to return her keys. Leave her alone. Every new intrusion is opening a wound. She feels like prey. The district nurse has given her a sort of plastic commode thing that sits on top of the lavatory seat, so she doesn't have to squat too far. She has a walk-in shower, and someone from the council or occupational health or whatever has put in a rail. One more visit from the physio, then she can stop doing these ridiculous ankle-flailing exercises. After that, she'll be fine. She's sure she will be fine. Her flat will resume its calm and order. Will feel like home again. She's sure it will.

Six long weeks in the hospital. Bedbound, with her arm in a sling across her breast. First the bone in her hip wouldn't set, so they had to operate, then she got a horrible urine infection to boot. Margaret averts her eyes from the pack of pads they sent home with her. Shameful, ugly things. An occasional wee accident does not an incontinent make. She's begged Zara to put them in the bin. *Let's just wait and see how you get on* was the response.

Margaret knows about decline. Bert had three strokes in all. Two smaller ones, then the final, huge one. It wasn't his fault, poor darling. But Margaret will never become . . .

She just won't.

She's refused the offer of a home help. Although she's not sure if it was offered as a gift or a service to be paid for. Which is out of the question, of course. Several reproachful envelopes loom on the table. Margaret doesn't hold with money flying out your bank willy-nilly. She likes to receive her bills, then, chequebook in hand, resolve them. But she's missed both her council tax and Scottish Power since she's been away. What if she's in arrears? Do they fine you? She knows she should open them, but it frightens her. Everything is frightening her. Money is tight, and getting tighter. If her fuel bills keep rising, by winter she'll be moving permanently to her bed. Her pension will not stretch to covering arrears, and she cannot face the embarrassment of explaining.

I am a Victim of Crime.

They should paint it on her forehead.

Margaret wants – needs – no one. After Albert passed, she found a wee quiet corner of herself to inhabit. Small, and self-contained. When you open up to others it tears a hole. You need to leave a space between folk. The day she has a carer is the day she'll simply give up. She'll ask someone who doesn't bully her – nice Gordon perhaps – to walk her to the bank. And the shops. If she goes down Duke Street with him on her arm, just for the first time, she'll be as right as rain. She's sure she will.

Thon Zara. She's a good lass. Without her, Margaret would still be languishing in a hospital bed. Zara is a force of nature, but she's so sure of what Margaret needs that she never actually asks her. Most of them are like that, her neighbours. Overwhelming.

That blonde woman, though. The lawyer girl who came before. Margaret liked her. There was a quiet coolness about her. Katie, was it? No, Claire. Zara berated her something terrible, went on about it afterwards too. Imagine having Margaret's dentures all that time! After her initial, daft panic, Margaret thought it was quite funny, actually. And, by hoicking them out in the first place, the girl did, technically, save her life.

Margaret's mind jolts violently to that boy, to the random cruelty of it, and she marshals her thoughts back to Zara. Dear God, if Zara had saved Margaret's life (and sometimes, you'd think she had), you'd never hear the end of it.

Claire might be her secret saviour, though. Unshowy. Reserved. Does the right thing, then discreetly retreats.

Perhaps Claire's should be the arm that takes Margaret back into the world?

But how to find her? She'll have to ask Zara. No. That will give her even more locus over Margaret's life. Zara is not her gatekeeper.

Ach, why don't they all just go away, and leave her with her thoughts?

Except Margaret's thoughts scare her.

She's hobbled full-circle, is in the living room once more. Flicks through a copy of *The People's Friend* that Jacqueline left on the table. A leaflet sits beneath it. A cloud with a sun poking out. It's from Victim Support Scotland. *It is normal to experience a range of physical, emotional and social reactions.* The leaflet is some kind of questionnaire; she can recall a young man handing it to her. Was it here or on the ward? She shuffles it under the local newspaper, the weekly freesheet. She'll not look at that either. News is never good. Her small television stares blankly. If she switches it on, she'll fall into a bigger void, of soaps and wars and desperate boat people and lingering pandemics.

She thinks she might scream.

Zara's computer thingy. It waits beside the newspaper. Zara insists Margaret will *love it!* Trying to get her all-mod-conned. Telling her the internet is *your window to the world!* (She imagines every speech bubble of Zara's to be liberally doused with exclamation marks.)

The thing's surprisingly light. Margaret turns the device over. A square of paper's taped to the back, with handwritten instructions about a passcode and what buttons to press. Of course there is – this is Zara we're talking about.

Ach, Margaret. Where's your softness? Did that bang to the head knock it out of you?

She remembers when Bert first told her his story. Late at night, a glass of brandy in his hand. How he described his mother and his brother. His grandparents. All gone. How she had wept with him. Wept, then raged, then wept again. How he'd held her in his arms, as if it were her pain, not his.

You can't taste only bitterness. There's sweetness on God's earth too. How else would I have made my way to you?

'Oh, Albert,' she says aloud, just so she can feel the syllables in her mouth. The magic power of his name fills the empty room. Conjures his presence, his hand on her spine, gently pushing. She locates her spectacles. Reads Zara's instructions. Reads them again, then presses the 'Big Circle in the Middle' button. Margaret types in the passcode, presses the smaller, multi-coloured circle that gives her access to 'The Web'.

She can't remember Claire's surname, but she does recall the firm she works for, mostly because Zara spent so long pointing to Claire's credentials on their website. Such a lovely, sing-song ring.

Murdoch, Murdoch and Black.

It takes a while for Margaret to realise she must move her finger on the tiny pad to make the hand symbol appear, but once she's got that, she's away. It's a matter of two clicks to find Claire's photo, then her surname, then one more click to find her phone number. Margaret jots it down. Shuts the computer, taking care to close all the little crosses in the windows first (as per instructions).

Carefully, she dials the number.

'Might I speak with Miss Urquhart, please?'

'Who's calling?'

Margaret hesitates. She hasn't thought of a plausible reason for calling. 'If you tell her it's Mrs Camberg.'

Without question, the receptionist puts her through.

'Hello?' Claire is brisk. Margaret is dumbstruck. 'Hello? Claire Urquhart here.'

'Claire!' she says, as if it's a surprise. 'It's Margaret. The . . . We met the other day. You returned my teeth?'

'Oh.' Then nothing.

'Hello?'

'Hello?' They both say it at the same time, adding to the confusion.

'I'm sorry,' says Margaret. 'Sorry for calling you at work.'

'No, no, it's fine,' says Claire, when it's clearly not; Margaret can hear a man in the background.

'Look, I won't keep you. I just . . .' She stops. Feels her cheeks flame.

'Margaret.' Claire goes very quiet, 'I just wanted to say how sorry I am. Again, I can only apologise.'

'Oh dear, no. I'm not calling to cause a fuss. I'm wondering if you'd like to come to tea?'

'Tea?'

'Or coffee. Or a sherry if you prefer?' Her voice sounds quavery. She presses her lips together. 'I want to say thank you. And . . . maybe we could take a wee walk?'

'A *walk*?' Evidently, Claire thinks she has gone mad.

'To get my confidence back.'

'But why . . .' Claire doesn't complete the sentence.

Margaret finds she is holding her breath.

'I work all week,' says Claire. 'Until quite late.'

'Ah.'

'So.'

'So.' Margaret exhales. Prepares her exit strategy. If her cheeks get any hotter, she shall self-combust.

'So, when were you thinking of? Would this weekend do? Say Saturday again?'

'Yes, please,' says Margaret. 'Saturday would be lovely. Say around three?' The bank won't be open then, but no matter. Margaret's in no hurry to confront her finances.

'Tea for two. At three.'

Is Claire making fun of her? 'At three,' repeats Margaret.

'At three,' repeats Claire. 'Do you want me to bring anything? Cakes? Buns? Dentures?'

Margaret laughs out loud. 'Only yourself,' she says. She replaces the phone on its cradle. Hears a raucous shout from outside. She moves herself closer to the window, side on, so she can peek. Just children, playing round the statue. She draws the curtains a little more. She's sure it's going to be fine.

Chapter Eleven

Gerard looks at the wee box they've given him.
'You each get your own trowel, mini-fork and gardening gloves,' the woman's saying. 'And there should be either a packet of wildflower seeds or a bee bomb in each trug too.'

'I'm no wearing these,' says Gerard, holding up a well-dodgy pair of purple mittens.

'But they'll keep your hands clean. Stop you getting scratches too.'

'Who else has worn them, but?'

'I'm sorry?'

'Look at them. They're rank. All crusty lines on the palms. I don't know whose hands have been in them. What about the COVID?'

'I'm not sure you can get COVID from old gloves.'

'Aye, you can. You can get it fae anywhere.'

There's a ripple of concern passing through the other kids. They're all checking out their gloves now. Gerard has started a revolution.

'Right, here.' The woman, Tracey, hands him a pair of green ones. Paradise-green and still in the packet. 'Will these do for sir?'

'Aye.' Gerard slips his hand into one of them. He wiggles them at Big Jiggy. 'Hail, hail, the Celts are here.' Jiggy grins. He'd sussed Jiggy was the unofficial group leader soon as he saw him. Clocked how the other kids were hinging on his every word.

Clocked the sandy hair and freckles too, and so took a punt that seems to have paid off.

Jiggy waves his arms, kids on he's on the terraces. '*Ceh*-l-tic. *Ceh*-l-tic.'

'Right, troops. We'll have none of that, remember?' Tracey has her hands on her hips. 'No football songs. No boys against girls – nothing. We're all guerrillas here, OK?'

'Ooh-ooh. Ooh-ooh.' Jiggy and some of the other lads start pure jumping like monkeys.

'*Guerr*, not *gor*, you eejits! *Guerr*-illas. Gardening guerrillas!'

'Here, miss, is that no offensive? Calling us eejits?'

'Aye, you're right, Gerard, it probably is. To eejits.' Tracey makes a face at him. But he doesn't take the huff cause it's like she's laughing with him. 'Right, my wee green army. Are we ready to roll?'

Craig is still there. Leaning against his Merc and watching. Gerard got some approving looks when they rocked up in that motor, and he's determined to capitalise on it for as long as possible. At the boxing gym, he was a marked man from the start. Boys can tell when you're making your body wee and unthreatening – even if you don't mean to, you canny really help it. It's in your walk – if there's no bounce to your step, you're doomed. Well, Gerard fair leapfrogged out that Merc, and it's meant he's been able to get a laugh out the group already. A wee nod from Jiggy and all.

Craig raises his palm. The universal man-signal that you're about to head. Gerard dips his chin in acknowledgement. *It's a jungle out there, Craig*, he doesn't say. Craig must of run out of reasons to hang about. He'd rhymed off a whole spiel when he dropped Gerard off. 'I'll just wait and see what you think of it. And then I'll just be round the corner, having a coffee, so you can phone me. Phone me if there's anything at all, yeah? Or if you want to go home.'

Craig's alright. He hasn't battered Gerard for smashing up the greenhouse. Hasn't even grounded him. Didn't do anything really, except hold on to Gerard until he stopped crying. Then telt him to wash the aubergines. He did make him apologise to the ginger kid, though. But he let him do it by phone, so Gerard didn't have to see the wee shit's face. Even helped him work out how he'd say it: *I'm sorry that I hit you. What you said about my mum was really rude and upset me, but I still shouldn't have done it.*

'That way you still get to tell him what he did was wrong too. See?'

Gerard would of much rather never spoken to the boy again. Or hear his snidey reply: *I accept your apology.* (Clearly, there was some adult in the background at his end too, coaching him on what to say.) It's funny, but. Afterwards, his shoulders felt less scrunched. Light, the way a balloon just lifts up when you pat it. It felt nice. Made him think of that CD with the wee dude floating on the cloud.

Gerard follows the rest of the guerrillas into the Transit. Leafgreen, painted with white flowers and a row of bubble letters. Craig told him what they stood for. Gerard reckons Craig knows. The way he spelled it out for him. 'See? Your chariot awaits! Grow For It! Gardening Guerrillas – South & East.'

Gerard will probably be getting another 'intervention' soon, where Craig sits him down with a diddy picture book for fiveyear-olds. Telling him how it's easy, really. A is for Apple . . . Not for a while maybe. Call-me-Craig knows he's pushing his luck with this one. The Gardening Guerrillas. Man. One minute Gerard's picking some willy-shaped vegetables, next thing Craig's all 'You like gardening, don't you? So how about this then?'

He knew it was coming. Heard Craig and Kris talking. Every Tuesday, Craig and Kris take turns to go to a support group for foster carers. Nice, eh? A support group – they actually call it that. Putting up with kids like Gerard is so flucken terrible, you need therapy. All they foster carers, rocking backwards and forwards in their wee circle, roaring and crying about how shite it is. But Craig aye comes back even more annoyingly smiley than when he went. It's like each greeting meeting gives him extra energy. And last Tuesday, Gerard heard him say to Kris how one of the other carers swears by a gardening group 'her boy' goes to. 'No teams. No competition. It's gentle, therapeutic. Creative.' His voice had speeded with excitement. 'And they give so much back to the community. Sounds like a winner to me.' He couldn't quite make out what Kris replied. He'd hoped she was saying about the football. Gerard had seen a football skills summer school that ran the whole of July. Four weeks of fitba, plus they threw in juice and crisps. Hours to himself, unsupervised (course he wouldn't go to it every day, but he wasny telling Kris that). Best of all – it was in Shawlands. He could walk down himself and maybe call in to see the weans too. When he asked them, he'd put on his best, wide-eyed, you-can-trust-me face, and Kris had said, 'We'll see.'

How 'we'll see' about football became 'you're going to dig up worms, boy' is not exactly clear. The football hasn't been totally discounted. It's just on hold until *we see how you get on with this*.

They say it like it's not a threat.

Ach, he doesn't mind. The summer holidays are stretching long. When he arrived here, they tried to put him into a new school called St Bride's, but they took one look at him . . . No, that's bullshit. He'd went there with Kris, and she'd been all yapping on to the teachers about extra support, how she'd been a teacher herself, and then they made him wait outside the heidie's office (as well getting used to that right from the off . . .) Anyway, the place seemed alright, but after a while Kris emerged and said it had *been agreed* she'd home school him for now. *It's only for a few weeks, really. I think this will be best, no?* So, in the mornings, she's had him sitting in the kitchen, watching videos about outer space or the Jacobite Rising and that. Or she'll get him to repeat adding-ons. Times tables, they're called. He minds them from school. Always repeating, not reading. Never words neither; they just do numbers, which is the only reason he's not done a runner. He reckons Kris has got him sussed too. Sometimes, if he's in the mood, he'll repeat the numbers in her funny accent, and that makes her laugh.

But now it's the actual school holidays, Kris says Gerard doesn't have to do his lessons any more. He thought he'd feel more happy about that. Their house is nice and all, but it's boring without your mates. He's not allowed to roam like he does at home. Doing what he's telt is in his contract. Every happy family needs a contract. Gerard has Rights and Responsibilities, by order of the Sheriff. Or the Reporter or the Children's Panel or the Social Work – he isny really sure. But whoever decided he wasn't getting locked up in some secure unit also gets to decide what goes in his Supervision Order.

It's a bit like being on probation – if you promise to be good, they give you another chance. But you canny just do a pinkie promise or be vague about it. No – they give you a big list of dos and don'ts. He's on an 8 p.m. curfew for starters. So if the garden monkeys want to stay out late for some midnight digging, Gerard will have to say no. He's also got to work with CAMHS, to 'deal with his anger issues' (yawn).

Luckily, there's a long waiting list for that, so he's managed to avoid sitting in an airless room with some old crazy-haired woman, listening to whales (well, that's what it was like last time). Gerard has also to 'engage with community activities relating to personal development', which means going one day a week to whatever shite Kris and Craig have planned for him next. Their boys have got a PS2, but playing on that doesn't count (though learning how to shoot down an alien invasion could be very useful in real life, Gerard thinks).

Restorative justice. Another thing they've talked about. He thinks it's to do with saying sorry, but nobody's really explained it to him. Craig says it will be part of finding out what happened to the old lady. Nobody will tell Craig either, but he says he'll keep asking. Anyway, Craig says Gerard can't even think about that till he's had his first session with CAMHS, so the mental health folk can check he's 'emotionally strong enough'.

'Are you OK with me saying that, Gerard? Do you understand what I mean? Emotionally strong just means you can handle it, you know?'

Craig does that a lot. It's what Gerard wishes teachers would do. He'll say something, then stop and ask if Gerard gets it, before going on to say the next thing. See if folk don't give you that wee space, but just keep blethering on and on, and you, getting more confused? Then you never get to catch up. That's when you switch off. Or get angry.

It's decent of Craig, he supposes. To tell him what folk are saying about him. But he doesny really like it. How the fluck does some social worker know how Gerard feels inside? Man. Gerard doesny even know that.

He just wishes someone would find his bike. And his mum.

He stares at the back of the seat in front of him. He has looked after his mum, his wee brother and the baby, all by himself. Because he had too. Because there is no one else. So how does a grown-up get to decide, now, what he can handle?

She's still alive, the old lady. They did say that. He can't speak to her, though. But he doesny want to. No way. Craig says he won't have to, that he can write her a letter or something. Well, he said 'you', then almost immediately, went 'we. I mean we can write it.' Craig isn't as patient as Kris. Gerard reckons he is itching to talk about the reading and writing bollocks, but, Jeezo, it's the summer holidays and Gerard has got enough on his plate.

Tell me, Gerard. Are you emotionally strong enough to handle that you're really, really thick?

'Shove up.' A tall, chubby boy plonks next to him on the Transit. Gerard wanted to sit on the outside of the seats, but he budges up. It's more like a minibus inside. There's about ten of them onboard. Ten kids and a cargo of feathery plants in a crate at the front. There's a door at the side that opens and one at the front, which you could climb over the seats to reach. Gerard's good at scanning for danger. He thinks he might be the youngest: they all look like secondary kids up close. Plenty plooks on show. One of the boys has got a definite shadow. If Gerard had known that, he wouldn't have been so gallus at the start.

'Alright?' says the boy. His thighs spill onto Gerard's side. 'I'm Ali. Jacqueline says I've to sit with you.'

Ali smells of chips and vinegar. Gerard budges over more. He nods at the woman who is doing the checks and counting heads. 'I thought her name was Tracey?'

'It is. Jacqueline's my foster. She's pals with your ones.'

'My ones?'

'Your fosters. Him, the dude with the big Merc.'

'Oh, Craig? Right.'

Ali opens a bag of crisps. 'Want one?' His fingers are manky.

'Nah, you're alright.'

Tracey shouts from the front, 'You all got your seatbelts on, troops? Let's roll!'

They drive for about fifteen minutes. Gerard doesn't have a clue where he is. The Southside is still a leafy mystery. Maybe it's exactly because he doesn't know it well, doesn't know which gang owns which corner, or whose granda got chibbed where, or what shops the dealers wait outside, that it feels so . . . unthreatening. There's nowhere that doesn't feel safe. It's a weird feeling to walk down a street with your head high. To own the middle of the pavement and not worry that you'll wind some psycho up in the process. They should put that in their wee anxiety CDs. *Move hoose.*

The minibus takes them to the community farm in Dalmarnock. There, they are unloaded, given a 'safety talk' and set to work within a walled garden surrounded by flats. Slave labour. Place stinks of shit, and Gerard has blisters before it's even lunchtime. They spend the morning howking potatoes out of trenches and making long furrows for lettuce seeds. Jiggy starts throwing clods of mud at one of the lassies, and is taken away for a 'cool down'. The girl's fair hair is peppered with earthy crumbs. She shakes and shakes it, head upside down, her pal batting bits of soil away. When she stops shoogling, her face is flushed. She's got shiny brown eyes. Gerard watches Ali try to chat the lassie up, offering her some Pringles. She takes a crisp, but is having none of his nonsense. Ali just grins and eats his Pringles. The girl sees Gerard staring and does the Vs. But she's laughing. He looks away.

Gerard listens to the birdsong, and feels the lukewarm sun on his back. He drags hessian sacks full of feed for the animals. Ali makes wee holes with a bit of wood called a divot or a dibble, and Gerard drops tiny seeds in the holes. He straightens his spine. Hears a donkey bray. The sky is a sugary blue. He plants some tubers – ugly wee clumps that could be alien babies for all he knows. They feel knobbly in his hand. It's quite good fun, actually. Here. There are mental chickens at the farm, running and scratching everywhere. The kids have to keep chasing them from what they've just planted. After a while, Gerard's blisters don't sting. A weird kind of rhythm takes over, where he lifts and bends and rises in time with the plants moving, with the breeze, and the buzzing in his head dissolves into buzzing insects, and it's really nice.

They eat lunch outside, after washing their hands at a 'cleaning station' – which is two sinks and a paper towel dispenser stuck to a wall. Kris has made Gerard a wholemeal wrap with hummus and red peppers. The hummus looks bogging, but it tastes delicious – and Gerard is so hungry he would eat anything. It's really garlicky. Better even than garlic bread. He wishes Anthony could try it. Tracey brings out a tin with lemon drizzle cake. Oh, man – he's never tasted anything so sharp and sweet. Says she made it herself, but he doesn't think you could. After lunch, they're allowed to walk in pairs round the farm. A couple of adult volunteers are mucking out an enclosure. The smell is bowfing. He sees more chickens. Rabbits. Some wee fat sheep. Two black and pink pigs, playing in mud like puppies. A nanny goat and her kid, suckling, which is gross and also gives him a tightness in his throat. Him and Ali walk together. He's not sussed out yet if all the guerrillas are no-hopes and bad yins like Gerard, or if some of them are just normal weirdos who want to spend their summer gardening.

There's a giant wooden carrot at the entrance to the farm. Ali insists they take a selfie, with the carrot in the middle, then he sends the photo to Gerard on his phone. They pass trees trained to spread against the high walls of the garden and long rows of soft fruit growing under nets.

'What school d'you go to?' says Ali, nudging aside the cobwebby net and helping himself to some raspberries.

Gerard stops walking. 'Em, I dunno. After summer I mean. I don't know where I'll be.' He doesn't want to talk about this.

Ali nods. Asks nothing more about school, or where he's from. 'What games d'you play?'

'You mean, like Xbox?'

'Aye.'

Gerard shrugs. 'Usual. FIFA. Call of Duty. GTA.' He's never had an Xbox, but Craig's boy Xander does.

'Fitba?'

'Aye.'

'Team? Hoops, is it?'

Dangerous territory, but he's admitted to it already. 'Aye. You?'

Ali pulls another raspberry off the cane. 'Partick Thistle.'

'Aye?' Gerard's never met one of those.

'Aye. Want one?' He offers Gerard a fat raspberry that oozes juice. Gerard doesny like fruit, but he takes it. Eats it. The berry explodes in his mouth: the seeds and the juice, each tiny, hairy segment singing. He takes another, then another. Oh, man. It's like a food and a drink. He imagines Miranda getting to eat a bowl of these instead of mashed-up gloop out a jar. He wants to fill his pockets with all these raspberries, and those wee blackcurrants, and white ones that look see-through pearly, just take hunners and hunners of berries, and feed them to his brother and sister. Think how strong and clever they'd grow if they got to eat berries like these.

In the middle of the afternoon, Tracey marches them all back onto the minibus. 'Great work, team. I hope you enjoyed your visit. A wee change of scene, eh? A lot of the food produced here goes to Food Share and the food bank. So you'll maybe never see it, but all the stuff you planted, all the stuff you harvested – everything you did, basically, will end up on someone's plate. So gie yourselves a big round of applause. Well done, guerrillas!'

'Even the donkey?' says Gerard.

'What?' says Tracey.

'Will the donkey end up on someone's plate?'

'Funny boy. OK, troops, home time.' She makes her way to the front of the bus, counting heads as she goes. 'We'll head back to the pick-up point now.'

There is a space beside the girl who got mud in her hair. She smiles up at Gerard. He waits a moment too long, and the seat is taken by another girl. He sits next to Ali, who is on his phone. He doesn't look up.

'It's alright that place, eh?'

'Aye. Wish we went there every week.'

'Do we not?' says Gerard. The girl is on the other side of the aisle from them. He hears her pal call her Jo.

'Naw, usually we're tidying up some clatty back garden or jumping out at the lights to plant leeks on roundabouts and that. Tracey loves her urban warrior stuff.'

Gerard's not sure what that means. The girl – Jo – is laughing. Twirling her long hair with her finger. The sunlight catches the top of her head and paints it pink. She is like one of Craig's paintings.

'Aye. Think they were short of volunteers this week,' Ali continues. 'You know, I wouldny mind working on a farm. When I leave school, like.'

'Can you do that?'

'Well, someone's got to, haven't they?'

'I suppose.' Gerard's never thought about that before. That you could be an artist and paint pictures or be a farmer and grow food.

That you could be anything.

'Ach, fuck.' Ali is typing away.

'What's up?'

'Ho, Tracey,' shouts Ali. 'My foster canny get over to pick me up. Her wee grandson's sick. Any chance you could drop me off near the house?'

'We're no really meant to, pal.' Tracey swivels round in her seat. 'You know that. We're no a taxi service. If I do it for you–'

'Aye, I know. But she's asked me to get the wean some Calpol. Quicker I get there, quicker the wee soul will stop puking his load.' Ali bats his eyelashes. 'Pleeease?'

'Och, fine. Seen as you're not everyone.'

'Love you, Trace,' says Ali.

'Love you, Trace,' shouts the rest of the bus.

Tracey blows them a kiss, then turns back round.

Gerard is fascinated by this exchange. What a simple, easy thing. No shouting. No threats. He stretches his feet under the seat in front. Lets his eyelids droop. The muscles in his legs are tight. Neck too. He feels that stiff-sore way, as if he's been playing football. His head bumps a little as the minibus rocks them onwards. Not dozing but not paying attention either. It is a good, tired feeling he's got, with the warm seat joogling and Jo and her mate chattering in the background.

'Alright, Your Majesty,' shouts Tracey. 'Duke Street do for you?'

'Aye, that's grand, Tracey, thanks. There's a Boots right there.' Ali pats Gerard on the shoulder. 'Alright, pal? See you next time?'

All Gerard can hear is *Duke Street*. He sits up, takes in his surroundings. Recognises the flower shop and the café. The fruit and veg shop where the boxes face onto the street. Sees people walking. He feels cold. Tries to breathe through his teeth and look straight down the bus. Sees Ali, head close to Tracey, then Ali is off the minibus and they start to shunt forward again, out into the traffic and along past the Rangers pub with all the Union Jacks outside, and then they turn right towards the river. He lets himself breathe out. He knows that this road will take you to the Calton, then Glasgow Green, then the Southside, and, eventually, he supposes, home.

Not home. To Kris and Craig's.

He shuts his eyes. Listens to his heartbeat until it slows. He is stupid. Stupid, stupid. His fingernails, pressing into his palms, tell him he's stupid. There is no such thing as ghosts. So how come he saw a yellow cardigan on the ground?

He didn't. He didn't.

A hand nudges him. It's the lassie, Jo. 'Wake up, you!'

He sits up. Can smell fresh air, coming from her hair. 'I'm no asleep.'

'Just as well. Jiggy was hovering. Aye, you,' she calls to Jiggy, who is sitting with a face of innocence.

She leans in close, to whisper. 'Guy's a prick, so he is.'

'How? What was he gonny do?'

'Fuck knows? Put a bogey in your mouth? His dick, maybe?'

'Nice.'

She nods. 'Aye.'

Gerard doesn't say anything else. His mind careers. Idiot. *Idiot.* Why did he say that? What if Jo thinks he meant that: that having a guy's dick in his mouth would be nice – and maybe it would, he's never really thought about it, though when he does, he thinks he probably wouldny like it, but that's not what he wants her to think. Shite, he was just being cool and sarcastic, and now he can feel his face going red, he's taking a riddy, and he stinks of sweat, and she's just sitting there, while all this is going on, like she's waiting.

His eyes have gone fuzzy. Ride it out, Gerard. Stare. It. Down. Inside his head, he counts to five. Breathes low. Speaks on the outbreath. 'Well, cheers for saving my life.' It works. His voice comes out steady.

'Any time. I'm Jo, by the way.'

'Gerard.'

'Oh, Ger-ahrd. Very posh.'

He laughs. 'No really.'

'Can I call you Jez?'

'Aye. If you want.' *Jez.* He quite likes that. It's jaggy like a knife.

'Alright, then, Jez,' she says. His new name zips through air to quiver at him. Yup, he could live with being a Jez.

'So. You coming back on Monday?'

'Nah . . . don't think so.' Ali lives in Dennistoun. Maybe he knows all about Gerard and his mum. About the weans being taken away. About him beating up an old lady. Or if he doesn't, he'll know someone who does. Oh fluck, fluck, fuck man. He canny take this. His tummy keeps flipping so he doesn't know what he feels any more. Part of him got excited when he recognised it was the East End. Relaxed, almost, which is mental, because Duke Street is not a relaxing place. But it was like putting on your comfy hoodie after a shower. Like a cuddle. And the other bit of him felt sick and scared.

'That's a shame,' Jo's saying.

'I might try something else,' he says airily, as if all the world is an option.

'You get made to do this, aye?'

'What? Naw.'

'So you just woke up one day and thought, *I know. I wanny be a gardening gorilla?*'

'Aye. Something like that.'

'Bullshit. Nobody wants to be a gardening gorilla.' Jo points at Jiggy. 'Diversion from . . . being a dick, probably.' Then she points at another two of the older boys. 'Him: anger issues, plus serial-absconding. Him: anger issues *and* self-harm.' Points to her pal across the aisle. 'Social Work-mandated "personal growth".' She points to a boy with thick glasses and a shaved head, who has spent most of the journey stroking the headrest of the seat in front of him. 'Zoomer, doesny speak, but possibly therapy? Me, social prescribing for mental health – oh, and Beth,' she says, indicating a girl with a long black ponytail sticking through her Nike cap, 'she's got a tag.'

'Right.'

'You?'

He stares beyond her, beyond her eyes which are brown with a wee fleck of green, beyond her friend across the aisle, through the window on the other side. Recognises the start of Queen's Park, with the boating pond. They are nearly there.

'Foster care,' he says.

'So they want you out the house as much as they can?'

'I guess.'

'Right, troops,' calls Tracey. 'That's us back at the ranch. Chop-chop. Gather your stuff. I've got a hot date tonight.'

'Aye. With the donkey off the farm,' Jiggy shouts. 'Donkey Kong, here we come!'

'Cheerio then.' Jo leans on Gerard's thigh as she stands. A bolt of pure sunlight shoots through him.

'I might,' he says, biting on his lip.

'Might what?'

'Gie it another try. This.'

'Cool.' She gives him a wee wave. 'See you, Jez.'

'See you.' He watches her sway towards the door. Waits a while, until everyone else gets off. As Jo is gesturing to someone he can't see, Gerard's phone beeps. Bloody fosters – fosterers? He canny mind how Ali said it, but it sounded cool. The bus is only a wee bit late. He can't see Craig's car, but. Man, he doesn't need all this babysitting. Kris and Craig get really narky if he ignores them. Kris has helped him sort his new phone, with symbols as well as names. Craig's number has a car beside it, while Kris has a frying pan. He takes the phone from his pocket and stares and stares. A heart shape. The sender is a heart shape.

It is a message from his mum.

Chapter Twelve

They are on their second outing. Claire and Margaret. Margaret and Claire. Without meaning to, Saturday afternoons have become a date. Claire will need to break the pattern before next week, but, ach, what was she doing with her time anyway? Most of her friends are coupled-up. Most of the world is coupled-up. She cannot face another awkward dinner party where some plus-one guy from someone's work is parachuted in to sit next to her. Nor does she want another dinner *à trois*, where, once the kids are in bed, they will sit and drink wine, and whatever pal and whatever pal's husband/boyfriend will toy with pasta and earnestly try to 'sort her life out'. With each glass of wine, whichever couple she's with will get more cuddlesome and reminiscey about their own relationship, and Claire will grow muted in her role as both mirror and salutary warning.

Margaret wants nothing more from her than a shoulder to lean on. Last weekend they simply walked down Duke Street. That was all Margaret wanted to do. She'd tried to tempt her into Coia's for a coffee, but Margaret was resolute. *Just a walk.* But it wasn't just a walk, of course not. They'd chatted a little, about nothing consequential, then grown silent as they neared the fruit and veg shop. Claire sensed the effort it was taking for Margaret to do this. Already arm in arm, she'd simply laid her other hand on top of Margaret's and helped her walk past the shop. They carried on to the next street, crossed over the road and stood for a while in front of a burger restaurant. 'That looks interesting,' Margaret had said. 'Pulled pork. What's that?'

'Wee strands of meat. A bit like hash?'

'Och! Corned beef hash. Ages since I had that. Used to eat it all the time. Quite a favourite in our house.' Then she'd grown quiet again and said that she'd like to go home. Claire felt the old soul shiver beneath her coat, although it was pretty warm outside. It made her uncomfortable, leaving her alone in her flat. She'd put a fresh cup of tea beside her, plus a slice of something wholemeal and earnest that Zara must have made.

'Can I get you anything else?'

'No, dear. I'm fine.' Eyes resolutely on the window. Her fingers, twisted in the blanket. Claire had switched on the lamp and prepared to leave.

But then Margaret asked if she'd come again next week, and how could Claire say no?

Next week is now this week. Claire doesn't mind, but she does need to get to Morrisons. 'So. What d'you fancy today?' She dangles her keys. Claire has already given this some thought. 'I've got the car – how about we drive over to the Women's Library. You like books. It's an old Carnegie library, but they–'

'Could I choose?'

'Yeah.' She stops swinging her keys. 'Of course. Sorry.' She notices Margaret is already wearing her coat, has her handbag clasped on her lap.

'Could we go to the West End? Is that too far?'

'No. No, that's fine.' Claire recalibrates. There's a Waitrose in Byres Road.

'It's just . . . I've been thinking. Quite a bit. And I've been . . . I've been having some funny dreams.'

'Did you contact Victim Support like we said? Or what about your doctor?' Claire is ill-equipped for this; this is why the whole arrangement is not a good idea. She never takes any of her own advice, so why should anyone else? Christ, Claire can't be trusted with a houseplant.

Probably just as well they never had kids.

Nico and Carole are delighted to welcome bouncing baby Catherine Maria to the world!

Maria was his nonna's name. Claire had forgotten to unfriend Nico's cousin on Facebook.

'Do you think we could?'

'Sorry?'

Margaret sighs. 'I want to see my old school. That's . . . I dream sometimes. I would just like to . . .' She shrugs. 'I don't know. I find it hard to remember, that's all.'

'Sure. Whereabouts in the West End?'

'I went to Laurel Bank.'

'Ooh, fancy! Up near the university?'

'That's right.'

'OK, then. Let's go be West End trendies.'

Claire drives cautiously along the narrow side street, negotiating tightly parked vehicles on either side. These tenements weren't built for two-car families. It's an awkward one-way system around the Drives; she's concentrating on squeezing round a blind corner when Margaret calls out, 'Wait! Stop!'

'Christ!' Claire slams on the brakes, terrified she's run over an unseen child. 'What?'

'Look! Look what they've done.'

Claire's struggling to follow her gaze; all she can see is a few shops below some flats.

'They've changed the name.' Margaret gazes, palms splayed on the passenger window like a crestfallen child. She's staring at the façade of a rather smart shop called Denholm & Serge. *Tailors of Repute.* Claire looks closer. The window is draped in swathes of lime brocade and turquoise satin. An old-fashioned Singer sewing machine sits alongside two headless mannequin busts, one sporting a tweed jacket, the other a Chanel-style bouclé blazer in heathery tones. It's stunning. Claire reads the copperplate gold writing on the window. *Specialists in Vintage Fabrics and Repurposed Denim.*

'That was Albert's shop,' says Margaret.

'Your husband? I didn't know he was a tailor.'

'He was. Made the best suits for miles around. Everyone came to Camberg's.'

'It looks amazing.'

'But they've changed it,' Margaret says wistfully. 'They never said.'

'Who's they?'

'Donald. Our friend. Him and his grandson run it now.'

'Is it still your business, though? If it is, they can't just arbitrarily change the name. I can–'

'No, dear. No, it's fine. They took it over completely. I suppose I knew it might . . . Ach. Never mind. It does look very nice, doesn't it?'

'It does. Might even have a wee nosey in it myself later on.' Claire moves the car off again. 'Do you fancy a rummage? Get a wee vintage denim jacket maybe?'

'No. Not really.'

'Fair enough.'

They carry on, up past the Royal Infirmary and onto the motorway, its concrete bulk ramming past Provand's Lordship and the Martyr's School. Two beautiful old buildings that don't deserve their daily battering of traffic. The car bumps over a rough patch on the surface of the road.

Margaret sits in silence, watching the city pass. 'Who's Mrs Pelosi?' she says suddenly.

'What?' Claire glances over. Margaret is flicking through some letters. Claire's positive she'd stuffed them in the glovebox.

'It just fell open. I was trying to put them back in.'

Pelosi. The name hangs there, being all exotic. Who wouldn't want to reinvent themselves as someone glamorous, begleamed with dolce vita? Claire concentrates on the grey concrete snakes of motorway.

'That's me. Pelosi.' She shrugs. 'My married name.'

'Ah. So you're one of those career girls – one name for work, one name for home.'

'No, not really.' She sooks her lip. 'We're getting a divorce. Well. Got it.'

'Oh. Oh dear. I'm sorry to hear that.'

'Ach, it's fine. He's moved on . . . I've moved on . . .'

She is in Tuscany. Breathing the faint, spiced scent of his neck. Vibrant with the pulse of electricity that used to spark between them.

'*Pe-low-si*,' Margaret says under her breath. 'Italian?'

'Yup.' Claire thinks of Nonna Maria, presiding over the kitchen table. All that beautiful outside, yet they were aye in the kitchen when they visited. Nonna, a couple of uncles, their kids, the cats. Baccio, the truffle dog. And Claire, not understanding much of the cut and thrust but feeling enfolded all the same. 'Mrs Pelosi, as was. Now I'm back to plain old Urquhart.' She can sense Margaret's eyes on her.

'Och, I don't know. Urquhart is a lovely name. A good, solid Scots name.'

'Aye – that nobody can spell!'

'True.' There is a heartbeat pause, then: 'Children?'

'Sorry?'

'Do you have any little ones?'

'Um . . . no.' Claire focuses on her driving. Senses their delicate equilibrium shift. This old biddy is trying to prise her open, like a tin can, and she's not having it. She checks her rear-view mirror. Takes the exit for Great Western Road. Margaret is silent, all the way to Kelvinbridge, and Claire knows she's waiting for her to say something, and she doesn't want to, cannot prolong this conversation or play confessional ping-pong.

Margaret remains quiet, so wee and patient in her seat, with the seatbelt near cutting her in two. Then, just as they're nearing their destination, she says, 'Did you want them?'

Claire feigns a casual air. 'Yes and no.' She imagines if Carole had never been, and it was her with Nico, babe in arms, receiving congratulations. Staring into a face which they had both made. She tries to relax her jaw. She's not even sure what she does feel. Cheated? Bereft? Best not to poke that particular bruise.

'Here we are.'

They turn into a car park. Lilybank Terrace sits a few streets above. Margaret's breath quickens.

'You OK?'

'Oh yes. Fine.'

The West End is sunny and vibrant. Pubs spill gloriously with bright-planted window boxes, and punters sup pints at pavement tables. Delis and bookshops abound, trendy home shops and ice cream parlours pout their pastel wares. Claire's heart plummets at the easy joy of it all. This should be the life she's living. They come face to face with a teenage boy in green tights, clad in a massive cardboard box. His face protrudes from the centre of a painted clock.

'Leaflet?' He thrusts one at them, toddles off.

'Have they changed when Freshers' Week is?' Claire watches the boy accost some tourists further down the street.

'*Time Flies When . . . ?*' reads Margaret. 'Oh, it's a retrospective.'

'Of what?'

'George Wyllie – the sculptor. I think the lad was meant to be thon clock on legs. You know the one outside the bus station?'

'Oh yeah. I've always liked that,' Claire laughs. '*Memento mori.* That's what it makes me think of. You know, how we're always chasing time, then suddenly it's chasing you?'

Margaret has stopped walking. She frowns. Holds onto a pedestrian railing outside the subway. 'I really do think someone should have said. About the shopfront. I mean, it's not right, is it?'

'Well, I–'

'We weren't rich, you know.' Margaret runs her hand along the railings. 'Me and Albert. I've never been rich. I don't want you to think that. My father . . . well, both of them. They saved really hard to send me to Laurel Bank. For my own good.' She glances down.

'Did you like it?'

'Och, maybe. For a while. But . . .' She begins to wobble

slightly. 'Oh, I wish I'd never thought of this. Can we just go home, please?' Margaret's face collapses. 'I just want to be young again. Just to be young and happy with my friends. Being old is so lonely.' She is crying a little, Claire holding her by the elbows. They end up in an awkward cuddle.

Margaret's hair is dry and scratchy. She smells of hair lacquer, and that makes Claire's heart fold. That Margaret stood there this morning, doing her hair and putting on her best dress, just to stand outside her old school, remembering girl-ghosts from long ago. A tiny breeze picks up, and it feels like desolation. One day Claire will be old and aching. There's a knot inside her. Any pity she felt for the boy who hurt Margaret burns clean away. He is a wee fucker, who deserves every shit thing he gets.

'Come on, Margaret. There's a lovely coffee shop in Byres Road. They do a cracking polenta cake.'

Margaret sniffs. 'What's polenta?'

'Cornmeal. But they zhoosh it up with lemon and pistachio. It's really good.'

'I can't eat nuts. They get stuck in my teeth.'

She resists the urge to kiss the top of Margaret's head. 'A scone, then? Let's go get a scone and a nice cup of tea.'

They spend an hour in Kember and Jones, a café filled with students and steam and ladies who lunch and glass cake stands full of meringues and giant cupcakes.

'I'm not sure I can afford this,' says Margaret the second they walk in, but Claire insists it's her treat. They talk about nothing much. Claire learns a little about lacrosse and how Albert would always hand-stitch his buttonholes, while Margaret is brought up to date on the housing market in Dennistoun and why it's worth getting Netflix. Turns out Margaret only watches terrestrial telly.

'I mean decent films, documentaries and that. I *hate* all that reality nonsense. Daft lassies in swimsuits dating random men. Surely love's . . . ach, I don't know. A private thing?'

'I know what you mean. It's like . . .' Claire hesitates. There's a lovely hum to the café, and this is not like a conversation with a friend, where your words will come back to haunt you, or be analysed with kind persistence. 'It's hard, you know? After me and Nico split, everyone kept saying, you need to get back out there. But then it was the pandemic, and we all just hunkered down – and now? I'm in a wee cocoon. It feels safer just to stay inside it.'

'Don't you want to meet someone else?'

'I don't know. I feel a bit bruised. We were together right through uni. Grew up together, almost. Like our roots and branches were woven.'

'Oh, that's a lovely image.'

'Aye, well, the roots got mildew. Plus someone else got their twiggy sticks into him. Then . . . well, I've kind of got stuck, I guess. It feels like the moment's gone.'

'Och, the moment's never gone. I grew up after the war, remember. I'll tell you – it was wild!' Margaret beams. 'As if we'd had new life breathed into us. We'd touched the void and come up laughing. Life is precious, you know.' There is a catch in her voice. A sudden shift in mood. 'Ach, don't listen to me. I'm just a daft old woman who doesn't know what she's talking about.'

'Rubbish. You make a lot of sense. You're a very good advice-giver, Margaret Camberg. I'm just not sure I'm ready.'

'You've got to grab life when you can – I'm sure your mother told you that.'

Claire changes the subject. 'So what did you do before?'

'Before what?' says Margaret, pouring more tea.

'The . . . your accident. Did you go out much? To, I dunno, to social clubs or groups or . . . classes?'

'Do you?'

'Um, no.'

'Well, why should you think I would? It's rather desperate, isn't it?'

Oh, she's sharp, that Margaret. Should Claire not have called it an accident? What, then? Attack? Mugging? Not mention it at all?

Margaret pats her mouth with a napkin. 'I read, mostly. I love to read and go to the library. I used to like crafts, but it's all a bit fumbly now. Used to garden too.'

'Really? Sorry – it's just, it's a bit . . . untidy, isn't it?'

Margaret snorts her tea. 'Untidy? It's a bloody pigsty!'

'Margaret!'

'Well, it is. It's a total cowp. Makes me grue to look at it. But I can't . . .' She pushes her plate away. 'I get dizzy now, if I bend.'

Margaret's hand strays to her collarbone. Her walking cane rests on the table-edge. If that wee shit were here right now, Claire would punch him. She cannot believe she felt bad about calling the police. She doubts the thought of what he did even crosses his mind. Why would it, if you'd no thought in your mind before you lashed out? She fork-stabs a final bit of cake. 'Does the garden not belong to the whole close?'

'No. It's mine. My responsibility. It was Bert's pride and joy. I've let it go, since he died. I can't bear to look at it.'

'I'm sorry. When was it he died?'

'Eleven months ago. He had a stroke. Well, a series of strokes.'

'I'm sorry,' Claire repeats. 'How long were you together?'

'Sixty-four years.'

'Jeezo!'

Margaret accepts this expletive with a quiet grace. They both concentrate on their teacups, Margaret stirring, Claire sipping. Struggling to comprehend a marriage that is almost twice as old as her. A delicate stillness settles. She should give Margaret another piece of her life story in return. But she reverts to the garden.

'I'm sure everyone would chip in, if you asked. The neighbours, I mean. In fact, I'm surprised Zara hasn't jumped in already.'

'Oh, but she has! She wants to make a whole bunch of horrid raised beds and grow her ugly vegetables! I'm not having that.'

'Ooh, get you, Mrs Camberg. Very feisty!'

'Well, it's true. Zara . . . she's very nice. So kind too – I know I couldn't have managed this last while without her. But she doesn't listen, just breenges in and does what she thinks everyone needs. But I want the garden full of roses again. Roses and dahlias and those wee rambling violets that go everywhere.'

'That sounds nice.' Claire signals for the bill.

'It does.' There is a wee pause. The wee pause becomes a bigger pause, which Claire fills with fiddling for her bank card and sorting out coins for a tip.

'But there's no real garden centres nearby, is there?' Margaret persists.

'I wouldn't know.' Claire leaves two pound coins beside her plate. 'Shall we, then?'

Margaret sits tight. 'There's the B&Q, of course, but it's all hybrids. You don't get the old-fashioned roses there.'

'Don't you?'

'No. All the best ones are out of town.'

Claire crosses her arms. Leans back. 'Would you like me to take you to a garden centre, Margaret?'

'Oh, that would be very nice, Claire, thank you.'

'Next Saturday suit you for a recce then?'

'Next Saturday would be lovely. Oh, and we'd better get a spade while we're there too.'

'A spade?'

'Well, that ground's not going to dig itself, is it, dear?'

Chapter Thirteen

Gerard stands outside the high flats. He puts his phone to his ear, listens once again. If you could wear away sound, he'd have done it. He doesn't know how many times he's listened to his mum's message.

Her voice is quiet. Not slurred. *Alright, son? It's me. Sorry I havny been in touch, but things are tough, know? I'm glad you're doing OK. Give the weans a kiss fae me when you see them, eh?* There is a gap when he thinks his mum is going to cough or choke or that, then more words come in a rush. *Look, I canny say too much but I need you to do something, right? Mind your Granny Lou? I want you to go to her house and get something for me, yeah? I canny . . . I think they're watching me. Just go into the back bedroom. My old room. There's a shoogly floorboard inside the press. The built-in cupboard, mind?*

Mind? How can he mind? He canny mind his granny, let alone the cupboard in his mum's old room. He's never even been inside the house. He thought for years his gran was dead, then, one day last year, his mum took the three of them on the bus to see her, all the way across town. 'You said she was dead,' he'd insisted. Furious. If he had a granny then why did him and Anthony end up in care? Why didn't his gran come and bring them sweeties and help look after Miranda?

'Aye. Good as,' she'd replied, ushering them into the lift. It had been a horrible visit. A horrible, smelly lift. A horrible, clatty man at the front door of the flat, screaming at his mum. He wouldn't let them in. How does his mum not remember that?

He listens to the rest of the message, although he knows it off by heart.

I used to hide things from her there. Anyroad, there's a packet, a brown envelope. I need you to take that. Dinny open it, mind. And do not *take anything else. Just the packet. But do it soon, right? Do not phone me before then, Gerard, you hear? Don't tell anyone what you're doing.*

Her voice gets a bit angry here, like Gerard has done something bad. Then she calms down.

OK, son? Just do that for your mammy and I'll speak to you soon. Just you go right on in, OK? She never fucking locks it, and it's your granny, so it's fine. Fucking free for all, that house.

She is getting in a bad mood again.

But don't you phone me, right? I'll phone you. In four days, I'll phone you, OK? Cheerio now.

He pretends she got cut off. That she meant to say *Love you* at the end. He thinks she was only pretending to be calm. He thinks she sounded scared. He wants, so badly, to phone her back, but she's told him that he can't.

How is that fair? For your mum to phone you and not want to talk and not want you to speak to her? When he saw the message was from her, his tummy flipped. Now he feels worse than ever. He was just getting used to . . . ach, he was just getting used to Kris and Craig and the big tall house and seeing the weans at the park and maybe seeing Jo. And now? Now he wishes she'd never bothered.

But she needs him. She must trust him a lot to do this. His mum knows how smart Gerard is, even if he canny read. What other mum wouldny even bother to say where his gran lived? Cause she knows that he'd remember it.

She knows his tricks. When Gerard has to go anywhere, he always works out the way back. (Just in case. Sometimes his mum would go off, and he'd be left with the weans some place strange). So he makes wee trails in his head. Bus stop over the road. Get her to tell you the number of the bus. Listen to where she says to the driver. Always listen. Always look.

One and two halves to Cardonald.

See what stop you get off at. Bus shelter beside a post box and a pub with a red sign outside.

Cross at the lights beside the scabby park.

He's standing at those lights right now. Watching the flats from across the road. He's waited until the Monday, cause he thought it might be quieter than the weekend. But this is where he gets stuck. There are three high flats, and he remembers it's the one in the middle. But he canny mind what floor. In his head, he can see his mum pressing a button, but, no matter how hard he screws up his eyes, he can't see what one. He's hoping when he's in the lift he'll recognise it. He remembers standing in the landing when the man was shouting at his mum, Gerard trying to distract the weans. There was a purple door opposite, and a wee side window, and he could see the tops of trees. So it canny be too high up then. He looks at the trees in the park, then looks again at the high flats. Halfway up, he reckons. Middle flat, halfway up. Purple door across the landing. Gerard pumps his hands into tight, tight fists. His skin is fizzing. His stomach is sick. He'll worry about what he'll say or how he gets into the flat when he gets there.

His mum is in trouble, and she needs him.

He waits for a break in the traffic, then runs across the road. He's told Kris he's with the Guerrillas. Hopefully she'll not check. Craig's away at some conference, and Kris is really busy on her computer, so he's not sure she even heard him right. It's best if you shout just when you're running out the door. Then go, *Home by six,* so it all sounds kosher. The numbers on his phone are 3, 3 and 2. Numbers are never as bad as words. It is half past three and he will be home by six.

Home. Not home. Tomorrow is the day he sees Anthony and Miranda. That is always the best day. He hopes it's dry, then they can stay at the park as long as possible. It's a door buzzer thing at the main door of the flats, but he just bashes loads of the buttons until someone lets him in. It's pretty grim inside – way worse than their old close. It feels like a school that's closed down. Got that sad feeling, because there should be loads of voices and stuff on the noticeboard and that. But there isny. The foyer is fousty, with pukey-yellow tiles on the wall, and a pile of old newspapers on the floor. Someone has drawn a rude picture of boobs and willies beside the empty noticeboard.

Gerard goes into the lift, which smells of pish. There's a long row of lights and numbers. He takes the lift to the number 8. Two round circles. Easy-peasy. It is near the middle of the row. He pushes himself into the far corner in case someone else comes in, but it's just him in the lift all the way up. Good. You never know what to do if someone else gets in a lift. If it's a lady with a pram, they tut if you're in the road. If it's an old lady, they want to talk to you, and he never knows what to say. And if it's a man or a bigger boy, and they're pure swearing or they smell of drink or there's more than one and they're loud and shouting and stoating about, well, that's when Gerard's heart starts to go mental and his throat closes over. Even if you are right tight in the corner, even if you close your eyes (and you never, ever do that, or they'll rip the pish right out of you), but even if you pretend you're on your wee floaty cloud, even though the lift is already stinking – they will smell your fear.

Today must be his lucky day. Eight floors up, and just him. But his heart still beats too fast. The lift pings and opens, and he's on the landing. Gerard looks for a purple door, but there isn't one. Jumps back in the lift before it heads off, goes up to the next floor. Nope. No purple door either. He checks out the window, just in case. He can see the tops of the trees. Tries the next floor. If there's no purple door here, he doesn't know what he'll do. Maybe chap one of the doors and ask for Lou? The thought terrifies him, but letting his mum down frightens him more.

He gets out the lift, and he sees it, he sees it! A door the colour of a new bruise. Facing a door which is meant to be white, and has a window with glass shaped like waves. There is brown sticky tape running from one side of the window to the other, where it's cracked. He thinks he recognises that glass. He remembers staring at wobbly glass when the man started shouting at his mum.

Gerard licks his lips. If this is his gran's house . . . For a wee minute, he just pretends. He pretends that he is knocking the door, and his gran comes and opens it. She is a wee, cuddly lady with white curly hair and she goes, 'Come away in, son. I've just made some pancakes.' And in that flat, he will have his own room – well, it's a room the three of them share, but it's his room really; he gets to decorate it. There are bunk beds for him and Anthony (Gerard is on top, obviously), Miranda has a cot over by the window.. The windows are squeaky-clean, and they have curtains with foxes and badgers on. He knows it's babyish, but the weans like it, and he seen a picture once in a magazine in some waiting room in some office in some social work place, where there was a room with yellow curtains with green trees and foxes and a matching duvet cover. So they'll each have a duvet cover like the curtains, and there's a big furry rug on the floor and tons of toys in a big wooden box, big fluffy rabbits and teddies and that, and maybe a train set for Anthony (though Gerard will have to help him set it up). And there's a big round paper shade on the light that is the colour of rainbows and a wee star nightlight too, to help Miranda sleep. (That makes him think – do Helen and Richard remember about how she needs a light on? They're dead old, so they might have forgot. He'll need to remind them tomorrow, when he sees them.) And maybe there's even some books in this room at his gran's house, maybe Gerard even has some books on a shelf, because, in this room, he reads stories to the weans. Then his granny will come in with toast and jam for them all and they brush their teeth and they go to sleep.

He blinks. Rubs itchy eyes. The dirty-white door looms. There is no bell. Should he chap it? What if that man comes and shouts at him? What is he going to say what is he going to say? He's worked so hard to get here, just to find, to find the stupid flat.

But he's not thought about this. Will his gran recognise him? Maybe she'll just know it's him. Would you just know? If you looked at someone who was made of you? Does his mum send photos of them to his gran? Maybe there'll be a photo of them on the wall.

There's a nasty taste in his mouth. He's chewing too hard on his lip. He doesn't think he can speak. He'll not chap the door, he'll not . . . he'll not . . . If he's meant to go in, it will happen. Quietly, he turns the handle and the door swings open. He stands on the threshold, listening. Can hear a telly. Smells . . . a toilet smell and . . . onions. There are four doors in the wee lobby. The one where the telly noise is coming from is shut. He can see a slice of shower curtain through another one, so that must be the bathroom. Two more doors, both slightly ajar. One has a red carpet. That one. He bets his mum had a red carpet. She used to wear red lipstick. If this is even his granny's house. Is he a housebreaker? Even if it is her house? Does it count, if it's your gran?

He creeps inside the lobby. Pee is bursting, prickles all over his skin. He wants to be sick, and he's pumping, pumping his fists and counting in his head. One step. Two step. He's nearly at the bedroom door, his foot is nearly on the red carpet when he hears the lift clang and open, onto the landing. He hasny shut the front door right. But it's too late, he's nearly at the bedroom, so he just swallows and closes his eyes and pushes the door and is . . .

In.

It's just a bedroom. And no one comes in the front door. It's just an old, damp-smelling bedroom, with a bed and some boxes and a mirror on the wall. He looks for the cupboard – there's a wooden door in the wall, so he tries that, and yes, it's a cupboard. There are some shoes and clothes hanging up. He moves the shoes, hardly breathing. Stops. Listens.

Get out!

The telly is still chattering – to someone or no one. There's no carpet inside the cupboard, just grey chipboard. He puts the flat of his hand on the floor until he finds a bit that wobbles. There's two squares, near the back, that quiver loosely under his touch. Carefully, Gerard presses the first one down, until the other edge sticks up enough for him to howk it out. The board makes a *flump* as he lays it down. Gerard holds his breath again. All his body is liquid. He is desperate for the toilet. His mouth is watery-dry. Sick is definitely coming up. The low voice of the telly burbles on. No doors open. No creaks. He lifts the other board. Looks inside the square dark hole. It's quite a shallow space. He can see the edge of a box. A shoebox. He moves it over. Sees a brown envelope beneath. He leans in, on his tummy, to sclaff it up towards him. But it's heavier than he realised, and it falls from his grip. There's a definite thud. Gerard freezes.

Get out!

Head half in the hole. *Shit.* Shit, man. What if she calls the polis? They'll lock him away for sure. Fuck, fluck, he'll never get to see the weans, not even if he says it's for his mum; even if he grasses her up, it will be Gerard's fault. Gerard steals from old ladies' houses – as well as beating them up.

He grabs the envelope with two hands this time and pulls it up. It feels hard and square, the thing inside

Get out!

but the envelope is sealed and he better not open it. His mum will know. He puts one piece of chipboard back, quiet as he can, then goes to slide the other one in place. Now he realises that he has to move across that hall again and get past the telly room and get to the door

Get out!

he just wants to stay inside the cupboard. Close the door and be safe and never have to move again.

He thinks that would be really nice actually. The blood is shooting round his veins so fast; lying down like a cat would probably stop the dizziness. When his gran finds him he could pretend he doesn't know how he got there. Doesn't remember a thing. Then she'll feel bad for him, and take him in.

What if she could cuddle him?

Some boys get cuddles off their gran.

He feels a sudden gush of fury. He fucking hates his mum. This is her fault. Everything is her fault. He tries to put the second board over the hole, but it won't go down flat. Fuck it, he'll just leave it and go, but then they'll know, somebody will know. Who is the *they* his mum is scared of? His poor, feart mum – and what if he leaves a clue, then someone will know whatever it is they haven't to know?

No way. Gerard would never hurt his mum. He thinks it is the shoebox sticking up. He slides it along more, so it almost disappears from sight. Notices a photograph stuck to the bottom. It is a teenage boy and teenage girl. They are smiling, the boy touching the girl's curly dark hair, and inside Gerard's body, something breaks. He scoops the picture up before he closes the hole and shuts the shoebox away forever. A shoebox that might be full of treasure. But his mum said not to take anything else. One hundred per cent on no account. This photograph is not an anything, though. He knows that hair. Those faces. It is his.

Silently, he closes the cupboard door. Takes envelope and photo in his arms, and creeps across the threadbare, sticky carpet. Out of the shabby room. Past the bed where his mum once lay, past the ceiling she must have stared at. And he is in the hall. And he is past the room where the tv chatters and he could reach out now and open the front door.

Get out, Gerard!

But he doesn't.

Gerard returns to the door where the telly plays. Pushes it gently. Just to see.

It is no curtains

It is *A Place in the Sun*

Bare floorboards and a gas fire (off)

Crushed cans on the floor

The back of an orange, stained recliner chair (up)

Short grey hair

A sickly smell that will finally make him boak (it doesn't. He holds it down with tears and confusion)

Two feet in pink slippers with toes coming out the front (Mules. The toes are inside tights. One of the big toes is poking through the tights. It is black and blue.)

An overflowing ashtray on a wee table

A bare arm, out to the ashtray

A wee glass phial, on its side

A needle in the crook of the arm.

Gerard stifles a sob. His gran stirs slightly. He doesn't think she can hear him, though, so he closes the door and leaves.

Inside the lift, he scrubs at his eyes. He couldny gie a fuck if ten neds came in right now and laughed their arses off at him.

Could

not

gie a fuck.

All his world is whirling. That was his gran. He sees her spinning past his mum, their arms and legs splayed wide; Gerard and Anthony and Miranda too, bobbing like bubbles in a bath. Gerard clutches the envelope tight, tears going pitter-pat.

They make the exact same sound as blood.

The lift pings. The door opens, and he lands back on the ground. Into the smelly foyer, which looks just the same as when he went up. Gerard leaves the lift, and the foyer and the high flats behind, walks over to the bus stop. There is a wee seat inside the shelter, just a bar to perch on, but it will do. The electronic sign is showing the number 4, so he guesses a bus is due soon. He doesn't really care what bus or where it takes him, just as long as it's away. No, he needs to get the right one. He has to be back in time for pick-up, or Kris will know he missed Guerrillas.

In the bright light of afternoon, Gerard stares closely at the photograph. He wants a nice picture to be in his head. Not the one of his gran's front room. He tries to concentrate. His mum is so pretty. She has big earrings in and is laughing up at the boy. The boy that turned into his daddy. But he's just a boy here, a daft laddie not much older than Gerard. They must have been in love forever. His dad is leaning across to touch his mum's hair, in fact he's holding a strand of it out, across his face. Kidding on it's a moustache. He's got the jet-black hair Gerard remembers, and that makes him so, so happy, because he didny make it up. The photo's too wee to see if there's a scar beside his dad's mouth. He's just wearing a T-shirt, his elbow bent to play with Gerard's mum's hair, and you can see dark squiggles on his forearm. A tattoo. Does Gerard remember a tattoo? There is something about it he remembers, about lines and a circle, but it's getting blurry; he can't see what's in front of him. Only what's in his head.

Her arm.

Grey hair.

Pink slippers.

Her arm.

He tries to stop the spinning in his brain, the what came first and the who is bad? He doesn't understand. Does it mean he'll be a junkie too? Is that what happens when they put that stuff in their blood? Does it just keep bleeding into your babies and their babies and their babies? When he thinks of babies, he sees Miranda, and the fucking fury that smashes up through him makes him want to kick out, keep kicking their fucking stupid bus shelter, trying to break it, but it just keeps bouncing back, twanging against his feet, hurting his knees, until he stops. Panting.

There are some mums in the park, watching. He gives them the Vicky, and then the bus comes.

Chapter Fourteen

Margaret's not been sleeping well. Her head jangles, hands, legs in constant agitation. She can't stop thinking about how they've ripped up Albert's shop. Wants to march in and speak to Donald, but she's afraid it might be Smirky Scott behind the counter. They'll say it's nothing to do with her anyway. And they're right. But surely Donald might have said?

Anyway. She never wants to set foot inside the place again. Bad enough before, when the lack of Albert permeated every surface, but now? Now she won't even find his ghost. Brutally, her headache ignites: a flash of smashed grey sky, Margaret holding the ladder, staring upwards as Bert paints furiously, clumsily over the sign. *Camberg and Son.*

Camberg—'s

She leans her brow on the window. Cool. Then the filthy mess of the garden outside makes her furious again.

Claire has cancelled their Saturday. Some excuse about having to work at the weekend, which is nonsense, of course it is. The woman sells houses. These things are planned, surely? People know when they're moving. Margaret can't imagine an emergency transaction arose. She was so foolish to get excited about plants and garden centres. Foolish to assume. Anyroad. It would've cost too much. Pennies she does not have, for fripperies like roses. Finally, she'd sent a cheque off for the electricity, but she forgot to sign it, so now she's got a red letter from Scottish Power.

Stupid Margaret.

She waits for the kettle to boil, fingers skittering beside her cup. She has never been a debtor. There were times when she and Bert thought they might lose the business, but things always picked up. Bert even got the contract to provide greatcoats for Strathclyde Police once. They went on holiday to Blackpool that year. Margaret always wanted to see the Illuminations, but her mother thought Blackpool was tacky. She wonders whatever would have made her mum smile? Could she have been a different daughter?

Stupid Margaret.

You can't reset the past, no matter how far back you send yourself. Standing there, in your old woman body, thinking about school.

She pours boiling water onto the teabag. Clear turns cloudy. Turns dark.

Faces in the dark. Margaret thinks of Stephen. Her son. He whispers until she plugs her ears. Over the years, Margaret's tamed the pain, packaged it to an ache. But that wee boy has shaken it all up, bashed everything out of her brain when he bashed her to the pavement. A weight settles on her. As if the boy's presence perches on her shoulder. Each day brings clearer, brutal fragments. The self-contained smugness of her wee cardigan. The pleasure of feeling apples in your hand. The rush of air, the confusion of sky, shifting as your head's thrown back and your mouth is jarred wide, eating air. Teeth in your throat. Blackened pain, your skirt, your thighs. Oh God. Her legs. There is something about her legs being open in a public place that has broken her. No matter how much Margaret crosses her ankles and folds her arms and is tight, tight, tight within herself, she cannot remake whatever protected the outside of her. She can't make herself whole.

Margaret takes two bits of shortbread from the tin. Balances them on her saucer. Carefully, she walks into the living room. Places her elevenses on the table, beside the catalogues for *Easy Living* and the local freesheets and the Victim Support leaflets that keep coming.

She hugs her cardigan tighter round her body. Did she offend Claire, asking her about children? The girl is struggling, with who she was and who she must be now. Is a divorcee sadder than a widow? Being the left-behind of a person who didn't want to leave you, as opposed to one who did?

Poor Claire. What would Margaret have said, if Claire returned the question? Would she have told Claire about her son? Paint herself ugly? Ach, how do you become friends with someone if you don't know the rules? Margaret wishes she was the kind of old woman who no longer cares, who wears purple and speaks her mind and does not suffer fools.

Maybe once. Now, she's the kind of old woman who keeps to herself and concentrates hard on being content. Even Zara gets narky if Margaret expresses more of an opinion than *thank you*.

Oh, it's fatiguing, being old. Too quiet, and you are ignored entirely. Too loud and you are an irritant. Too dribbly, slow or unfragrant and you're a harbinger of death.

What can she do, what can she do? Her mind is uneasy. Will not behave. She finds she can no longer concentrate on novels. Her nose tickles. From the sleeve of her cardie, Margaret withdraws a yellowed lace hankie. The one with the embroidered thistles. She's taken to carrying it with her. Feels nice to have it up her sleeve. A gift from Pitlochry. Scout camp, Stephen's first time away from home.

She closes her eyes. A thin veneer: that's all that separates you from the world. There is nobody in this tenement block who knows Margaret had a son.

Has a son.

Perhaps that boy was sent on purpose. Shaking her head to give it a good clear-out. She hears them all, knocking. Come in, come in. Family. Love. The bright hope of it.

Opening the door makes it worse. Recriminations, remorse. The should-haves, would-haves, they're all too late. So it's easier to be furious – or simply forget. Today finds Margaret full of bitterness. Angry, bitter bubbles. They fizz inside. She is all astir in broken pieces. Bitterness bubbles her belly. It scours its way through, up and out, in a visceral groan.

She stuffs a bit of shortbread in her mouth. Jacqueline might hear and come running. Or worse, send that boy she's got staying with her. Margaret's noticed him loitering outside the close. One of Jacqueline's foster waifs. Tall boy. Pudgy. Eyes too close together. Looks a bad lot. And why's he in care anyway? What bad things has that one done? She unclasps her fist. Her shortbread is crumbled to dust. *Love, don't hate, yekirati.* Whenever Albert was having a bad day and she was asking, hopelessly, what could she do? *Just hold me*, he'd say. *I need love, not hate.*

'Well, you're not here now, are you?' Crumbs spray from her mouth. She is shocked at this angry outburst in her front room. Holds the handkerchief to her lips.

The clock in the hall chimes twice, and her cup goes flying. Threat is incipient. It is everywhere, constantly, no matter how well she behaves, how much she minds her own business and has occasional jaunts out and does not take up too much space. A wee boy saw her and thought to hurt her. He looked at the smallness of her shoulders, her neat grey hair, and thought, *she'll do.*

Margaret begins to weep. Her chest gropes for air. How could he? The cramping in her chest expands suddenly, rips outwards, into rage. How dare he?

She rummages through the bumph on the table. The Victim Support cloud flutters. Margaret seizes this latest leaflet they've sent, before it falls to the tea-soaked rug. *Restorative Justice – Driven for you, by you, at a pace that's right for you. We don't manage this service, but can put you in touch with organisations that can help.*

In the hallway, her telephone rings. She's in no state to answer. Let it go to the machine. She doesn't listen, pretends it's Stephen. Pretends she could slip through time itself and talk to him. Just pick it up.

Mum? You there? Mum, please. I'm sorry. Dad, will you pick up? We're just about to– A tannoy interrupts. *Fucksake, will you just pick up the bloody phone? I know you're there.*

Bert's face, stoic and distant. Wet eyes glistening. Margaret's effervescent wrath.

Serious? Is that it? I honestly thought you'd be here. You know? Jesus, Mum, we're getting married in a month. The tannoy again. *Fuck! Seriously, fuck you. You have any idea what you're doing to us? Right, fine. Well, just remember – it was you who did this, not me.* Them, listening to his voice, until it faded, and the beep came. Filling the flat with loss. The snatch of grief. A whole world they could have shared had things been different.

But things are never different.

All those years. There were times when she could sense the air softening, each searching for ways to fill the cracks. Albert and Margaret were so careful how they danced round one another. His pride, his hurt. Her aching, wrenching grief.

No words.

Why don't good things come back to you? Why is it only regrets?

Stiffly, Margaret rises from her chair. It is two o'clock in the afternoon. Sunny outside. 'Ta-dah!' she whispers hoarsely, as she pulls her William Morris curtains shut.

Doof-doof-doof. The noise of the French girls' stereo begins to pump from upstairs.

Chapter Fifteen

'OK, Gerard.' They are in Kris and Craig's shiny kitchen, in the tall, thin house in the fancy street. Kris is handing him an onion without its skin. All gross and shiny like an alien space egg. 'Now I want you to chop this. Quite finely.' There is a big knife on the counter and a wooden board. Ugly brown trails move across its surface. It is olive wood, Kris told Gerard. The edges of it are like lizard scales. It shimmers and swirls, and he doesn't want to touch it. Upstairs there is an envelope which is hard and humming. He touches it all the time. It is begging to be opened, and he cannot, must not. But it's been one whole week, and his mum's still not phoned. He spoke to her last Friday, and now it's this Friday, and she's still not phoned him back. The onion smell makes his eyes nip.

He's not seen Anthony and Miranda either; they'd to change the day because of dentists or something, but it is today now. He is going to see them right now, soon, just as soon as he's made the stupid lunch. Guerrillas is Mondays and Fridays, which means he's missing that again. Kris says it's not ideal, but if she knew he'd dyked it to go to his gran's flat too, she'd do her nut. He'd a story all ready. But no one's bothered to check up on him. Jo will probably think he's chucked it, but Gerard doesn't care. He is thirsty to see the weans.

'Slice it first, like this. See?'

Who cooks stuff for lunch? Lunch is a sausage roll if you're lucky, or a cold piece and crisps. Or sometimes, nothing at all.

'Now you try.' Kris passes him the knife, goes to stir a pot on the shiny cooker. The gleam of the kitchen is overpowering – there is even a mirror on the wall behind the hob. How can a house be so clean? How come there's no smudges or piles of broken crap or empty loo rolls by the toilet, when folk actually live in here? Like, all the time? It's a wee bit creepy. And it smells. Every room has a jar with wee sticks and they all stink of lemon. Some days he feels he's walking through a telly programme. Gerard picks up the knife. It's really heavy. The blade's so big he can see his face in it.

He makes sure his room is extra messy – just to see what they say. But Kris says nothing at all. Every day, she picks his clothes off the floor, takes his squashed juice cans and plates downstairs. Gerard stabs at the onion, but it slips away. The knife slips too, gliding swift and smooth across his fingertips. He sees a line of blood, then a trickle, then pink goes on the onion. Then it hurts. He's made a mess, he's made a mess of the cooking and the clean kitchen. Why the fluck did she make him do that? Man, it is flucken fucking louping, his finger, as the onion juice gets in. He sees red blood push along the board, feels his heart vibrate. Each beat is a pistol, pumping out this blood. Raging. It's as if a big block of angriness had burst above his head. He is blinking and blinking until his eyes go funny. He holds his breath and focuses on the kitchen cupboards, which start to jiggle and buck the way the words do on the page.

'Now, look at the recipe book,' Kris is saying. 'Can you see how many eggs it says?'

He doesn't answer.

'Hey! What's up?' She comes closer. 'Oh no! You've cut yourself. Here–' She goes to take his hand.

'Don't touch me!'

'Alright!' she says in her curt, clipped accent. Kris steps back. He thinks she goes out the room. Gerard holds his bleeding hand in to himself. Stares at the jaggy cupboards until they're only dancing a wee bit. Finally, they stop moving. He cannot look at the blood.

'Here.' Kris again, sliding a box of plasters under his nose.

He shakes his head. 'I canny . . .'

'Will you let me?'

Gerard nods. She takes his hand, runs it under the tap. It stings a wee bit, but she holds him there until he can't feel it. She dries him with a paper towel, sticks the plaster on. Only then can he look. First at his hand, then her. Kris is scowling, but not in a bad way. She looks worried for him.

'Sorry,' he says. 'I don't like blood.'

She pours him a glass of water. Gets another onion from the wire basket. Starts to chop. 'This thing, with your reading. And the writing. It's hard, I think?'

He's about to put on his *I don't know what you mean* face. A cross between glaikit and rude. But he feels so exhausted, he just shrugs.

'What did they tell you it was? When the words dance?'

Another shrug. What they? he wants to say. There are so many theys.

'Did they say it was dyslexia?'

'Aye. I think.' Gerard unfurls a bit of onion skin.

'But were you actually diagnosed?'

'I don't know.'

Kris makes a clicky sound with her mouth. He must've said the wrong thing. Should he just have said *yes* to keep her happy? 'They got me to use different colours – a plastic thing over the words. It helped a wee bit.'

He remembers feeling like a dick. Him and the support teacher in a wee corner of the classroom. Cheeks on fire, head down as per usual. It would never work in real life. No way was he going to wheech out a big blue 'reading aid' in front of folk. But, for a minute, it did stop them leaping. He felt he was holding the letters down somehow, squashing them under the plastic film. Doing battle with *Bouncing Ben the Bunny*. Flucken take that, Bugs.

'I'm not sure it is dyslexia, though,' Kris is saying. 'Other stuff also moves, yes?'

'How d'you mean?' He's picking at his plaster. Picking and blinking.

'Well. Just now for instance. You were looking at that cupboard for ages. And you seemed really upset.'

'Did I?'

'I thought so. Also, your eyes were moving the way they do when you look at a page. And I thought perhaps you were saying *stop*?'

'Stop what?'

'I don't know. I wondered if the cupboards might be moving also? Like your letters do?'

Gerard can hear the chop-chop-chop of her knife, slicing through the onion. His eyes are stinging. 'I have been wondering that for a while, Gerard. Because it happens other times too, I think? If you feel upset, maybe?'

Why would you pure stare at someone like that? When they wereny even looking anywhere near you? That's just rude. Staring and poking with your big beaky nose until you peck a person's skin off. What's wrong with this lady? She's like a flucken witch.

'Do you think it might be anxiety?'

'Can we just have lunch, please?' he says. 'Please? I really, really want to go and see the weans.'

Kris smiles at him. 'Of course we can, sweetie.'

*

Gerard's tummy is full of bees. Happy, buzzing bees, and he's running and running across the park, Queen's Park, past the boating pond, and there he is! He sees his brother; there is Anthony, over by a bench, and he's waving and running too; they are both running and running until they bump-stop together, head to chest, and he breathes his wee brother's hair which is apple shampoo, is tangle-free and shorter than before, his wee face beaming. 'Oh man,' says Gerard, kissing Anthony's forehead. 'How you doing, wee man? You got a haircut? Let me see.'

But Anthony won't let go. 'Hey.' Gerard can feel him crying.

Feel the trembly heat of his mouth, lost in Gerard's chest. 'Hey, it's OK.' He hugs him tighter.

'I thought you wereny coming.'

'How?'

'It was meant to be before. Mandy showed me. On the stickers.'

'What stickers? Who's Mandy?'

Anthony lifts his head from Gerard's breast. 'My famly lady.'

'Your whit?'

'We made a chart. With stickers to tell me stuff. Your sticker is a bear.'

'A bear?' He laughs. 'How am I a bear?'

'Cause you're cuddly.'

Gerard has to look up at the trees then. A big black bird is watching them. He can hear Kris come up behind. 'I'm just going to talk to Helen,' she says. 'Hello there, Anthony.'

'Is Mandy a social worker?' Gerard takes Anthony's hand. The sky is a bright, happy blue. It is summer. Folk float wee toy yachts on the boating pond and there are dugs and people everywhere. Gerard has a sudden urge to go on the swings. 'M'on. I want to see the wean.'

'I don't know. She comes to famly centre.'

'What d'you do at family centre?'

Anthony sniffs. 'Play.'

'That sounds good. And have yous–'

'Where's my mum?'

Gerard keeps walking. 'She'll come soon.'

'She didn't come to famly centre. Her sticker was a star. But she didn't come any of the star days. And then you didny come too.'

'They telt me you'd the dentist. Were you no at the dentist last week?'

'What's that?'

'Kindy like a doctor? The man who looks at your teeth? They telt me I couldny come cause you were there.'

Anthony stops. Gerard can see his tongue move inside his mouth, poking about, as if that will help him remember. 'Naw,' he says finally.

The black bird caws. Gerard's jaw clenches. Gerard's ears are singing. Gerard is getting close to the bench, to the stupid old fosters that've told lies and taken his family away, and the stupid beaky cow who is keeping him prisoner too, and there's fucking Naggy, his new social worker – *fuck off, the lot of yous, we're not a show, we're not a 'thing' you've got to do* – and they're all blethering and laughing at him; the old woman has Miranda strapped in a stupid pram, when all she wants is to be out on the grass. He can see it, he can fucking see that from here, the way she's straining forward, squeaking and shoogling her chubby wee arms.

And then he realises. She's waving at him. She recognises him!

He quickens his pace, squeezes Anthony's hand. 'Well, they were talking shite. I'm here now, so I am.' He gets to the pushchair, drops to his knees. 'Hey, baby!'

'Geh!' she replies. Her face is like a flower. Her tiny hand reaches up to him. 'Gaar!' It definitely sounds like *Gerard* this time. He kisses her fingers, then begins to unstrap her.

'Ho! Gerard.' Naggy gets in between them. 'Paws off!' She says it like it's a joke, big stupid grin going over his head, to the grown-ups. Does she think he canny see? He's not even sure Naggy is a proper social worker. She was 'shadowing' the other one until she went off sick, and now she just comes on her own.

'Ho, Natalie,' he replies. 'Piss off.' He continues to undo his sister, lifts her out of the pram.

'Wait, Gerard.' Naggy touches his elbow. 'You're not . . . What if you drop her?'

Gerard ignores her. Holds his sister. Miranda is heavy and gorgeous in his arms; she is like holding a massive warm bucket of McNuggets. Her slobbers slick his face and he doesny even mind. He has forgot the smell of her. Every time he sees her, he forgets, and then remembers that she smells like she's just out the washing machine, and he doesn't understand how that talcy sweetness can make him happy and sad all at once. Sweat on his skin. He stares them all down, with the sun at his back and kids playing football over by the trees. Naggy is twittering, the old couple look stern. Kris stands a wee bit apart, with her blank face on. What is it they want him to do?

'Have I ever dropped her in her life?' he says.

'Well . . .' Naggy is so desperate to take her from him. She is quivering almost.

'Anthony, have I ever dropped the wean?'

'Gerard, you don't need to–'

'Naw,' Anthony says. 'Gerard does the baths and everything. He's really gentle.'

Kris comes right up beside them. So close, she's almost pushing Naggy away. 'You just want to hug her, don't you? Gerard?'

'Aye.'

'Because you love her, yes?'

Do they really expect him to answer that?

'I think maybe Natalie is worried because she doesn't know how careful you can be. Why don't you put Miranda on the grass and see what clever thing she can do now?'

Kris is all lilty and sing-song. She is trying to hypnotise him into being good. But Gerard is already being good. He's not grabbing Anthony by the hand and shoving the pushchair forward and running as hard as fuck so all three of them can get away, is he? He's doing what he's told, all these rules, all the time – *here's the box we want you to be in today, Gerard, here's the place we need you to be, Gerard, here's the thing we need you to say, Gerard*. Other kids don't get moved about like bendy fucking toys.

If they don't treat you normal, how're you meant to be 'normal'? Gerard is bad. Watch him be bad. Watch him think about being bad. Watch him being bad even if he doesny think he's being bad.

Watch

Watch

Watch

Why did his mum not just watch *them*?

'How come I couldn't see the weans before?' He asks it loud, to them all. He is still holding Miranda. He sees Naggy pulling out her phone.

'I didny have the dentist,' says Anthony. Hard and steady. Man, Gerard has missed their wee double act. He loves that Anthony's voice sounds the same as his. You don't mess with the Macklins. Not this double act. Miranda is wriggling now. There is three of them. The three of them, holding each other up like one of they toy wigwams you used to get to play in at . . . what was it? Group Action something? Action Man, Family Action. Whatever. They did good pancakes there too.

'No, it was me,' says Richard. 'I had the dentist.' The old boy wrinkles his nose. 'An abscess. It was horrible. Thought my mouth was going to explode.'

'Bit of an emergency,' says Helen. 'But we did say.'

Gerard sees Anthony's face go white. His bottom lip is quivering; he thinks he's going to get into trouble.

'Aye, did yous say to Anthony, but?' Gerard lets Miranda slide from his arms, places her slowly so she's sitting on the grass (he checks for dog shite and glass first, obviously).

There is a pause.

'It was a bit of a rush,' says Helen. 'We had to get there quick, or Richard would have missed his slot.' She glances at Anthony. 'I'm not sure we did explain it, exactly.'

Two other boys are running on the grass behind them, kicking a ball. They dribble it back and forth, the older boy taking his time to pass. The way Gerard would with Anthony. Kicking hard at someone when they're learning is just shite. It's just showing off. Gerard can see a woman – the boys' mum, he guesses, holding a couple of cones. Ninety-nines they are, thick brown flakes he can almost taste. White ice cream dribbling down her wrist. She's shouting after the boys, but it's not an angry shout. They don't look feart or nothing. They all just look happy.

'OK,' says Naggy. 'Well, that's perhaps a lesson for us all. Improve communication between the various parties, yes? Gerard, I apologise that you were given the wrong information. And thank you, for putting Miranda down.'

'She wanted down,' says Gerard. He's watching his wee sister, fascinated, as she begins to roll onto her knees, bum sticking up in the air. Then she pulls herself up to standing.

'Are yous going to say sorry to Anthony, but?' He's not letting this go.

The old boy seems flustered. 'I don't think–'

'Of course,' says his wife. She squats down, so she's face to face with Anthony. Maybe Helen's not that old, even though she does have grey hair. 'Anthony, we're sorry.' She takes his hands in hers. 'We should have said it was our fault you couldn't see Gerard before. Because Richard had a sore tooth, and we needed to make it better, remember? I promise you if we break a date again, we'll make sure you know why right away – and that you'll see Gerard as soon as possible afterwards, OK?'

Anthony nods. Helen pulls him in for a wee hug. Gerard notices how his arms go round her, how his eyes close for a minute. So he doesny mind the woman doing it.

'OK, Gerard . . .'

Here it comes. Another lecture from Naggy McNagnag. Apparently *piss off* is a swear, which is daft, when you're only saying it so you don't say the actual *fuck off* you were wanting to say out loud. He readies himself. And then . . .

And then, his little sister does something miraculous. She puts one wobbly wee leg out, first to the side, then the front. Moves forward. Does the same with the other leg. Gerard holds his breath. It takes a third step before he speaks.

'She's walking,' he whispers. 'Miranda's walking.'

Kris is clapping her hands. 'I know! Isn't it wonderful?'

Gerard can't take his eyes off this wee creature who is no longer a baby. His heart pulses in time to her tiny hands opening and closing. As if she is holding the air for balance. After four steps, she is gurgling with joy, but also swaying dangerously close to falling, so he gets down on his hunkers and wraps his arms around her and tells her what a clever girl she is. 'Geh!' she replies, her sun-sparkled eyes wide and ever-changing in their blue-green-grey. He is so proud of her. He is so scared for her.

'She just started the other day,' Helen's saying.

Holding Miranda's hand, Gerard lets her parade in a circle. She's so funny with her bandy legs. Like a wee gnome. He is listening and not listening to the women blether until it dawns on him Kris is talking about a video.

'You all seen her?'

'Sorry?'

'You seen her walk already? You . . . and him?' He points to Richard.

'Oh, come on,' Kris is saying. 'You can't predict when a baby's gonna walk. We thought it would be a nice surprise.'

'Aye. But you've already seen her?'

Of course they have. Everyone knows the Macklins' business. Nothing is private or special. Or theirs.

For one, daft moment he thought Miranda had saved it up just for him. She wriggles her hand away, totters over to Helen.

There is a low ache in his belly. He is happy for Miranda and sad for himself. Sadder yet for his mum, whose baby is walking into the arms of strangers. Miranda teeters, stumbles to the grass, bum first, then on her back, her yellow cardigan splashed like egg yolk on the green. She giggles, tries to sook her foot.

A bright flare inside him.

He shuts his eyes, but the yellow cardigan is still there, flowing out as she falls.

Gerard has many horrible pictures playing in his head. They are not constant, but they are frequent – and, even though he carries them and was there when they got put inside his napper (obvs), they still have the power to surprise him. Bit like riding on the ghost train – you know, at some point, some horror will come bowfing out – you just don't know what, or when. But the knotted fear in your gut sits with you every day. Waiting. Knowing it's coming.

Honest to God, Gerard would be the shitiest cinema, so he would. *Now showing: blood, guts and tears! See a junkie granny pass out. See a screaming wean with no nappy. See a head crack wide.*

Why did they put Miranda in a yellow cardigan? He sees that

the grown-ups are busy, cooing round the wean. 'Natalie,' he says quietly, pulling on her elbow. 'Did you find out any more about the old lady? Do you know how she's doing?'

Craig said he'd find out, but nobody tells him nothing. Gerard steels himself to be lectured yet again that it's not his business, that there are issues of confidentiality and blah blah blah (but there's never any confidentiality for Gerard, is there?), that it's best to move on and focus on his own actions for the time being. But they *were* his actions: that's the actual, flucken point. Gerard's actions have put an old woman in hospital. Put his brother and sister in care. They made his mum run away and not want to talk to them any more.

He must be so, so bad.

You're as bad as your fucking father.

His mum used to scream that at him, if he'd got caught by the polis, or cheeked a teacher. Even if he noised up a neighbour, sometimes. And his daddy ended up in jail. He thinks his grandpa maybe did too, though nobody talks about him. So, probably that's where Gerard will go. One day.

He shivers in the sunshine.

Sometimes he just thinks, if he could only tell the old lady, how he didny mean it. *But you have to accept responsibility, Gerard, before there can be constructive dialogue.* Aye, well, you can still say sorry and explain, can't you? Explain so she knows he didny mean to hurt her. Because maybe if she knew about the electric, and Miranda's bum being red-raw sore . . . Aye. Maybe.

'Well, actually . . .' Naggy is fishing in her big bag. All social workers must get issued with a Big Bag – they either come in flowery canvas or squashy leather. 'That's one of the things I wanted to talk to you about. Craig mentioned you'd been discussing it.'

His heart quickens. But then she starts talking over his head to Kris. 'She got back via Victim Support.'

'Did she? Wow. And?'

'Gerard . . . Here it is. It literally came in just as I was leaving.'

Natalie pulls out a folder. Plonks her arse down on the bench and pats the seat beside her. 'Come, sit.'

Anthony and Miranda are being taken to the ice cream van. He wants to say to Natalie, *Ho! I only get to see them twice a month. Can we no do this another time?* But part of him is also desperate to know, yet equally desperate to not know, and if he doesn't get to know now, then the waiting to know will be too much and he will bottle it and not want to know at all.

'So the lady has said . . .' Naggy is reading as she's talking. He's pretty sure he's not meant to be able to see the form she's reading from, but, hey ho, it's only thicko Gerard who canny understand what all they squiggles mean anyroad.

'OK, so what she's saying is . . . she doesn't want to meet.' Naggy looks up at him. 'Well, that wasn't going to happen for starters, was it? Honestly!' She starts muttering into herself. 'That wasn't what we were suggesting, dearie.' She clears her throat. 'Right, anonymity, no details . . . except . . . Hmm, OK, well, no, lady. Absolutely not. We don't want your Victim Impact statement, thank you very much. It's a child, for . . .' She's muttering again. Not to him. Gerard could just get up and go over to the ice cream van. He could not hear anything at all about the old lady. Surely the fact she's writing anything is good? She must be alright, eh? If she's written down a whole letter or filled in a form or whatever. So it doesn't really matter what's in it. He just wants to know she's alright.

'Right.' Naggy lifts her head from the sheaf of papers. Kris is hovering too. 'Sorry, Gerard. I should have read this on the way . . . Anyhoo, what it is is, the old lady is doing quite well. She's agreed . . . OK. We can tell you she was in hospital for a while because she hurt her head, her shoulder and her hip when she fell, but she's on the mend now . . . is back home, able to live independently. Two-bedroom flat. Oh.' She stops. 'Not sure if that bit was . . . Well, where else would she be, eh? Point is she's doing fine. She doesn't want to write back or anything but has agreed you can write her a letter if you want, saying what happened. Well,' she glances at him, 'I'm not sure about explaining what happened.'

Kris interrupts. 'Does that mean admitting any kind of liability or guilt?'

'I'm not sure.'

'But could that jeopardise–'

'Well, there was agreement not to report this jointly, remember?'

'Sorry?'

'The Fiscal's not involved? Just the Reporter. But there does need to be an acceptance of responsibility for restorative justice to work.'

'Yes, but what exactly does that involve him doing? Surely apologising would be enough?'

'Um . . . I've not done one of these before. I'll need to check.'

Gerard is watching a swan land on the boating pond. It's incredible. Soaring belly-low to the water, it is a beautiful kite. Then it transforms into a crazy-kicking monster, splaying out stumpy legs as if it were stopping a bike. Splash-splash-splash before it folds up its wings and glides along, transformed once again into long-necked elegance. He wonders who else is listening to these women tell the world that he's in trouble with the law.

Dangerous criminal, park-goers. Do not approach.

'Sure,' says Kris. 'And his . . .' She mouths the word *mum*. Kris thinks Gerard canny see, but he can see everything out the corner of his eye. *Flucken red alert, folks. Do yous people not get it? You think I'm just watching stupid swans?*

Naggy uses the same tactic. *Still AWOL*, she mouths back.

The swan ruffles its wings at a duck.

Thicko Gerard Macklin. Canny read. Canny hear. Canny think. He hugs himself. Aye, well, they two do not have a clue. Him and his mum can get round them all. They have their own secret communication channels. They are super-spies. She'll definitely message him tonight. She's got to, otherwise he'll open the envelope by himself. He will. He canny bear it, knowing it's there, under his bed. A secret from his mum. A secret message, or a sign. Or a precious, precious thing from when she was wee. If he breaks his promise and opens it, it's only because she broke her promise first.

Days can run away with her. He knows that. Days for his mum are not the same length as for other people.

'OK, so, Gerard, what we're thinking is . . .'

Gerard is allowed to join the conversation now. What about Helen and Richard who are returning from the ice cream van with the kids? Can they chuck their oar in too?

Naggy smiles encouragingly at him. 'You can maybe write and tell the old lady that you're sorry? I mean, if you want to. We could try some shuttle mediation?'

'What?'

'Do you want to? Write to her, I mean.'

'I canny write.'

'Ah, good point.' Naggy thinks for a minute. 'Well, you could dictate . . . you could say what you'd like to say, and I'll write it down.'

He doesn't want Naggy listening in.

'Or what about my phone? We could make a wee recording. If you like.' She's not really paying attention to him any more. Head back in her folder, rustle-rustle. 'Ah, hold that thought. In fact, I think there might need to be another meeting.'

'Why?' says Kris.

Anthony is back, shoving a wafer under his nose. 'We got you a nougat.'

'To discuss if . . . well, if this is the sort of approach that will be helpful to you, Gerard.'

'But why? It's up to me, sure?'

'Gerard! Gonny take it?'

He jerks his head away from his brother's dripping hand. 'Can I no just say something to her on your phone the now, and get it over with, and that's it done?'

Suddenly, the urge to say sorry is very strong. They are not letting him say sorry, and he wants to fucking say it.

'Gerard! *Is meltin!*'

'Fucksake!' Gerard shouts, pushing the ice cream out of his

face. He doesny mean to be rough, but the nougat goes flying out of Anthony's hand and straight into Naggy's folder, where it lands with a splat, the two wafers separating. Nobody speaks. They all watch the ice cream pool and spread across Naggy's Very Important Papers, and then Anthony does his wee bull impersonation and headbutts Gerard in the stomach.

'You are a horrible stinky pig!'

'Boys!'

'And you're a wee shite,' Gerard yells back. 'But I love you!'

Anthony stops ramming him and looks up. They both burst out laughing.

The rest of the afternoon is so, so good. Naggy buys Gerard another ice cream and him and Anthony go on the swings together. He begs for a shot on the rowing boats too, but Naggy says there would need to be a risk assessment. So they take them for chips instead, and Gerard gets to push Miranda in her pram, him and Anthony play some football with old Richard, and the sun is blazing up the sky. It is the best day. Even when it's time to go home, he's not sad. Naggy says she's going to see if they can make it weekly meetings from now on. And she promises she'll look into what they need to do next, so he can write to the old lady.

He thinks he'll feel better if he can write to the old lady.

It's getting past teatime, and Miranda is looking zonked, so they kiss their goodbyes (not Naggy obviously. That would be *gross*).

Kris has her hand on Gerard's shoulder as they leave the park. 'You have a good time, Gerard, yes?'

'It was brilliant.' His face is sticky with ice cream. Tight with too much sun. 'Thank you, Kris.'

She squeezes his shoulder. 'Well, no thank yous necessary. But thank you.'

They walk across the main road to where the car is parked. Kris's car is a daft wee purple Citroën. Nothing like Craig's Merc. Gerard would love the Broncos to see him in that motor, swanking about the East End. His tummy lurches, a feeling like he is falling down a drain. They seem so distant now, those boys. Not just far away as in across the river, but far away in time. It's not fair, how pals that've been your pals forever can just be rubbed away. But they have. He doesny know what he'd say to Colm or Drew or any of them if he saw them now. Yet school will start back at the end of August. What if he does go to St Roch's after all? They'll no let him do lessons with Kris forever. Or will they send him to school near Kris and Craig's house? How can they if he doesny know a soul? No one's told him.

Just if his mum's back. Just if she's back and they can all be together, then he doesn't care where he is. He could get a job even, a paper run or something. To help out. Could just quit school altogether. Who would care? Gerard will want to be at home as much as possible anyway, to keep an eye on things.

As him and Kris are getting into the car, Gerard sees a man, standing right by the park gates. They must have walked past him. He is smiling at them. Gerard looks at Kris to see if she knows the guy, but she's busy fiddling with the radio. Must be someone else he's staring at then cause Gerard doesny know him. The man takes off his sunglasses, then raises his hand at Gerard, as if he is saying hello. Kris pulls away from the kerb, does a U-turn. For a second, they are right beside the man, and, as the car passes, Gerard sees his glass-grey eyes, boring in. Sees the tattoo on the man's forearm. A gallows and lines and a circle. Same tattoo he has seen before, in the picture of his dad. On the arm of the man outside their flat in Dennistoun.

The sun goes out.

Chapter Sixteen

Claire parks outside Margaret's close. She went a bit mad in Dobbies. Hard not to when the sun's shining and the garden centre was flaunting a purple haze. Buddleia, lavender and some leggy thing called nepeta (which it turns out is actually catnip). Claire has also bought a spade, a fork and trowel, four bags of compost, violets and two rose bushes, which she hopes will start to smell of something soon. She specifically asked for scented ones.

Unload her extravagant guilt-purchases first or knock the door? The morning sun remains strong, beating on the windows of the surrounding tenements, causing the panes to shimmer. Seagulls stalk the ridgelines like Weegie vultures. Across the road, a woman on the second floor practises yoga. Dogs bark as their owners blether on the bench in the little park where Buffalo Bill is master of all he surveys. The desire to chap Margaret's door fades. Gathers again. Gathers and recedes. Margaret might not even like purple. But she hasn't replied to any of her messages, and Claire's called three times.

Work is definitely manic. Last Saturday was a great opportunity to catch up. Claire had time to go through a big executory file too, which had been glowering at her for months. Satisfying, yes. Essential? No.

It is just a thing she does, does Claire.

She does this dance. For every move forward, she takes two steps back. She does it with her friends. Never visiting spontaneously.

Not returning calls or messages until at least one calendar day has passed. She does it by keeping her door shut at work. She does it by cultivating an aura of insurmountable *busy-ness*, where she simply Does not. Have. Time (for impromptu cinema, chats, drinks, coffee or strange men).

Claire did it with Nico. Maintaining just enough space around herself that she could never be fully lost in intimacy. But he still got in to hurt her. She did it with her mother too. Dad was always a distant enigma, but Mum? Oh, how her mum tried. How earnestly her mother loved her. How panicked it would make wee Claire, unsure of how she should return this intensity. Conscious of the unsteady ground beneath her feet, or the shifting sands, or serpentine water or whatever wobbly metaphor she'd chosen.

Nothing is unconditional. Everything is impermanent. So you should never assume.

Margaret assumed. In the normal, friendly way folk do. Thus, Claire dug a wee, subtle channel, just to mark her boundaries. Which she knew instantly, was wrong. Hence the phone calls and the buddleia.

It's a full-time effort being Claire.

She opens the boot, removes the showiest plants first. Claire aims to dazzle Margaret with her largesse. Smooth over any bumps so quickly they won't even be noticed. At the unkempt hedge, though, she stops. Her day could be her own. She doesn't need an old lady buddy. Or a surrogate gran.

Margaret's been making her think more about her grandparents. Two people of whom Claire has only the vaguest memories. Her mum was older than all the other mums at school, her grandparents ancient. Her grandfather lived with them for a while before he died. A shady, stooped man with liver spots on his head, who spent most of the time in a chair. Claire had been a little embarrassed by her family. Theirs was a quiet house. Bungalow. Neat. Patterned carpets. Not joyless, no. But not the sort of house you'd bring pals home to. Her grandfather had an old family bible, with a family tree inside. Mum showed it to her one day.

Sophia Matheson m Anthony Black. Amanda, Colin branching off below. *Amanda Black m Jonathon Urquhart. Claire (Alison)* underneath.

Why's my name Alison and *Claire?* she'd asked.
Well, that's the name you had when we got you.

Other names. Linked to other names. Claire, obliquely looking on.

She wonders what happened to the bible. If her mum took it with her, to her new life in Devon. If she's scored out Nico's name yet. She's not been to see her in ages. Claire doesn't like surfing and she doesn't like cream teas. Nor does she like her new stepdad much. But good on her mum. Going for it, at her age.

A strange, hollow feeling settles. Might it be best just to leave the plants and go? Or not leave the plants at all? For whom is she doing this? Why does she constantly ask herself questions? Claire, forever prosecuting her own defence.

When she was wee, her mum would attempt to answer all her interrogations, her own anxieties building in relation to Claire's increasing demands. *But what holds the sun up? But why is it round? Will it come back tomorrow? Will it always be there? But how do you know?* Her mum would usually burst at some point and shout: *Just because.*

Despite her industriousness, her mergers and dissolutions Claire is always her first self. That small girl, painfully aware that belonging is not a given. She'd thought she'd found it with Nico, a place where you could let your shoulders drop, and think, *yes, this is home.*

Aye, well. She got careless.

Claire continues up the path. Margaret's garden is packed with its usual clutter, and her arms are too full to see the steps properly. The main door swings as she's climbing up.

'Can you hold that door!' she shouts, through a mouthful of leaves.

'Nae bother.' A tall, chunky kid waits for her at the top of the stairs. 'You flitting or flogging?'

'What?' She's alongside him now. One rose bush is slipping from her hands. She nudges it with her knee.

'They flowers. You selling them?'

'I'm just visiting. You live here?'

'Aye.'

'I'm here for Mrs Camberg?'

He shrugs.

'The lady on the ground floor.'

'Oh, *her*. Aye.' There's a slight hardening in his stance.

'Right, I've got it, cheers.' Claire slides along the door, holding it open with her back.

He lets go the door. 'Nice buddleia by the way.'

'Um, thanks?'

The boy grins. He can't be more than fifteen. The writing on the label's tiny. Is he taking the piss?

'Aye. Is it for here, like?'

'It is.'

'Mind and keep it away fae the hedge then.'

'Sorry?'

'They like full sun.'

He saunters down the path.

'Here! You know about gardening?'

'Wee bit.'

'So how come this one's such a tip?'

'No my garden, missus. Cheerio.'

She watches him close the gate, then disappear behind the high hedge.

Inside, the close smells of bleach. Claire can hear a child wail behind the first front door. Forcefully, she presses Margaret's doorbell. The storm doors are shut. A pair of young women clatter down the stairs and eye her suspiciously. She hears a lilt of French as they close the outside door. Claire rings again. The plants in her arms grow heavy. A third time, she presses. Eventually, she hears a bolt slide, and one half of the green double doors creaks open.

'Hey, Margaret. It's me.' Margaret looks confused. God, she looks *old*.

'I didn't . . . Had we arranged—'

Claire bustles past, kicking the doormat flat with her foot. 'No, but I hadn't heard from you, so . . . Here. Look!' She jiggles a rosebush. 'For your garden.'

Margaret turns away. Her hair is dishevelled. Claire dumps the plants in the hall, follows her into the dimly-lit living room. 'Did I wake you? Are you OK?'

'No. I'm fine.' She lowers herself into her chair. No offer of tea is made.

'Margaret, I'm really sorry I had to cancel last week.'

No response.

'But I thought we could make up for it this week? If you weren't busy?'

Margaret shifts her head slightly, looking from under lowered brows. 'Are you trying to be funny?'

'Please.' Claire drops on her hunkers, takes Margaret's hand. It hangs loosely inside her own, but the old woman doesn't withdraw it. 'I'm sorry it was last minute, but sometimes my work's like that. It's just, there aren't enough days in the week, you know? Some days it feels like I meet myself coming back. Or that I just shouldn't bother going to bed at all. So weekends are . . .'

The curtains are half-drawn. They are both looking at the stained-glass panel rather than each other. Outside, a football beats against the wall, a low, continuous thud.

'You need your weekends to recuperate. I understand.'

The heat in the room is oppressive. Claire would grow crazy if she were sealed up in here all day.

'No, it's not that. I need eight days in the week just to catch up. So I can't commit . . .' She corrects herself. 'Rather than let you down, how would it be if we met up once a fortnight? Just till you're feeling better, eh? Then we could—'

'Revise the offer?' Margaret tilts her chin. 'I'd really rather you didn't, thank you.'

'Oh. Right.'

'There's no need for you to feel obliged to me, dear. I'm the one who should feel obliged. You saved my life, and you got that wee toerag off the streets and hopefully put behind bars.' Margaret smiles, a brave, haggard thing. 'Though they still won't tell me when the trial is. I hope you'll come to that with me at least? Oh no – well, you'll be a witness anyway, won't you?' Her speech is becoming a little frenzied. 'The Victim Support people said they could send someone, and Zara's offered to come, but–'

'Margaret, I don't think there's going to be any trial.'

'What do you mean?'

'Well, I'm not a criminal lawyer, but I'm pretty sure a kid of that age will be dealt with by the Children's Panel.'

Margaret blinks. 'Is that Borstal?'

'It's more . . .' Claire sits on the couch. 'It's a group of people who're trained to make decisions in the best interests of the child. They'll talk to police, social workers, health professionals, check out his family situation and so on.'

Margaret's hands twist in her lap. One thumb rotating round the other, repeating. Reversing. 'What about me?'

'What do you mean?'

'Will they talk to me?'

'No, I don't think so.'

'But I need to know why he did it. And *they* need to know how I feel. I've already–'

'What?'

'Nothing.' She looks directly at Claire. 'Why not? Why wouldn't this Panel talk to me?'

'I don't know.'

Margaret's eyes are liquid with hurt.

'Will we open the curtains in here? Get a wee bit light in. It's a lovely day outside, you know.' Claire goes to sweep the heavy curtains back, but they stutter and sway.

'There's a cord,' says Margaret from her chair. She sounds like a sullen child. 'You need to pull the cord.'

'Ah.' Claire tugs on the cord, and the curtains glide apart. Sunshine spears the room, shafting light onto the velvet chairs, the dusty table.

Margaret screws up her eyes, raises her hand for shade. 'Shut them. It's too bright.'

'Away. It's gorgeous.' Claire is *exuding* jollity. She will make amends whether Margaret likes it or not. Feels a small, sharp twist inside her. She never thought Margaret could slip into despair again so quickly. There's no spark to her. Part of that – perhaps all of it – is on Claire.

'So, let's grab your gardening gloves and get out there, eh? What d'you say, Maggie May?'

'What?'

'Sorry. It was a vain attempt at rhyming.'

'My birthday's in May.'

'Is it? Well, there you go. I'm clearly psychic. Right, up you get.'

A flurry in the hall, the doorbell ringing at the same time as a key scrapes in the lock. Claire sees Margaret stiffen, both hands on the arms of her chair.

'Hello,' calls a deep male voice. The living room door opens. Enter one man, carrying a cling-filmed wooden bowl. 'Hi, Margaret, it's only me. Oh.' The man smiles at Claire. 'Hi there.'

'Hello,' says Claire. Jaw compelled to hing wide. God, but this man is handsome. A walking cliché of handsomeness. He dominates the room. Is well over six feet, with dark hair, obligatory chiselled cheekbones. His shoulders suggest he might play rugby, but artfully and with grace, escaping the blunt nose or cauliflower ears of more cumbersome men. His arms flex with manly, dark hairs, which complement the manly, dark hairs sprouting at his neckline.

'Who's this then, Margaret?' The man's teeth are straight and white – not luminescent white, but the colour of perfect white that is just right for perfect teeth.

'Just a friend,' Claire simpers, holding out her hand. 'I'm Claire.'

'Hi, Claire.' He puts the bowl he's carrying on the table by Margaret's chair, then shakes Claire's hand. 'Ian. I live upstairs.'

'Ian is a doctor,' says Margaret.

'I am indeed. And how's my favourite patient?'

Margaret giggles. 'Ach, not so bad.'

'Look, I can't stop – I'm on a backshift. But I made this, and there's loads left. It's a spinach and quinoa salad? Bit of goat's cheese, beetroot – all very soft. I thought it might tempt you, madam?'

'Ooh, that sounds lovely,' says Margaret. 'Thank you, Ian, that's very kind.'

'And don't worry about the bowl – I can pop in and get it any time.'

'Or I could bring it up?' says Claire. 'That could make us a nice lunch, Margaret, eh?'

'Sure,' he says. 'If you've got time. Just leave it on the mat if nobody's in.' Ian holds the back of his hand to Margaret's brow. 'You sure you're alright? You're looking a wee bit peaky.'

'No, I'm fine, honestly. I just didn't sleep very well last night.'

'Did you go to your GP yet?'

'No. Not yet.'

'What are you like?' Ian puts his hands on his hips in mock disappointment. 'Claire, I don't know what influence you have, but will you try to persuade this very stubborn lady that it's OK to ask for help sometimes? Oh shit.' He pulls his bleeping phone from the back pocket of his jeans. 'Sorry, I really need to go. I'll see you soon Margaret, yes? Lovely to meet you, Claire.'

And he's gone, in a cloud of rich aftershave. The room takes a moment to settle itself around Dr Ian's departure.

Margaret's peeled off the cling film, is peering into the wooden bowl. 'What's keewah when it's at home?'

'Quinoa. It's a type of grain. Like barley.'

'In a salad?'

'He seems nice.'

'Who, Ian? Oh yes, he's very kind. They're all very kind. I just wish . . .' She's tugging the cling film, stretching it and kneading it.

'You wish what?'

'I wish they wouldn't pass my key round like that. I gave it to

Zara, right at the start when I came home, and now I can't seem to get it back. They all have some kind of rota, or maybe they've made copies, I don't know. Nobody tells me – they just turn up.'

'Is it making you nervous?'

'Yes! I could be in my nightie or . . . or on the toilet. But I can't say anything, can I, because then I'll feel terrible? They're all being so kind.' Her hands are skittish. Scrunched-up cling film wafts to the rug.

'Do you want me to say something?'

Claire has no qualms about confronting Zara. Although relations have been frosty since Teethgate. Or possibly Dr Ian? He seems more sympathetic. Yes, when she returns the bowl (not today, as he expressly told her he's on backshift), she can drop it into the conversation.

'He's married, you know,' says Margaret waspishly.

'Sorry?'

'Dr Ian. Married, with a wee one.'

Claire feels her face grow warm. 'Good for him.'

'Away. I could see your wee eyes light up when he came in.'

'Very funny.' Claire goes to make some other flippant comment, because a bantering Margaret is a much happier prospect than a huffy one. But the bridge of her nose grows tight. Is she so transparent? She sits on the couch again. It was hardly a passing thought. It wasn't anything. A man being married is not a rejection, Claire. You're *fine*. You are fine as you are. Why does she do that? Imagine the possibility of something else? Even fleetingly? All it does is crush you. Birling you in this catastrophising circle, where you start gouging at what was barely a scratch.

Claire holds her eyes shut. Then she begins to cry. She senses Margaret at her side. 'Oh dear. What is it? What's wrong?'

'Just leave me.'

Irrational tears, which refuse to stop. Claire's roasting face, pressed into her hands. Rejection terrifies her. But it's omnipresent. Why does she think every imagined slight, every misstep, is intentional? The springs on the couch dig into her arse. The cushions smell musty.

'Why do we do it?'

'Shh.' Margaret is cradling her head. 'Do what?'

'I don't know. *This*. All this. Life. Work and home and sleep and work. All this pretending. It's just shite, isn't it?'

Margaret rubs her back. Claire doesn't want to push her away, but will not allow her body to relax. Tears cascade. Her skin feels raw.

'Seriously. What's it for?'

'Lots of things,' says Margaret. 'Hope, for one? Yes, hope.'

'In what?'

'I don't know. In change? Beauty? Joy?'

'My ex just had a baby.'

'Oh, Claire. My poor Claire.'

She burrows deeper in. Margaret's jumper is perfumed with lily of the valley. 'What did being with Albert give you?' she sniffs.

'Comfort? And kindness. Definitely kindness.'

'And what did you give him?'

'Peace, I think.'

'That's lovely.' Claire wipes her eyes. The clock in the hall chimes. The football outside has stopped its drumming. Eventually, she trusts herself to sit up. 'I'm just so tired. Of everything.'

Margaret pats her hand. 'I know, dear. I know.'

'Do you?'

'Och, aye. It gets awful lonely now. There's days when I . . . you get sad, you know? Lonely and overwhelmed. Days when you feel wee and fragile. Or stupid. That's the worst, I think. Those are the days when I shut myself in.'

Claire laces her fingers through Margaret's. Her eyes trace the repeating motif of the curtains. Green and navy and gold. Pomegranates, birds and peacock feathers. A pattern you could get lost in.

Margaret speaks again. 'My husband used to say you need days where you're closed-in. Where you must *sit with the darkness*, was how he put it. But only so you're stronger. Then you can go back into the light.'

'He sounds like a wonderful man.'

'Oh, he was. He lost most of his family in the Holocaust. Yet he was the gentlest, most loving soul ever. I miss him terribly.'

'Mine hated any time I was having a down day. He just couldn't leave it alone, you know? We'd to talk about *every* tiny thing. Following me about, all, *Don't shut me out.* Just before he went and shagged another woman.'

'So his . . . indiscretion was your fault?'

'Apparently.'

'Och, love. Don't ever think that. We can't control what other folk do. Only how we respond to it.' Margaret unclasps her hand from Claire's. 'I'm sorry I teased you about Dr Ian.'

Claire's palm is damp and sweaty. She can feel her hair sticking to the nape of her neck. 'Don't be daft.' Her head feels empty after the crying. 'But I hate the thought I'm stoating about with a big flashing light on my head. *Single and desperate.* Am I that obvious?'

'Not in the slightest. But I'm no deid yet, dear. Dr Ian is a hunk. I wouldn't kick thon out of bed either.'

'Margaret Camberg!'

Margaret cackles. 'Right, then. I believe you have some plants for me? Shall we get on while the sap is stirring?'

The two women go outside, into the brightness of the day. Claire fetches the spade and compost from the car. Margaret finds some gardening gloves and bin bags and they begin to work methodically through the undergrowth. Claire refuses to let Margaret lift anything heavy, but she is able to say where there used to be a little patio, and, sure enough, once Claire has moved the broken toys and scraped back the moss, she finds a stretch of crazy paving. Then scary Jacqueline from the other downstairs flat comes out and says she'll get Gordon from upstairs. Soon there are five people working in Margaret's garden, for the tall, chunky boy returns and he must belong to Jacqueline in some way, because he too is inveigled into proceedings. He proves invaluable with the spade, plunging and turning with gusto – and a surprising degree of skill. He – Ali his name is – says he can get a whole team to come and help, but his mother, or gran or whoever Jacqueline is to him, says she *doesny want the whole place overrun with they gorillas* (Claire guesses it's a football team?) and that they can do it themselves, if they work hard enough. And they do. Despite this being too late in the season, according to Ali, they dig the soil and add the compost and plant the buddleia in the centre. The catnip and violets go beneath the bay window. Ali suggests planting the roses either side of the old patio, because they'll need a bench, obviously, and it will be nice to have the scent of the roses on the breeze. The lavender is dotted here and there to fill the gaps, and Ali asks Margaret if there's any chance she'd let him grow some herbs, and she says only if he keeps them in planters; she's not having mint running riot like a weed, and he says *OK*, then *thank you, Mrs Camberg*, and Margaret looks surprised. Then beams.

Chapter Seventeen

Gerard circles the shelves of the Co-op one more time. He needs to be positive Craig's gone. He told him he wanted some snacks. *Keep my strength up, know?* Kris gives him a few quid pocket money (which they probably put on expenses and claim back, but money's money, so he's not saying no). He's saving it for the weans, but Kris keeps saying, *treat yourself*, so they can't complain if he spends it on crap.

Craig said he'd wait till the minibus came, but Gerard went *naw*. Came out well harsh, so he panicked, said, *There's a girl I like*, like a total dick, and Craig went, *Ah! Enough said*, and got back in the car.

What a fanny. Why would Gerard tell anyone about Jo? She wasn't even . . . she's just a lassie who was nice. Now Kris will be asking him questions. Plus Craig, doing his stupid winking act.

Towers of Pringles sway. So many rounded lines of green zooming at him. Gerard can't see properly, and his heart is galloping. What's the time, what's the time? Oh, he canny be doing with any of this crap right now. Every second is a wasted beat. The man behind the counter coughs. Right, he better buy . . . salt and vinegar. They're the green ones, aren't they? That'll do. He goes up and pays. Puts the crisps in the shoulder bag thing Xander's given him. *I've got two, mate. Here you go.* It's a leather satchel. *A manbag*, Xander said. *You look really cool. Old school.*

Aye, right. Gerard fiddles with the strap. Well seen this is the

Southside. Get your head panned in in Dennistoun if you strutted up the street with a handbag. But today, he needs it. The crisps crinkle against a big brown envelope as he closes the flap.

Outside, the street is clear. They're not strict, but Kris and Craig like their schedules and planners. He supposes busy folk have to find more room to do more stuff when you're doing so much stuff anyroad. He thinks of the unfilled days his mum lives in. Weeks, sometimes, where getting washed or dressed could not be fitted in, where the telly (if it was working) rolled out endless garbage, DIY stuff or shit cartoons, and the squeaking of the music made him want to scream. Gerard could at least leave the house on those days, and she wouldn't notice. But not for long, because of the weans. He learned to get used to yawning days. Learned to sense when bedtime might be. Learned to be in his head. Time is weird.

He crosses the road, cuts through into the park. Kris and Craig are definitely not into zoning out. They do so much: work, cooking, gardening. Music too. The whole bunch of them play instruments. Piano, trumpet, drums. Serious, they could have their own band. Craig's even given Gerard a go on his guitar. (It made his fingers sore.) Brunches, lunches, tennis. Theatre, clubs. Good works.

Gerard is a 'good work', he gets that. It's their job to fill his days – them and Naggy's. To pack his brain with mince. Godknows how he'll ever fit in going to school once the holidays are past. Each Thursday evening, after the ironing, Kris sits him down and they go through the week to come. At first, she did it on a Sunday, but that wasn't enough time for Gerard to get his head round stuff. Some weeks are pretty quiet; others – like this coming one – are rammed. Gerard will be seeing Derek the Safeguarder – who tells Gerard to think of him like his guardian angel. Gerard thinks he's the same person as the man from Who Cares?, but he's not really sure. They all look and sound the same. There'll be the usual chat with Naggy – either on the phone or at Social Work. Naggy calls it 'The Unit'. He reckons her job is so rubbish she likes to kid on she's a secret agent or Dr Who something. *Call me at the Unit! Roger. Over and out!*

He walks faster. CAMHS finally came back with an appointment, so he's off to see a mental health dude as well, which'll be a riot. Maybe they'll give him another of those CDs with the clouds on it. He'd like that. Naggy says he has to be 'assessed' before they'll let him write to the old lady. *So make sure you answer all the questions . . . you know, properly.* Which is code for 'don't act up'. Naggy reckons he's moved up the queue because of their 'positive engagement with' – he fumbles for the word – 'restraining justice'? 'Reformative'? With any luck he'll get to see the weans more too, if Naggy can get the contact arrangements changed. But only if Gerard continues to be *good*.

He thinks saying sorry will be a good thing. His mouth floods with saliva. He wonders if she'll say it to him.

His mum.

He skirts past an old man, sitting eating a sandwich. You can sense the loneliness hovering on him. As if a miserable cloud perches on his head. The old boy looks up – whoa, he's about to speak – but Gerard has his own head down. Keeps walking. He's no time for anyone else's problems.

Bloody Kris has went and got him a literacy tutor. Didn't even ask. Well, she can piss right off. What a cow. She knows how much letters freak him. Course she does. She took him to a library, and it got that he couldny breathe. Feeling all those words in all those books, packed in one room. Tottering, pure looming over you. All piled up, frowning, hammering his head with blocks and blocks of dancing squiggles. He could hear the books laughing. Feel the walls tilt, until his heart was racing and he couldny speak. Kris seen all that, yet still she won't let it go. The tutor is coming next Wednesday, and Gerard knows if he refuses to see her, Kris will tell Naggy. Naggy *is* a flucken spy, actually. They all are. If Gerard doesn't 'engage' with any and all of the pish they line up for him, it gets reported back. To the Reporter, the Panel, the Management. God, probably. *Gerard is non-compliant.* They better not find out he dyked Gardening Guerrillas again.

He hurries up the grassy hill, towards the flagpole. His stomach is in spirals. It is how a fish would feel, once it's snagged on a rod, being drawn by a line it cannot see, a line which is aching his belly, is properly hurting him. But he can't not go. He squints up to the top of the hill. Can see a few people there, but they are only shapes. His knees feel trembly. This is the exact same park it was when he was here with the weans. When it was a happy, sweet-grass and sunshine kindy place. It is. That's why he said to meet here. It was his idea. He refuses not to let this place be lovely, to be overshadowed with a stupid fear. Gerard was just being paranoid about the man. Of course it wasny him he seen at the gates. Shawlands is miles away from Dennistoun.

His lips are salty. Sometimes, Gerard gathers things up like a hoover. Memories, images, bits of junk: they all get mangled in his head, and then project themselves in dense and glowing colours, so he can see them, outside his eyes. But they're not true. He is determined that man was not true. He's just a picture that was in Gerard's mind, and when Gerard's mind wasny looking, he sneaked out.

What kind of place is the park now, then? Not happy . . . he's not sure what. The weather has turned, is cooler and cloudy, which casts everything in a different light. Damp air sneaking under your clothes. The grass and trees seem drabber than before. More sludgy. That's it. Despite the crazy jittering bombing through him, Gerard feels dull. It's almost like the moment before you are hit: when you know it's coming, but you're so wasted with the fear of waiting, you just want it over and done. So you go way inside yourself. Just zone out. Even though your body is still pumping adrenaline, you make yourself numb.

He doesn't like it. You could float off into the air when you go that way. Dissociation. That's the word they telt him last time he saw a therapist. *Are there times when you feel your body doesn't belong to you, Gerard? It might manifest in other ways too. What about gaps in your life that you can't recall?* Why do they speak all posh like that? To a kid? Really brainy folk have so much cleverness crammed into their heads they have to show it off. Or maybe they forget other people are not like them. Ha. Maybe they have it too. *Dissociation.* It's a difficult word to remember, but he'd seized on it immediately, grabbed it hard because it seemed to make so much sense. To have a word like that, which said someone else knew how you feel – and that other folk felt it too – had astounded him. To have doctors give a name to a feeling that was so big and scary it drowned you? Man. For the first time, he'd seen how words might be useful, might hold power that could help instead of threaten.

He smooths down his hair. Should probably have brushed it this morning. Licks his lips. The final event of this week is that they have a family meeting scheduled at the Unit. They've had a family meeting scheduled ever since Gerard came to live with Kris and Craig. But it never goes ahead because his mum isny here to come to it.

His mum.

She messaged him last night. Late. Three whole weeks she's made him wait. Gerard lying there, almost asleep, watching the moonlight cut a slash through the ceiling. Then the vicious wee ping, which broke across the air and made him jump.

U get it?

As soon as he'd realised it was from her, all drowsiness dissolved. But why was she messaging? How was he meant to know what it said? He didn't want to make her angry. He could work out the U. *You.* He knew the squiggle at the end meant a question. He had to respond, what if he didn't answer and she went away? Panic rising. Concentrate, concentrate. T. He recognised that. Two Ts. Was she trying to trick him? She must be asking if he'd done what she asked. Or even if she was asking if he was alright. The thumbs-up emoji would do.

Then another message. M, mm, Ts. A number 2 or a 5. His eyes began to smart. It was no good. She was going to be mad at him whatever he did. Fearfully, he'd pressed the little phone symbol, swallowing hard. It began to ring.

'Hey, Mu–'

'I telt you no to phone me!' Her voice came in a low hiss.

'I know, but I couldny read what you said.'

'For fucksake, Gerard.'

That's what she said. Not *how are you?* or *God, I've missed you* or *Oh, sorry, pet. I wasn't thinking.*

Imagine if his mum talked like that? Imagine if his mum cared he couldn't read?

She had kept the conversation brief. It sounded noisy where she was, but he was feart to ask. 'You got it?'

'You said four days. You said it would be four days.'

'What?'

'That you'd phone me.'

'Jesus, Gerard. I had to go away. But did you get it?'

'Aye.'

'Right. Meet me tomorrow at one o'clock.'

'Where?'

She'd hesitated, then gone, 'You pick. Somewhere near you,' and he'd thought instantly of the park. He'd not been back, and he wanted to prove that he could. Wanted to show her the boating pond, thought they could maybe call into Richard and Helen's to see the weans, if she'd time. Wouldn't that be a brilliant surprise? And if his mum was there, the park would be the best place again.

'There's a big flagpole, Mum, right at the top of the hill—'

'Aye, aye. See you then. And Gerard . . .' Her voice was so soft at this point he'd to strain to hear her.

'Yes, Mum?'

'Don't tell a fucking soul where you're headed.'

He's nearly there now, at the top of the big hill. But he still can't see her. What if she doesn't come? His eyes blur. Blood rushes in his ears. More saliva pools in his mouth; all the juice from his body is gathering in one place. He thinks he'll throw up if she isn't there. *Please come, Mum. Please, please, come.* A man and a lady walk past with their dog. No sign of his mum. He kicks about for a bit, waiting. Walks round the whole thing, just in case. Nobody else about. The base of the flagpole is surrounded by a black wire fence and cobblestones, with some big numbers at the front. You can go in alright, there's spaces in the fence, and benches there. There's no flag, but, just some scribbled graffiti on the white pole, which is pretty mahoosive. It has a strange skirt-shape at its base, rises into the sky like a skinny space rocket. If you bend your neck upwards to see the top, it sends you dizzy. There are trees dotted round the flagpole, behind the fence. But not much else going on, which is annoying. Craig had said there was an Iron Age fort up here; that's the main reason Gerard had wanted to come up. It didny look so far from the park gates. His mum is going to be raging he's made her climb all this way. His chest begins to flutter. He doesn't want her to be angry with him. He's done what she asked. He wants her to say he's been good. Three whole weeks, and he's never even opened the envelope. Each night, when he was tempted, he'd think the same thing. *If I don't open it today, she'll phone.*

When Gerard turns to face the way he came, to see if he can see her, the view makes him gasp. There's the whole sweep of the park. Then a great big church steeple and lots of sandstone tenements. The long straight stretch of Vicky Road, which takes you into town. But you can see right across the whole city. Far away, he can make out high flats and rolling green hills. He can see the river, skirted by silvery bridges and green swathes. Can see other spires and turrets and towers. Glasgow could be a fairyland from up here. So many tenements: they spill over the city like battlements and castles. Fortresses and prisons. Dividing lines. Somewhere down there, way over to the left, is Gerard's old flat and the statue of Buffalo Bill and Duke Street, and the Broncos. His primary school will be there, and the fruit shop, and an old lady in a yellow cardie, and Celtic Park (he thinks maybe that's the tip of it there, that shiny curved structure he can see, but it could be a shopping centre). Paths seem to converge on the flagpole from every side of the park. People move like ants. Any one of them could be his mum. He doesn't check the clock on his phone. He will just keep waiting.

Gerard sits on one of the empty seats. Hunches his feet up too, so his chin can rest on his knees. She will definitely come.

*

'Christ, that was some climb.'

He is staring at the seagulls, feels a dunt on the back of his head.

'Hi, Mum.' Sharp stab of his fingernails, pressing through his jeans. It feels like on your birthday or Christmas, when you wake up and do not know what's to come. Hugs or hitting. Presents or puke. He daren't move.

'You cold? Jesus, I'm roasting after that.' Her voice is sharp, not slurred. Good. That's good.

Gerard looks up at her. 'No.'

'You're shivering.'

'No, I amny.'

'Christ, Gerard.' His mum plonks down beside him. 'Why d'you always have to argue with me?'

The trick is to not say it. Too late.

'I'm not.' The press of air between them. He fights his body, not to coorie in. He still does not know what mood she's in. What she wants. She has to make the first move. He steals another glance. She's wearing jeans. Clean jeans and a pink hoodie. Her hair is caught in a ponytail, but not one of those vicious, witchy ones. That's good too.

She touches his elbow with hers. 'You alright?' Stinging nettles, flaring up his arm.

'Aye.'

An empty Coke can lies on the ground beneath their bench. Gerard can see it through the slats, shiny red crushed over in a grumpy mouth. Razor-blade tongue that would cut you clean away. The ground pulses. He tilts his chin up. Leaves shimmer on the trees. His ears sing.

'Oh, and I'm fine, son. Thanks for asking.'

Already, she's making him want to cry. Of course he wants to know how she is. That's *all* he flucken wants to know, all he has flucken thought about for weeks.

She touches him again, and he tries not to flinch. Or fold. 'You no speaking?'

He shrugs.

'Fucksake.' She removes her hand from his arm. Stretches her feet in front of her, like they are sunbathing. Gerard counts his own breaths. Waiting. He senses it's important to wait. There's nobody else up here. Just a boy and his mum, on the top of the world. Eventually, his mum breaks the silence. 'Look, I'm sorry, right?'

Gerard slams his foot down onto the Coke can. He no longer knows if he is counting or holding his breath, but it all bursts out of him. 'How come you never came to see us? No even Miranda. You didny even phone us or nothing.' He's staring right at her now, deep into her eyes. She has painted them a pretty blue, and there's make-up on her cheeks as well. He wants to stroke her face and slap her.

'I've had to keep my head down, alright? Christ, Gerard, it was for your own good. I shouldny even be here now.'

He stiffens. 'How no?' She is going to run away again. His mouth goes dry. What can he . . .? Fumbling, he reaches into his manbag.

'Did you see your gran?'

'Aye.' He pulls out the envelope. Holds it close.

'Is that it?'

He nods.

'Gonny gies it, then?'

Gerard shakes his head.

'Look, son, stop dicking around, eh? Have you opened it?'

'No.' Driving his teeth into his bottom lip. Does she know how hard it was, how he could feel it, burning? He crushes his arms around the envelope, pushing the hardness of it into his chest. 'Are you no even gonny ask how the weans are? Or where we've been living or anything?'

'I know where you've been living,' she says quietly.

This surprises him, but he almost doesn't hear it. 'Aye, well, do you know where my bike is? Or the wean's Ingiefant?'

'What? No,' she laughs.

'So are you not at the house?'

'I told you. I've had to lie low.'

'Well, see when you've been lying low, d'you know our Anthony's been pissing the bed again? Or that Miranda's walking? She's walking, Mum, and you didny even see it. And neither did I cause I only get to see them once a fortnight.' His mouth is sore, brimming with angry words.

'Aye, and whose fault is that?' she snaps.

'What?' He can no longer contain the sting behind his eyes. Hot tears spiking.

'If you hadny fucking kicked off at that meeting. Fucking decked that social worker, didn't you? Stupid cunt.' Gerard's eyes are closed by this time, his brain aching. Full of storms. He feels her wipe under his eye. 'Funny, mind.'

He relaxes into her touch. Allows his body to unclench. His mum is tracing the outline of his cheek. 'You're some boy. You know that? Just like your da.'

Gerard takes hold of her fingers, but then she pulls away.

'Och, son, I'm sorry. I canny always . . . It's fucking hard, know? Sometimes it's really hard when I . . . then I feel so shit. So utter shite I canny bear it. Then I know . . . I shouldny be near yous.'

'Mum! Don't say that.'

'But it's true. Cause I hurt you, I know I do. And that hurts me. So it's better if I just leave yous alone, know? Just gie you space and leave you be.'

'No! No way. It's always better when you're here. It doesny matter what you do. We don't care. You're our mum.' He can barely see. The hill begins to undulate, a white sun-moon above, pale and searching him out, while the sky bears down, slate-grey, and vast, too vast. It's pouring like an ocean. The sky is going to drown them both.

'That's bullshit, Gerard, and you know it. I'm bad news, always have been.'

'Mum!'

'Fucksake. Stop your greeting. Crying doesny get you anywhere in this life, Gerard. Fucking toughen up.'

'Mum, please don't shout,' he begs, trying to coorie into her again.

'Right, enough.' She shoves him off. 'Gie me that envelope.'

'Is it about my dad?' He grabs at her hoodie.

'It's none of your fucking business.'

'Like my gran wasny none of my business? How come you get to decide?' he shouts. 'It's my life. My gran. It's *my* fucking dad!'

A belt across his face.

'Because the less you fucking know, the better.'

Gerard wants to die. He cowers, waiting for more.

'I'm trying to protect you, you stupid bastard.' His mum snatches at the envelope, but he won't give it to her. Once she takes it he will never see her again. She keeps tugging, harder, is always stronger than he is. Of course she will win. He hears the paper tear slightly as it's yanked away. 'This is what got your father killed, alright? And now they're fucking after me. So the further away I am fae yous, the better. Do you not fucking get that?'

'Aye, and what's your excuse for all they other times you left us?' Gerard is screaming at her, does not care who is staring. He's aware someone else is there now, near to them. A man who is watching, closely. A man who has walked all the way up the hill and is leaning on the black iron fence that surrounds the flagpole. He draws on his cigarette. Enjoying the show. Gerard's mum clocks him at the same time Gerard does. The man smiles at them both. Raises his hand in greeting.

'Alright, Marissa? Good to see you.'

Against the white circle of the sun, Gerard sees the black circle of the tattoo that's beginning to haunt him. He opens his mouth. The sky yawns. There is a long hill. A man. A boy. A woman. The man flicks his cigarette in a burning arc. Takes one slow step. Unhurried. The woman shrinks. Gerard watches his mother melt. The man glides forward, yet no one is moving.

'You got something for me, doll?'

'Fuck off, Davey,' his mother roars. Urgently, she thrusts the envelope into Gerard's breastbone. 'Run, son. Fucking run!'

The ground is surging, green grass and mud. He is falling, she is screeching. One leg tumbles before the other and he is racing for the trees behind the flagpole. Crack of twigs underfoot, rustle of envelope jostling. World spinning. Gerard tunnelling through myriad skies: blue and white and green light ticker-taping. And yelling. So much yelling. His feet pounding on and on.

Chapter Eighteen

It is becoming dusk when Gerard emerges from Queen's Park. Disorientated by the fading pink light, and the wrong direction, he stumbles into the road. He's come out past a big greenhouse, onto another hill, a busy, sweeping road with tenements facing the park. Up or down? He chooses up, simply because it feels further away. At the summit of the hill is a roundabout, with a long column in the middle. There are stone eagles, and a big lion on top. The road branches into three. One road skirts more of the park to the left, while another veers right towards some big houses. He recognises nothing on the main bit, where the road slopes down the other side of the hill. Just more tenements and some new flats. He is shaking. Trousers damp where he pished himself.

A guy looks at him funny. 'You alright, son?'

Gerard doesn't answer, just slinks away, following the line of the road that edges the park. If he walks right round till he finds the gates he knows, then he won't be lost. He coughs, and his whole body shudders. It is too loud. He is terrified the man will hear him. The man is everywhere. He is in the dark leaves that whisper as Gerard passes. He is in the purpling sky. His eyes will be in the stars when they come out too, and he is somehow . . . his fingers are somehow laced round Gerard's throat. They have been choking him these past hours, forcing him down on grass, quivering like a feart, trapped rabbit, in poisonous bushes with glossy green leaves. Gerard ran until his lungs were bursting, his mum's voice pushing him further and further forward, even when he could no longer hear it. He has no idea what the time is or how long he's been hiding. The one thing he did before he stopped thinking was turn off his phone. If it rang, he would be caught. If he moved, he would be caught. He tried to pant as quietly as he could, gulping and hissing out the air until everything slowed down. He tried not to think what the man was doing to his mum, or how he had found them.

It is Gerard's fault he found them.

He walks on trembly legs, at times holding the park railings if he thinks he's going to fall. He's tied his hoodie round his waist, to disguise the wet patch on his jeans. Why did they come to this fucking park? Why is he so fucking thick, kidding on the things he sees aren't the things he sees? *You're too big for fairy tales, Gerard.* His hands are agitated; every so often, they fly to his scalp, scratching for bits of greenery or beasties. He is sure he's crawling with them. Eventually, he limps his way to a place he recognises – the huge fancy gold gates at the top of Vicky Road. From here, he knows his way. Keep going left. And then it will be Shawlands and the boating pond.

He thinks of the weans, probably tucked up in bed at Richard and Helen's, and his legs buckle. He can't go anywhere near Shawlands. What if the man is stalking him right now, and follows him there? Fuck, the man seen Anthony and Miranda already, didn't he? When they were all at the park before. The man's been watching Gerard all this time. But how? How the flucken-fuck does anyone know – or care about Gerard Macklin?

Numb, he leans against one of the massive pillars that support the gates. Paper cups and crisp pokes litter the pavement, gathering in the corners where the pillars meet the fence. Where can he go? Where's safe? When he breathes, it is cotton wool. The space inside his ribs swells as he fights to stay calm. What does he need to be safe from? He doesn't have to look down to remember it's there. The torn flap of the envelope kisses his hand. Carrying it and not dropping it and hiding it and hating it is all he has done. Whatever is in there is what his mum wanted. Is probably what the man wants too.

Gerard swallows the saliva that thickens his throat. He wants to spit, but he's so weak it will only dribble down his chin. *Davey. Wee Davey. Daft Davey.* You canny be feart of a name like that. Yet he is. Names are stupid. They mean fuck all. The man could be nameless, or called Trevor or anything, and it would not change the slow menace of him. Gerard knew Davey wouldny chase him. Not really. Men like Davey, hard men, do not run. They remember faces, and get other folk to do their running. They bide their time. Gerard puts one finger in the envelope's ragged slit. He needs to know what this is.

He glances up and down the street. The grey skies of earlier have turned luminous. Stormy washes of purple and gold. Plenty of folk, going about their business. A group of workies loading cones on a truck. A few dog walkers. Couples strolling arm in arm. Folk heading for the pub. It all looks so normal. Nice. Folk just chug along, doing their thing, with not a clue what the person next to them is going through. He tears his finger viciously along the crease, opening the envelope completely. There's enough glow from the setting sun and the juddery street lights to see inside. It feels like ripping off a plaster. He's past caring. Let Davey come ahead, if he's lurking.

Square. Hard. It's a book. Gerard takes the thing out, shakes the envelope. Nothing else inside. It's just an old hardback book. He squints at the cover. There's a silver fish leaping on the front, and a castle, and a queen. A weans' story book. Man, he must of picked up the wrong thing. This can't be what his mum was wanting. As he stares at the cover, another image shimmers into view. A golden ring, encircling the title. The letters bump and grind as usual, but he doesn't need to read them to recognise the title.

The words will say *A Fish of Silver,* and *A Ring of Gold.*

The book falls to the ground. The pavement warps, rushing fast like pleated water. Gerard stares at the sky. His daddy read him this book. It's as if someone's sliced open the top of his head. Memories spurt, Gerard powerless to stop them. His daddy used to read books to him before he went to sleep. He had a wee shelf with books on. One about a cat who was a lollipop lady. There was a mouse called Maisie and stuff about farms and tractors and spaceships . . . and this. If Gerard opens the pages, he will see a river. There is a wee river and a man called St Mungo and a lady who is crying. There is his daddy's finger on the page, following the words. Gerard can smell his shirt, smell the sweat of his oxters, the lager on his breath. Gerard is under the covers, his daddy leaning on the pillow. He has been away but is back now, so Gerard's getting his stories again. His daddy always says it's real, this story; that's why Gerard likes it so much. Together they trace the letters on the page, his daddy's words soft in his ear. Sometimes he gets Gerard to practise too, copying the letters with a pencil and a piece of paper as his daddy reads them out. *That's it. You're such a clever wee boy.* It is the best thing in the world, to feel the hum of his breath as he speaks to you, so Gerard tries to block out the commotion at the door. Men shouting, feet running up the stairs, his mum yelling *no, please no,* over and over, while his daddy shoves him roughly, he's taking the pencil off him, and Gerard hasny finished yet, but he's spoiling his book, then he throws it under the pillow, jumps up as the door bangs open and hands pull at his daddy and a big dark stick swings down, onto his face.

If Gerard opens the pages, he will see blood.

He doesn't open it. He just picks the book up, and starts walking. Gerard walks as fast as he can, leaving the memories piled among the rubbish by the gates. He refuses to see the pictures in his head; there is only the road and his feet; he has to get somewhere, anywhere. It's like when you're about to puke. Fucking look straight ahead, and swallow it down.

Gerard walks and he walks, all the way down Victoria Road. Past the shops and the cafés, with their flats up above. Every window is somebody's house. He passes the bus stops and the Star Bar and the voids where tenements used to be. He passes under the concrete jut of the motorway bridge, past vast gaps where high flats used to be, past stranded pubs and the bricked-up railway arches and the new flats with sky-diving angels above their doors. He comes to the river, and a bridge, and he crosses. Gets halfway, then checks behind him. There is nobody there. He leans his elbows on the bridge. Buses go past. Drunk men shout. A woman whoops. His legs don't belong to him any more; he doesn't think he can lift them. Lights glitter in the river below. It is properly nighttime. He is in so much shit. Craig and Kris will be going ballistic. They'll have phoned Naggy by now, and Tracey at Gardening Guerrillas. Probably the polis too. When he thinks of the polis he thinks of his mum. What if that man has really hurt her?

Gerard leans over a little, until he can see a watery image of his own face. It is long and distorted. He hoicks up some spit and gobs a big, stringy greener. Right between the eyes. Of course the man will have hurt her. And there is nothing Gerard can do. Who can he tell? Who will help him? Folk like Naggy, Kris and Craig – they havny a clue. People like that would say *Oh, go to the police*, if something bad happens. They live in nice houses. Work hard, have a holiday, a car. Folk do things when they ask, and the streets they live in are not warzones. Honest to Christ, Gerard would love to see Naggy round his bit. Not like dropping in for a snoopy visit but properly, permanently, marooned there. Learning what bits it's OK to walk through. Learning what it's OK to say, and when. Learning how to move and stand so you are tough enough to be left alone, but not tough enough to be challenged. Learning to live with the nausea of fear, all the fucking time. And then you go home, and those feelings just get bigger. Aye, Naggy. Gerard would love to see how your 'coping strategies' work then. The head in the water grins at him. Gerard would totally *love* to see someone wipe the stupid smile right off Naggy's stupid face. Torch her stupid files.

Fuck you and your degrees and your flowery dresses, Naggy. You canny learn what it's like to be Gerard. His fists grind against the stone parapet of the bridge. Enjoying the sensation of his knuckles being skinned. Man, he wants so badly to hit her. Hit anyone really. He wants to smash that guy Davey's head in with a concrete block.

He wants his dad.

Waves of pain build inside his brain. Desperately, he crushes the images down again. He's lived with them long enough. Fucking disappear. He canny lose it here.

Man up, Gerard. He can't stay dreeped over a bridge. He can't go near the weans' house. If he goes back to Kris and Craig's, he's fucked. He'll be grounded for a month, or worse.

He doesn't think of the alternative. *Gerard, we loved having you. Just one of us, in our fuzzy family home. But you are in breach of contract, so FUCK OFF.*

Think. Think. The book is back inside its torn envelope. It would be so easy, just to let it slip over the edge. One wee splash. Then whatever the bad thing is, is gone.

But he knows that won't be true. He can't keep lugging it about either, mind. He needs to find his mum, and give it to her. She'll know what to do.

Aye, right.

He almost laughs out loud.

He switches his phone back on. A stream of cheery pings burst like bubbles in the night sky. Hunners and hunners of messages, his phone is alive; you can feel the urgency buzzing in your hand. Tonnes from the witch symbol. But if he does phone Naggy, she'll only send the storm troopers in. Is this like probation? No one's really explained how it works. Or if they have, Gerard's not been listening. Does not coming home (aye, home-not-home) count as non-compliance or your standard 'high jinks'? Gerard knows he is under supervision. He thinks it's instead of being charged. He doesn't think he was ever charged. But if he fucks up now, do they charge him anyway?

He stares at all the messages. Can hear them, jabbering. There is no loveheart for his mum, but. She's not tried to call him.

He shouldny of run away. He should've stayed and protected her. He feels his body topple further forward. Hot chocolate.

That's what the muddy churn underneath him looks like. Would the River Clyde be warm?

Gerard just needs to sleep. He cannot face any of this. Not right now. Not one single person in the world will ever know how small and alone he feels. Here. Now. He is small, and he is massive. He is filled with this whole city, and blood and swirls of rage. Imagine just having a laugh. He thinks of his pals. Daft wee boys, the lot of them. All the Broncos live with their mum or their dad. Colm lives with both. Gerard fingers his phone. He is seriously considering dropping it in the Clyde, because that will solve one problem (and it's better than dropping himself in), when he notices a picture of a carrot in the middle of all the WhatsApps. Ali, that boy from Guerrillas. He's messaged Gerard too. That was decent of him. He's sound, that guy. Ali's got no one either.

Gerard contemplates the river. His crotch has dried. He is shivery. Rank. Scared. He presses the carrot. Surely Ali wouldny grass him up?

Chapter Nineteen

The night air is delicious. Honeysuckle, mixed with the frondy herbs in the planter. Margaret only came out for a sprig of mint, but the evening is so beautiful, she's been sitting this past while on her new bench. Longer than a while, perhaps. She emerged when flares of deep orange and bands of purple-gold hung across the sky. Now the air is soft, and navy blue. The novelty of her garden is snapped-stem fresh. There are still patches of dark earth, but they'll soon fill up as the plants bulk and grow.

Albert insisted that nature was healing; Margaret never believed him – well, she'd never experienced it for herself. All the times he had her hoeing and weeding, she'd smiled, and felt happy, but it was because she saw him being happy. Albert held a profound sadness within him. Being outdoors, being active, lit his face with a kind of peace.

Tenderly, she touches the back of her head. It's healed fine, but she's still protective of it. She feels closer to Bert, here in this resurrected garden, than she has for a long time. Nobody tells you how that ache expands, the longer you're apart. When he died, Margaret felt numb, then utterly alone. Grief didn't hit properly until after the funeral, when the dismantling of his life began. Writing replies to the condolence letters, telling the bank, the pension people, packing his things away, it all still gave her a connection. There was a purposeful link between them; folk could see he remained tethered to her. She's not sure, now, why that felt important. For all his long life, there were few people at the funeral. Fewer at the purvey. She only told those who needed to be told. Donald from the shop had read out a poem about a ship, and the folk welcoming it as it sailed beyond the horizon, and she'd embraced that image – even though she didn't believe it. But she liked to imagine Bert's lost family, waving to their boy.

Real grief had struck weeks later. A literal blow. To come into their lounge one morning, and double over. That jolt to her gut. The utter emptiness she'd been left with, reeling at the waste of it all. This same room, this same home – and him, not in it. None of them in it. The intense pain beneath her skin. All that life, never in it again. His hand on hers at the dinner table. Not once more. Their nonsense burble of chit-chat, dammed. Mashing up Weetabix, clearing up clutter. All past, and empty. These walls, which knew their secrets. Silent. She knew then that she had lived her best life with him. For a time, she'd known nothing but the loveliness of love. All their yesterdays, all their tomorrows, together. Only Albert could recall her long-gone mum and dad, or how prettily she danced, or that time she had thought to study French, and he'd gently encouraged her, then she'd decided not to. Only she and Albert shared the months and years of trying, and failing, and rising. Only Albert had kissed her belly and her breasts as they changed shape. Only she and Albert knew the deafening shatter of a slamming door. Knew the depth of their grief, and their righteousness. Their business was nobody's but their own. Only Albert stood between Margaret and the world. Once the smell of him faded from the overcoat she'd hung onto, there would be no physical trace.

The foreverness of it was too much, and she had crept quietly back to bed.

She thinks she can understand Albert's thirst for stillness better. When demons lurk in every corner – with the worst ones inside your head – it's unbearable. She's glad he wasn't here to see her shamed in the street like that. By that wee boy. It would have hurt him too deeply. To not protect the people he loved, to not hold them close and keep them safe, was the very worst thing on earth.

Which is why their son broke his heart.

Zara spied a photograph of Stephen once. Not long after Albert died, when Zara first began to poke her nose in. Getting the hoover out of the hall press – Margaret hadn't even known the girl was tidying up – but she'd knocked Margaret's satchel off the shelf, and a wheen of old photos had come spilling out. *Oh, he's so cute!* Zara cried. It was a small snapshot. Stephen, on his trike on Christmas morning. It suits Margaret to let her neighbours believe she has a nephew in Australia, not a son. Too many questions. Why had they never seen him? Why was he not at Albert's funeral?

Because Margaret never told him, that's why. Margaret has never spoken to her son, beyond that awful night he left. Stephen has been gone twelve years now. Not even Jacqueline has lived in this tenement that long. So there are no witnesses to the Camberg family of before.

It's simpler that way. Margaret leans over to pluck another leaf of mint. Crushes it, inhales the freshness. She wishes she'd tackled this silly strip of mess sooner. It's just a patch of soil and a few plants, but it is filling up her heart. Daring to make something good, not worrying it'll be spoiled. She wonders how many times this has held her back, how many lifelines altered or curtailed from fear of over-reaching. She's hardly Icarus for dreaming of a nice space to sit and breathe now, is she? Daft to think there's safety in ignoring ugliness. She thought she'd be looking out the window constantly, getting flustered at every piece of litter that floats in. But she hasn't. She's had to pick up the odd bit of rubbish, yes, but, in the main, people have been respecting her garden. So maybe if you create some wee, brave thing, it makes folk care? Jacqueline's grandson has been taking in his toys at night. She thought it would kill her to hear him outside, but it's like a gurgling stream below her window. Margaret takes pleasure in him playing there. Every flat-dweller should have access to a garden. Back courts are for bins and clotheslines. Front gardens like this one are rare – and posh.

She raises an imaginary glass. *Look, Mum! I got there in the end.*

Over the road, the gateposts of the old school wrap round new flats. Whitehill Secondary, a handsome, solid piece of Victoriana. Razed to the ground. Glasgow is an expert in razing its heritage to the ground. All those fine buildings lost since she was a girl, or suspended in façade-form only. Walking through the city, Margaret notices gaps and skeletons everywhere. And it never feels like progress.

By all accounts, Whitehill was a great school. The flat Margaret grew up in was only round the corner. It would've been so handy; Margaret could have gone to school with the lassies she played with in the street. But, no, her parents decreed she must schlep all the way to the West End, and be with rich girls who had ponies, and sneered at Margaret's shoes.

Stephen might have gone to Whitehill too, but it closed when he was at primary. The new secondary was all mod cons, mind. Had a wonderful technology department. Stephen virtually lived there. Top of the year for science. Margaret could never find the words to say how proud she was of his achievements. Such a smart boy. But practical too, excelling in metalwork and technical drawing. And the way he could sketch an outline on fabric with tailor's chalk? Like he was born to it. This longed-for, brilliant creature, who came from them. How could it be? From douce, dull Margaret and Albert?

When Stephen was born, they were reborn too. Immediately, Albert grew taller, straighter. As if he deserved more space in the world. So many disappointments, before this one, perfect boy took breath and ignited their world. Glittering, multi-faceted Stephen, made of diamond. Of course he was indulged. He was their only baby. Always pushing at boundaries they created to keep him safe. They indulged that too. Margaret never wanted to repeat the mistakes of her own mother. Which of course, you're destined to do: DNA stitching and looping back. Love in a chainstitch. Until someone breaks the chain.

An abyss threatens to open, here in Margaret's lovely garden.

She toys on the edge of it, not knowing how far she'll plummet this time. The depth varies; she has to steel herself, like plunging into an icy loch.

It begins with an ache in her cheek. Clamped teeth. Always her back teeth, trying to withstand the overwhelming, purple rush of pain.

Stephen began to disappoint them when he was twelve. *But I don't want to be a tailor, Daddy. I want to build things.* So they laughed, and let him chatter, and Bert would put him to work after school. Confident his son would see that the quiet craft of turning a seam was also a form of building things. Building a business too. A legacy. When you are the older parents of an only child, you consider these things.

Stephen disappointed them at eighteen, when he decided to leave home. Bert had got the new sign painted up as a surprise, for the day Stephen finished school. *Camberg and Son.* The lad had been studying so hard. He'd done them proud. They'd put enough money aside to help him through college, which is what they thought he wanted. He could stay home, learn useful skills in retail, production, design, that kind of thing, then bring that new knowledge to Bert and Donald at the weekends. Evenings too – *I worked all the hours God sent, my boy. Three jobs I did, before I got this shop.*

But no. Without saying a word, Stephen applied to study civil engineering. Five years. In Dundee.

Dundee?

He told them it was one of the best degrees, that he'd come back home as often as he could. She remembers Bert, swallowing down his hurt and bewilderment, clapping his boy on the shoulder. Telling him he was proud. She remembers the very fingernails of her, cutting into her palms. Wanting to slap her son. But they tholed it, as they always did. Their bright boy would want for nothing. Bert worked doubly hard to supplement Stephen's grant. They made sure he'd somewhere decent to stay – a grey harled tenement, hunkered by the river. Told each other that he'd be back. That he'd remodel Camberg and Son (Bert insisted the sign remain). No, that he'd return and build a chain of shops for Albert, an empire!

Stephen came home rarely. So they went up to visit him, awkward trips where they seemed to get in his road, so stayed mostly in their motel. *He's working really hard,* said Bert. University was where Stephen, her soft, gorgeous baby boy, finally became a stranger. With every clumsy effort to connect, Margaret and Albert seemed to make a greater gulf. The worst of it was watching Bert, becoming small once more.

And university was where Stephen met Lauren – lovely lass. Australian. Warm and tanned against the chilly braes and clear, wide skies of Dundee. Oh aye, a lovely lass, Margaret thought. Lauren brought their boy back to them. His visits home became more frequent, his demeanour more relaxed. Lauren wound her magic round them all. After graduation, it was Lauren who insisted they came back to Glasgow, and the joy – oh, the utter joy – that flooded them. The gratitude, for this girl who was closer than a daughter, because she'd *chosen* to be near them.

Margaret and Bert relaxed into their roles, Mum and Dad again, fully. Oh, they were careful not to live in Stephen's pocket, but meals and money and love were always on hand. Lauren struggled to find work, grew paler as Stephen's career flourished. But Margaret was there, with tea and sympathy and knowing smiles.

You're expecting, aren't you? And the girl had gleamed.

Margaret's grandchild will be, she calculates, fifteen now. A man, almost. Off to university soon. Perhaps a sports scholarship, he was such an active wee boy. Used to run around this garden like a human dynamo. *Chase me, Nana!*

Paul was three when Margaret last held his hand.

They used him as a human shield. Thinking Bert and Margaret would meekly accept their decision. How little Stephen understood his parents. How little they understood him.

Lauren wants to go home.

They kept thinking it wouldn't happen – right up until it did.

When her son first mentioned going to Australia, the words took a moment to connect. Then Lauren had ruffled Paul's hair and made a joke. *My mum's forgotten what this one looks like.*

But you were there at Christmas, said Margaret.

And we were here the Christmas before, smiled Lauren, *and the one before that.*

Margaret had spent the rest of that day in a daze, a massive hole torn through her body. Desperate to know if they were serious. Terrified to ask.

We'd like to get married out there, Stephen told her the next day. *And we want you guys to be there.*

But you're coming back?

He'd shaken his head. *I don't know, Mum. I've been offered a job. It's a brilliant opportunity.*

The hole in Margaret's chest increased as the weeks progressed. It was an erosion. Australia? A day, a life, away. How could she live without them? Her only son. Her grandson?

The love she'd felt when she first held her grandson was exquisite, unlike anything she'd felt before. That familiar-strange child. She could feel the membrane of the world, pulsing in his heartbeat. That tiny heartbeat, reconnecting with your own.

She and Albert clung to one another in their misery. He was the worst she'd ever seen. Withdrawn. Agitated. Haunted at the thought of losing another family.

Can't you see what you're doing to your father?

Stop using Dad as your crutch, Mum.

Margaret had appealed to Lauren. *Aren't you happy here? What more could we give you?*

Nothing. Lauren had held her hand. *You guys are wonderful. It's just . . . I need my own mum too. Look, you can visit any time. You'll have your own room. And we'll come back whenever we can.*

All the soft light that had filled her up, from the moment her son, her grandson, was born. When Margaret had looked and thought, *I know you.*

Gone.

Weeks went by. Weeks of preparation. Weeks of crammed-down despair. That last night they spoke, here in the flat. Albert, hunched on the settee. Margaret, sitting beside him, Paul snuggled into her. Her Bert, who had given everything and asked for nothing in return. Three days before they were leaving for good, Lauren had been showing them pictures of a fancy hotel with a swimming pool. *This is where we're going to have the wedding. There's a waterfall fountain they can switch on–*

It came as barely a whisper. *Don't go*, said Albert. *I'm begging you. Please don't go. I don't think I can bear it.*

Dad, come on, said Stephen. *That's not fair. I've got to do what's best for my family – just like you did for us.*

But we're your family.

It was the pleading in Albert's voice. Narrowing the room. Channelling Margaret's anger.

Stephen, please, will you listen to your father for once? He's begging you. She didn't know her voice could be so cold.

Jesus. Why do you have to be so selfish, Mum?

Selfish? We've given you everything. You're our life, can't you see that?

I know. And I love you both very much.

Aye, do you?

What?

Do you, though? Years of anger, flaring. *What have you ever done for us, Stephen? Do you even see us? All you do is take, take, take. Such a greedy little bastard – always have been.*

Margaret! That's not fair, Lauren had remonstrated.

And you – she'd pointed at Lauren *– you're worse! Coming here and wheedling him away. Ripping up our bloody lives. Your mum has plenty other grandweans over there. We don't. If you leave, we'll have nothing. Can't you see that?*

Right, I've had enough. I'm not listening to this. Come on, Lauren.

And what about Paul? Margaret was half-demented. *Have you asked him what he thinks? Eh, Paulie? Do you want to leave Nana and Grandpa behind and never see us again?*

Mum! Stop, please. Don't drag him into this.
You're the one bloody dragging him! she'd yelled.

Lauren had begun to cry; Paul too, his wee arms tight around Margaret's neck. Harsh words upon harsh words spilling, a flurry of hatefulness. Margaret hasn't chosen to make it a blur: it just is. Blazes of that night return in the sharpest detail, but her brain has obliterated the end. Only the last of her words hang, suspended.

This will kill your father, can't you see?
Christ, Mum, enough!
Margaret, please. Lauren had the cheek to go over to Albert, who was weeping. *You're upsetting everyone.*
Me, stop it? Both of you, you're selfish, cruel, ungrateful bastards. If you go, we will never speak to you again. And we certainly won't be coming to your wedding.

That vile, defiant look on her son's face. *Well, if you don't come to our wedding, I'll never speak to you. I mean it. Mum. Never.*
Fine!

Atoms of herself dissolving, Margaret drained and vacant, like everything she'd ever known had been erased. Realising Lauren was gathering up her grandson. Then a door. Just a door. Just their living-room door, a threshold they'd passed through a thousand times, moving them into another dimension. Margaret never got to kiss wee Paul goodbye. There was the imprint of them, framed in the door, but she could not move. Then it was only the slam. The wooden panels. The slight, residual tremble of the doorknob.

Her flowers whisper. Margaret's hand strays to her neck, to touch the wee gold locket. She's taken to wearing it again. It carries a photo of Paul as a baby. But she's snipped out the image of Stephen, from the snapshot with the trike. Added it to the locket. She doesn't know why; she just wants to have him near her.

Why does the end shadow the beginning? You don't read as many books as Margaret without knowing that it does. The end shines a light back over everything. Changes all the colours in the story. It's the ending that lingers, long after the book is closed.

What will be Margaret's ending? All she can see is struggle. Struggle and solitude. No matter how hard she tries, she can't shake this feeling of dread. Money is a terrible worry, yes, but it's not that. It's the stomach-plummet fall outside the fruit shop. Again and again, she relives it. Coldness of pavement on spine. The weight on her. She holds the locket to her lips. The boy who broke her bones: he must have a mother too.

It's getting chilly. A black shadow flits below a streetlight. A bat! Another tiny darting blur. Definitely bats! Who knew there were bats in the city centre? See, if she was cooped inside with the telly she'd have missed that. She must learn to enjoy small segments of life. Forbid herself from looking too far back or forward. Margaret will be like Burns' wee moose. *The present only toucheth thee . . .* Something something. *An' forward, tho' I cannot see . . .* Something something. The end.

She can't not worry about her finances, though. It's getting worse since she fell behind with her bills. There's never enough money to last the month. It's confusing because she thought she'd get all of Bert's pension after he died. That doesn't appear to be the case. The letters keep referring her to some website, and whenever she's tried to phone all she gets is a disembodied voice telling her to press damn buttons.

Perhaps she should ask Claire? Mind, she's becoming as bossy as Zara. *You really should make a will.* Apparently the new garden is an asset to the flat. Asking her about all sorts – Power of Attorney too. It had infuriated Margaret.

Can we stop discussing my potential dementia and ultimate demise, please?

She thought that was quite a witty riposte. They don't like it, Claire, or Zara, when Margaret stands up for herself. Ach, that's not true – they don't expect it. She does it partly so they don't think she's a charity case. But also – and this is the most frustrating thing – she does it because that's what they tell her to do! *Be honest, Margaret. Don't let me steamroller you, Margaret. It's OK to say no, Margaret. Times have changed, you know.* She's had a lecture on MeToo from Claire. Merely because she'd the temerity to say there are worse things than a man pinching you on the bottom. She thinks of Handsy McGuire, the music master at school. You just took sensible precautions and went to the instrument store in pairs.

Being in the company of younger women has been a revelation. Take gin, for instance. Never touched the stuff, not until Zara brought home a clump of borage (*not porridge, Margaret. Borage!*) and a blue-glass bottle of gin. What a delight! The things you can put in gin! You can have it with lemon or orange, with apple and – Margaret's personal favourite – mint. Apparently, you can also get pink gin, but she thinks that might be taking it too far.

Buoyed by two G&Ts, Margaret asked if Zara would mind dropping off her house keys next time she came round, and, wonder of wonders, Zara shrugged and went 'no bother'. Just like that. She thought Zara would've been angry. Expected her to be cross about the garden too, seeing as Claire instigated that. On the contrary, Zara seemed pleased. Promised not to add anything new without Margaret's say-so and says she and her husband will do the weeding. Margaret feels a little foolish, the way she's been fretting. She brushes a stray petal off her lap. A breeze rustles the leaves. Nice Gordon from upstairs is going to fashion a sort of trellis behind the bench, so she can trail some jasmine over it.

Margaret crosses her ankles. The wooden slats of the bench are getting uncomfortable. She's come out in her sheepskin slippers. She looks at the lumps and bumps of her calves. How did a girl who played hockey end up with legs like this? Yet Margaret can see her old gym shoes as clearly as she can see her varicose veins. Memories are tidal. They push past textures and time and sandstone and sleep. She doesn't think there's any way to change that.

The slam of the close door startles her. 'Alright, missus?' A hooded figure emerges from her tenement. Margaret's right hand flies to her locket, the other steadies her body on the bench. How can she get past him? Will anyone hear? Then she realises it's Jacqueline's foster son, the one with green fingers.

'Oh, hello, Alistair. Lovely evening, isn't it?'

'Aye.' He lumbers down the steps adjacent to where she sits, tucked in the lee of the tenement. 'But watch yourself. It's getting late.'

'Och, you've all made this place so pretty, I just don't want to go in.'

Margaret feels safe in her garden. Even though she's exposed to the elements, forbye the boy just gave her a fright, it's as if a fine silver orb encases her here. Her garden is enchanted. Only through the gate lies the real world.

Alistair sniffs. She braces herself. The boy has an awful habit of spitting.

'Even so. I wouldny want my gran sitting out here by herself. No in the dark.' He looks up the street, as if he's checking it. 'Here.' He offers his arm. 'You want a hand up?'

'Honestly, I'm fine. Two more minutes, then I'm away in.' Margaret smiles at him. 'I promise.'

'Will I get Jackie to come out and gie you company?'

'No, really. I'm very content here on my own. But thank you.'

'Fair enough. I like my own headspace too. It can get helluva crowded in there.'

She can never work out what age he is. Beefy boy. Plump, smooth skin. But eyes that are old.

'How long have you been with Jacqueline now?' she asks.

'Going on six month.'

'Really? That long? And where were you–'

'Got to go, Mrs C. Meeting a pal.' Alistair rummages inside the front of his hooded sweatshirt. There is a large patch pocket there, like a kangaroo pouch.

'Goodness. At this time? Does Jacqueline not mind you going out?'

'Auld Jackie's cool. She knows the score.' He bends his head. Cups his hand, and she sees he is lighting a cigarette.

'Alistair! That's a terrible habit.'

He flicks his lighter shut. Winks at her. 'That's no my worst one. Cheerio now.'

She notices him finger the lavender as he passes. 'We should get some nicotiana,' he calls from the street.

'What's that?' Margaret calls back.

'Tobacco plants.' Alistair grins. 'Serious. They smell great at night.'

The boy has a curious gait. She watches him, swinging up the road, his arms loose, shoulders rolling. Is that . . . his underwear? Should she shout after him, to warn him that his denims are in danger of falling down? Surely he can feel the draught about his nether regions? But she thinks better of it, does not want to embarrass him.

Half a year he's been here. He's actually quite a nice lad, though you wouldn't know from looking at him.

Limbs creaking, she rises to go indoors. Ach, she doesn't mean to be judgemental, but sometimes, Margaret is her mother's daughter. She catches a glimpse of her side window. Sees lamplight glowing through her stained glass sun. She's never looked at it from the outside before. It really is beautiful.

She massages the base of her spine. If tomorrow is sunnier than today, Margaret thinks she will sit on her bench and read a book. With a cushion, mind. But, yes, her brain feels ready to return to reading. She inhales her garden one more time. Under the streetlights, the colours are bleached, as if she's stepped into a sepia photograph. You could imagine a horse and cart trotting by – or even Buffalo Bill's travelling circus. At the top of the road, past the wee park, she notices Alistair greet his friend. Another waif. Alistair towers over him. She places one hand on the railing the council have fitted, so she can climb her steps. Pauses to look again. Are they fighting? They seem to be in urgent conversation, then Alistair puts his arm across the shoulders of the smaller boy. What a kind lad he is. Margaret lets herself into the house, leaving her garden to itself.

Chapter Twenty

Two boys sit on top of a wall. It is waist height, so their legs only dangle slightly. Silhouettes of crosses rise in the foreground, the looming Celtic kind, which are slightly pagan and all the more foreboding. Velvety black sky, with the glow and outlines of the city beyond. Gerard can see the lights from the big hospital by the cathedral. His mum could be in there. Lying on a trolley. Wings swish, an owl hoots, and both boys pretend not to jump. Creatures snuffle in the undergrowth. At least Gerard hopes it's creatures. They have walked all the way to the Necropolis, which should be locked, but Ali knows a way in, a bend in the railings through which they squirmed, so it is fine. The animal (or ghostie) is making a kind of grunting.

'Badger,' says Ali knowledgeably.

It is the spookiest place Gerard's ever been. How has he lived in Glasgow all his life and not known this graveyard's here? How could you miss it? Crazy, like a whole secret town. For starters, it's on a hill full of trees and bushes – and it's ginormous. It appears to go on for miles, with paths and stairs circling up and round. Not just gravestones either; there are proper buildings, actual houses for dead folk, palaces with spires and roofs and great big towering monuments wending their way up the slopes.

'This is mental,' he whispers.

Ali shines the light from his phone beneath his chin. He keeps doing this creepy voice. 'Welcome. To. The Village of the Dead.'

'But why all the weird buildings? I don't get it. You could build proper houses instead.'

'It's all for rich bastards, pal. They couldny take it with them, and I guess they didny want to give it away. Here.'

Ali passes him the bottle. Gerard doesn't like the taste; it makes him think of medicine, but he takes a swally. He's dragged the guy out his house and been gibbering shite at him for ages, so the least he can do is be sociable. He's tried cider and that – he thinks this is just Buckie, so it's not like he's on the hard stuff. Plus he likes how Ali's treating him like a big boy.

Come on, Gerard. Big boys don't say 'big boy'.

He hands the bottle back. Wishes he could phone his mum. There is an unacknowledged terror, beyond the squatting, permanent terror of Mad Davey, that his mum is lying undiscovered in some bushes, life ebbing, as Gerard sits here drinking tonic wine made by monks.

'Right,' says Ali, wiping his mouth. 'So we've talked about the fitba and we've talked about gaming, and I've slagged your manbag, and you've talked about how great your fosters are, and I've even blethered about fucking gardening. D'you wanny tell me why you really called me up? You said it was important.'

Where to begin? Ali knows he wasn't at Guerrillas today, because he seen the barney when Craig turned up to collect Gerard.

'Was he angry? Craig, I mean.'

'Nah. I wouldny say angry. More worried. Tracey was doing her nut, cos she hadny done the register, she was on a course the day. We'd some new lassie called Charlene, and Jiggy had just shouted yes to your name for a laugh. But the girl didny even do a headcount, so by the time Craig turned up looking for you at the finish and Charlene phoned Tracey and Tracey had driven all the way in, it was all kicking off.' Ali picks at the label on the bottle. 'They'd called the polis by then, mate. I'm sorry.'

'Fuck.' He knew they would. 'What did they say? Did they ask yous anything?'

'Ach, just the usual patter. Had anyone seen you the day? Just to say if we had cause nobody would get into trouble. Usual shite. They asked if you'd been upset about anything, and . . .' Ali sniggers. 'That dick Jiggy said, *Aye, he didny get his hole off of Jo.*'

Gerard feels his face grow hot. 'What did she say?'

'Nothing. Nobody said a word. I'm no talking to the pigs, man. Not for nothing. No way.'

'Cheers.'

'Here. Finish it.' Ali gives him the dregs of the bottle. Gerard chugs it down. While the drink rasps his throat, it is beginning to warm his chest. Warm clouds are gathering inside. He feels a wee bit floaty. Everything bad that's happening to him is still there, but it's fuzzy. Like the shadows on the gravestones. There's one over there that looks like a bus shelter.

He hears Ali cough, then spit. 'So, you alright, wee man? What happened?'

Gerard's not sure he can put today into words. Maybe it will make sense, though, if he tries. 'Know my mum, right?'

'Aye.'

'And how I'm no with her. How I'm under supervision, that's how I'm wi Kris and Craig, right?'

'Aye.'

'Well, she's no been in touch for ages.'

'Junkie.' It drops from Ali's mouth, flatly. Unremarkably. The floaty feeling bursts.

'What did you say?' Gerard slides from the wall, ready to defend his mother.

'Cool it mate, alright? Ali also stands, but only so he can push Gerard back onto the wall. 'Cool your jets, OK?'

Gerard is shaking. He stares straight ahead, trying to focus on all the different layers and veils of grey he can see. A tree, gnarled and lush with darkened leaves. A triangular pillar. The bus-stop grave, which, now he looks closely at it, seems more like a mini bandstand, the kind you get in old parks. Sweet malty smells coil up from the brewery on Duke Street. His house used to be on that street. He wonders if his bike is still locked inside, or if some other family lives there now.

Ali taps his arm. 'It's no your fault, pal.'

'I know. But I hate when folk say that.'

'Yir maw's a junkie hoor.' Ali does a whiny chant, as if they're in the playground.

'No, she's not!'

'No, that's what I used to get.'

'Oh.'

'Anyway. Your maw's went off the radar–'

'Aye, but that's just it. Then she messaged me out the blue. Telt me I'd to go and . . . ach, shit, man. Ma heid's mince. Point is' – Gerard pats his manbag – 'I've got this thing she wants, and I didny even know what it was, but she telt me to get it off my gran, and I went to meet her the day, to give it to her, and this guy jumps us. Fucking battered my maw.'

'Shit, man.'

'I know.'

'She OK?'

Gerard shrugs. It is the tiniest gesture, yet it threatens to ripple through his ribcage. He is going to cry, he knows he is, so he rushes over the thought he cannot think: that she's lying there, alone, and he has left her. 'I don't know. I never seen him hit her, but he pure went for her, and she told me to run, and now I think he must be after me, the guy, and I canny go home – back to Craig's, I mean, and I'm feart he's gonny go for the weans too so I canny go there and . . . fuck, I don't know where my mum is now and I don't know what to do.'

He is squeezing the life out his manbag. Swallowing snot. He wants to spit like Ali, like he doesn't give a shit. Through blurry eyes, he sees a carving of a skull and crossbones on a tombstone. His mouth twitches. Now he can't stop thinking of all the rotten bones beneath his feet too. Why would they want to remind you what happens when you go in the ground? He feels Ali clap his back. 'That's some heavy shit, mate.' Ali makes a sucking sound with his teeth. 'Right. You need to lay low for a while. Get your head together.'

'But I'm gonny get into so much trouble.'

'How?'

'I skipped Guerrillas.'

'Ach, just say you got your days mixed up. Or some boys chased you the day, before the bus came.'

'But I've not went back to my fosters.'

Ali thinks for a little bit. 'How about you banged your head? Naw, the boys chasing you banged your head. Here, I could gie you a couple of bruises–'

'No. And I've no answered any of my messages. There's hunners from my social worker too.'

'Concussion. Definitely. Go for the sympathy vote, man. It's no really a lie anyroad. You got scared, then you got confused.'

Gerard isn't sure. He's so very tired, though, and his head is so sore that he needs to have Ali tell him what to do.

'Two things. One, where you gonny go the night, and two, what the fuck's in your gay-bag?'

Gerard takes the book from the satchel.

'What is it?'

'A book.'

Ali slaps the back of Gerard's head. Not roughly. 'I can see that, smart-arse.'

In the murk of the graveyard, Ali shines his phone torch on the cover.

'It's a book I had as a wean,' Gerard explains. 'My da–'

No more words. A lid goes down. A clanging explosion of light and dark and sparking metal. He shakes his head, furiously, trying to jettison the image of the gun that's been lurking there all day. Trying not to see the blood, not hear the screaming. He can't remember if it was his mum or his daddy. He thinks the loudest screaming is his daddy, because he hears it right inside his ear, his ear was hurting and shapes were moving above his bed, angry angles of elbows, grabbing, his daddy roaring and greeting, Gerard's face, his pillow, wet with red. His daddy canny walk. He must of fallen because blood's pouring from his knees. The bedroom smells of butcher-shop, is hot and moist with terror. His daddy's on his bleeding, broken knees, being dragged away. Gerard tries to reach or push, his arms are hurting; he is swimming through spinning air, as if he's tied and hurtling on a wheel. He knows it is cold, yet he is boiling. And he knows it is a gun, a big, long brown one, because he sees it raised and swung and smashing into his daddy's face. In the distance, he hears a voice call his name. He can't remember his daddy's voice, but he doesn't think it's him cause his dad's mouth is gushing blood and the voice is saying his name again, but he does not want to leave nor unsee the crimson gouts of blood because it is the closest he has ever been; he could reach out and wipe the matted hair from his daddy's eyes; it is like a hologram around him, and his daddy is the brightest, most vivid person he has ever seen with his bright blue eyes which do not leave Gerard's face, not even as the men are pulling him away from the mess on Gerard's bed.

'Ho! Jez, man!' Arms, shaking him. 'Gerard. Fucking quit it!'

'Leave me alone!' He lashes out, makes contact with a fleshy cheek.

'Jesus fuck, ya mental case – it's me!' A greater bulk than he is forcing him to the ground. Gerard, lying in the dirt in a graveyard, looking at the stars. Angels glare down at him. Stone wings. Unmoving faces. The shouting in his head abates, becomes the low roar from the motorway.

'What the actual fuck, Damien?' Ali helps him sit up. 'You been taking something?'

His teeth are chittering, or maybe they are totally still and it's the ground that jerks and spasms.

'Just breathe, pal. Breathe.'

'I'm alright,' Gerard mumbles. If he presses his face into his knees, really, really hard, that will make the jittering stop. Drive his kneecaps into his brain. He could. Black stars burst from the pressure on his eyes. He follows Ali's instructions. *In* and *out*. *In* and *out*. Nudges the image of his dad back to the surface, testing himself, like after a doing, when you're checking your bruises. Seeing if your legs can take your weight. Usually, a silence would fall after his mum had given him a battering – a kind of muffling – and in that space, Gerard's learned the art of bringing all the scattered pieces of himself back together. He rocks a wee bit. Breathes. This is no different.

'I think I seen my dad get killed.' His lips vibrate against his jeans. He can't look up yet.

'What?'

'I think we were reading that book when my da got shot.'

'Jesus fuck.'

'I think, if you open it, there'll be blood inside. I can mind it spraying. He was sitting on my bed when they came in. Kind of sprawling. I think he was trying to put the book under my pillow.'

'Fuck, man. What age were you?'

'Maybe four?' Was he at school? He canny mind. Each fragment of life entwined with his dad is vague, apart from this one, which is vicious-bright. 'Four or five.' He raises his head, in time to see the horror on Ali's face.

'Can I see the book over?' Gerard asks.

'What? Aye, aye.'

Slowly, Gerard flicks through the pages. 'Can you hold your phone up?'

'Aye, sure.' Ali is crouched beside him, shining a light on the book and Gerard's fingers. When you open it, there are words on one side and a picture on the other. There is a picture of a lady in a barrel, or a wee boat? He thinks it's a boat. Then one of a boy with a robin perched on his finger. Another page shows a man with a cart and two bulls. Then there is a lady, a queen, crying, and the same man, pointing to a river. There is other writing too, pen writing, scrawled over the whiteness of the water. It is only when you turn to the back of the book that the spots of blood begin to show. By the time you close it and look at the back cover, you can see most if it is crusted with a spreading, dark stain. Gerard rests his finger on the stain.

'Don't, man.' Ali takes the book off him.

'I don't think they killed him.'

'No?'

'No. Not then. I mind his eyes were moving, and he was

making noises. Right up till they took him away.' Gerard nods. 'I'm positive.'

'But he never came back?'

'Nope.'

'Fuck. man. Who were they? Where did they take him?'

'I don't know.'

'And you're only just remembering it the now?'

Gerard considers this. 'I can mind wee bits of it, sometimes. Just like wee bits of smashed glass, know? But then I make myself forget.'

'I get that.' Ali rubs his chin. Then his hand travels all the way up his face and through his hair. 'Fucksake, wee man. I'm sorry.'

Ali's torch dances little cones of light across the graveyard. Glances off mossy columns and blackened vegetation. Gerard holds the night air in his mouth. Two eye-shaped glints return the reflection of the torch, less than twenty feet from where they sit. Must be the beastie that's been rummaging in the brambles. The badger. Gerard's never seen a badger, not a live one anyway. He's seen a dead one by the side of the road. Big as a dog, but its wee paws were curled soft, like a cat's. Ali's torch bounces on, but now Gerard knows where to look. He lets his gaze become accustomed to the gloom. Can see a glimmer of gentle motion, perhaps the curve of its back as it turns and shuffles off. He doesn't think Ali's seen it. Possibly no one's ever seen this badger except Gerard. Somehow, this makes the wound he's opened bearable. He can still feel it hurting, throbbing away inside him, but it's always been there. Pretending it isn't doesn't stop kitchen cupboards from wavering in and out. Doesn't stop words from melting or his nails from digging in. He loves how the badger doesn't give a toss, how it's just been snuffling and eating slaters as Gerard's soul is smashed to smithereens. Brock the badger, rocking on, living his best life. It feels a wee bit like a miracle to have seen it.

He realises he has no idea where his dad is buried. If he is buried.

'Mate, honest. I'm really sorry.'

The storybook was about miracles. Gerard's sure. The boy brings the robin back to life.

'It was a long time ago. I never really knew him.'

'Aye, but even so. You were just a wean.'

'Yup.'

'Here.' There is a soft *phut*. 'Have a can.'

Gerard drinks greedily. The lager tastes fishy, but he doesn't care. The more he drinks, the easier he becomes. It's like the alcohol is painting him a different colour. Brightening him. Soothing him.

'What did your mum say?' Ali asks.

'What d'you mean?'

'Afterwards, like. What did she tell you?'

Gerard thinks a while. There is a gap there. 'I don't know. She went away, I think. Aye, she must of been expecting my wee brother.' He tries to concentrate. 'I think that must be when I went into foster care. The first time. But, no . . . wait.' He shuts his eyes. Another memory is forming. He's in his room, and there's a woman crying, but it's not his mum. She's crying and cuddling him and rocking him, and there's something hard in his chest. He can see her arms around him, arms in a stripy, scratchy jumper, and fingers with orange-painted nails, clasping his hands, which are holding tightly onto his book. This storybook. Men with dark trousers and boots are stripping the covers from his bed, and telling them to get out, saying they've *told* her to take him back downstairs. He can hear the man's gruff voice distinctly say *Take the kid to yours. We'll question him later.*

'I think I maybe went to my gran's?' How does he know it was his gran? He doesn't, only that he can sense himself lying in the hollow below her heart. And she doesn't feel like a stranger. 'Anyway.' Purposefully, Gerard seizes hold of the nearest gravestone, yanks himself to his feet. 'My arse is getting corners sitting here. D'you think I should just go back to my fosters? Tell them everything?'

Craig and Kris are clever people. They'll know what to do. What they'll do is send him away.

'Christ, man, I dunno. What if the guy *is* after you? Do you no mind anything about him?'

'Only that he's got a tattoo on his arm–'

'What of?' Ali is sparking a cigarette. Maybe he'll offer him a draw. Fucking aye. He wants a fag. Gerard is enjoying this . . . looseness in him. He tries to pinpoint what, other than the wobbliness, is different.

It's his head. His heart. They've stopped clamouring.

'What's it of?' Ali repeats.

'Ach, dunno. Some weird symbol. I seen him before too, outside our house. Our old house.'

'When was that?'

'Couple of months ago. When we stayed out this way.'

'Did yous? Whereabout?' Ali blows smoke through pursed, pinched lips. He looks cool as fuck.

'Duke Street. Above the burger place.'

'That right? How come I've no seen you kicking about?'

Because I'm just a baby. Gerard holds his fleeing head. His body is fluid with Buckfast and beer. No one talked about their age at Guerrillas. Should he admit he was only a primary seven? Was in a gang called the Broncos? He's not even that now; he's in limbo. If Ali were to laugh at him, to look at him like he's even less than he is, Gerard will . . .

He doesn't know. So he ignores the question.

'Oh – and I seen him again a few weeks back, in Shawlands. His name's Davey. That's all I know.'

'Was your mum there? At Shawlands?'

'Not that time, no.'

'So he *is* following you then, right enough?'

'I guess. Fuck.'

Ali's pretending not to, but Gerard can see him looking at his phone. Excluding him. 'Listen, mate. I'm on a curfew.' A drift of laughter comes from the slope below. Three or four figures weaving their way up the path.

'That'll be the nightshift,' says Ali.

'What?'

'Plenty folk use this as a howff. We should probably head.'

'Where?'

Ali begins to walk. Did he not hear him? Ali's sorted; he has a place to go. Has he not listened to a word Gerard's said? The drunken men approach their level of the graveyard. Ali acknowledges them with a brusque *How's it going, guys?*, but Gerard presses himself into the rough bark of the tree until they pass. The nice, floaty feeling ruptures. He thought Ali would help. Gerard's either bugging him, or boring the arse off him. Why is he such a misfit? He can never read signals. What has he done so wrong, to make him so apart? He feels the tree shiver, sees the gravestones swaying, rocking back and forth, and his body rocks with them. Falling back into the loneliness that engulfs him. He wants to curl into a wee ball. Pull the covers over and hide until the morning.

'Look,' Ali's by his side again. 'Headcase. Why don't you come back to mine?'

The graveyard glides slowly to a stop. 'Won't your foster mum mind?' Tiny crumbs of bark are on his lips. The tree is surprisingly smooth.

'She'll mind more if I stay out all night or if I leave you here. She's sound, Jacqueline. Trust me. She'll know what to do. C'mon, tree-hugger.'

They make their way along the path, clamber down the stone steps and cut out through the gap in the fence. Past the back of the hospital, down the broad road which will take them on to Duke Street.

'Did you know,' says Ali, 'there used to be a river here? See how we're in a dip?'

'Aye.' Gerard eyes Ali's cigarette. There's not much remaining. Ali is devouring it. 'Can I get a draw of your fag?'

'Naw. Well, the river gushed down here, wide as the street, all the way to the Drygate. That's how there's a brewery there – they used the water to power it.'

'How no?'

'It's my last one. Och, fucksake. Here.'

The cigarette is on him too quick. He's been watching how Ali held it. Not with V-shaped fingers, but tight and mean. Gerard tries to emulate Ali's thirsty suck. Immediately, his head swims. He suppresses a cough. Holds it, holds it, then speaks. 'Cheers, man.' Hands the cigarette back. 'So where is it now? The river?'

'Under the ground, I suppose.'

The taste in his mouth is disgusting. He's not eaten anything since breakfast. 'How d'you know this stuff? About plants and that too?'

Ali stops for a minute. Grinds the fag dowt out with his shoe. 'Do folk think you're thick as shit, Gerard?'

'Aye.'

'Me too. And does it make you fucking sick?'

'Aye.'

'Well, don't let them. You can learn stuff anywhere. You can google anything you like – at the library if you've no got data on your phone.'

'Aye, I do that sometimes.'

'Good. You can go to community centres too, get stuff off TV. You can just ask folk questions, know? I got talking about roses to a parkie, this old boy working at Tollcross. Thought I was taking the piss at first, but when he seen I wasn't, he pure loved it. Let me in the greenhouses, do a wee bit of potting.'

'Ha ha, very funny.'

'Whit?'

'Potting? You and some old boy, smoking a spliff.'

'Prick.' He slaps Gerard's head again. Gerard quite likes it. It's a language he understands. Sort of thing a big brother would do. 'Brand new, so he was. Got me signed up for a gardening course and everything.'

'Was it any good?'

'Havny a scooby. Couldny be arsed going. But that's no the point. I could of, if I'd wanted to. You can even go into museums and that, for free. I done a history walk round here. I canny mind who ran it, but I do mind the woman saying this road used to be a river. Look – there's a bridge to prove it.'

Ali points upwards. Sure enough, the dark arch of a bridge stretches from the graveyard, which rises over them now, to span the road, and lead to the cathedral on the other side. They pass underneath. Gerard feels woozy. He's not sure he likes cigarettes. Or Buckie for that matter.

'Seriously, Jez. Knowing stuff is addictive. It gets like joining the dots after a while. All they wee random facts folk tell you, all the crap they say you've got to learn? Well, fuck that. You learn what *you* want to know. Tell you, folk look at you different when you can tell them . . . well, anything really. Anything they wereny expecting to come out your mouth, know? Just show them you're no dumb. Plus, the more you do it, the more stuff you learn, then it all starts to make sense. All they wee bits kindy join up. Knowledge is power, my friend.'

Shouts, and a bottle smashing somewhere in the graveyard. Wavery bridge, wavery road. They are both definitely a wee bit pished. Gerard hasn't a clue what Ali's talking about, but he does like the fact he's walking over a hidden river. He really hopes those drunks don't find the badger.

*

'Wake up, fannybaws.' A low and urgent voice. A hand, roughly shaking him. Sticky eyes, blearing at an unfamiliar wall. Mouth in which a badger has definitely died.

Gerard rolls over. Realises he's on a floor. Carpet burns his elbows. Bed above, shielding him. He is tucked in the space between the divan and the window.

Ali's face looms. 'Right, listen,' he hisses. 'You just turned up, alright? You've been wandering the streets all night and I've just let you in, OK?'

'Aye. OK.' Gerard is struggling to right his brain; it's as upside down as the rest of him. Gradually, then rapidly, yesterday comes flooding back. 'Why?'

'No point in us both getting an interrogation, is there?'

'Are the polis here?' he whispers, sitting upright.

'No. But I can hear Jacqueline moving about.' Ali tilts his head. Sounds of banging. A child, wailing. 'That's Ryan, wanting his Frosties. So we're just gonny go through and face the music, OK?'

'OK.'

Ali is pulling a sweatshirt over his head. Gerard tugs his arm. 'But what do we say?'

'We say . . . *you* say . . . fuck. See the less lies you say, the more it works, right?'

'Right.'

'So. Do you want to say about Mad Davey? And the book?'

'No! No way, man. Not till I've spoke to my mum. I don't want to make things worse.'

Ali sniffs a sock, then tugs it on. 'Fine. Gonny pat your hair down or something? You look mental.'

Gerard smooths his fingers through his hair. Catches a flavour of his teeth. Man, his breath is putrid. He needs to find some toothpaste. Or a drink of water.

'So,' continues Ali, 'say you dyked Guerrillas cause you were meeting your mum, aye?'

'But why will I say I was meeting her then?'

'Cause you wanted to see her, ya fud! You've no heard fae her in ages, then she calls you up. Course you'd want to see her. No questions asked. And if they do ask anything, just say you were feart they wouldny let you see her. That always works.'

'OK.' Gerard fumbles for his trainers. His fingers shrink from something soft and crispy. Crusty hankies, under Ali's bed. 'What do I say about Davey, but?'

'I dunno. Just say some randomer jumped yous. How would they know any different?'

'True.' It's nice to have a person to bounce things off of. Somebody a wee bit smarter, but totally on your wavelength. Who doesn't make you feel like a dick. Despite what he's heading into, Gerard relaxes a little. It's as if he can take off his anxiety for a bit, just give it a wee rest. Someone else is taking the load. It's what he used to do for Anthony.

'So. You were absolutely terrified, and you ran away. Pure lost your mind, forgot where you stayed. You decide. Here' – Ali indicates the manbag. Gerard's forgotten all about this; his guts twist. 'You want me to keep your book? Just till you talk to your maw?'

'Aye. OK. Maybe.' What will he do with it? The book with his dad's blood inside.

'Well, stash it under my bed the now.'

He does as he's told. 'What age are you?' Gerard asks stupidly. But age is important.

'Fifteen. How?'

'No reason.'

'Right. Let's do this.'

Gerard doesn't want to leave *A Ring of Gold* with jizz-soaked tissues. He removes the book from its hiding place. Returns it to his manbag.

'I'm just gonny keep it on me.'

'Fair enough. M'on then.'

'But, Ali, what will I say about–'

'Fuck, man. Let's just wing it, eh?'

They go through to the kitchen. Blue cupboards, chipped worktop. Yellow strip light and a smoke alarm overhead. The kitchen is neither big nor small, just comfy enough to take a round table, four seats and a baby's high chair. Cooking smells fill the air. Dishes are piled in the sink and on the draining board. Bright magnets cover the fridge, pinning pictures and letters in place. Scuffed boots lie on a grubby vinyl floor, beneath a row of coat hooks piled with jackets. A woman in a floral quilted dressing gown has her back to them. Elbow raised as she butters toast. He feels at home here. The room shrinks to give him a hug. You could fit four of these kitchens into Kris and Craig's big white one, in their shiny house the size of a tenement. If you don't count Gerard, there's only four of them. Four people to fill three whole floors of house.

Four people in this room too, for there's a fat toddler in the high chair, banging his fist and demanding food. When he spots Ali and Gerard he waves and goes 'Bye-ya.'

Gerard feels his breast expand. Such an urge to cuddle his wee sister again. Tuck her head below his chin.

'Oh, hello.' The woman turns round. 'Look what the cat dragged in. And who's this?'

'My mate, Jez. Jez, meet Jacqueline. Jacqueline the Terrible.'

Jacqueline pretends to swat Ali with her buttery knife. 'I'll gie you terrible.'

'How you doing?' Gerard says shyly.

'Nice to meet you, son. I take it yous'll be wanting some breakfast?'

Ali pulls out a seat, nods at Gerard to do the same. 'Aye, lovely, Jacqueline. That would be lovely, please and thank you. Good morning, little Ryan. How are we?'

'Lally!'

'Lally yourself.'

Jacqueline puts some fingers of toast in front of the toddler. 'What time did yous stroll in, then?'

Gerard can't believe she's so casual. Kris and Craig would have a fit if they didn't know where he was, or when he got home.

Are having a fit.

'I was home by midnight. As per instructions. Jez just came round the now.'

'Did he, by God?' Jacqueline squints at them both. 'Funny how I never heard him. And I've been up for hours.'

'Aye, aye. Came round dead early so he did. We've just been talking in my room.'

'That right?'

'Aye!' Ali hams up the indignance. 'Swear to God.'

'When was the last time you were in church, Alistair McDougall?'

'Fucking Sunday just past.'

'Don't swear in front of the wean. And don't tell me porkies either.'

'Straight up.' He gives Jacqueline a huge and charming grin. 'That's how come I know Jez. We go to the same church. Ave Maree-ee-a.'

Jacqueline pure glares at him. Gerard tenses. Waits for the shouting to begin. It's so obviously bullshit that Ali's flogging. The cue for a leathering, if he took the piss out his mum like that. Occasionally, his mum would open her mouth to shout, and simply deflate instead. Gerard, draining the life from her. Either way, it was horrible, and never worth the brash, glorious moment of cheek that went before.

Jacqueline lays a plate of toast and scrambled egg down for Ali, then Gerard. 'Would you like to say grace, son? Before we eat?'

'What?'

She and Ali both burst out laughing, then Ryan joins in, spitting toast.

Gerard studies the table, which isny even proper wood; it's fake, the edges peeling to reveal chipboard underneath. His lower jaw begins to tremble; he can see his petted lip, not see it but sense it, hazy through his eyelashes.

'Ach, you don't have to say grace, son. We're only bantering. Only way I can deal with this yin. Here, what is it? Don't look so upset.'

Ali speaks through a mouthful of food. 'He's run away fae home.'

'What?' Jacqueline clatters cutlery on the table. 'Use a fork, you.'

'Well, no exactly run away. But he's in a wee bit of bother. And I telt him you were the woman to know what to do.'

Then Jacqueline is leaning over Gerard, one flowery arm cuddling his shoulder. 'What's up, son? What is it?'

He goes rigid. Jacqueline persists. She strokes his hair, fingertips barely making contact, and he wants to scream. Ali begins to feed Ryan. Fury creeps its way around Gerard's body, undercut with longing. It is the worst feeling, pushing you and pulling you until you break. Folk touching him do that. Jacqueline smells kind, and safe. But she doesn't know a thing about him.

'You tell me what you want to tell me, son. Let me see if I can help.'

Son and sun. Gerard needs warmth, needs light. Gerard is too tired. Unless Davey kills them, there is nothing worse that can really happen. He goes to explain the story as he and Ali discussed: that a man started shouting at his mum, and Gerard got scared and fled. It doesn't come out that way, though. He's been having the conversation in his head already, and what if Jacqueline thinks he didn't protect his mum? So he embellishes it some more. Gerard's mum asked to see him, and he waited and he waited. But she didn't come. So he started crying. Then some big boys chased him, and he got scared and ran away. Hid for ages, had a panic attack. Forgot where he was and everything. Jacqueline soothes him with tuts and *och, pet*s. When he gets to the end, he feels unburdened, though he's barely told any truth. In the embrace of this kitchen, nothing feels as bad. He never even saw his mum get hit. Maybe it's all going to be fine. He doesn't know for sure if Davey *is* mental. He might be her boyfriend. So even if he did hit Gerard's mum, it might not be that bad.

'Well, pet.' One final mauling, then Jacqueline releases him. 'First things first. We need to phone your mum. She'll be worried sick.'

'I don't live with my mum.'

'Oh.'

'Oh, did we not say?' Ali chips in. 'Jez is in my gang. One of the reject brigade.'

'Aye. I live with foster carers. That's how I was so keen to see my mum, know?'

'Fucksake, Alistair. Could you not have told me that at the start?' Jacqueline's fists are on her hips. 'Right, son. Who's your social worker? What office do they work fae? I need your full name. And I want the name of your foster parents too.'

The change in tone unsettles Gerard. Why is she angry? He's the same boy she was cuddling two seconds ago; the same shit just happened to him. Same as when social workers call Anthony cute and cheeky for the exact same behaviour that gets Gerard branded a thug. It isn't fair, and he doesn't understand it.

'You know them, actually,' says Ali. 'It was you who telt his foster to try out Guerrillas. That's how come we really know each other.'

'Christ, Alistair! What the hell were you thinking?'

Ryan begins to cry. Jacqueline scoops the toddler out the high chair and onto her hip. 'How d'you think this looks for me? Harbouring a runaway? I could lose my fucking registration!'

'We havny done anything wrong, you auld bitch!' Ali leaps from his chair, nose inches from hers. 'You're aye saying *ooh, come to me* if I've a fucking problem. Fucking giving it all *trust me, Ali. I know you've been let down*. Well, we had a fucking problem–'

Gerard canny take the shouting; he's forgot how calm it is in Kris and Craig's, he cannot move but he wants to disappear and his fight or flight is kicking in, the adrenaline souping up his brain.

'Aye, but it's not my problem, is it?' Jacqueline shouts, loud enough to stun Ryan into silence. Gerard recognises the shock, then the crumple of the baby's face. Sickened, he slides from his chair, makes his way to the door.

'Here! Wait, son,' Jacqueline calls. 'Och, I'm sorry. I didny mean that. Take the wean, you.'

She catches Gerard's arm, draws him back into the kitchen. 'I shouldny have said that. I'm sorry. Please don't go. And Alistair . . .' Jacqueline turns to Ali, who is cradling Ryan. Face scarlet. She rests the back of her hand against his flaming cheek, but soft, like. Gerard doesn't think she's going to hurt him. 'You're right, son. You're absolutely right. I'm sorry to you too. I am an auld bitch.'

'No, you're no.' Ali looks away from her, his eyes too bright and gleaming.

Jacqueline still has her mitts on Gerard too. He doesn't know what to do. 'Right then. Jez, is it?'

'Mmm.' His heartbeat slows. But his brain's still hyper. The kitchen shimmers. Jelly walls. He forces his mouth to work. 'Gerard.'

'Gerard what?'

'Gerard Macklin. My foster's Craig?'

'Craig? Oh, posh Craig wi the big car? Lives over on the Southside.'

'That's him.'

'Do you know his number?'

Gerard shakes his head. 'It's on my phone.'

'Where's your phone?'

'Here.'

'Do you want to phone him or will I?'

'You. Please.'

'Right you are.' She fiddles with Gerard's mobile. 'It's no working.'

'I switched if off.' He takes it from her, presses the button at the side, then chucks it back as another string of messages beep and trill, filling the kitchen with angry birdsong. Gerard faces the wall as she speaks. Would stick his fingers into his ears too, if he thought he could get away with it. Bouncing on the balls of his feet, staring at a wallpaper of fake bricks. Desperate to run.

Jacqueline is kind. She notices, goes into the hall to make the phone call. Neither Ali nor Gerard speak. Only wee Ryan keeps chattering his nonsense, until Gerard hears a long, low-pitched *oh* coming from the other side of the door, and Jacqueline saying, 'Yes, yes. I'll tell him.'

She enters the kitchen, Gerard's phone held against her mouth. 'Oh, son,' she says, with her face all warped. 'It's your mammy.'

Chapter Twenty-One

Claire removes her specs. The flicker of her computer is giving her a migraine. She checks through the glass partition. All the lights in the main office are off. She doesn't like this sugar cube of an office she's been moved to, but at least she's visible to the casual glance. They locked her in the building once. Before she got promoted, when she worked upstairs, the last person out had locked up and set the alarm, assuming no one else would still be there.

Claire was. Catching up on Saturday mornings (having now learned the alarm code off by heart) is much less embarrassing than staying late. She wasn't totally lying to Margaret that time she cancelled. Weekends, she can work uninterrupted – no calls, no emails. Nobody to notice how far behind she is. She's trying hard to accept she will always be behind; that's the nature of her job. To constantly plate-spin while catching every random new dish chucked at her from leftfield. Having some semblance of being in control makes her less anxious. Claire will never reach the bottom of her in-tray, but she can at least rotate the papers in the pile.

One last thing before she heads. She clicks on the Registers of Scotland website. After this, she's going to see Margaret, but she can't stay long. For this evening, Claire Urquhart Has A Date.

Kind of.

Her stomach corkscrews when she thinks about it. Twice she's considered cancelling, especially here, in her office where she can legitimately say *I'm really busy at work*. But she hasn't. Both times, something has stayed her hand. She's got the email written. Could send it at any point.

Hope, maybe? Yes, hope.

Margaret's words, not hers.

Hope in change. God, how she wants that. Can't imagine any human being who does not.

But she's frightened.

Dateman is really nice. Grant. She's met him once before at a CPD seminar on Contract and Property Disputes (a hotbed of sexual tension). There might actually have been a hint of low-level flirting, but Claire being Claire advised herself she was imagining it. He works with one of her pals from uni, who's throwing a thirty-fifth birthday dinner, twenty folk, mostly couples, blah blah blah, the usual. She swithered about accepting, but then Grant himself emailed to say how pleased he was she was going, and that it would be great to see her again. Done via their respective work emails, but even so. A kind of date, with a kind of man she kind of already likes. Hence the knotted stomach.

She scrolls through the Search Sheet again, just to be certain. A lot of properties in Dennistoun haven't yet been moved to digital and can only be found on the old Sasine Register, which involves a whole faff of sending off for copy records. But the premises at 45 Hillfoot Street are definitely listed on the Land Register. What's puzzling Claire is that she's downloaded the title sheet, and it's still listed under the name of Albert Camberg, owner. She's checked with Companies House too, in case it's the registered business name which hasn't been changed, although the shopfront has. But Camberg Tailors ceased trading nine months ago – which is presumably when Albert's 'boy', Donald, took it over.

Despite Margaret insisting she doesn't need a will, Claire has been pulling bits and pieces together, just to show her the value of her assets. So many old folk don't bother when they've no one left to inherit their estate. But you still need to make provisions.

She's compiled a folder with a rough valuation of Margaret's flat, some suggestions for how she may wish to itemise the contents. She'll simply leave the information with Margaret, no pressure. Stress that, given her assets, a will really is a good idea. Of course it's for Margaret to decide. What kind of a friend is Claire, though, if she doesn't try to advise? Methodical, lawyerly Claire. Who diligently did this one final trawl to make sure Margaret has no outstanding interests with her husband's former business.

She stares again at the screen, pen tapping teeth. When she checked Companies House for Denholm & Serge, there was nobody by the name of Donald listed. The sole director is a Scott Brown. Claire scribbles down the exact wording on the title sheet. Then takes a screenshot too. Just in case.

*

Margaret's made scones. Lavender scones.
'From my garden.'
'Very nice.' Claire doesn't like them. Too perfumed. 'Listen. I can't stay long. But there's something I wanted to talk to you about.'
'That's fine, dear. I was thinking of taking a walk to the library anyway. There's a thing called Stitch and Bitch that looks quite fun. Thought I might give crochet a go. Make a wee old lady blanket for my knees.'
Claire regards her. 'I never know if you're joking or not.'
'Just assume I am always sweetness and light.'
'Someone's in a good mood.'
'Well, I am feeling better. I . . .' Margaret stops mid-flow. Half rises from her chair, pushing up so she can see out of the window. 'There's a police car outside.'
'Could be for anywhere.'
'No, I think they're coming in here. Maybe it's about the court case?' Her eyes widen.
'I told you. I don't think there's going to be any court case.'
'Did I tell you I've asked to speak to him?' Margaret keeps

her gaze on the window. 'My juvenile assailant? Well, for him to write to me.'

'Why on earth would you want to do that?'

Margaret's distracted. She makes her way into the hall, though the doorbell hasn't rung. Claire follows. 'Margaret, I'm not sure about this.'

'Shh!' They hear a loud rap, but it comes from across the close.

'They've gone to Jacqueline's,' Margaret hisses. 'Oh dear. I hope nothing's wrong.'

'Maybe that boy she fosters? Did you not say he was a bit dodgy?'

'He's a very nice lad, actually. It might be about those French girls, I suppose.'

'What French girls?'

'The ones up the stairs. They like their music loud.'

'Can we get back to the whole getting in touch with your attacker scenario, please?'

'Why?'

'Well, have you really thought it through? I thought . . . I know it made you scared, and unsettled. But you're doing awful well now. Will this not rake it all up again?'

Margaret unpresses her ear from the front door, the better to stare at Claire. There's a haze of tiredness there. 'Do you think it's gone away?'

'No, I suppose not. I'm sorry. Forget what I said. You do what you think's right. You don't have to answer to me.'

Margaret returns to the living room. She stands in front of the bay window, which affords the best view of the street. 'No, dear, I don't. But I do appreciate your concern. I've thought about it. A lot. I can take it at my own pace, they say. All I've done is initiate the process. I've said he can write to me, if he wants.'

'But why?'

'Because I want to know if he's sorry. I want to understand why he did it. Why he picked on me.'

'Oh, Margaret.' Claire catches her by the elbows. 'Look at me. It was a totally random thing. He saw your purse in your bag, and went for it. Not you. I bet he didn't even *look* at you.'

'Well.' She is defiant. 'Maybe I want him to.'

'Fair enough. I get that.'

Margaret crosses her arms. In the light from the window, she is gossamer. 'It's done via a third party. I can respond to his letter, if I want to. Tell him how I feel. I imagine it'll be censored, mind – like the war!' She smiles wanly.

'Do you think a kid like that would agree to it, though?'

'The thing is – he has.'

'Really?' Claire unpicks this. The boy's expression when she passed him in the street. It's been a while; it doesn't haunt her any more. But she can remember the glaze of tears. How distraught he seemed. If it was an act, who would he have been acting for?

'I did wonder, though – will it mean he gets a reduced sentence?' says Margaret. 'Would that be why he's doing it?'

'That's not how it works. Because he's under supervision, he'll have a whole load of conditions attached, sure, but like attending social work meetings or anger management. I doubt they'd coerce a child to get involved with . . .' She doesn't want to say *victim*. 'I'm surprised he's even eligible to take part. Are you positive?'

'They say it's a pilot scheme. And, because he's a minor, it's unlikely we'll have any sort of face to face. But, if I ever do meet him, I'd really like you to be there with me.'

'Oh.' A wee punch of joy in Claire's solar plexus. 'Yes. Yes, of course, I would.'

'Good. That's settled, then.' Margaret resumes her seat.

'Are you sure you'd want me? Not someone like Zara? I mean, I'd be all, "Right, you, I'm about to interrogate you"–'

'You'd be looking out for me. And hopefully you'd let me do the talking.'

This seems as opportune a time as any. Claire settles her buff folder on the oak side table. 'Talking of looking out for you – and I know you said you didn't want one – but I've put a wee package together about the benefits of a will.'

The room cools. Margaret clasps her hands. 'Why? I told you I wasn't interested.'

'Because I'm your friend, Margaret. And it's my job.'

'Are you expecting a commission?'

'No! For goodness sake. Of course not. Look, can you just forget going in a huff with me, please? Just for a wee minute.'

'I'm not "in a huff". It's a perfectly legitimate–'

'The point is, when I was digging about, I came across this.' Claire slides her phone over. The photograph of the title sheet is open, zoomed in on the name of the owner. 'There. Will you look at it, please?'

'That's the police away,' Margaret says, head cocked at the sound of the close door. 'That was quick.'

'Margaret! This is important. Honestly, I don't care if you get a will or not. But I do care about this.'

Margaret stares at the screen. 'What is it?'

'It's a picture I took today when I was checking Registers of Scotland. It's a website solicitors use, that lists property transactions and ownerships.'

'So?'

'So, the name registered against your husband's old shop is Albert Camberg.'

'So? It was his shop.'

'Stop with the petted lip, please. This isn't a rental agreement. The record's saying that Albert owned the shop.'

'Owned it? No, I don't think so. That's not possible.'

'See when Albert died, what was left to you in his will?'

Margaret frowns. 'Everything, I suppose. I don't know.'

'Can you remember what the solicitor told you? About the business for example. Do you have any paperwork?'

'I don't know.' Margaret is growing agitated. 'I don't understand. What is it? What's wrong?'

'Nothing's wrong, don't worry. Well, it is, but, judging by this, Albert owned the shop. He didn't rent it.'

She pauses. Margaret is twirling one thumb across the other, rotoring them over and over in her lap.

'With your permission I can do a bit more digging – and I'll speak with your solicitor too, to see the terms of the will. But the point is, according to Registers of Scotland, Albert still owns the shop. As of now. Which means you do. As well as the flat, you own the shop. Outright. As far as I can tell, there's no mortgage held against it.'

'I own the tailor's? How?'

'Not only that, but whoever's using the premises currently, has no authorisation to do so. Plus they must owe you nearly a year's back-dated rent.'

Margaret's features are inscrutable. Claire doesn't want to add to her distress, but she needs to appraise her of everything. 'I checked to see who owns the business operating out of there now, and it's a man called Scott Brown.'

'Smirky Scott.' Margaret's voice is almost inaudible. Claire can hear music drifting, faintly, from a flat above.

'Right, come on.' Margaret rises from her chair.

'Where are we going?'

'To the shop.'

'No. Margaret wait. We need to approach this properly–'

'Did you not just say it was my shop?'

'Well, I think so.' Claire had not expected to unleash this firebrand. 'But we can't go accusing folk in public.'

'Maybe *you* can't. Anyway, I have no intention of causing a scene.'

Margaret fetches her handbag from the sideboard. 'I just want to look him in the eye and ask him if it's true. Donald, I mean – not that horrible boy.'

'Do you want your stick?'

But Margaret's already out the door, moving with surprising speed. Claire goes after, scooping up the buff folder in case they need it, then thinking better of it, and leaving it in the hall. She is methodical, not confrontational. This needs to be sorted by sternly worded letters and a much greater abundance of facts than she has at present. At the gate, she sees Margaret falter a little. Claire takes her arm, and together they walk across the road and down Hillfoot Street towards the tailor's.

The shopfront display for Denholm & Serge has changed. Today there is a Black Watch mini kilt, paired with an evening gown made entirely of patchwork denims. 'Will you let me do the talking?' says Claire.

'Nope.' Margaret is grim. She scrutinises the gilded lettering on the window, then thrusts the shop door open. Inside is a cornucopia of gorgeousness. Drapes of vibrant fabrics billow across the ceiling. Exposed iron columns are wound with brightly coloured skeins of braid, fairy lights and bobbly trimmings. The counter is all scrubbed wood and battered brass. The beardy man behind it looks up from his phone. He's younger than Claire, wears a burgundy T-shirt and green woollen waistcoat. Hanging round his neck is a frayed fabric tape measure.

Before Claire can stop her, Margaret leans across the counter and snatches it from his neck. 'That's Albert's!'

'Christ! What are you doing? You near choked me.' He peers closer at them. 'Margaret! Long time no see. Sorry.' Pats his throat absently. 'Just a wee tribute to the man. I didn't think you'd mind.' Dark, trimmed beard. Big twinkly teeth. He reminds Claire of a TV presenter, one who's too groomed to be true.

'Is Donald here?'

'Granda? Och no. Haven't you heard?' His features drop. 'Heart attack. He's no been in here in ages.'

'Oh no! I'm so sorry. Is he alright?'

'Getting there. Slowly. Doubt he'll be back at work though. Anyway. How can I help you, ladies?' He turns up the wattage on his smile. Attention shifting to Claire. She makes no acknowledgement of him.

'I want to talk to you about the shop, Scott.'

'What about the shop, Margaret? Do you like it?' There's nothing offensive in his words, but his whole vibe is supercilious. He talks to Margaret as you would a child. Claire wonders if she ever adopts this tone. She fingers one of the beautiful tweed jackets hanging on a rail. The tag says £299.

'It looks like a cheap brothel.' Margaret's cheeks are mottled.

'Didn't think you were the sort of girl to frequent one of those—'

Claire cuts across him. 'OK, that's enough. I'm Mrs Camberg's solicitor. I'd like to enquire as to your landlord.'

'Sorry?'

'Who is it you rent the shop from, Mr Brown?'

'Eh, that would be none of your business.'

His stance is more aggressive now, palms planted on the counter, pecs swelling. But Claire senses a faint beading on his forehead. There are definite dark half-moons under his oxters.

'Actually Mr Brown, it would be, given the owner of this property is my client. Furthermore, it seems you've been using her premises for almost a year – a lease you appear to have obtained by deception and which equates to a considerable debt in terms of rental. We'll obviously be talking to the police regarding a potential investigation of fraud, as well as launching a civil claim for damages and recovery of rent arrears.'

'Fucksake, Margaret.' Scott's voice grows louder. 'This place was a shithole, you know that. Bert was a waste of space these last few years, ran the whole place into the ground. You fucking *know* that. It was my granda kept the business going.'

'That's a subjective opinion, Mr Brown,' says Claire, 'which, in any case, doesn't give you any claim or title whatsoever over the property. We'll also be obtaining a court order to have you evicted from these premises within thirty days of receipt.'

'Margaret, come on! It's only a wee bit fucking rent. Be reasonable. We were going to sort it.'

'Tell me one thing, Scott. Whose idea was it? Yours or Donald's?' Margaret's bony fingers twist-twist the measuring tape she holds. Claire aches for her. She looks so wee and dignified.

'We were going to pay you back. But you never even asked us for it!'

'I didn't know!' Margaret shouts.

'Well, there you fucking go. I telt Granda to hold off settling what the rent would be, that's all. Just till we got set up. And then he took no well. But, Jesus, man, why are you making such a fuss? You canny have missed the money if you didny even know you owned the shop!'

'But your grandfather presumably did?' says Claire.

'Oh, fuck off, you!' He looms forward, filling her field of vision. Claire positions herself so she's in front of Margaret, but Scott just cranes his head around her. 'Of course he did. Bert talked to him about it, years ago.'

'You're lying.' Margaret is visibly distressed. 'This is just a mix-up. Bert would never buy this place and not tell me. We shared everything.'

'Clearly not. Jesus, how did you not know? Bert bought this place for Stephen!'

Margaret gives a sharp little gasp.

'Aye – remember him, do you? Coming here and shouting the odds at me, ya selfish cow. Granda was right about you. What kind of a woman cuts off her own son? Bet you didny even tell him when his dad died, did you?'

'Margaret, I think we should leave.' Claire begins to usher her out, while her brain careers wildly, rewinds. Absorbing what the man just said.

'How do you know about Stephen?' says Margaret.

'Bert! He used to fucking greet to my granda all the time, saying how much he missed him. How you wouldn't let him even talk to his boy, for I don't know how many fucking years.'

'That's not true!'

'Bullshit. Bert even tried to write to him. Did you know that, Margaret? Soul was shit-scared of you. Fucking used the shop address and everything so you wouldn't find out. But it just fired back "not known at this address". Christ, I telt him he should hire a private detective or something. Auld witch that you are.'

Finally, Margaret crumples. There is a visible weakening of her spine, like she is snapping, and Claire catches her just in time. 'Right. Out, now. Come on.' She helps the old woman to the door, suddenly vulnerable herself, now her back's to the raging man. The air is a soup of violence. But she forces herself to stop. Turns in the doorway. 'We'll be in touch, Mr Brown.' Then she gets Margaret outside.

'Just keep walking. Please, Margaret. Let's get you a seat.'

There's a café a few doors along, the formica and jars of boiled sweeties type that's not yet been swept away. They find a table. Margaret is shaken. Grey. Claire waits until they have tea before them. 'Are you alright?'

'Not really.' Margaret tries to lift her cup, but tea splashes into the glass saucer. She sets it down again without drinking.

'Do you want to talk about it?'

She shakes her head. They sit a while, Margaret staring into space, Claire drinking. She's worried the old woman might pass out.

'Are you sure you wouldn't like a wee biscuit? Or a scone?'

No response. Tiny, puckered lines run from Margaret's pinched lips. Wiry eyebrows touch hooded eyelids, which must constantly curtain her view of the world. Her skin is pale. Claire watches as tears run, tracing all her lifelines, channelling her face. Claire reaches for her hand.

'I didn't know,' Margaret whispers.

Claire waits.

'We never really talked . . . I thought Bert didn't want to. So I never . . . Oh, when I let myself think about them it's like falling into a black hole. So it was easier just to shut them away. I thought that's what he wanted too.'

'You're saying *them*?' Claire says gently.

Margaret wears a look of blank desperation. 'I did it for him. To protect him. Bert was so very fragile. Stephen tore his heart out when he left.'

'Tell me about them?'

She swallows. 'I have a son called Stephen. And a daughter-in-law Lauren, and a beautiful grandson Paul. They live in Australia. And we don't talk. I haven't seen them for twelve years.'

'Oh, Margaret.' Claire caresses the back of Margaret's fingers with her thumb. 'I'm so sorry.'

She lets this information settle. Does not know what to do with it.

'Well,' she eventually offers, 'I have an adoptive mum and dad. Dad dead. Mum down south. No siblings. And a birth mother somewhere who I've never met. I don't even know her name.' It comes out clumsy, like she's in competition with Margaret.

'We're poor things, aren't we?'

'I don't know. Maybe we're really strong?'

'Maybe.' Margaret drifts again, distant. The door chimes as a mum pushing a double buggy comes in, and Claire shuffles her chair a little to let her pass.

'Albert was a war orphan,' Margaret says. 'He came here as a refugee – lost his parents, his brothers and sisters in the camps. Family was everything to him. And me. We tried so hard to have children. It nearly didn't happen . . . but then it did. Just when we'd given up hope. Can you imagine? How wonderful that was?'

'I can.'

'And then to have a grandchild too? It was like a miracle. Albert just transformed. It was like all the hungry ghosts inside him vanished. Me too. I didn't . . . I didn't have a good relationship with my mother. She was forever trying to make me into something I'm not. Then tell me she was doing it for me, you know? But I think she was doing it for her.' Slowly, Margaret lifts her cup in both hands. Takes a long draught of tea.

'We had a terrible fight when Stephen decided . . .' She clears her throat. 'They moved overseas, when my grandson was little. Awful, horrible things were said. We never wanted them to go. I was so scared. And you lash out when you're scared, don't you? Our son told us to fuck off. We never even went to their wedding.'

'Oh, Margaret. I'm sorry.'

Her voice breaks. 'So am I.'

'But maybe he deserves forgiveness? Stephen, I mean. Maybe you do too?'

'I never told him when his dad died.' One hand goes over her mouth.

Claire is shocked. She tries to conceal it, plucking a sugar sachet.

'Never told him when Bert had his first stroke either.' Margaret's eyes dart. 'I wanted to punish him, I suppose. The way he'd punished us. But I could have given him and his dad a few last months together. Bert wanted me to find him. Speech was difficult then, but I knew he did. How could I, though? Too much time had gone by. How could we even try to make things right? It felt more unbearable somehow. And I had enough with . . .' She shrugs. 'So I lied. I said to Bert I'd tried. But I didn't. And now it's too late.'

'It's never too late.'

'That's such a cliché. How could I . . . how could my son ever speak to me now?'

'Well, just be honest. What would you tell him, if Stephen was me?'

For a long while, Margaret contemplates. The café moves on around them, babies squalling, folk chatting. The schoosh of a coffee machine spurts delicious smells into the air. Claire finishes her tea, sets the old-fashioned glass cup down on the saucer.

Then, with profound focus, Margaret replies: 'That I was hurt. That he left us made of nothing but broken edges, and I wanted to hurt him too. That I learned to numb myself and not remember. That I grieved for my son and my grandson as if they were dead – and couldn't bear to be reminded they were not.' She grimaces. 'How obscene is that? I threw out all Paul's toys. He had wee rubber ducks round our bath. And building blocks, and a train set. Albert was making him a rocking horse. I chucked the lot. It was easier to pretend we no longer had a family, because if I did . . . I wasn't sleeping. I'd lie, curled on my side in the spare room, on the sheets wee Paulie had lain on, trying desperately to breathe him in. And I would miss my son with a passion and hate him for what he'd done.'

'And what would you say to him about the funeral?'

Margaret toys with a teaspoon. 'That I didn't know how to find him?'

'Really?'

'That he didn't deserve to come? That he'd forgotten us?'

'Did you feel rejected?'

A violent, tearful *yes*.

'Hey, it's OK.'

'But I never . . .' She is sobbing. 'It was me that rejected them. I never even sent a thing for wee Paul. Not for Christmas or his birthdays. Nothing. Ignored the fact he existed. Oh God. Oh God. What did I do?'

People are beginning to look in their direction. The waitress comes over, Claire steels herself for an argument. But the woman puts a slice of chocolate cake on the table beside Margaret, then stoops slightly to put her arm round her. 'There you go, hen. On the house.'

They sit in the café another hour. Claire doesn't know if she'll make her dinner. How can she leave Margaret? She was meant to get her hair cut, but she's missed that. They'll probably charge her. Blade and Co. are not sympathetic that way. You get shiatsu head massages and endless cappuccino, but you pay for it, you pay for it. Ach, her hair doesn't seem important.

'I do want you to make a will,' Margaret says suddenly.

'OK.'

'I want everything to go to Stephen and wee Paul.'

Claire nods. 'Would you like me to see if I can track them down too?'

'Oh, I don't know. Can I think about that?'

'Of course.'

'Alright. Good.' Margaret blows her nose.

'And what do you want me to do about the shop? I'll need to speak to the solicitor who drafted Albert's will.'

'Can we not talk about that just now please? I'm founert.'

'Founert?'

'Yes. It means wrung-out. Spent, you know?'

Founert. A guid Scots word that Claire will henceforth adopt because it describes perfectly how she's feeling. She has no conversation left in her. Pity the poor man who sits beside her tonight.

Margaret glances at her watch. 'Oh dear I'm so sorry. I've taken up all of your afternoon.'

'And you've missed Stitch and Bitch.'

'I'd better get home. Let you get on.'

'I'll walk you back.'

As they approach Margaret's street, Zara cycles past them. 'Just the person,' she shouts to Margaret, waving. 'I've something yummy for your tea. See you in a minute!'

Claire has never been so pleased to see her. If she passes the baton now, she still has time for a bath.

On the way home, she calls her mother.

Chapter Twenty-Two

'Where in your body do you feel the anger?' Gerard stares at the man with the glasses. He has been in a waiting room with sticky kids' toys and stained bean bags and magazines nobody reads, and now he is in an office. *Stay calm, Gerard. You're at CAMHS!* Do they think the name is funny?

He has been sitting in the waiting room for twenty minutes, watching teenagers bite their lips or pick skin from their nails. One girl got taken in, then ran out crying a wee while later. Kris has come with him this first time, but she is waiting outside. His jailer. He plans to say *Up my bum, you wanker*, but then the man looks at him. Really looks at him, like he can see Gerard sitting there, and not just the chair. Gerard can see two tiny Gerards, reflected in the man's glasses. His fingernails dig into the sides of his thighs. He is real. He is here.

'In my tummy,' he says. 'And in my head. It's like bees buzzing.'

'And do you feel that all the time?'

He nods.

'Does it ever change?'

'Sometimes.'

'When does it change?'

'When I get scared. The bees get louder and they go into my eyes.'

'I see.'

Although they're near a busy road, the room feels quiet. It doesn't have the usual strip lighting. Instead, the man has put a lamp in the corner, the kind of light you'd get in a nice living room, and another, smaller lamp on his desk. But they're not sitting at his desk; they're sitting on soft chairs which scoop you like a circle.

'Why is it you think you're here, Gerard?'

'Cause I hurt folk.'

'Why do you say that?'

'I beat up an old woman for starters.'

'I see.'

'Aye. I did.'

The man puts his fingers to his lips: an arrow for him to rest his chin on. 'Would you like to talk about that?'

'Nope.'

'OK.'

Gerard waits for the next question. But the man doesn't talk for a wee while. Gerard isn't sure what to do. Or what to look at. There are some pictures on the walls, ships at sea and crap like that – nothing like the pictures at Kris and Craig's. He never gets tired of looking at their paintings – you can always see something different in them. These ones the man has are just coloured splodges. He doesny even think they're real paint. The sun on one of them is stretched out in orange and yellow lines. You're supposed to think it's melting away, but it just looks squashed. He thinks of the old lady's yellow cardigan, how soft it felt as he grabbed her, smelt her old lady smell of peppermints and fousty perfume. How he kidded on he couldn't feel her falling as he ran away, as he was falling too; he could feel *her* falling in his stomach.

'I didn't mean to,' he blurts.

'Mean to what?'

'Hurt her. I did . . . I kind of pushed her. Or pulled her. She fell over, but, and it was my fault, I know it was.'

'And how did you feel, Gerard?'

'Scared. Scared and bad.'

'I see. And how do you feel about it now?'

He slides his hands beneath his legs. 'Shite.' He looks up. The man is watching him, but he doesn't seem angry. 'I want to say I'm sorry.'

'How do you feel when you say sorry?'

Gerard shrugs.

'Does that help? Do the angry feelings change?'

'Sometimes.' He thinks of all the times he has said it to his mum. To stop her shouting or hurting him or going away. 'Sometimes you just say sorry, but.'

The man doesn't answer, so he's probably said it wrong, made it sound like he's at it, and he's not, he's really not.

'I do want to tell her, cause it's true, alright? I feel shite and I wish I hadny done it.'

'Alright, Gerard.'

Gerard pushes his feet out in front of him, heels scuffing the floor. 'It's shite getting hurt.'

'Does that make you angry too?'

'Aye.'

'Can you tell me what other feelings you have? In your body, when you get angry. Or anxious.'

'My eyes go funny.'

'Funny how?' The man is holding his pen.

'Like everything goes all wavery – wobbling and that? Know, like stuff dances about and goes big, then goes wee?' He sounds like a dick, but he canny stop. 'And I feel like I'm on a wave. I'm in the sea and it's fucking crashing all . . .' He stops. 'Oh, sorry.'

'It's OK, Gerard. It's fine to swear. You can say anything in here.'

'Anything? Aye, right, then you'll just write it all down and that'll go in my file too?'

The man puts his pen back in its stupid wee holder. An old-fashioned car on a piece of marble. It is so tacky. Craig would hate it.

'How about we take no notes today? Nothing at all. I promise.'

Gerard eyes him up and down. He wants to test this. 'I hurt my mum too,' he says. 'I ripped her open.'

The man says nothing.

'When I was born. She says I ruined her.' Gerard shakes his head. 'She doesny like me.'

He thinks of his mum, lying with her eyes shut. When the polis picked him up from Jacqueline's house, they took him straight to the hospital. Kris and Craig were waiting for him. He thought he was going to get a bollocking, but Kris pure swooped him up. Her face was puffy. They took him in to the wee side room, where his mum was. Her hair was all lovely, laid out on the pillow like a starburst. But she had this mask thing over her mouth or up her nose; he'd turned his head away quick cause she looked like a Dalek.

'She's sleeping just now,' Kris said.

'No, she's no.' He'd felt really calm. Nothing else could hurt him. Or her. He knew where she was. 'She's OD'd.'

'Well, we don't know that.'

'Who found her?'

'The police did.'

'Where?'

They'd not wanted to say, but he'd went on at them. 'In a public toilet,' Craig said eventually.

The man with the glasses is talking again. 'Why do you think that? That your mum doesn't like you?'

'Because she keeps trying to leave us! She's out her head half the fucking time and the other half she's crying or yelling or . . .' He's about to say *hitting* but he stops himself in time. This bastard is clever. He nearly tricked him into spilling his guts. The dude's probably recording him anyroad. Why else would you have a big fuck-off stunt pen on your desk? So you can go I'M NOT GOING TO USE IT, BUDDY! Obvious. It's just a con. Gerard bets he does this *we won't take notes* shite with every kid.

'That's a lot of emotion to feel,' says the man. 'Strong emotions are like waves. You're absolutely right. And what we're gonna try to do here is help you manage those waves.'

'How?' Gerard hates the way he says *gonna*.

'Well, there are lots of practical tools we can look at. Being able to recognise what you're feeling instead of pushing it away is one. Sitting with those feelings, then letting them pass. Meditation might be good to try. And there's CBT and DBT.'

All the Ts, thinks Gerard.

'Group therapy, family therapy, NLP.'

Now the guy's just showing off.

'Occasionally, EMDR.'

'What's that?' Gerard challenges. Man, he *has* to be making that one up.

'That's working with your eye movements. And there's medications too of course. These are all areas your whole care team can look at and discuss. But one of the main things I'd like to work on is simply helping you to understand and regulate your emotions. Together we can look at where these feelings come from – and why. Then we can work out ways to think about what you do with them. How does that sound?'

Gerard shrugs. He'd like to say *it sounds like flucken hard work, mate.* He wonders how it would feel just to give in to it. He keeps trying to be good, he does. But he's so tired. It would be a relief to stop fighting it. Because it feels so brilliant, when he lets his fists fly. To spit and scream and feel his feelings, and just not care. Be a right hard bastard. That is the problem. It's not when he gets angry or tunes out; it's how he feels afterwards. He gets upset by being upset. So how will thinking about *why* he gets upset that he's upset not just make him more upset? *Would you like some extra upset on your upset burger to go with your upset sauce?*

Normal folk don't need to pull their feelings out their heads and ask them what they're doing there. *Hello, mad ball of anger. How did you get into my head? And what am I going to do with you?* He thinks of all the hard men, all the tough guys he knows from round Dennistoun. What must that feel like? To swagger and punch your way through life and not gie a fuck? For folk to be feart of you? Then you're not scared of anything at all. He cannot conceive of what that must be like, is not sure what would be left of him, if all the fear got burned away. He imagines it doesn't go, but hardens, the way a jaw or eyes or skin can harden. Would the fear be like bones inside you, then? Gone hard and angry to hold you up? He doesn't know if he wants that either.

'How do you think your mum feels?' the man asks.

'What?'

But the man just sits there. Blinking behind his big glasses.

'Fuck knows.' Gerard looks at the ceiling. 'I don't care.'

Outside, in the waiting room, a baby cries. Everyone probably heard him shouting about his mum leaving. He bets Kris's got her nebby ear pressed up against the door.

'OK. Well, I think we'll leave it there for today, Gerard. I'm going to give you a wee worksheet to take away. More of a questionnaire–'

'I canny fucking read.' He says it as though it bores him. And it does a wee bit, actually. It pisses him off that he has to embarrass himself again and again and say it all the time, but also that it's IN HIS FILE. If all the various tossers that pretended to give a toss about him bothered to actually know him, they'd know that, wouldn't they? Then he wouldny have to keep on admitting it out loud.

'No problem,' the man says. 'We can do it next week.'

Gerard shuffles out. 'Canny wait,' he says, shutting the door. He goes back down the corridor, to where his jailer waits.

'How was it?' says Kris brightly, handing him his jacket. It is roasting in the waiting room. 'Was Dr Lumsden nice?'

'Alright.'

'Want to talk about it?'

'No.'

'OK Gerard. But I am here if you need me, yes?' she says in her sing-song accent. Where is she from again? He thinks it's Sweden. He's heard her on the phone to her sister, speaking a whole other language which is sharp and clipped. He wonders why Kris came here, to Scotland. If she misses home? He struggles with the sleeves of his jacket.

'Let me–'

'I can do it!' he snaps. They walk out to the car through drizzling rain. The ground shines like metal. How could Gerard possibly know how his mum feels? It's not his job to know. It's her job to look after him. When she gets out her face, she doesn't care how *he* feels. Or Anthony or Miranda. He gets it, though. Man, it's scary. Such a brilliant feeling, like finding a hidden doorway. Him and Ali, dizzy with the drink. Invincible. All you have is the instant you are in. Everything else melts away.

Is that why his mum does it? To get away from them?

Loving his mum is like quicksand. A teenage girl in a pink anorak walks past them, arm linked through an older woman's. He sees the flash of scarring at the girl's wrist.

'I'm hungry,' he says. There's a McDonald's nearby. He might get a burger out of this trip. He's not even missing school, so there has to be some upside. There's not much of the summer holidays left, and he still doesn't know what high school he'll be going to. Nobody's asked him. Will it be with his old pals, who know he's been in trouble? Who he can boast to about his summer on the run from the law. Or something. But who also know his mum's a junkie and owes money and once tried to set fire to Gerard's bike. And they'll know by now that the weans have been taken away. Gerard's family will be the talk of the steamie, as per usual. (Though everyone also knows that Brian's dad beats up his mum. But folk don't whisper about that in the same way.) If he went to a brand new school in a brand new place, Gerard could be brand new too. He could be Jez. He could be a somebody or a nobody, all on his own efforts, living in a tall thin house with a stark white kitchen and real paintings on the walls.

He'd still be Gerard, but. Daftie Gerard who can make words dance, but canny get them to make sense. But he'll be that wherever he lives, and in a nicer place, he could be a nastier person. He's seen the way Kris and Craig's boys watch him, sideyways. As if he might bite. He knows they let him play their PlayStation cause they're feart he'll just take it if they don't.

It's a big deal where he lives. Where he goes to school. And none of it will be for Gerard to decide. He bets they'll just tell him at the Hearing. Naggy says there will be one soon, on account of him going AWOL. She's been pretty decent too, surprisingly. He didn't do what Ali said. He hasn't told anyone about Mad Davey. He doesn't know if it will help his mum or make it worse. Gerard's sticking to his story. His mum failed to trap, and Gerard flipped out. Just got really freaked about everything. Couldn't handle it and ran away. Oh, and some unknown boys chased him.

So far, it seems to have worked. Though it has meant he's to go to the speccy psychologist for the foreseeable.

'Well, how about we get some lunch?' Kris opens the car door for him. 'Then I thought we could go see your mum – if you like?'

'Don't care.'

'The hospital phoned when you were at your appointment. She has woken up a little.'

His heart flips. 'Is she OK? Are they letting her out?'

'She's still, um, drowsy.'

'Are they keeping her in, though?' Gerard starts to panic. In hospital, she's safe. There's good folk helping her, and bad folk can't find her. He thinks it would be a genius idea if they put the grown-ups in care, not the kids.

'I think they will keep her for a while, yes.'

'Can we just skip lunch and go straight there?'

'Sure.'

Happy-sad. Happy-sad. He feels like he's sinking. It's not simply waves that are battering him; it's an avalanche of water, hitting him in the face each time he comes up for air. He was safe too, when his mum was sleeping. But now he has to face her. What's he meant to say? Did you try to kill yourself so you could leave us? Did Davey try to kill you? Why d'you love drugs more? Or are you too stupid to care?

Busy traffic. No one stopping. Kris is waiting at the junction. The indicator tick-ticks.

'Wait!' says Gerard. 'Could we nip home first?'

'Sure.' Kris turns her head. 'Why?'

'I need to get . . . I want to pick something up. To show my mum.'

'Well, I'm not sure she'll be up to–'

'Please? It's important.'

In the hospital, his mum can't run away. He can make her listen to him. He has to try. Gerard has to work out where his feelings come from; that's what the speccy psycho said.

'Is it a card? Oh, pet, did you make her a card?'

'Something like that.'

'Alright, darling.' Kris flicks the indicator in the opposite direction.

*

They don't let them in the room at first. 'She's having a bed bath,' the nurse tells Kris. They sit on two plastic chairs and wait. Gerard holds the manbag tight. The book about the ring of gold waits inside. The corridor smells of Dettol. It is literally squeaky clean. A regular, rhythmic thud fills the air. Gently, Kris puts her arm across the top of his legs. It's him. The noise is Gerard rocking the chair back and forth. He stops. Kris removes her arm. The nurse motions for them to come in.

Kris goes first. Gerard hears her say, 'Hello. My name is Kris. I've been looking after Gerard for you. He's here. He'd like to see–'

Gerard pushes past her. Flings himself on the bed. He doesn't need an introduction to his mum. At first, he just lies there, pressing his face into her tummy, but then he feels his mum's hand fall upon his hair.

'Here, son.' She sounds croaky. 'Here. What's all this?'

'Oh, Mum.' He wants to lose himself in crying. The covers are so soft, so white, his mum is there, stroking him. It feels like being in heaven. But he mustn't. Never let your guard down. One wrong move and that hand will strike him. A memory opens – of cot bars. No, the playpen. He was too big for the cot. Baby-jail, she called it. She put him in there if he'd been bad. Sometimes if she was going out. This one day, he'd been in it so long, he was starving. He'd tried to shoogle it over, so he could get out, but it had fallen on him. He remembers his head being stuck, cheek shoved against the bars, and her hand swiping down to leather him. Not to lift him up.

'I'll give you two a moment.' Kris is muffled, but he can still hear her beyond the soft, crisp covers and the rushing in his ears. It sounds like the sea, but it is the blood inside him he can hear, mingling with the blood inside his mum.

He lifts his head from her belly. 'How are you feeling, Mum?'

'Och, no so bad.' Her tongue moistens her lips. It is white and swollen. 'You?'

'I'm fine.'

'Good.' She looks down at the covers. He thinks she's a wee bit embarrassed.

'Did that man hurt you?'

Sharp fingers seize his wrist. 'I telt you not to say. Have you told anyone?'

'No, Mum, no!' He tugs his wrist away. 'I promise. But what happened?'

'Doesny matter,' she slurs. 'Have you still got that envelope?'

'It's here.' He taps his bag, slung round his shoulder.

Greedily, she reaches for it. Gerard shifts further down the bed. He takes out the book, no longer in its envelope.

'How come you opened it? Fucksake, Gerard.'

'It's my book.'

'No, it's no.'

'Yes, it is. I remember it.'

'Bullshit.' She makes a snort like a horse.

'Mum.' He speaks slowly, opening the book, flicking through the pages till he's near the end. 'I want to ask you something. And I want you to tell me the truth.' He takes her hand. 'Please.' There's a plaster on the back of her hand, covering a huge needle. He tries not to cringe when he sees it, but it is gross. The needle goes into a tube, which spirals up and into a machine he doesn't want to see either. She's still dopey; it's putting other drugs into her.

He takes a deep breath. *Don't think, Jez. Just say it.* Uses the air inside him to push the words into being. 'Did I see my dad get killed?' The metal-glass-shiny room shudders.

'What? Christ, Gerard. Jesus.' His mum tries to sit up but can't. 'Fucksake,' she says, flopping back on the bed.

'Did we?' He holds the open book in front of her. 'Look. That's his blood, isn't it? You were there too.'

She turns her face into the pillow.

'Fucking look at it, Mum!'

'What the fuck're you asking me that for?'

'I remember it.'

'No, you don't.'

'Aye, I do. I was in my bed and he was reading me this book and you shouted and then men came up and there was a bang. I can remember it, Mum, it's in my head.' He's banging his finger above his ear, an angry bird pecking. His mum's mouth is open, but no sound comes out. She might be crying, but he doesn't care. He shoves his nose right up to hers. 'I remember the warm blood, spattering on my face.'

'Fucking leave me alone,' she whispers.

'Tell me!'

'Yes! Alright! Yes!'

'Is that his blood?'

'Yes,' she whimpers.

He allows himself to return there, with his dad and the blood and his dad leaving the world. Did his dad's blood go into him, through his pores? Was it inside him now? His dad and his mum made him; he was made of them and stars. And then his dad went back to the stars, or the earth. His dad gets to fly in the wind while he and his mum stay behind. 'Is that why you kept it?' He's all choked.

A tiny shake of her head. Her eyes are rolling backwards. 'It's our treasure, son. I'd forgot about it, till he came looking.'

'Who? Davey?'

'You canny give it to Davey. It's our protection. Our way out.'

He sits back on the edge of the bed. 'What d'you mean, Mum?'

'S'a key. The key'll make us rich.' Wee bits of froth are coming out her mouth.

'What do you mean?' He shakes her, but she's fleeing.

He shouts for Kris, who runs in. Then a nurse comes, and they get hustled out. In the confusion of the corridor, he gives Kris the slip. She's talking to a man in blue scrubs, and Gerard walks, at normal speed, towards the lift. If she sees him, he will say he's going to the toilet, but she never calls his name. The lift opens, swallows him up, and he is on the ground floor in seconds. The hospital's called the Death Star – so huge it has its own roads and bus stops. People think Gerard is stupid, but he's not. He knows this hospital is on the Southside of Glasgow. And it's not that far from Cardonald. All he has to do is look for a nice lady in the queue and ask her which bus to get. If he sees Kris coming, he can just jook behind the bus shelter.

Back where the book came from. To his gran's house. That's where he'll find the answers. He has to find some answers. They owe him. All of them. The bastards owe him.

Chapter Twenty-Three

It's no bother to find his gran's flat this time. Gerard knows exactly where he's going. He takes the stairs to the tenth floor, because he doesn't think he can be in a lift going that high. There's a weird thing going on with his breathing; it's almost hiccups in his lungs; they feel too shallow to do much good, but he'd still rather be wheezing on the stairs than inside a metal box. His damp jacket steams as he climbs, the satchel bumping his thigh. The stairwell is clean one minute, dirty the next: wee puddles of cans and broken bottles on one landing, a broad-leafed shiny plant inside a ceramic cart and donkey on another. At one point he sees a familiar symbol woven within the graffiti: a gallows with half a circle and a snake. The tattoo his dad and Mad Davey share.

He's in their territory now. He cannot shake this feeling of being observed. Unseen jungle drums thumping in unpeopled streets. If a big boy jumps him, he thinks he'd burst into tears. Which is no way to build your street cred.

Gerard pauses by the purple door. Lets his breathing settle. Hands sticky with sweat, and the residue of other people's hands on the banister. This time, his gran's door is locked. His plan was to barge in, march right up to her chair and confront her. He wants to fill the flat with righteous anger. Gerard seen a cowboy film where the guy killed a whole gang due to *righteous anger*, and it got him off with the Sheriff. But he'll have to knock politely instead.

He makes a fist. Dunts the door three times. Doesn't know why, but three times is a charm.

'Hang on.' That does not sound like an old lady junkie. The voice is female, yes. But bright.

The door unlocks, slowly – two key turns and then a chain. A woman appears in the gap. What Gerard will remember of this later is the steady glow behind her, illuminating her dark curly hair and round, pink cheeks. She is definitely not old.

'Yes?' she says.

Gerard's totally thrown off course.

She gives him a wee smile. 'Cat got your tongue?' Then she frowns. 'Here – you're not one of Johnny's lads, are you? I telt him to piss off.'

'Naw. No. I'm here . . .' He looks wildly past her, searching for the hunched figure in the chair, but all the doors from the hall are shut. 'I want to see my gran.'

The woman draws in a slight breath. She studies him. Opens the door a little wider. In the tilt of light, a shadow passes her face. Beyond, the tatty hall beckons, its single lit bulb hanging shadeless from the ceiling.

'Come in, come in. Your gran?' she says, closing the door.

'Aye.'

'Lucille is your gran?' The woman's wearing a purple tunic, the kind that gives off static. It's a bit tight across her belly. A home help. He's glad his gran's got a carer. It worried him to see her alone like that. Gerard fidgets with his manbag. 'Aye. I think.'

'You think?' She's pure staring at him, walking round him in a spooky ring.

'Lou. The woman that lives here. I don't know if her right name's Lucille.'

'Well, it is. And how do you think she's your gran?'

'Cause my mum telt me. And I mind her bringing me here one time.'

'Do you? When was that, then?'

He begins to explain. The woman is in uniform, so she's the

boss here. But then this is his gran's house, not hers. So maybe he is the boss.

'I don't have to tell you nothing.'

'Fair enough.' She's still examining him. He can't understand what her expression is trying to do. Is she laughing at him, or about to greet? She has the nicest face. It makes him think of a friendly apple.

'Is she in?'

'Oh aye. She's in. Doesny get out much does Lucille. Or at all, actually. That's why I'm here.'

'I came before. Few weeks ago.'

'Did you indeed?'

'Aye. You wereny here then. The door was open.'

She tuts. 'Christ.' Then softer. 'I know, she did that sometimes. That's how I needed to come and look after her.'

'Can I see her, then?'

'She's sleeping the now.'

He tuts even louder. He can play tut-tennis all day if she wants to. 'It's fine. You don't have to fib. I know she's a junkie.'

'Who told you that?'

He shrugs. 'I seen her. Last time. With a needle sticking out. She didny see me, but. She was out of it.'

'Lucille's a diabetic.'

'What's that?' He rests his back against the wall. He doesn't like how the woman keeps circling him. Makes him feel examined.

'It means she's not very well. Her body can't make the stuff it needs to keep going.'

'How d'you mean? Is she gonny die, like?'

The woman looks a bit surprised.

'It's alright. You can say. It doesny bother me.' He scans the hallway, searching for clues, a sign he's related to the woman who lives here. He was too scared to scrutinise it last time. There are no photos on the wall, only ugly striped wallpaper and an unticking copper clock, which is in a blob shape, with elephants and giraffes stuck on it. He thinks it's meant to be Africa.

'So why are you here, then,' she says, 'if you don't care?'

'I want to ask her something.'

'Can you ask me instead?'

'Naw.'

She crosses her arms. 'Can I level with you?'

'Aye.'

'Then you can level with me?'

Gerard purses his lips.

'Lucille *was* a drug addict.'

'Knew it.' He says it triumphantly, but it's bitter-tasting. Like he is spiting himself.

'I'm sorry to say all this, because she's your gran, but she drank too much too. Way too much. And because she didn't look after herself, now she's no very well. She's no very well at all, son. She can't really see for starters.'

'She canny see?' This gives him chills. To be lost in a world of black, where folk could do anything they wanted to you, and you don't even see it coming.

'Only shadows. Diabetes does that to you. She can't walk any more either.'

Gerard nods, absorbing this. A dark thought steeps inside him. One day, this will be his mother. If she lives to be old at all.

'Come on through the living room.' The carer takes him through to the room with the manky chair, but his gran is not in it. 'Have a seat.'

He sits on the edge of the couch.

'Want some juice?'

'Naw.' He catches her smiling at him, a tiny wee smile at the edges of her mouth, and it's like a giant big light comes out of nowhere, dissolving the dark. He changes his mind. 'Aye. OK, then.'

She's only gone a wee minute, but a glimmer unzips inside him. A thing he needs to remember. She comes back with a can of ginger. 'There you go.'

'Ta.'

The carer sits on the couch next to him. 'When I say she's

not well, Gerard, I mean she's really not well. You're right. She is going to die. I think we'll be moving her into a hospice soon.'

Gerard scooshes the bubbles of his drink round his mouth, then swallows. 'Can I talk to her, but?'

'She's coming and going, you know? Maybe later. What did you want to tell her?'

He sighs. Unbuckles the satchel. 'You'll no be able to help.'

'Try me.'

The space around her is calm. Capable. She feels like a person he might trust. The book is in his grasp, and he's just about to draw it out when his brain catches up with the conversation.

'Hey! How did you know my name?'

The woman makes a cup of her hands. A heart shape. Puts Gerard's face inside. 'Oh, son. I know you don't remember me pet, but I'm your Auntie Ran. Your mum's sister. Your gran's my mum too.'

He shrinks away from the woman, deep into the couch. She lets him be, but is ever watchful, eyes hovering, darting. Attempting to read his face. Gerard tries to look away from her, but he can't. Now he knows it, he can see his mum everywhere. She glistens in eyes which are clear instead of dull. A complexion that's not pitted or blotched. She shines in veins that give pink light to healthy skin, and do not rupture in livid patterns. It is how his mum might look if she was happy.

'It's true, Gerard.'

He blinks and blinks, expecting revolution in the room. But the couch stays where it is. The window does not shimmer, nor the carpet rise. He does, though. A floaty draught takes him up above himself, and, just for the tiniest second, he is watching a woman and a boy sit millimetres and miles apart. He sees they have the same colour of hair. Then he blinks again, and crashes down.

'Can I give you a hug?' Her arms are extended. Hopeful.

Violently, he shakes his head.

'OK. OK.' She tucks herself away. 'Oh, my wee lamb. You've no idea how much I've missed you.'

'Missed me?'

She looks so sad. 'Do you no remember me at all? I used to babysit for you.'

'Nuh.' He is freaking out. How can he have an auntie?

'How's your mum?' She asks it so quietly, he thinks she doesn't want to hear the reply – which reminds him to be angry.

'How come you don't know, then? If you're her sister, how come you don't look after her too?'

'God, I tried, Gerard. I promise you. I tried so hard. But she wouldn't let me.'

He knows this sounds true, but he has to punish her. 'Well, why didn't you look after me, then, eh? How come you didn't come and help us and not just leave us with her?'

'Oh, pet, I tried that too. I promise you. But they wouldn't let me.'

'Who wouldn't?'

Steepled hands over her nose. A prayer. Then she wipes her thumbs across her eyes. 'Can we start at the beginning, please?'

'If you want.' *Auntie Ran, Auntie Ran.* Chanting it in his head, a train of *antirans*. His childhood is a damaged blur. Folk come and go, names change. Hands hold or hit you. Voices go soft or hard, but there were arms holding him occasionally, arms that may have been his mum's or his gran's. Or they could have been hers. Antiran. The name is daft, sounds like a nickname. Gerard might have said it once. The rhythm sounds familiar. But there's so much about his memory he doesn't trust.

'I mean your beginning, Gerard. You tell me. About you. Where you are, why you're here. What you know about us. Then I'll try to fill in the blanks. How's that?'

It seems as good a place to start as any. There's a strange blankness in the room, as if time no longer ticks there either. Gerard has another long glug of his ginger, then he tells her where he lives now, and how he got there. He tells her about Kris and Craig and all their paintings. He tells her about the flat in Dennistoun that used to be his home. How long they lived there. Where they lived before. He tells her about Anthony and the baby, and she starts to cry. *I didn't know*, she sniffs, her mouth all ragged. He tells her about his first time in care, and how his life has chopped and changed. He tells her he can't read. He never tells people that, but she's his auntie so it seems OK. He doesn't say about the old lady or the police, because he doesn't want her to hate him. And he tells her about his mum. Not everything. Not about when she put a cigarette out on his arm or locked him outside in the rain. But he tells her about his mum's struggles, how she is never really OK but she does her best. Because it's true, he thinks as he's saying it. He's not really making excuses. When he tells her his mum is in hospital, right now, the hospital just up the road, she cries again. She wants to go and see her, but he says to wait. He hasn't told her about how his mum went funny, and he legged it. The more he talks to Ran and sees the altered angles of her face, the more he can pretend it's his mum there. So nothing he says feel like a betrayal. Gerard's just about to launch into Gardening Guerrillas and ask Ran if she's ever eaten aubergine, when the doorbell goes. Immediately followed by hammering. It sounds like the polis.

'Stay there,' says Ran, jumping up. He hears the chain slide, then Ran goes, 'You again. Fucksake.'

'She's fucking in here, isn't she?'

A man's voice. Harsh. Gerard recognises it, and his insides turn to water. Davey.

'I seen her fucking wean come in.'

Gerard darts into the hall, in time to see his Auntie Ran grind her elbow into the concave space beneath Davey's chin.

'Haw you, ya cunt.' Forcing him against the door frame, where there is no give and no escape. It is grotesque, yet Gerard is fascinated. Horrified and transfixed at how his auntie is transformed. Davey squirms. Ran presses harder. He ducks, trying to release himself, using her weight to force her backwards. But Ran is really, really strong, and Davey, he sees, is quite small and weedy beside his aunt. He is all bluster and tremors, all glazed, dull eyes, and she slams his head back against the metal frame. 'I've telt you. You fucking stay away from me and my family. You understand?'

'Rissa owes me.'

'Does she fuck. Her man is dead, and you're alive. What the fuck do you want from her now?'

'I want ma fucking life back,' he roars. 'I've been stewing in a fucking cell, and she's out spending ma money.'

'There is no money, you daft cunt. She's a fantasist. D'you not think she'd've fucked off somewhere else if she had money? Why would she still be kicking her heels in this shithole?'

'Naw, she'd just be shooting it up her fucking veins.' Davey lunges forward, his fist high. He makes contact with Auntie Ran's cheek, and she howls. Bends down and brings her head up beneath his chin. The crack rings out across the landing. Davey's fingers are at his nose, blood pumping. Gerard yells, propels himself forward, his skull impacting with Davey's gut. Every ounce of his anger is honed, bitter-welded to every shit thing that has ever hurt him, desperate to destroy the fear Davey instils. Davey reels in the doorway. Smashes his toecap into Gerard's shin, and Gerard drops. Curls in on himself. Wishes this monstrous, yawning threshold would disappear, but Auntie Ran is solid at his spine. With one fluid movement she sweeps him up, brushes him behind her and seizes Davey by the throat.

'Listen to me, you fucking maniac.' The door across the landing opens. An old man peers out. 'It's fine, Jimmy,' Ran yells. 'It's fine. Get yoursel inside.' The old man obeys, just as she's shaking Davey's neck. 'Fucking listen to me.' Another shake.

Gerard huddles in the hallway, arms across his head. 'Please, please, please,' he whispers, but he doesn't know what to do.

Ran shakes Davey harder. 'There was never any money. Rissa is skint. Her weans are terrified.' Her grip moves from his throat to his chin. There is spit and blood at the side of Davey's mouth. 'You may have lost a few years in the jail, but they've lost their dad. He was your fucking mate, ya cunt. Why would you want to terrorise his weans?'

'She fucking owes me!' His eyes are lost, unfocused.

'No. No, she doesny. And I'll tell you this: if you ever come near me or my family again, I'm gonny phone the polis.'

'So fuck?'

'So you're out on fucking parole, you dick. Aren't you? One word fae me, and it's straight back to jail, do not pass go.'

She lets him go, and the momentum sends Davey spinning into the landing. He clatters against the far wall.

'I am. Not. Fucking. Joking.' Finger tapping the side of her skull. 'Are you really mental, right enough? You want to go back inside? If you think you're owed any money, then take it up with Frank fucking McGraw and his mates.'

He blanches. 'Fuck d'you know about McGraw?'

'I know you're his bitch,' she sneers. 'And that he's been taking you up the arse for years.'

Gerard's fingers are in his ears. He thought she was nice; he hates hearing those ugly words come from his auntie's mouth, but Davey is rubbing his teeth and shaking his head. Gerard can see the power leach from his body, until he is nothing but a skinny, troubled smout, wreathed in confusion.

'So get the fuck out my face right now.' Ran waves her mobile phone at him. 'I pressed record the moment I seen your ugly face at the door. Don't think I won't send it to the polis, cause I will. And any time you try this again, remember I've got this video. Pathetic wee Davey Carr threatening a woman and her nephew in glorious technicolour.'

'Aye, but they'll see you doing the same,' Davey blusters. It's the whimperings of a beaten man. Gerard hates violence, yet his adrenaline is coursing, part of him is relishing the thrill of this; it's why guys fight and join gangs and kick the shit out one another. It is terrible and wonderful.

Then Ran charges at Davey, the full force of her hefty torso sending him reeling. 'Get to fucking fuck,' she shrieks.

It works. Amazingly, Davey folds. He staggers towards the stairs. 'Fuck yous,' he shouts. But he goes.

'Here.' Gerard helps his aunt back into the flat. Together, they lock and bolt the door. She is scarlet-hot, the patch of cheek where Davey struck her a deeper puce. 'I need to check my mum,' Ran murmurs. She leaves Gerard standing in his gran's hall. Shaking.

Who is she? All that viciousness, under the skin. His stomach heaves. *Focus on your breathing. Focus on your breathing.*

'Sorry about that.' Ran returns. 'She's still out for the count. Man, that guy is off his fucking skull.' She seems befuddled. Distracted still, as if her thoughts are back in the fight, or with her sleeping mum. Gerard's been there too. Fighting is like waking from a horrible, head-down nightmare. 'Oh God.' Ran grabs his arm, and he recoils slightly. 'I'm so, so sorry you saw that, son. Come back through to the living room, yeah? Let's just get our breath back, eh?'

They sit down. Gerard's lungs are stabbing him. Neither of them say a word. The atmosphere inside the flat is frayed. Davey has made it threadbare. He notices Ran's got the shakes too.

'You got a fag?' asks Gerard eventually.

'What? No! Don't you dare–'

'I'm joking.' Palms up, his Italian gangster pose.

'Not funny.'

'I think he was after this.' Gerard takes *A Ring of Gold* from his manbag. 'I found it last time I was here.'

'Oh, Jesus God.' Ran's hand flies to her mouth. 'I thought we'd chucked that years ago. How on earth did you get that?'

'It was in my mum's bedroom. In the cupboard, under the floor. She telt me to come and get it – that's how I was here. I think that man Davey is after it as well.'

'Of course he fucking is,' she says under her breath. 'So you know Davey?'

'No really. I just seen him hanging about outside our house and that.'

'Christ.' She sighs. 'Right.' Ran blows the hair out of her eyes. Gerard likes how cleanly it bounces.

'Tell me. What d'you remember about your dad, Gerard?'

He shuts his eyes. 'I mind him getting killed.'

'Oh, Jesus God. Jesus God, wee man. You don't remember that?'

'Aye, I do.'

'You were only, what, four? How could you?'

'Cause I was there? It was in my bedroom, wasn't it?' He points to the back of the book. 'That's his blood. Look. And there's writing there too. I mind him writing in my book, just before the men came in. My mum says that's the key. That's why Davey's not to get it.'

'Oh, man.' His auntie groans. Runs her hands through her curly, long hair. Gerard is fascinated by it. He bets it will feel like candyfloss. 'Will it never stop?' She says it into herself. 'Do you always believe what your mum says, Gerard?'

He half-laughs. 'Naw.'

'Do you know anything about Davey?'

'Only that he's got this funny tattoo and he's after us.'

'Right. See when you were a wee boy? Your daddy and Davey were in a gang.'

He nods. 'I thought so. I seen the tag on the landing downstairs.'

'Yup. The S. Car Toi. Big toys for wee boys. They kind of resurrected it from the old days. Anyway, and I hate saying this to you, Gerard, but they wereny very nice. Especially Davey. Got your dad into all sorts of trouble.'

'Did you know my dad then?'

'Aye!' She smiles that smile again. 'He was my big sister's boyfriend. Of course I did.'

'What was he like?'

'Nice. Good-looking guy. Smart too. Too nice for round here. Big softie to be honest. Doted on our Marissa – though Christ knows why. She was always such a bitch to him. I think he only joined the Toi to impress her.'

'I've got this photo of him.' He feels shy all of a sudden. 'The both of them, cuddling. It was hidden with the book. They looked dead happy.'

'Aye, they were some pair. Oh, wee man, this is really hard. But I want to be honest with you. Your mum owed a fair bit of money.'

'To dealers?'

'Aye.'

'No change there.' He crushes his empty can. Sets it, see-sawing on the table.

She gives him a long, slow look. 'You're no daft, are you? Aye, following the family tradition.'

He wonders if she means not being daft or using dealers.

'Well, for whatever reason, your dad and Davey ended up getting involved in an armed robbery. Hired muscle for real gangsters, if you know what I mean.'

'Aye.'

'We're talking thousands and thousands here. I mean, your dad had been in trouble before, but this was big time. Cut a long story short – it all goes tits-up. Some of the gang get arrested, but the money's never found.'

'What about my dad?'

'I don't know, but he was never arrested. Davey was, but. And he never grassed your dad up. But your stupid fucking cow of a mother put it about that your dad had hidden the money. Probably off her face at the time. I think she was trying to be some kind of Mrs Big. A proper gangster's moll or something. Godknows why. I don't know if she thought it would make her untouchable – but it didny.'

'Is that how those men came and hurt my da?'

'I think so, son. Aye. But it was the folk your mum owed money to. Nothing to do with the robbery. Except they thought your daddy had money, of course.'

For a wonderful moment Gerard grabs on to the idea that maybe his daddy is still alive and in jail. Unable to reach him, waiting for the day he can get out and come to Gerard's aid. But he knows this not to be true.

'They did kill him, though, didn't they? I mind his eyes were all jumpy when they dragged him out. But I don't . . .'

His auntie puts her arm round him. 'Oh, pet. They killed him alright. Your mammy . . . she kind of went . . . even more loopy. I don't–'

A noise comes from down the hall.

'Hold on. I need to go and check on my mum again.'

He watches his Auntie Ran leave the room, then follows her because he doesn't want to be on his own. He's frightened if he can't see her, she'll disappear. And if he sits here in this clatty living room, surrounded by the residue of Davey's thick rage and the dying embers of his grandmother's wasted life, all that will remain will be his auntie's words. He needs her to keep talking to him. The lull of her voice dampens his anxiety. What she is telling him and what he has seen is horrible, but it's like they're in a forest full of wolves and she's got him by the hand. If she leaves him there alone, the wolves will get him. Auntie Ran can fight off wolves. She has to lead him to the end.

She's left the bedroom door ajar. Quietly, he pushes it further, so he can stand unobserved and watch them, these two strangers who are connected to him by blood. The room smells sweet. His gran is grey all over, hair and face blending in a sickly mess on the bed. Skinny arms stick from a flowered nightie, but her face is bloated, double chin drooping loosely to her wrinkled chest. Ran is deft and expert in how she lifts, then lays, her mother, making her more comfortable on the pillows. She takes a cotton wool swab, dips it in a cup of water. Then, gently, she runs it along the old woman's lips, squeezing it until drips of water run into his gran's mouth.

Without looking up, she holds out the swab to him. 'Here. Do you want to do it?'

Gerard shrinks away. Returns to the living room, where he waits, holding a cushion to his belly. His auntie comes through with another can of juice and some biscuits.

'Caramel Log or Penguin?'

'Caramel Log. Ta.'

'I get that you don't want to see her. It's not a pretty sight, is it? Look, pal, I'll level with you. She's not got long, your gran, know? I'm just here to . . .'

Gerard peels the wrapper from his biscuit. Tiny crumbles of coconut fall to the floor. The couch judders as she plonks herself beside him. 'To be honest, I don't really want to look at her either. She wasn't the best of mums, put it that way.'

'But you still want to help her?'

Auntie Ran unwraps her own biscuit. 'There's no one else. Plus I do it every day as my job. What kind of a person would I be if I couldn't do it for my own mother?' She takes a bite. Speaks through a mouthful of chocolate. 'Don't get me wrong. I didny want to come back. I live in Aberdeen, see. Got a nice wee flat. I haven't spoken to my mother in . . . what age are you, Gerard?'

'I'm twelve.'

'Twelve? Jeezo. Well, I haven't spoken to either of them in about eight year then.'

'Not my mum either?'

'Nope. I only just came back here. It was your gran's doctor got in touch, to say how bad she was. They must've had me as her next of kin.'

'So my gran knew where you lived?'

'Aye.'

'And did my mum know where you lived?'

'Doubt it.'

'So none of yous talked to each other?'

She finishes her biscuit. 'Nope.'

Was that what happened to families? Would him and Anthony and Miranda end up scattered and alone, none of them knowing what the other was doing? Not knowing each other at all? How could you go from that fierce love he felt for the weans, the bone-deep pain he got when he thought how much he missed them, to this . . . shrug?

He watches his aunt lick her fingers. 'Did you not wonder about us, but?'

'Course I did. But Lucille's no really been compos mentis enough since I got back to have a catch-up chat, put it that way. She thought I was *her* mother last night. Right,' she slaps her hands on her thighs. 'This book of yours.'

'I can mind it. I think it was my favourite.' He realises now, that he used to love books. Gerard, who's feart of words, once got excited by these strange packages of colour and shape.

'It was. You'd three books you used to get every night. One about a mouse in a bath, another one I canny mind – and this.'

'You put me to bed?'

'Sometimes, aye. You were my wee champion.'

A lurch, a stone slipping and shifting. A woman, singing *champi-own-ee*, waving his arms aloft.

'I remember that!'

'You do!' She laughs, a joyous, bubbly sound. 'That was me, wee man.'

'Why did you leave us?'

Her eyes cloud. 'After . . . when your daddy got killed, your mum went to a really dark place. Convinced herself he really had hidden the money. That he'd written a code in your wee book there.'

'A code?'

'A code, a key. A message from beyond the grave.' She fingers the back page of *A Ring of Gold*. 'See this?' She's pointing at the writing his dad did, just before the men came into his bedroom. The letters don't blur or shimmer, but they don't make sense to him either.

'What does it mean?'

'Well, according to your mother, first it was a safety deposit box number. Then it was the number of a road the money was buried under. She even decided he'd stashed it in an old tunnel she used to shoot up in at one point and this was the code to tell her how many bricks up and along he'd hidden it.'

'But maybe she was right? If they didn't find the money?'

'No, Gerard. I told your mum over and over she was talking shite, but you know what she's like. I'm pretty sure him and Davey were just cut out the loop. I know a few of the boys that were jailed. But the real gangsters they were working for would've kept their hands clean. They aye do. That money will have been divvied up all right, otherwise your mum would've been a dead woman walking. She just totally lost it. Your mum's always kindy lived in her own head, know? But this was off the scale. We'd find her at night, wandering. Asking folk to help her find *the treasure*. That's what she called it. She went to a fortune teller down the Barras, was lighting candles to St Anthony, the works.'

He starts slightly, at the mention of his brother's name. He squeezes his eyes, trying to think if any of this story is truly part of his life. When his mum went out, he thought she was at parties. Maybe she was. But maybe she was also moving like a ghost through Glasgow, looking for treasure.

'Here, och, don't cry, Gerard, please. Oh, come here, son.'

He lets himself be cuddled. His aunt is pillowy-soft and squashy once more. 'I'm trying to remember what happened afterwards. But I canny. Did they take me into care right away?'

'Oh no, son. You came here. At first, your mum was catatonic, so yous both came back to ours – here, I mean. You only lived across the way.'

'Not in Dennistoun?'

'No. Right here.' She releases him. 'But the polis had come and sealed off your house. Taken all your bedding and that. For evidence, I suppose. I found you sitting, clutching your wee book. Christ, I think they even made you change out your pyjamas so they could take them too. But nobody thought about the book. It was days later we seen the blood on the back of it, and then Marissa seen your dad's handwriting too, and that's what sent her totally fucking loopy. Sorry.' She pats his knee. 'I shouldny swear like that.'

'It's OK. I'm used to it. I live with my mum.'

They both do the same wee half-smile.

Gerard takes the story book from his aunt. Studies the ink markings which were the very last thing his father ever made. 'What does it mean, then?'

'Well, you read it. It's obvious, isn't it? What do you think?'

'I told you. I canny read.'

Gently, his aunt pushes his hair back from his forehead. He catches a faint floral scent from her wrist. His limbs go loose and easy. The bickering chatter that loops inside him, stops. He wants to curl up here, on this stained couch, and go to sleep. With her stroking his hair.

'Yes, you can,' his aunt encourages. 'You're your father's son as well as your mum's. And your dad, despite his faults, was pretty smart. Look. Watch my finger.' She traces a straight line down, then across. 'What letter's that? Did you not used to have a Letterland Book too? Mind Lucy Lamplady?'

Gerard concentrates. He can see a vague image of a woman with a lampshade on her head. 'L?'

'That's right. Now what about the next one?' She drags her finger down, along and up. 'Come on. You used to know these. Mind the Ugly Umbrella or whatever it was?'

'U?'

'There you go. Now, this one's a number.'

'I can do them not so bad. That's a four.'

'It is indeed. See. You're cooking with gas! And the last one?'

The last letter is quite angry and jaggy-looking. Sideways teeth. He shakes his head.

'It's an E,' she says. 'L. U. 4. E.'

'Right.' He waits for the world to move, but it doesn't.

'*Love You Forever.*' The way Auntie Ran says this makes Gerard's throat ache. 'I think your dad knew, soon as he heard your front door being kicked in. He knew what was going to happen. I think he just wanted to leave yous both a message.'

Gerard places the book on his knee. He copies his aunt's movements, drawing each symbol with his finger. 'St Mungo,' he says.

'Sorry?'

'That's who this book's about. He gets a lady's ring out a fish. And he brings a wee robin back to life.'

'That's right.'

'He made Glasgow.'

'He did.'

'Maybe my mum should've prayed to St Mungo.'

'Maybe.'

'Did my dad die right away?'

'I don't know, son. Pretty soon. They found his body a few hours later.'

'Where?'

His aunt shakes her head. 'I canny mind. In the back court of some tenement.'

'Where's he buried?'

'Not far from here, actually. I'll show you one day.'

Gerard reaches for the *one day*. Catches it the way you'd catch a dandelion spore. That means he will see her again. He leans forward, so he can stare right inside the specks of his dad's blood. It's brown, not red. He must have been so scared. 'Was my dad a junkie too?'

'No! I mean, he dabbled a wee bit. But your mum was way worse.' Auntie Ran hunches forward so her forearms rest on her thighs. She picks at her nails as she talks. 'Your mum was always trying to be somewhere she was not. Ever since . . . well. She used to be good fun, when we were wee. I mind us playing some brilliant games – princesses and dragons. Spaceships. She was really good at making things up.'

There's a catch in her voice. He feels the tension in her body. Gerard tries to picture his mum as a kid, a lassie having fun with her wee sister. He concentrates really, really hard until he is there, in the most unguarded heart of himself, and she is there too. Marissa. They are holding hands and they're the same age, birling each other wide, and she is smiling just like Auntie Ran, and then he's immediately consumed by sadness, because he will never know his mum like that.

'What happened to her?'

'Don't be too angry with your mum, eh? She aye lived in a bit of a fantasy world – even before the drink and drugs took over. Your gran wasn't very nice to us. Neither were the folk she hung about with.' She looks away. 'Marissa aye got the worst of it.'

'Why did you leave us?'

'Self-preservation? Christ, you've seen what happens when I come back here.' She cradles her sore cheek. 'Gerard, I swear on my life, I tried. Your mum ended up . . . she just couldn't look after you. And your gran was no use either. In fact, I couldny leave the two of them alone with you. When they get together, they two either go on massive benders or try to kill each other. Sometimes both.'

Ran takes a long slug of Coke. Relaxes into the cushions. Gerard is glad of the rest. His brain feels it's been mugged. Was all of this awfulness in his files? Did every person know this when they were peering at him over their grey folders? When they were passing judgement, every time, on what should be done with him next? It pierces a hole right through him. The desolation he feels for that wee boy. But he takes a breath, stoppers up the wound. Otherwise folk can smell it on you.

'I asked the social work to let me have custody of you,' his auntie says. 'Begged them. But I was only seventeen. Stuck here with the two of them. There's no way they'd let me have you in the house. I thought they might give us our own wee place, but, no.'

'That's no fair.'

'No, son. No, it isny.'

Imagine if he'd always had this? If being with Ran was no big deal. It startles him, how comfortable he feels beside her, even after she's went full tonto. What if he'd always known that feeling, so normal he'd never even notice how precious it was? How different his life might have been. Why do clicky-pen strangers get to decide who's allowed to be a family? Kris and Craig are nice, but Gerard is forever a guest in their home. He's their work. He knows for a fact Kris keeps receipts for every pair of socks she's bought him, any bus ride or ticket for the cinema. They claim it back. Gerard's never sure what seat to sit on, in case he ruffles a cushion, and the telly's mostly on BBC2 (which is shite). And they're all so bloody . . . *shiny*. He feels brittle in their home. Dazzled by bright, clipped smiles and clever questions, those constant wee nudges to be productive, be polite. Kris and Craig are Gerard's sheepdogs. Only in his room can he relax.

'When they took you into foster care, it broke my heart,' Ran says. 'It happened so quick – it was an emergency order. But I thought, maybe it's for the best. Maybe wee Gerard will get out of this shitehole and make something of hisself. Then I thought, well, maybe I should too. So I did. I went up to Aberdeen. Got into college. Made new pals. I never knew your mum was pregnant then. I'd never have . . .' She covers her face with her hands. He doesn't think she's crying. She's just bone-weary. He recognises that feeling.

'But did you not keep in touch or anything? Not even to see how I was?'

'Your mum and I had a big fall out. She didny want me to go, called me all sorts for abandoning her and my mum. But I knew they'd just drag me further down if I stayed. With you gone, there was nothing for me here. So I just pissed off. Didn't tell anyone. Just up and left one morning. I did send my mum my address later on, once I'd got settled. But I never heard back.'

She taps the book. 'Marissa wouldny let this out her sight at times. My mum promised me she'd burn it.'

'What am I going to do?'

'About what?'

'This? My mum? Mad Davey? Does Davey really believe my dad took the money?'

'Guess he must. Guy always was a prick. No the brightest tool in the box, put it that way. I thought he'd still be in the jail, to be honest.'

'So what do I do?'

His auntie's thinking. Her eyes flit that same way his mum's do. 'Nothing. If he comes near either of you again, I will break his fucking neck.' She rises majestically. There is no other word for it, the way her strong legs power her upwards and her chin juts high and clean. 'But I reckon we won't see Davey again.'

'Serious?'

'Aye.' Auntie Ran flounces her mauve overall. 'Guy's a bullshitter. But, then, so am I.' She winks, waves her phone at him.

'Did you not record him, then?'

'Naw. I only thought of it once I was saying it. But, hey, he doesny know that. I may work as a carer, but inside he knows

I'm a fucking Bell. Aye ready for a ding-dong. We're animals, us Bells! Hard as nails.' She actually growls, and Gerard bursts out laughing. 'You and me both, sunshine. How d'you think we've managed to survive, eh?' She wanders over to the window. 'Look at they bloody seagulls. At the bins again. It's carnage.'

Gerard comes over to join her. Scores of huge white birds, wheeling and diving around the black hopper bins. One of them is tugging and tugging with its yellow beak. Its wings flap in triumph as it tears a huge strip of cardboard from a pizza box and makes off with its prize, dripping tomato gunk on a car parked below.

'You know, Aberdeen's by the sea, but I seen more seagulls here in a week than I've seen in a year up the road.'

The two of them watch the birds fly, playing tig with one another in figures of eight. Seagulls are elegant. Fierce. Gerard doesn't like their beady eyes, but he likes the way they strut. There's one swaggering across the car park, the hook of its beak saying *Come ahead*. Pigeons scatter, and even the cat that was stalking them slinks behind a Volvo. You wouldny mess with a seagull.

'Who's St Anthony?'

'The patron saint of lost things.'

'Huh.' Gerard's head is louping, but he feels calm. His lips breathe against the window glass. There is nothing but the seagulls and the sunlight, which has broken through the drizzle, burnishing the cars. A glint of metallic green, a pulse of blue, flash of beat-up dusty yellow, more blue, a slash of red. It's mesmerising. The motors make a rainbow. The flitting seagulls stitch land and air and sea. Birds can go anywhere they like. Gerard stands beside his auntie, their elbows touching, in a cluttered room which has plenty things in, but no soul, while his grandmother hovers on the edge of someplace else. She had a family once, but she's alone. He tries to feel sorry for her. Nothing comes. Gerard knows what sorry feels like. You can't magic it; it has to well up, bubble through like water from a spring. It's what people call your conscience. If he was drawing it (which is just the sort of stupid thing Dr Lumsden might make him do), his conscience would be a pale, feathery hand, turning you round. Forcing you to look at what you've done. Your conscience makes you imagine the other person, the one who's not you, and how they might feel. Tells you to ask if you could change that. It's funny, but he cares more about the old lady he knocked over than his own gran. He doesny need to care about her. Auntie Ran won't mind; he knows this instinctively. Gerard steals another look at this new miracle. Finally, his pulse is steady. His heart luminous.

'What does Ran mean? Is it short for anything?'

'It's short for Miranda.'

'That's my wee sister's name!'

'I know, you telt me.' His auntie's eyes are shiny. 'Maybe next time you go to see them I could come too?'

'Oh, man! I'd love that. But . . . I'd need to check with Naggy.'

'Who's Naggy?'

'My social worker.'

'You leave her to me.'

A sensation of release. Like the time Gerard had a broken arm and the doctor cut off his plaster. His healed arm had flown up, weightless with delight at being free.

'Will you phone my foster mum too, and tell her where I am, please?'

'You are some chancer, boy. Just like your daddy. Right, what's her number?'

A secret joy reverberates through the walls. Ran sees parts of Gerard he doesn't know are there. He has an auntie. It's mad how your life is one thing and it can only ever be that thing, with no other paths for you to go on, and you accept it'll never change, because change is impossible. You are stuck with what you're given. Then, all of a sudden, it does. Change happens, just like that. Then it becomes the real thing, and you are living inside the dream that was further than the moon.

He's terrified to ask when she's going back to Aberdeen.

AUGUST

Chapter Twenty-Four

Traffic rumbles, imposing a steady rhythm on the day, exuding exhaust fumes so you are breathing carbon monoxide to the boom and grind of constant buses. But the effect is like being by the sea. Lulling you with broad, fixed beats. Providing a vast background for your wandering thoughts.

Claire examines her fingers. They're threaded through those of a man, and they are walking down Duke Street, in full view of the world (the couple, not the fingers). If she had feathers, she would preen. Puffed chest too, courtesy of new and better underwear. Damp, close, beginning-of-the-end-of-summer air. The street is shiny with her gladness. Folk can see how easy her strides are, matching pace with the man at her side. Drops of rain begin to fall. She turns her face towards the corrugated sky to stop from laughing out loud. Teenage Claire felt the same when she got her first boyfriend.

Complete.

She knows it's superficial. Transient. These passers-by do not know her, nor she them. To be fair, she doesn't know Grant completely either. Who knows how long this will last? It matters not one iota how she presents herself to the denizens of Duke Street, and yet it does, it does. They walk past the brewery nestled in the shadow of the Necropolis, past the pizza-by-the-slice place and the disused Grecian-style church. Being alone is a delight, sometimes. But it should never be your default. Shopping on your own, cooking on your own, eating on your own, walking on your own. Claire is aware of how defensively she moves, the barriers of book or mobile phone she deploys to intercept the space between her aloneness and other people. Solitude is a place of calm escape. Loneliness is spikes on the outside, and yearning within. Hurtling you straight back to childhood and a bustling playground. You, unmoving in the corner, not knowing how to join in.

Claire wears her loneliness in many subtle forms, and her hurried gait is one of them. But today has slowed. Today is sleepy with deliciousness. Another human, choosing to spend time with her. And folk *seeing* it. That shouldn't validate her. Yet here she is, sparkling. She and Grant chat about the hulking new flats on the site of the abattoir. *Is Meat Market really the name to entice the buyers?* They bemoan the state of the beautiful old hospital opposite, derelict and held together by metal rivets. Say how glad they are it's not a match day, or the street would be hoaching with football fans. They reach the new vegan bakery that's appeared beside the vape shop. Check out the charity shops further along.

Grant looks left and right. 'It's got a nice buzz, this place.'

'It does.' Seen through his eyes, Claire is proud of the bleached-wood cafés, hunkered by the bookies and overflowing bins. The tenements lour benignly: slightly drunk but affable. Beaten up, but with good bones beneath. They are going for lunch at a Middle Eastern deli. Claire has never been for lunch in Dennistoun (except a café with Margaret, which doesn't count).

Most of her encounters with Grant have revolved around meals – she is savouring food now, not using it as ballast. The first dinner they had was . . . great, actually. Her skull had felt huge and echoey, and full of another person's life. Margaret's hidden life. By the time she'd got Margaret settled, rushed home and had a quick shower, Claire was fair founert herself. So much churn within her. Once she finally made it to the birthday party, she was just too spent to try. Her usual excitable energy (which tips into manic chattiness as the wine flows and nerves jangle) never materialised. She was relaxed, light, with fashionably dishevelled hair. They'd blethered. Had a laugh. Then he'd taken her phone number – and actually called. They met that Friday for cocktails after work (in a very nice gin bar in town). That went even better. They've had a date most weekends since. Claire and Grant will shortly be heading for falafel, and, today, she feels the very best version of herself.

Maybe that's the way to do it.

Life: don't try too hard.

'Do you mind if we nip in here first?' Claire asks, nudging Grant's arm to turn left, up Hillfoot Street. It feels nice, this connection. Not quite a frisson, but there is a press of anticipation. They are not that far from her flat. Maybe they'll go there after lunch. 'I've something I need to drop off.' They've stopped outside Denholm & Serge. The theme du jour is full Culloden, with a velvet Bonnie Prince Charlie jacket atop a black denim kilt, and two criss-crossed claymores suspended on wires. Drippy Gothic lettering on the window hammers the unsubtle point: *Outland-ish.*

'Sure.' Grant's reflection is imposed on a Royal Stewart tartan ball gown. 'Are we going to a ceilidh later? Should I practise my Strip the Willow?' He offers her his crooked arm. Sandy hair half-covers his left eye, but the right one sparkles and is coloured like the sea. He really does have a lovely smile.

'Nah, don't worry. I'm just handing in a client letter. Won't be a sec.'

'Working on a Saturday? Hope you're billing them extra hours.'

She jingles the shop door. Scott emerges from the back shop, wielding a large pair of scissors. Claire raises her hands. 'I come in peace. Here.' She slides the envelope across the counter. 'This is for you.'

'That me got my marching orders?' The shop is piled with boxes. Half the shelves are empty. There has been some limited correspondence: Scott can't afford a lawyer.

Claire shrugs. 'Open it.'

He tears the envelope, unfolds the sheet of paper. Lays it flat on the counter. Claire can see the start of the paragraph she dictated earlier that week. Scott begins to read aloud.

'*Dear Sir,*

With regard to our meeting of blah, during which it was established that my client is the owner of the property at blah . . . Having consulted with my client . . .'

Then he stops. Lifts the letter closer to his face.

Claire knows how the rest of it goes.

'*As a gesture of goodwill, and in recognition of the long service of Mr Donald Aitken, my client has decided to allow you, if agreeable, to obtain a three-year lease on the premises on the following favourable terms, to be renewed annually. Furthermore, my client will agree not to proceed with any civil or criminal action, provided back-dated rent is recovered at the rate of £700 per calendar month – to be paid in full within twenty-one working days.*'

Scott mouths the last few words, then conceals his mouth behind his hand. 'You're kidding?'

'Nope. But you will need to engage your own solicitor so we can draw up the lease.'

'Aye, aye, of course. Jesus, man.' He shakes his head. 'This is *amazing*. I was not expecting this.'

Claire has remonstrated with Margaret in the strongest terms. 'You could sell the shop. Make a fortune.'

'But what would I do with it?' she'd said. 'Anyway, he bought it for Stephen.'

'Well, you don't know that. There was no mention of that in Albert's will.'

'But that's the only bit that makes sense. It's Stephen's legacy. It's what Bert always wanted. So, when I go, Stephen can do what he likes with the place.'

'Well, at least consider new tenants then. Ones that are trustworthy.'

'No. I've thought about it long and hard. Now I've calmed down. I feel bad for them. As long as thon Smirky Scott makes sure Donald's looked after, and I get a wee bit of rental each month, then we're all winning.'

'Jeez, you've mellowed.'

'Maybe I have.'

Through Denholm & Serge's window, Claire can see Grant, watching her. He sticks his tongue out. Smiles. The soggy street outside, the little tailor's shop. Her. All suffused with warmth.

Scott rubs his beard. 'What changed the old dear's mind?'

'Honestly? I don't know,' she lies. 'Maybe you should ask her.'

'Nah.' She hears Scott sniff. 'I feel shite for what I said. About her son and that. I'm not sure she'd want to talk to me.'

Claire raises her hand in a little shy wave. Grant waves back. 'Yeah, well, I don't think she's doing it for you. I think she's doing it for your grandad. Even though he shafted her too.'

'That your man out there? Here, does he want a shirt? We've a really good offer on poplin button-downs. I can do you two for one?'

'No, thanks.'

'No bother. He looks a bit like that Sam Heughan, though, doesn't he?'

'Who? Grant?'

'Aye.' Scott waves at him too, while still holding the scissors. Grant looks a bit puzzled. 'Oh aye. Check out that brooding brow. D'you know, now that we're staying, I'll be looking to update the website. Highlight our Culloden chic range. Would your man be up–'

'No. And, in future, we'll be doing everything via letter or email, OK? Talking of which, Margaret asked me to ask if you knew what happened to Albert's letter? The one that got returned from Australia.'

'Havny a clue. Sorry.'

'Any chance it's still kicking around? In here?'

'Not after two humungous clearouts and a grand refurbishment, no.'

Claire leaves Smirky Scott to his scissors, opens the door. The shop bell jingles. The air is smirred with moisture. She takes Grant's hand. 'Sorted,' she says.

In years to come, when she thinks of Margaret, she will think of this day too. How the light shone through prisms of rain and glittered the longest street in Glasgow, Scotland, Europe, wherever. How it lit the sandstone walls and gilded the heart of her, revealing millennia of quartz and feldspar, all the silicate grains compressed by time and wave and gravity. Great blocks dug from a Dumfriesshire quarry, shaped by dexterous hands. And she will think of all the layers of life that have lived within those walls, and the light that shone out of them, beating its hopeful pulse into Glasgow. Warm bowls of light, saying *this is home*. Folk cheek by jowl, above, below. In their boxes. Their bay windows, their truckle beds. In the mouths of their closes. All those people, going forth into the world. She will recall the press of a man's hand in hers, the texture of his skin, how his pinkie cupped the tender edge of her palm. And she will smile at the memory of Margaret's kindness. Her fortitude.

At how Margaret rarely took her advice.

Margaret will be one of those rare, complex women whom Claire remembers fondly, and with frustration, whom she'll wish she'd known when they were both the same age. It would have been fun to go dancing with Margaret. But, for now, all she plans to do is to walk along Duke Street, turn right with Grant, and take him to meet her friend. And then, they will go for falafel.

Chapter Twenty-Five

Gerard rests his cheek inside his folded arms. Head on the table. They're doing it differently this time. Instead of being marched in as the accused, they've got him waiting inside the room. The naughty kid at his desk. His primary two teacher would make him sit like that for ages. Head down, thumbs up. *If you won't participate, Gerard Macklin, then we'll just pretend you're not here.* Whole mornings wasted gazing out the classroom window. Only seeing a slice of sky, listening to his schoolmates' chatter. Them, having fun. Whispering about him – the boy who could not sit still. There must've been others like him, who'd got themselves up and dressed. No breakfast, no jacket. Running out the house, being chased by a screaming mother trying to belt you with a hairbrush cause you'd drunk the last of the milk. Then, knees trembling as the adrenaline surged, trying desperately not to overturn the desk – because that is what you wanted to do, so desperate were you to jettison that energy, just run and tear your hair until you'd calmed down enough to think.

The teachers must've seen that, surely?

A door behind him opens. Footsteps. A murmuring ripple, echoing in the lofty space.

'Sit up, Gerard!' Naggy dunts him with her elbow.

He sits up. Another big old room, another horseshoe-shaped arrangement of tables. Gerard is flanked by Naggy and Kris. Craig's at work but will be here shortly. On his right is a row of four people: man, woman, woman, man. One looks like his old teacher from Dennistoun. Shit, does that mean they're punting him back to the East End? He's not sure it's her, but. His neck feels clammy. Kris says they'll be starting the home-schooling again, until they decide on his 'transitional arrangements'. He's quite looking forward to it actually. She's got that literacy tutor in too, and the guy's brand new. Got Gerard up to reading age seven. It is so much easier when the letters don't jump. The tutor gets him to do slow breathing before they even start, but he honestly doesny think he needs it. He just thinks of his dad's finger, moving smoothly beneath each word, and it calms the letters right down.

Every day, as well as his words, he's been practising thinking of his dad. If wee flashes of him cuddling Gerard or throwing him up in the air until he squeals keep coming, it helps to lay down layers, covering over the memories of blood. It doesn't rub them out; nothing will do that. It's like painting over the top. His grief counsellor bangs on about the need to 'sit with his emotions'. Him and Dr Lumsden should do a double act. What with the grief and the anger, plus Naggy and his fosters, and the weans' fosterers and all the counsellors and that, it's a pretty big seat they'll need.

To his left is a man Gerard doesn't recognise and a woman he does. Glint of gold tooth. Matching gold bracelet. The woman acknowledges him, now he's come up from his dwam. 'Alright, wee man?' It's the hackit policewoman, the one who chased him. Got him into all this mess in the first place.

A simpery voice inside his ear. *No, she didn't, Gerard. That was you. You have to accept responsibility.* The voice is neither male nor female. It could belong to any of them in here cause they've all said it to him at one point. Or will do in the future.

It has to be your own voice, Gerard.

Words are powerful.

Your voice is powerful.

So when will yous listen to me? Gerard wonders.

The policewoman's not in uniform. She looks awkward in her

skirt and blouse. Gerard scans the room for Auntie Ran. No trace. He dies a wee bit inside. He knows there is a train strike and it's three hours' drive from Aberdeen. He's not seen her much, since his gran died. Ran went with him to the hospital to visit his mum. Mum was horrible to her. Just kind of grunted and turned over. Gerard tries to imagine if he hadn't seen the weans for years and years, and a bright, spiky feeling fills his chest. He would never turn away. When Ran told her about his gran, his mum had laughed. Pure cackled like a mentalist witch, until Gerard had to leave the room.

Straight after the funeral, the Council papped Auntie Ran out of his gran's flat. She said she'd 'no option' but to go back home. *I've a flat there, Gerard. My own place.* He thinks she might be at college there too. He canny mind. *Lots of stuff to sort*, she told him. *But I'll be back. I promise.*

Aye, right. Said in the days after the funeral, when his auntie was sore and teary. Gerard didn't go to the funeral. Why would he? His gran was just a raddled old woman who was nothing to him. He'd still felt a bit funny, but. On the day. A strange kind of heaviness in his bones. Kris offered to take him, but he didny want to.

Three sets of footsteps move round the wonky tables. His psycho psychologist Lumsden is reclining in his seat, polishing his glasses. Gerard wants to kid on he's lobbing a ball of flame at him. *Here's all today's anger, matey. Catch!* The Panel members take their seats.

'Good afternoon, everyone,' says the lady in the middle. 'I'd like to welcome you to this Children's Hearing, in respect of Gerard Macklin.'

Roll up, roll up, for Gerard's Shite Show.

There is the usual round of introductions. Gerard tunes out, as they begin to recap his misdemeanours. There is nothing good about it. One by one, the adults speak. They talk about *GIRFEC Principles* and his *Child Plan*. One woman insists that *the Wellbeing Wheel must be core,* She is very clear on that. Another woman mentions *a triangle* of something or other. He recognises

Kris's voice above the drone, telling them all about his dirty stop-out ways. She sounds sad actually.

'Would you say there is a failure in general to adhere to boundaries?'

'No,' Kris says firmly. 'Gerard is a bright and intelligent boy. He knows when he . . . when there is a need to correct his behaviours. And he is trying, really hard.' A flash of her kind, white teeth. In that moment, he loves her.

The door opens again and Gerard's pulse speeds, but it's only Craig, smiling sheepishly as he shimmies in. Whispering, 'Apologies, Chair.'

Then it's Naggy's turn to give her report, and he hears her saying that she doesn't think he's ready for *Reaching Out* after all. He hasny a clue what that is. Just as long as they let him keep doing Gardening Guerrillas.

'I may have been a little premature in suggesting it,' Naggy continues. 'On reflection, I think, as lead professional, given the death of Gerard's grandmother and the fact of his mother's recent hospitalisation–'

The Chair interrupts: 'I believe his mother is unable to attend today?'

'That's correct. She's currently an inpatient in a rehabilitation programme, over in Midlothian. It's very intensive, and her doctor felt–'

'No, no, that's fine.' The Chair waves her hand. 'Please continue.'

'We just feel that Gerard needs to work on himself for the next wee while. He's doing very well with his literacy, and his relaxation practices, as well as attending the Molendinar Centre once a week.'

'Yes. We'll be hearing from Dr Lumsden shortly.'

'Indeed.' Naggy is putting on her posh voice. 'So, to ask him to participate in a scheme where he's required to make himself vulnerable, and analyse his actions in a potentially censorial fashion–'

'That's not the object of the pilot at all,' says another person.

'It's entirely non-confrontational. Very much a reflective and healing process for all concerned.'

Gerard's legs begin to jitter under the table. He pumps them a little harder, trying to see if he can get the table to move using only his knees. Make them think the place is haunted – and it could be; it's a creepy old school they're in. This room might have been the old gym hall or dinner school. It has wooden arches like whalebones above his head and long thin windows. They are three floors up. The outline of wings in flight is ghosted on one of the uppermost glass panes, along with spattered birdshit. He bets some wean will have fallen over the banisters of the stairwell at some point. Or more likely been pushed. There are many nooks and crannies for bullying in this building.

'Even so,' Naggy's saying, 'asking a traumatised child to relive part of that trauma, however sanitised–'

'What about the victim's trauma?' says the hackit policewoman.

Trauma, trauma, trauma. You could make a wee tune out of that. Whoa, yes, there it goes. The table rises slightly, causing Naggy's papers to drift to the left. Without looking at Gerard, she jabs her hand out to push them back in place. He can feel the pressure of her pushing down on the table too.

'Do we have any further updates there?' says the lady in the middle. The one they call Chair. He imagines her with a cushion on her head.

'Only that she's keen to proceed and feels it would be beneficial to her own rehabilitation.'

'And Gerard is aware of this?' asks the Chair.

Naggy hisses at him, 'Gerard!'

'What?'

Everyone is staring. He slides his hands beneath the table. Under his thighs.

'They're asking you a question.'

'What?'

'Your social worker Natalie is suggesting you may not want to proceed with the Reaching Out scheme?' says the Chair.

'What's that one again?'

Naggy speaks quietly in his ear. 'Where you write a letter to the old lady.'

'What? No, but I do. I want to say sorry to her.' Gerard panics. They'd already said he could. He wants to stand up, so they can tell how important this is, but he knows that will get him into trouble.

'Why is that, Gerard?'

'Because I do.' His breath is sore in his throat.

'But why?' Two different folk are talking at him now, on purpose. Trying to confuse him.

'Because I am, right?' He is jerking his head from one to the other. Who's meant to be in charge here? Who is it he's got to convince?

'How do you know you're sorry, Gerard?'

He looks at the man who says this as if he has two heads. And the other one is up his arse. 'How do you?'

'I'm sorry?' The guy's nostrils flare.

'Aye, are you, but? Are you really? How do you know?'

'Gerard . . .' Naggy's doing her warning growl.

'I know I'm sorry because I wish I hadn't done it, right?' Gerard leans forward, forcing his words out hard. He senses the others back away. 'I think about it loads, right? What if she was someone's gran? What if she hadn't got up again? It makes me feel really, really crap that I hurt her, and I want to tell her about the leccy meter and the card and the wean's arse being red raw, and I want her to know I didn't mean to push her. I didny fucking mean it, right?' He's shouting now but he cannot stop. 'I want her to know I'm not BAD!'

Before they lead him out again, which they surely will do since Gerard is being a *Disruptive Presence* and Naggy is drawing him daggers, the door to the big room bangs opens for a third time, and a heavy, out-of-breath woman batters in.

'I'm so sorry I'm late. Hi, darling! Hi, Gerard!' His auntie waves, trailing a suitcase behind. The trundling wheels squeak as she makes her way over to Gerard.

'Excuse me,' says the Chair. 'And you are?'

'I'm Gerard's Auntie Miranda. Miranda Bell.'

'Well, we've been in session for a while now, Ms Bell. It's a shame you couldn't join us at the start.'

Gerard hates the snidey way the woman says this. Craig was allowed to come in late and nobody said bugger all. His Auntie Ran is not dressed in a posh designer blazer, though. She's in a sort of combat jacket-thing, flapping loose over her purple overall. Overweight and a wee bit sweaty, hauling a lime-green suitcase with daisies on. She ignores the Chair. Kisses Gerard on the top of his head. A candle flares inside him, burning up to where she is, and the room shimmers. Goes soft like after snow falls. She is here.

'Budge up,' she says to Naggy, pulling up a seat. Their knees bounce against one another. Gerard takes a sip of water.

'So,' Auntie Ran addresses the room. Her chin is jutting out the way his mum's does when she's about to let rip. But he can tell Ran is nervous. Can see how tensely she grips her shoulder bag. 'What have I missed? Sounded like you were getting my nephew a bit distressed out there.'

'Ms Bell, we were made aware by Gerard's social worker that you may be joining us. And you *will* have the opportunity to talk later. However, if you don't mind, we'd like to–'

'Well, I do mind, actually. I apologise for being late. I got held up at work due to an old lady having a seizure. Which meant I then missed my bus from Aberdeen and, as the trains are currently on strike and I don't have a car, I'd no option but to wait for the next one. I did call the number I had for Social Work to explain.' Auntie Ran looks at Naggy.

'Well, I'm sorry. The message wasn't passed on.'

'That's a shame. Anyway, I'm here now. And we all want the best for Gerard's future, right? So what I have to say is important. It's got an impact on everything else you decide here today.'

The Chair sighs. 'Very well, Ms Bell. Go ahead.'

Auntie Ran clears her throat. Stands up.

'That won't be necessary, Ms Bell. Please sit down.'

'No, thank you. I've prepared a statement.' She takes a piece of paper from her shoulder bag, and as she does so, Naggy begins to pass more papers round the table. She raises her eyebrow at Ran, and they both do a wee smile. Gerard's heart is beating so fast he thinks he might explode.

'OK, can I start? Right. My name is Miranda Bell. I am the younger sister of Gerard, Anthony and Miranda's mother, Marissa. I'm currently in my final year of a social sciences degree at the University of Aberdeen. I supplement my studies by working part-time as a carer for Aberdeen City Council. I have a two-bedroom flat which I rent along with a female student friend. Because of my job, I am fully Disclosure Checked for working with vulnerable people and have no criminal convictions.'

'Ms Bell–'

'Can you let me finish, please? My late mother and my sister both have drug and alcohol addictions, and I've been estranged from them both for a number of years. However, when Gerard was a baby, and up until the age of four, I was fully involved in his welfare and development, regularly babysitting and caring for him. It was only when Gerard was taken into care following the violent death of his father – and despite me begging at the time to be allowed to look after him – that I moved away.' She stares hard into Gerard's eyes when she says this, and he feels all the years she was apart from him just shrink away. He wants to tell her it's fine, but he can't.

'I believed him to be safe at that time.' Ran's voice wavers. Roughly, she pulls one hand down the side of her nose. 'Sorry.' Steadies herself. 'I returned to Glasgow to care for my mother in the last weeks of her life. My mother is now dead, and I have no dependents.' She drops the paper on the table. Her breath wheezes. Gerard can see beads of sweat dripping on her forehead. She is so beautiful. 'Please.' Her voice goes quiet. So quiet he's worried that they won't hear. 'I want to look after them. Let me look after my family.'

Once, Gerard was standing in a church when a bell rang. He thinks it was a first communion. Not his – he doesn't know why he was there. Just a handbell, clanging too close to his ear, and he got a fright. But it was such a clear, pure sound, chiming on into the hush that came after. It was like star-song. He thinks his auntie sounds like that.

'What age are you, Ms Bell?' says the man beside the Chair.
'Twenty-five.'
'And you live in Aberdeen?'
'I do. But I've spoken to the uni. They'll let me defer for a year. Or' – she becomes bold again – 'if you might be able to assist me in securing suitable rented accommodation here, the university say they'll consider letting me transfer to the BA Honours at Glasgow Cally. My adviser of studies is writing to them this week. Or we can live in Aberdeen – but I realise that means he'll be away from his support networks – all the support you're giving him, which I really appreciate, I do.' She's out of breath again. 'I want to be a kinship carer.' She glances at Gerard. 'Please. I'm his auntie. If his mum can't look after him, then he should be with me.'

Naggy interrupts: 'Chair, if I can just draw everyone's attention to appendix four, you'll see that Ms Bell has already started the kinship process. All appropriate suitability checks are before you.'

'Ms Bell,' says the Chair. 'I'm not quite clear on this. Is it your wish to care for Gerard only?'

'No! No way. For his brother and sister too. I want them to be together.'

Gerard closes his eyes. He is in a tunnel. A triangular tunnel, arched high in the belly of a whale and all the people in the room are rushing at him faster than a train. Gerard's in the dark bit, with his eyes shut tight, and they are all bright white headache light behind them, swooshing over and past him, great white waves which will flatten and crush. If he crouches down, though, crouches and keeps his eyes shut and digs in his heels and holds his auntie's hand, he can withstand them. With the other hand, he can hang on to Anthony – or Miranda, he doesny mind. But Auntie Ran can take the other one and together they can make a wall.

'Have you ever met Gerard's siblings, Ms Bell?'

Gerard leaves his mental wee tunnel behind, returns to the mental wee Panel. Ran waves her arms about when she talks, so he'll not be holding her hand any time soon. He tries to work out what he knows about Aberdeen. Cold. Oil. Decent football team. No Gardening Guerrillas. No Jo or Ali. Nowhere near his mum.

'No, not yet. What with my mum dying, and me having to go back up the road . . .' Ran falters. 'Term's starting back in October, you see, and I'd a paper to write. And there's my job. But I've asked Nat – Gerard's social worker – to see if we can arrange a meeting soon.'

'I see. Your other nephew's seven – is that correct? – and yet you've never met him?'

'Chair,' Naggy butts in, 'Ms Bell has not been in a position to get to know her nephews and niece, due to her estrangement from her sister. But that shouldn't preclude–'

Helen and Richard never met the weans before they fostered them, Gerard thinks. This is bogus. Why are they being nasty when Ran is only trying to help?

'Are you married, Ms Bell, or in a relationship?'

'No.'

'But you may want to be in the future? What about children of your own?'

'I'm not sure this is appropriate,' says Naggy.

'Kris and Craig have got their own children!' Gerard shouts. 'And Helen and Richard never met the weans before they fostered them either!'

'Gerard, please.'

He can feel it slipping away. Tears pool behind his eyes. He stares straight ahead. Imagines a superpower where he could smash in all they long windows, just pure stare at them and watch them shatter.

'Look,' says Ran. 'No one was there for my sister and me when we were growing up. And I'm pretty sure no one was there for my mum when she was a wee lassie either. I'm not going to go into all that – it's there, on the back of my statement. Yous can all have a good read of how shite my family's lives have been. But the point is: *I can*. I can be there for my nephews and my niece. Please let me. They're my blood,' she whispers, sitting down. Without pause, she reaches for him. Automatically Gerard leans into her, hiding his face in her belly.

'Shh, wee man. It's OK.'

Silence fills the cavernous room. He can hear them all, gawping at him. Wants to give them the finger.

'Gerard,' Naggy says gently, 'Gerard, do you want a wee break?'

'No,' he sniffs. 'I want you to ask me.'

'Ask you what?'

He glares at her.

'Gerard,' Naggy says, in a much louder voice. 'What do *you* want?'

'I want to live with my Auntie Ran.'

Chapter Twenty-Six

Gerard lives in other people's homes. Today is the day he moves from one house to another. But, this time, it's different. The tall, thin house he's spent the summer in seems even taller when you're sitting in a car and looking up to say goodbye. Auntie Ran has hired a nice blue Nissan, especially for the occasion. Kris and Craig stand on the pavement. (The boys are at school.) Kris has her cardigan hugged tight around her. Her eyes are red. Craig is very cheery, using lots of big words and hand gestures. Twice he has clapped Gerard on the back and called him *young man*. The car door remains open. Gerard will shut it when Auntie Ran starts the engine. He just needed a wee seat. But he likes that the fresh air is keeping them connected. Now he's leaving, Gerard feels a bit sad. Happy sad. They're really nice folk, Kris and Craig. Imagine having a huge, big house and all that money. You could totally shut the world outside. When you don't need anything else, why would you bother about other people? They've let him stay for months. They've gave up a room in their house, and made their own boys share their PlayStation and put up with Gerard's tantrums. *They are* not *tantrums*, he hears Dr Lumsden say. *They are an expression of an emotion you're finding difficult to process.* Aye, he bets Auntie Ran won't be saying that if he kicks off with her. But her too. Ran does it. She cares for folk she doesny have to. He thought she was his gran's carer at first, but she says she was only wearing that overall to keep her own clothes clean. When you hear *clean*, you think of *dirty*. Oh, man. Bad enough having to take your wrinkly old mum to the toilet. But if it's a total stranger? That's what carers do. It's just being kind, his auntie's told him. *Wouldn't you want someone to do that for you one day?*

Kris is giving Auntie Ran a hug. The two women hold the embrace for quite a long time. Craig stands to the side of his wife, patting her shoulder. When you think about it though, toilets and that, Gerard's done it for Miranda, and it hardly bothered him at all. But that wasn't kindness, that was just your wee sister, which is really a part of you. If you are properly kind like his Auntie Ran, or folk like Kris and Craig, then there's a difference. You are giving so much more. Caring for people who're nothing to you, folk you might not even meet, like if you were giving to charity or a food bank or that. Putting a blanket round another person. Even if you're cold too. That's kind. A deep, velvety blanket like the throw on Kris's couch, just throwing it wide and wrapping it.

He's not sure if kind and generous are the same. The adults come right over to the car. Auntie Ran is getting in the driver's door. She has to be quick, as it's on the roadside and there's a car coming. Kris looks in the open passenger door. 'Bye bye, special boy,' she says, taking his hand and kissing it.

Gerard feels embarrassed by the fuss. 'Where's Craig?' he asks.

Craig has disappeared, and it's really important Gerard says goodbye to him. Kris squeezes his hand, half-turns towards the house. 'Here he is,' she says, and there's Craig, emerging from the front door with a picture frame in his arms. The wood is dark, and gilded.

'This is for you,' Craig says, leaning in. He gives Gerard the painting.

It's the one Craig's dad did, of the blue ripples with the smashed orange sun. Gerard cannot speak. He brings the picture close to his face. The paint is thick and lumpy; it looks like actual waves.

'To remember us by.'

It is magic. Gerard puts his finger against the sun.

'Keep in touch, young man, alright? Things are going to be OK. I promise.' Craig sounds very gruff, and he's stepping backwards, but Gerard pings his seatbelt.

'Wait!'

Carefully, he lays his picture on his auntie's lap – *watch that* – then gets out the car. Craig kind of bends and flings his arms open all at once, and Gerard dunts his head against Craig's chest, cuddling him as hard as he can. Because he can't say what he wants to say. He hopes Craig feels it, but.

'Thank you.'

'Away. It's been a pleasure. Come back any time, you hear?' Craig ruffles his hair, then gives him a wee nudge. 'Right. Off with you, young sir. You have new adventures on which to embark. Go now. Stand not upon the order of–'

'Oh, wheesht, Craig,' says Kris. It sounds funny in her accent, more like *veest*, and everybody laughs.

They're going to drop his stuff off at the new flat, then go to see his mum. It's a Family Day, but the weans have both got chickenpox, so it's just him and Auntie Ran. It's a shame Ran's missing seeing the weans again, but the four of them have had one nice afternoon together already. Instead of some crappy office, Naggy let them do it at a soft play. The weans loved it. Miranda can be funny with folk she doesny know, but she let Ran dandle her on her knee and everything. Anthony was really quiet, but, until Gerard had a word with him. Put him straight. *You can trust her, Anthony. Promise. Just like you can trust me. She's not a bit like Mum*. He whispered that bit, in case anyone else was listening. Cause it's no a very nice thing to say. It's true, but. Except when Ran goes crazy and beats folk up. Even then, she was only hurting some prick that deserved it. He's pretty sure she wouldn't hurt him. Nearly ninety-nine per cent sure.

They can all go to the next Family Day. The Rehab Centre do them once a month. It'll be brilliant to have his mum and his auntie and the weans, all in the one room. It's quite a long drive, mind, and he doesn't know if Ran can get car seats with a hired car. You all sit about at Family Day, and have cups of tea and cakes, and there's a display of the crafts folk have done – pottery, photography, sewing. His mum did a really nice flower arrangement last time. She's going to do a poem today. When Gerard spoke to her on the phone, she told him it's called 'Proud'. He's quite excited about that. He didny know his mum was proud of anything. Hopefully, no one will have to go to the next one after that because his mum will have got out by then. Maybe. She is awfully thin, thinner than he's ever seen her, and she keeps saying she's cold.

On the way, his auntie asks if he want to make a wee detour. 'Since we're on the Southside anyway?'

'Where to?'

She indicates, stops the car. 'Well, if it's all too much in one day, just tell me. But I know you said you'd like to see where your dad's buried. It's not that far away? If you want?'

At first, Gerard's a bit freaked out by the suggestion. The thought of his dad, lying under the ground. The dead bones of him. He's not prepared for that. He wants to ask if he'll be a skeleton yet. All he knows of bodies is zombie movies, and they are gross. 'Can I no just remember him like he was?'

'Of course! There's nothing to see, pet. It's just a gravestone.'

'OK. Well, I'd still rather not.'

'That's fine.' Ran moves off again. 'I think you're going to like the Townhead. It's dead close to the shops and that. You can walk right into town. And St Mungo's is a very good school. Fresh start.'

'Yeah.'

'It's not that far from Dennistoun either. You could probably walk there, if it's a nice day. See some of your pals?'

'Hmm.' He doesn't know if he wants to meet up with the Broncos. Some folk are your pals just cause of geography. Or because you need some kind of posse to protect you. The Broncos were alright for mucking about with, but they used to slag off his mum too. Take the piss about how Gerard stunk of nappies. Yes, they'd some laughs, but he can't forget the way he'd aye have to mind what he said or how he stood. Not mind when they said his bike was bent. Gerard, up for any nonsense that would get him a laugh. Kidding on he liked the things they liked. There was always a faint threat hanging in the air, Gerard adjusting his behaviour to suit the mood. The dread of having to fight to guard their territory. The Broncos never actually did, not with weapons anyroad. But even grabbing a boy and pulling his head down so your mate could give him a kicking. A circle of kids, the mad cheering. It made him ill. Gerard wants pals that are for keeps. He hopes Ali might be one – though he's just got lifted for being in a stolen motor. So who knows how that'll go. But Ali's been really decent to Gerard. Kind about his dad.

Sound. Not kind. You have to say *sound* or it sounds wank.

'No, wait!' he says. 'I do want to go.'

'Where? St Mungo's? But you are going there. They're going to buddy you up–'

'No. My dad's grave.'

Ran checks the clock on the dashboard. 'Aye, alright then. We've still got time.'

She drives them through Shawlands and down onto the motorway. They come off almost as soon as they get on. The area seems familiar. Gerard recognises some of the high flats. 'Is this near where my gran's house was?'

'Aye.' They go down a wide, tree-lined street, turn into another road. Lots of new buildings on either side, and one old stone mansion stranded in its garden. Everything else is grey. Facing the mansion is more old stone: gateposts to the cemetery. It's on a busy main road, with a bus stop outside. There's a row of modern brick flats with glass balconies, right next to the graveyard. Who'd want to be living next to hunners of dead people? Gerard's about to make a joke, when Ran beats him to it. 'At least the neighbours will be quiet, eh?'

Above the brick walls are grey roofs, and in front of the flats are grey walls, with all their recycling bins lined up. It looks like a prison, actually. Gerard definitely wouldn't want to stay there. Ran drives past the gates, finds a place to park.

'Can I put my painting in the boot?' says Gerard.

'I don't know if there's room, with all your stuff in. Why don't we just slide it under the seat?'

He isn't sure, but she promises it will be safe. They wrap it in Auntie Ran's sweatshirt first, just in case. The cemetery is nothing like the one Gerard and Ali got drunk in. This one is neat, more of a park, with wide paths and trees and grass and benches. And rows of dead people under the rows of gravestones. Auntie Ran leads him along the main path, then onto a smaller one branching off. 'I've not been here in ages,' she says. 'But I know you come in this gate – and it's near the Jewish bit.'

They walk for ages. Gerard's worried about his painting. What if someone saw them hide it? Anyone could take it, if they were watching them, or following them.

'Does my mum know you spoke to Mad Davey?'

'I *spoke* to him?' Ran grins.

'You know what I mean.' He's glad she did it, but Gerard really doesn't like to think about his banshee auntie going mental in his gran's flat.

'She does now.'

'What did she say?'

'Well, she wasny very happy with me, put it that way. But I just went on and on at her, told her I'd definitely take yous to Aberdeen if she didny . . .' Ran stops. 'Anyway, I said I would go to the polis, if he ever comes back. And your mum agreed if Davey comes anywhere near her, she'll make a complaint too.'

He knows she's only said that to get Ran off her case. There's no way his mum will grass anyone up to the pigs. 'But what about the robbery money? Does she not still want us to . . .' He shrugs. 'I dunno. Look for it or something?'

'There *is* no money, Gerard.' Auntie Ran smiles at him. 'I think that's finally dawning on her too. One benefit of your mum being in the happy hoose. She's learning to let go. Right, wait. Down here, I think.'

They turn down another path, pass under a huge oak tree. Gerard can see the fence of the cemetery at the far end, and high flats further on. There's another smaller wall, separating a small rectangular part of the graveyard from the rest. At one end is a white building with a black shuttered door. Could be a garage. Probably where the workies keep their lawnmowers. He smiles as he remembers the Broncos, tearing up the grass as they rampaged across Alexandra Park.

'Here we go.' Ran squeezes his arm. 'That's your daddy, there.'

It's a simple stone slab, with a pair of praying hands carved at the top. Ran reads it out for him, but he can work out the *Macklin* no bother.

'Daniel Gerard Macklin. Rest Well.'

'Wait. His middle name was Gerard?'

'It was. We all called him Jed.'

'Jed?' He likes the way it feels on his tongue. Jed. It's kind of cool. Not jaggy like Jez. Not old-mannish like Gerry. He repeats it. 'Jed.'

Gerard is transfixed by the ground in front of the gravestone. He wants to bend down and touch it, wants to press his cheek into the soil and whisper *hello*. But he won't. This is enough for now.

'Can that be my name? Jed?'

'Sure. If you like.'

'You don't think my mum would mind?' He fiddles with the zip on his jacket.

'Gerard, sweetie. Sorry, Jed. You listen to me. You need to stop worrying so much what your mum thinks, OK?'

'But I want her to be happy.'

'I know you do, darling.' She kisses the top of his head. 'Only your mum can make herself happy. You just be you, alright? Be Jed Macklin. Be anyone you want. Just do it for yourself. Not her.'

He nods. He doesny really understand what she means, though.

'You want a wee minute to yourself?'

'Is that alright?' He didn't know how to ask.

'Aye. I need to make a quick phone call anyway.'

Auntie Ran leaves him, goes over to a nearby bench. When she's dialling, he reaches out to touch his dad's gravestone. It's cold. Rough at the top, then smooth on the surface. He puts his finger in the letters. Traces them one by one. Blackbirds chatter. Cellophane rustles in a bin full of crispy brown flowers. They should have brought flowers. Through the trees, over by the workies' garage, he sees a flash of yellow. A figure in yellow, doing what he just did. Touching the top of a gravestone. His heart begins to pound. The ground on which he stands swells in an ocean of grass and soil and bone-dust and does not move at all. But he does.

The figure wears a yellow cardigan over a flowery skirt. There's something in the stoop of her because it plays on a loop in his brain. He threads his way through the ranks of gravestones, past other people's dads and grans and daughters and pals. Moves swiftly towards the strange garage building, which has a pointed black star above its metal door. Opens the gate which separates that plot from this.

*

Margaret lays a pebble on top of Albert's grave. It's one of the new chippie stones from her garden. 'You should see it,' she says, dusting off the gravestone. Imaginary dirt, but she's not been here in a while. She tells Albert most things. But she could never tell him about the accident. That's what Margaret has taken to calling the attack. He'll notice her stick, mind. Her hip's been playing up again.

'The garden. Back to its full glory. In fact, it's even better than before. There's a lovely bench, and a few trellises to give some height. I think I'm going to put a firethorn in – you know, with the wee white flowers? Or is that a pyracanthas? With the leaves like flame?'

It doesn't matter. They rarely knew the correct names of the plants they put in. Each was chosen because Bert or Margaret liked the picture of the flower on the label. Some took, some didn't.

'I know where Stephen is.' She bends to tidy the plastic flowers she stuck in the marble planter. It was supposed to save time and keep the place bright, but the roses have faded to the pink of pork chops. Albert would hate them.

'He's a professor in "Infrastructure Engineering", whatever that is. At the University of Melbourne. My friend Claire tracked him down.'

She's not visited the grave in weeks. It's quite a trauchle to Cardonald, but it's where the Glasgow Reform Synagogue bury their dead. At first, Margaret attended religiously (if that's not too irreligious), boarding the two buses it took to get from Dennistoun to here. An hour each way, and a fair time on her feet to boot. She felt it was expected. By whom, she does not know.

'I was thinking I might go there? To Melbourne. What d'you think?'

A thrush darts from a thicket of bushes to peck at the ground. Why is she havering aloud? Och, she's not embarrassed; plenty visitors do that; no one bats an eye. But Margaret knows that Albert isn't out here, in this Southside cemetery between Abraham Winetrobe and Melvin Wiseman. She's not declaiming for comfort. She's just unspooling her thoughts. Such a tranquil spot, despite the busy roads which surround the cemetery. A veritable oasis. He is here, of course, if you're being literal. Traces of Albert will have permeated this ground. If she picks a blade of grass, he might be in that too. Or mingling with the sky, with the clouds and rain and the air she's currently breathing. Perhaps Albert has helped that bush to grow, and the insect the thrush is pecking at. It may be also that vestiges of him dwell above ground. She read a wonderful novel, where President Lincoln's in a graveyard mourning his son, and all the spirits are blethering furiously away. She wouldn't mind if Albert leans against his gravestone now and then to chew the fat with Mel or Abe. Do him good. Just as long as he's not lonely. Or trapped.

She never wants their connection to be broken. But she worries that the thread she holds him by might slow his progress.

'I think I will go. Oh, Bert. I don't know. I haven't told him about you. I don't know how.'

Margaret has written several letters to Stephen. Posted none. She hasn't got the courage. Can't form the perfect words to make it better. Far easier to shrink inwards and tend her pain than tend her son.

She thinks about arriving unannounced. Just flying off to Australia and standing on the threshold. Arms held wide. Would that be enough? She has that money from Smirky Scott. She could afford the ticket.

What would it be like, to hold her grandsons? Two. She has two grandsons, Claire tells her. Claire has been diligent in her research. Margaret feels the air rise in her lungs. Big, grown boys. Two strangers. What is she supposed to do? What is necessary? Star-shaped leaves shine from a scarlet acer. She loves the way they shimmy. There's such a livid hole inside her, and she can stop it up with bitterness and grief. Or she can . . . she can never sort it. Never. But she could mend something.

The Prayer House sits over-by. Funny wee place. Perhaps she should pray. But Margaret's not Jewish. She's not anything. The thrush trills. Whatever it ate, it's happy. Margaret pushes up the sleeves of her cardigan. Late August. Pleasant enough to not wear a coat. It's the anniversary of when she and Bert met. She wasn't going to go up the dancing, but her friends insisted. *Come to the Palais, Mags! Come with us!* Joe Loss was playing. Her mother even lent her an evening bag that night. Serendipity was in the air.

She sits on the bench which faces Albert and Melvin and Abe. 'I want you to forgive me, Albert. For Stephen.' The brightness of her grief surprises her. 'We could have made it right. All that wasted time, each holding our private hurt. We should have been honest. Even when you were ill, Bert, I lied to you. I told you I couldn't find him. But I never even tried. Oh, love, I pretended it was to protect you. But really, I was protecting me. My pride, my hurt. That's what kept him from us. And I'm sorry.'

A bank of clouds scud behind the high flats. No rainbows. No celestial fireworks. Merely a steady Glasgow sky. Albert's not here. He only exists in Stephen and their grandsons. In Margaret too. In the end, there's only love.

'Excuse me.' She hears a child's voice. A fleeting hand against her elbow. Margaret jumps.

'It's you, isn't it? Oh my God, it is you.' The boy goes crimson, head down.

Margaret doesn't understand. 'Who, dear?'

His thin, drawn face rising to confront her. That singular gaze.

Horror registers. She wants to scream. Tries to pull her handbag to her breast with rigid fists. There must be others in the graveyard – living others? Her breath drains. Grey curtains of her hair, coming in to blind her. She is staring into pinprick. The boy is too close, close as an arrow: the sharpness of his chin a blade. The boy and Margaret blaze with pain; she cannot fight him.

'Please!' he says, stepping away. 'I only want to talk to you.'

'It's you,' she mouths.

'You're the lady, aren't you?'

Margaret shakes her head. 'Go away.'

'I stole your purse.'

'You stole my life! Get away from me.' She thinks she's shrieking, but her voice won't work properly. The harder she tries, the thicker the blockage in her throat.

'Please. I never meant to hurt you. I promise. I just seen your purse on top of your bag.'

'It was *my* purse,' Margaret whispers. She cannot recoil any further, the wooden bench pinions her neck.

'I know. I just needed money. I wasny thinking about nothing. My wee sister needed nappy cream, and the meter had went off. They needed their dinner, see?' He is pleading with her. The boy's hands are writhing beneath his chin. Thumbs pointing upwards. It is a bizarre sight. Snakes in prayer. Ugly, ugly, ugly.

'Leave me alone!' she begs, steeling herself for him to hit her.

'I will,' he says. 'I just needed to tell you. Please, missus. I'm sorry. It was an accident. Can you please let me say I'm sorry?'

Sorry. She hears it echo in the depths of her fear. Waits for what will happen next. Not sure if her eyes are open. The boy is silent, but she's aware he's crying. Margaret understands that if she does not force her body to unfreeze right now, then it never will. In stutters, she moves her head. Observes the child obliquely. He's not very tall. His hands no longer flail. They are clasped neatly in front of him. Brown, tousled hair. Wearing an insubstantial jerkin, and jeans that skim his anklebones. He is painfully thin.

Sorry.

Such a little word. You can pad it out with all manner of superlatives: *deeply, abjectly*. Pepper it with *so, so, so*. But it's worthless, if not accepted. She notices a plump, anxious woman striding towards them. Feels herself fractionally unthaw. Afraid.

'Is that your mum?'

'What?' He follows the direction of her gaze. 'No. That's my auntie. My mum's not here.'

Momentarily, Margaret is flustered. Her shock made awkward. Sunlight balances on the tip of the Prayer House roof. 'Is it . . . are you here to visit your mum?'

'No,' he says dully. 'No. She's just . . . not well. She's in rehab. She takes drugs.'

'Ah.'

'My auntie's looking after us. Well, just me. They won't let her take the weans yet. Building up to that, know? If this all works out.'

'I see.' Which she does not.

'She's doing a degree,' he blurts. 'She's nice.'

'I'm sure she is.'

'It's my dad I'm visiting.'

'Oh, I'm sorry.' Convention dictates she must be. 'When did he die?'

'When I was a wee boy.'

But you are *a wee boy*, she thinks.

'What about you?'

Margaret is at a loss. 'Um . . . this is Albert.' She points at his grave. 'My husband.'

'I'm sorry for your troubles.' A stilted, old-fashioned homily for such a young lad to say. But it sounds genuine.

'What's your name?' she asks him.

'Jed. Jed Macklin.'

'I'm Margaret.'

'They wouldn't let me talk to you. I wanted to.'

But I don't. She is spinning on the rim of an intense and distant edge.

'Naggy said you might write to me.'

Now that you're here, I really, really can't. I cannot do this. Margaret never wanted him to be real. Only a letter in a file. She does not need his explanations. She wants no more strife.

'Is everything OK?' The aunt is upon them. 'Jed, what's going on?'

Margaret can simply get up and walk away. She owes this child nothing.

'We were just talking,' says Margaret. 'He was telling me about his dad, and I was telling him about my husband.'

'Can you give me a wee minute more, Auntie Ran?'

'But we need to go, son. Or we're going to miss Family Day.'

The boy twists, then is motionless. Flexing tendons in his wrist. His aunt regards him, trying to assess the situation. 'No. I think this lady's probably wanting left in peace.'

What can Margaret say?

The boy fixes desperate eyes upon her. The aunt's mobile phone starts to trill a jaunty melody. 'Shit. I need to get this . . . Sorry. Jed! Come on!' She swishes the air with her hand as she turns and takes the call, and begins to walk away.

'Jed.' Margaret catches his wrist. Can feel the sinewy whole of him. 'What would you have said? If they'd let you?' It's the tone she used with Stephen, when he was that age. Brisk. Encouraging. Oh God. It's the tone Margaret's mother would use with her.

'I'd have told you I heard the crack on the pavement when you fell. Even though I kept running, I could still hear it. And how I kept thinking you were probably someone's gran.'

'I am.' Her throat is dry.

He nods. 'You look like a gran. A nice gran. I get so scared. I have nightmares that you're dead, and . . .' His face crumples.

'Here.' Margaret hands him her embroidered hankie.

'Thank you.'

'And thank you, for saying you're sorry. That was brave.'

He bites his thumbnail. 'Did you get your purse back?'

'No. No, I don't think I did.'

'I can get you a new one?'

'That's alright. You don't have to. I've got plenty purses.'

The steady Glasgow sky stretches over gridded streets and high flats. Over running clocks and hidden streams and dear green parks and rooms without carpets.

Auntie Ran shouts, 'Move it!'

The thrush flaps at this commotion. Flies on to find another treasure.

'You reached into my life.'

He nods.

There is so much more she wants to say, here where he is open, and she, half-shut. *You ripped the veil I live behind. I want doesn't get.* But it will spiral in a tirade. She needs no vitriol on her tongue. Margaret can never be within this boy's head. He has done it again: made that rupture. Disturbed her self-containment. *It was an accident* he says. The accident is that she fell and shattered bones. Not that he invaded her. She could say actions have consequences, or *Here I am. Your salutary tale.* Force him to truly see her. She could tell him about the nightmares and her commode. The indignity, the *why me* outrage. The shock, the shame. But venting her spleen will seal him harder. Will weaken her. He sees her.

He sees her.

The boy and the old woman don't say goodbye. He breaks first, teetering between his desire to follow his aunt and his need to continue. Margaret dips her head away, retrieving the faded plastic flowers from her husband's grave.

In the undergrowth of another graveyard, a badger stirs. A refugee rides a scratched, donated child's bike past Glasgow Green, to deliver fast food to slow people. In Campbell's clothing store, private schoolkids shop for new blazers. Bagpipes drone on Buchanan Street while Council gardeners sort pale pink bedding for George Square. Outside a betting shop, a tattooed man holds his head, bewildered.

The boy and the old woman both leave the cemetery by different gates: Gerard, to all the places he will go to, and Margaret, to her garden in the shabby, bustling, faded East End of the city.

Which is on the cusp of up and coming.

Acknowledgements

As with raising a child, it took many people to help make this book. First, a huge thank you to my mates Helen Fitzgerald and Liz Njie, and to Diane Gray for all their social work and child protection input. I found the system complicated to navigate, so how hard must it be for a kid? But your advice was kind and patient, and any procedural mistakes are my own. Grateful thanks also to Linda Lane, for detailed information about Children's Panels, and to Graham Goulden for insights on restorative justice and bystander engagement. Hello to the real-life Craig Thomson, who 'won' having a character named after him by supporting the brilliant Hansel Village social care charity. I hope you're happy with the good works your namesake does here! Shout out to my lovely nephew, Stuart MacLean, for advice on teenage-boy stuff and topical swearing! Thank you to my own Dr Ian, my brother-in-law Dr Ian Campbell, for medical guidance, and thank you to my beloved daughter Eidann Campbell for not charging an hourly rate for solicitor inside knowledge. My gratitude to Professor Alan Riach for kind permission to use his quote, channelling what Hugh MacDiarmid might be saying to us via his poems, and to my friend Glen Murray for the connection. Much love as always to my most excellent former agent Jo Unwin, Daisy and all the team at JULA, for pushing, persevering, praising and prodding. It's very much appreciated, and I will miss you all. And huge thanks to my brilliant new agent Juliet Pickering, Finlay and all at Blake Friedmann for their warmth in welcoming me into the fold for an exciting new chapter. A massive thanks to my kind and clever editor Leah Woodburn, and to Francis Bickmore, Aisling Holling, Alice Shortland, Leila Cruickshank, Brodie McKenzie, Valeri Rangelov, John McColgan, Anna Frame, Jenny Fry, Rali, Alan, Mel and everyone at Canongate for making me feel so at home, and to Alison Rae for thoughtful copyediting. Finally, to my girls Eidann (again) and Ciorstan, and my husband Dougie – first readers, wise counsellors and foremost people in the world: thank you, thank you, thank you.